PRAISE FOR
WHERE THE CRAWDADS SING

'Owens combines high tension with precise detail about how
people dress, sound, live and eat – the case studies in her book are
both human and natural . . . Surprise bestsellers are often works that
chime with the times. Though set in the 1950s and 60s, *Where the
Crawdads Sing* is, in its treatment of racial and social division and
the fragile complexities of nature, obviously relevant to
contemporary politics and ecology. But these themes will reach a
huge audience though the writer's old-fashioned talents for
compelling character, plotting and landscape description'
THE GUARDIAN

'The strength of the story comes from the sympathetic
portrait of its heroine who cannot fail to captivate,
right up until the surprising end'
***i* NEWSPAPER**

'A painfully beautiful first novel that is at once a murder mystery, a
coming-of-age narrative and a celebration of nature . . . Owens here
surveys the desolate marshlands of the North Carolina coast
through the eyes of an abandoned child. And in her isolation that
child makes us open our own eyes to the secret wonders – and
dangers – of her private world'
NEW YORK TIMES BOOK REVIEW

'Unsettling and tinged with sadness, yet astonishingly fresh,
powerful and mesmerising – with a surprising ending that
will haunt you. I couldn't put it down'
THE LADY

'Heart-wrenching . . . A fresh exploration of isolation and nature
from a female perspective along with a compelling love story'
ENTERTAINMENT WEEKLY

'Both a coming-of-age story and a mysterious account of a murder investigation told from the perspective of a young girl ... Through Kya's story, Owens explores how isolation affects human behaviour, and the deep effect that rejection can have on our lives'
VANITY FAIR

'A stunningly beautiful novel. Owens brings the North Carolina marshlands to lush, exquisite life'
THE BOOKSELLER, 'BOOK OF THE MONTH'

'A lush debut novel, Owens delivers her mystery wrapped in gorgeous, lyrical prose. It's clear she's from this place – the land of the southern coasts, but also the emotional terrain – you can feel it in the pages. A magnificent achievement, ambitious, credible and very timely'
ALEXANDRA FULLER, *NEW YORK TIMES* BESTSELLING AUTHOR OF *DON'T LET'S GO TO THE DOGS TONIGHT*

'This is a heart-wrenching coming-of-age story, perfect for book clubs'
CANDIS

'A story that's evocative and sad and with a remarkable heroine'
IMAGE

'A nature-infused romance with a killer twist'
REFINERY29

Delia Owens is the co-author of three internationally bestselling nonfiction books about her life as a wildlife scientist in Africa. She holds a BS in Zoology from the University of Georgia and a PhD in Animal Behaviour from the University of California at Davis. She has won the John Burroughs Award for Nature Writing and has been published in *Nature, The African Journal of Ecology* and *International Wildlife,* among many others. She lives in the mountains of North Carolina. *Where the Crawdads Sing* is her first novel.

WHERE THE CRAWDADS SING

DELIA OWENS

corsair

CORSAIR

First published in the US in 2018 by GP Putnam's Sons
First published in Great Britain in 2019 by Corsair
This paperback edition published in 2022

1 3 5 7 9 10 8 6 4 2

Excerpts from "The Correspondence School Instructor Says Goodbye to His Poetry Students"
from *Three Books* by Galway Kinnell. Copyright © 1993 by Galway Kinnell. Reprinted by
permission of Houghton Mifflin Harcourt Publishing Company. All rights reserved.

"Evening" from *Above the River: The Complete Poems* © 1990 by Anne Wright. Published by
Wesleyan University Press. Used by permission.

A CIP catalogue record for this book
is available from the British Library.

ISBN: 978-1-4721-5736-2

Printed and bound in Great Britain by
Clays Ltd, Elcograf S.p.A.

Papers used by Corsair are from well-managed forests
and other responsible sources.

MIX
Paper from
responsible sources
FSC   FSC® C104740
www.fsc.org

Corsair
An imprint of
Little, Brown Book Group
Carmelite House
50 Victoria Embankment
London EC4Y 0DZ

An Hachette UK Company
www.hachette.co.uk

www.littlebrown.co.uk

To Amanda, Margaret, and Barbara

Here's to'd ya
If I never see'd ya
I never knowed ya.
I see'd ya
I knowed ya
I loved ya,
Forever.

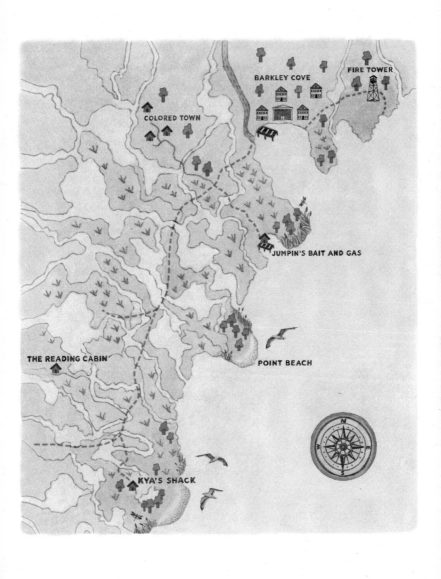

WHERE THE CRAWDADS SING

WHERE

THE

CRAWDADS

SING

PART 1

The Marsh

Prologue

1969

Marsh is not swamp. Marsh is a space of light, where grass grows in water, and water flows into the sky. Slow-moving creeks wander, carrying the orb of the sun with them to the sea, and long-legged birds lift with unexpected grace—as though not built to fly—against the roar of a thousand snow geese.

Then within the marsh, here and there, true swamp crawls into low-lying bogs, hidden in clammy forests. Swamp water is still and dark, having swallowed the light in its muddy throat. Even night crawlers are diurnal in this lair. There are sounds, of course, but compared to the marsh, the swamp is quiet because decomposition is cellular work. Life decays and reeks and returns to the rotted duff; a poignant wallow of death begetting life.

On the morning of October 30, 1969, the body of Chase Andrews lay in the swamp, which would have absorbed it silently, routinely. Hiding it for good. A swamp knows all about death, and doesn't necessarily define it as tragedy, certainly not a sin. But this morning two boys from the village rode their bikes out to the old fire tower and, from the third switchback, spotted his denim jacket.

1.

Ma

1952

The morning burned so August-hot, the marsh's moist breath hung the oaks and pines with fog. The palmetto patches stood unusually quiet except for the low, slow flap of the heron's wings lifting from the lagoon. And then, Kya, only six at the time, heard the screen door slap. Standing on the stool, she stopped scrubbing grits from the pot and lowered it into the basin of worn-out suds. No sounds now but her own breathing. Who had left the shack? Not Ma. She never let the door slam.

But when Kya ran to the porch, she saw her mother in a long brown skirt, kick pleats nipping at her ankles, as she walked down the sandy lane in high heels. The stubby-nosed shoes were fake alligator skin. Her only going-out pair. Kya wanted to holler out but knew not to rouse Pa, so opened the door and stood on the brick-'n'-board steps. From there she saw the blue train case Ma carried. Usually, with the confidence of a pup, Kya knew her mother would return with meat wrapped in greasy brown paper or with a chicken, head dangling down. But she never wore the gator heels, never took a case.

Ma always looked back where the foot lane met the road, one arm held high, white palm waving, as she turned onto the track, which wove through bog forests, cattail lagoons, and maybe—if the tide obliged—eventually into town. But today she walked on, unsteady in the ruts. Her tall figure emerged now and then through the holes of the forest until only swatches of white scarf flashed between the leaves. Kya sprinted to the spot she knew would bare the road; surely Ma would wave from there, but she arrived only in time to glimpse the blue case—the color so wrong for the woods—as it disappeared. A heaviness, thick as black-cotton mud, pushed her chest as she returned to the steps to wait.

Kya was the youngest of five, the others much older, though later she couldn't recall their ages. They lived with Ma and Pa, squeezed together like penned rabbits, in the rough-cut shack, its screened porch staring big-eyed from under the oaks.

Jodie, the brother closest to Kya, but still seven years older, stepped from the house and stood behind her. He had her same dark eyes and black hair; had taught her birdsongs, star names, how to steer the boat through saw grass.

"Ma'll be back," he said.

"I dunno. She's wearin' her gator shoes."

"A ma don't leave her kids. It ain't in 'em."

"You told me that fox left her babies."

"Yeah, but that vixen got 'er leg all tore up. She'd've starved to death if she'd tried to feed herself 'n' her kits. She was better off to leave 'em, heal herself up, then whelp more when she could raise 'em good. Ma ain't starvin', she'll be back." Jodie wasn't nearly as sure as he sounded, but said it for Kya.

Her throat tight, she whispered, "But Ma's carryin' that blue case like she's goin' somewheres big."

The shack sat back from the palmettos, which sprawled across sand flats to a necklace of green lagoons and, in the distance, all the marsh beyond. Miles of blade-grass so tough it grew in salt water, interrupted only by trees so bent they wore the shape of the wind. Oak forests bunched around the other sides of the shack and sheltered the closest lagoon, its surface so rich in life it churned. Salt air and gull-song drifted through the trees from the sea.

Claiming territory hadn't changed much since the 1500s. The scattered marsh holdings weren't legally described, just staked out natural—a creek boundary here, a dead oak there—by renegades. A man doesn't set up a palmetto lean-to in a bog unless he's on the run from somebody or at the end of his own road.

The marsh was guarded by a torn shoreline, labeled by early explorers as the "Graveyard of the Atlantic" because riptides, furious winds, and shallow shoals wrecked ships like paper hats along what would become the North Carolina coast. One seaman's journal read, "rang'd along the Shoar . . . but could discern no Entrance . . . A violent Storm overtook us . . . we were forced to get off to Sea, to secure Ourselves and Ship, and were driven by the Rapidity of a strong Current . . .

"The Land . . . being marshy and Swamps, we return'd towards our Ship . . . Discouragement of all such as should hereafter come into those Parts to settle."

Those looking for serious land moved on, and this infamous marsh became a net, scooping up a mishmash of mutinous sailors, castaways, debtors, and fugitives dodging wars, taxes, or laws that they didn't take to. The ones malaria didn't kill or the swamp didn't swallow bred into a woodsmen tribe of several races and multiple cultures, each of whom could fell a small forest with a hatchet and pack a buck for miles. Like river rats, each had his own territory, yet had to fit into the fringe or simply disappear some day in the swamp. Two hundred years later, they were joined by runaway slaves, who escaped into the marsh and were called maroons, and freed slaves, penniless and beleaguered, who dispersed into the water-land because of scant options.

Maybe it was mean country, but not an inch was lean. Layers of life—squiggly sand crabs, mud-waddling crayfish, waterfowl, fish, shrimp, oysters, fatted deer, and plump geese—were piled on the land or in the water. A man who didn't mind scrabbling for supper would never starve.

It was now 1952, so some of the claims had been held by a string of disconnected, unrecorded persons for four centuries. Most before the Civil War. Others squatted on the land more recently, especially after the World Wars, when men came back broke and broke-up. The marsh did not confine them but defined them and, like any sacred ground, kept their secrets deep. No one cared that they held the land because nobody else wanted it. After all, it was wasteland bog.

Just like their whiskey, the marsh dwellers bootlegged their own laws—not like those burned onto stone tablets or inscribed on documents, but deeper ones, stamped in their genes. Ancient and natural, like those hatched from hawks and doves. When cornered, desperate, or isolated, man reverts to those instincts that aim straight at survival. Quick and just. They will always be the trump cards because they are passed on more frequently from one generation to the next than the gentler genes. It is not a morality, but simple math. Among themselves, doves fight as often as hawks.

Ma didn't come back that day. No one spoke of it. Least of all Pa. Stinking of fish and drum likker, he clanked pot lids. "Whar's supper?"

Eyes downcast, the brothers and sisters shrugged. Pa dog-cussed, then limp-stepped out, back into the woods. There had been fights before; Ma had even left a time or two, but she always came back, scooping up whoever would be cuddled.

The two older sisters cooked a supper of red beans and cornbread, but no one sat to eat at the table, as they would have with Ma. Each dipped beans from the pot, flopped cornbread on top, and wandered off to eat on their floor mattresses or the faded sofa.

Kya couldn't eat. She sat on the porch steps, looking down the lane. Tall for her age, bone skinny, she had deep-tanned skin and straight hair, black and thick as crow wings.

Darkness put a stop to her lookout. Croaking frogs would drown the sounds of footsteps; even so, she lay on her porch bed, listening. Just that morning she'd awakened to fatback crackling in the iron skillet and whiffs of biscuits browning in the wood oven. Pulling up her bib overalls, she'd rushed into the kitchen to put the plates and forks out. Pick the weevils from the grits. Most dawns, smiling wide, Ma hugged her—"Good morning, my special girl"—and the two of them moved about the chores, dancelike. Sometimes Ma sang folk songs or quoted nursery rhymes: "This little piggy went to market." Or she'd swing Kya into a jitterbug, their feet banging the plywood floor until the music of the battery-operated radio died, sounding as if it were singing to itself at the bottom of a barrel. Other mornings Ma spoke about adult things Kya didn't understand, but she figured Ma's words needed somewhere to go, so she absorbed them through her skin, as she poked more wood in the cookstove. Nodding like she knew.

Then, the hustle of getting everybody up and fed. Pa not there. He had two settings: silence and shouting. So it was just fine when he slept through, or didn't come home at all.

But this morning, Ma had been quiet; her smile lost, her eyes red.

9

She'd tied a white scarf pirate style, low across her forehead, but the purple and yellow edges of a bruise spilled out. Right after breakfast, even before the dishes were washed, Ma had put a few personals in the train case and walked down the road.

The next morning, Kya took up her post again on the steps, her dark eyes boring down the lane like a tunnel waiting for a train. The marsh beyond was veiled in fog so low its cushy bottom sat right on the mud. Barefoot, Kya drummed her toes, twirled grass stems at doodlebugs, but a six-year-old can't sit long and soon she moseyed onto the tidal flats, sucking sounds pulling at her toes. Squatting at the edge of the clear water, she watched minnows dart between sunspots and shadows.

Jodie hollered to her from the palmettos. She stared; maybe he was coming with news. But as he wove through the spiky fronds, she knew by the way he moved, casual, that Ma wasn't home.

"Ya wanta play explorers?" he asked.

"Ya said ya're too old to play 'splorers."

"Nah, I just said that. Never too old. Race ya!"

They tore across the flats, then through the woods toward the beach. She squealed as he overtook her and laughed until they reached the large oak that jutted enormous arms over the sand. Jodie and their older brother, Murph, had hammered a few boards across the branches as a lookout tower and tree fort. Now, much of it was falling in, dangling from rusty nails.

Usually if she was allowed to crew at all it was as slave girl, bringing her brothers warm biscuits swiped from Ma's pan.

But today Jodie said, "You can be captain."

Kya raised her right arm in a charge. "Run off the Spaniards!" They broke off stick-swords and crashed through brambles, shouting and stabbing at the enemy.

Then—make-believe coming and going easily—she walked to a mossy log and sat. Silently, he joined her. He wanted to say something to get her mind off Ma, but no words came, so they watched the swimming shadows of water striders.

Kya returned to the porch steps later and waited for a long time, but, as she looked to the end of the lane, she never cried. Her face was still, her lips a simple thin line under searching eyes. But Ma didn't come back that day either.

2.

Jodie

1952

After Ma left, over the next few weeks, Kya's oldest brother and two sisters drifted away too, as if by example. They had endured Pa's red-faced rages, which started as shouts, then escalated into fist-slugs, or backhanded punches, until one by one, they disappeared. They were nearly grown anyway. And later, just as she forgot their ages, she couldn't remember their real names, only that they were called Missy, Murph, and Mandy. On her porch mattress, Kya found a small pile of socks left by her sisters.

On the morning when Jodie was the only sibling left, Kya awakened to the *clatter-clank* and hot grease of breakfast. She dashed into the kitchen, thinking Ma was home frying corn fritters or hoecakes. But it was Jodie, standing at the woodstove, stirring grits. She smiled to hide the letdown, and he patted the top of her head, gently shushing her to be quiet: if they didn't wake Pa, they could eat alone. Jodie didn't know how to make biscuits, and there wasn't any bacon, so he cooked grits and scrambled eggs in lard, and they sat down together, silently exchanging glances and smiles.

They washed their dishes fast, then ran out the door toward the marsh, he in the lead. But just then Pa shouted and hobbled toward them. Impossibly lean, his frame seemed to flop about from poor gravity. His molars yellow as an old dog's teeth.

Kya looked up at Jodie. "We can run. Hide in the mossy place."

"It's okay. It'll be okay," he said.

Later, near sunset, Jodie found Kya on the beach staring at the sea. As he stepped up beside her, she didn't look at him but kept her eyes on the roiling waves. Still, she knew by the way he spoke that Pa had slugged his face.

"I hafta go, Kya. Can't live here no longer."

She almost turned to him, but didn't. Wanted to beg him not to leave her alone with Pa, but the words jammed up.

"When you're old enough you'll understand," he said. Kya wanted to holler out that she may be young, but she wasn't stupid. She knew Pa was the reason they all left; what she wondered was why no one took her with them. She'd thought of leaving too, but had nowhere to go and no bus money.

"Kya, ya be careful, hear. If anybody comes, don't go in the house. They can get ya there. Run deep in the marsh, hide in the bushes. Always cover yo' tracks; I learned ya how. And ya can hide from Pa, too." When she still didn't speak, he said good-bye and strode across the beach to the woods. Just before he stepped into the trees, she finally turned and watched him walk away.

"This little piggy stayed home," she said to the waves.

Breaking her freeze, she ran to the shack. Shouted his name down the hall, but Jodie's things were already gone, his floor bed stripped bare.

She sank onto his mattress, watching the last of that day slide down the wall. Light lingered after the sun, as it does, some of it pooling in the room, so that for a brief moment the lumpy beds and piles of old clothes took on more shape and color than the trees outside.

A gnawing hunger—such a mundane thing—surprised her. She walked to the kitchen and stood at the door. All her life the room had been warmed from baking bread, boiling butter beans, or bubbling fish stew. Now, it was stale, quiet, and dark. "Who's gonna cook?" she asked out loud. Could have asked, *Who's gonna dance?*

She lit a candle and poked at hot ashes in the woodstove, added kindling. Pumped the bellows till a flame caught, then more wood. The Frigidaire served as a cupboard because no electricity came near the shack. To keep the mold at bay, the door was propped open with the flyswatter. Still, greenish-black veins of mildew grew in every crevice.

Getting out leftovers, she said, "I'll tump the grits in lard, warm 'em up," which she did and ate from the pot, looking through the window for Pa. But he didn't come.

When light from the quarter moon finally touched the shack, she crawled into her porch bed—a lumpy mattress on the floor with real sheets covered in little blue roses that Ma had got at a yard sale— alone at night for the first time in her life.

At first, every few minutes, she sat up and peered through the screen. Listening for footsteps in the woods. She knew the shapes of all the trees; still some seemed to dart here and there, moving with the moon. For a while she was so stiff she couldn't swallow, but on cue, the familiar songs of tree frogs and katydids filled the night. More comforting than three blind mice with a carving knife. The darkness held an odor of sweetness, the earthy breath of frogs and salamanders who'd made it through one more stinky-hot day. The marsh snuggled in closer with a low fog, and she slept.

For three days Pa didn't come and Kya boiled turnip greens from Ma's garden for breakfast, lunch, and dinner. She'd walked out to the chicken coop for eggs but found it bare. Not a chicken or egg anywhere.

"Chicken shits! You're just a bunch of chicken shits!" She'd been meaning to tend them since Ma left but hadn't done much of anything. Now they'd escaped as a motley flock, clucking far in the trees beyond. She'd have to scatter grits, see if she could keep them close.

On the evening of the fourth day, Pa showed up with a bottle and sprawled across his bed.

Walking into the kitchen the next morning, he hollered, "Whar's ev'body got to?"

"I don't know," she said, not looking at him.

"Ya don't know much as a cur-dawg. Useless as tits on a boar hog."

Kya slipped quietly out the porch door, but walking along the beach searching for mussels, she smelled smoke and looked up to see a plume rising from the direction of the shack. Running as fast as she could, she broke through the trees and saw a bonfire blazing in the yard. Pa was throwing Ma's paintings, dresses, and books onto the flames.

"No!" Kya screamed. He didn't look at her, but threw the old battery-operated radio into the fire. Her face and arms burned as she reached toward the paintings, but the heat pushed her back.

She rushed to the shack to block Pa's return for more, locking eyes with him. Pa raised his backhand toward Kya, but she stood her ground. Suddenly, he turned and limp-stepped toward his boat.

Kya sank onto the brick 'n' boards, watching Ma's watercolors of the marsh smolder into ash. She sat until the sun set, until all the buttons glowed as embers and the memories of dancing the jitterbug with Ma melted into the flames.

Over the next few days, Kya learned from the mistakes of the others, and perhaps more from the minnows, how to live with him. Just keep out of the way, don't let him see you, dart from sunspots to shadows. Up and out of the house before he rose, she lived in the woods and water, then padded into the house to sleep in her bed on the porch as close to the marsh as she could get.

Pa had fought Germany in the Second World War, where his left femur caught shrapnel and shattered, their last source of pride. His weekly disability checks, their only source of income. A week after Jodie left, the Frigidaire stood empty and hardly any turnips remained. When Kya walked into the kitchen that Monday morning, Pa pointed to a crumpled dollar and loose coins on the kitchen table.

"This here'll get ya food fer the week. Thar ain't no such thang as handouts," he said. "Ever'thang cost sump'm, and fer the money ya gotta keep the house up, stove wood c'lected, and warsh the laundree."

For the first time ever Kya walked alone toward the village of Barkley Cove to buy groceries—*this little piggy went to market.* She plodded through deep sand or black mud for four miles until the bay glistened ahead, the hamlet on its shore.

Everglades surrounded the town, mixing their salty haze with that of the ocean, which swelled in high tide on the other side of Main Street. Together the marsh and sea separated the village from the rest of the world, the only connection being the single-lane highway that limped into town on cracked cement and potholes.

There were two streets: Main ran along the oceanfront with a row of shops; the Piggly Wiggly grocery at one end, the Western Auto at the other, the diner in the middle. Mixed in there were Kress's Five and Dime, a Penney's (catalog only), Parker's Bakery, and a Buster Brown Shoe Shop. Next to the Piggly was the Dog-Gone Beer Hall, which offered roasted hot dogs, red-hot chili, and fried shrimp served in folded paper boats. No ladies or children stepped inside because it wasn't considered proper, but a take-out window had been cut out of the wall so they could order hot dogs and Nehi cola from the street. Coloreds couldn't use the door or the window.

The other street, Broad, ran from the old highway straight toward the ocean and into Main, ending right there. So the only intersection in town was Main, Broad, and the Atlantic Ocean. The stores and businesses weren't joined together as in most towns but were separated by small, vacant lots brushed with sea oats and palmettos, as if overnight the marsh had inched in. For more than two hundred years, sharp salty winds had weathered the cedar-shingled buildings to the color of rust, and the window frames, most painted white or blue, had flaked and cracked. Mostly, the village seemed tired of arguing with the elements, and simply sagged.

The town wharf, draped in frayed ropes and old pelicans, jutted into the small bay, whose water, when calm, reflected the reds and yellows of shrimp boats. Dirt roads, lined with small cedar houses, wound through the trees, around lagoons, and along the ocean on either end of the shops. Barkley Cove was quite literally a backwater town, bits scattered here and there among the estuaries and reeds like an egret's nest flung by the wind.

Barefoot and dressed in too-short bib overalls, Kya stood where the marsh track met the road. Biting her lip, wanting to run home. She couldn't reckon what she'd say to people; how she'd figure the grocery money. But hunger was a pushing thing, so she stepped onto Main and walked, head down, toward the Piggly Wiggly on a crumbling sidewalk that appeared now and then between grass clumps. As she approached the Five and Dime, she heard a commotion behind her and jumped to the side just as three boys, a few years older than she, sped by on bikes. The lead boy looked back at her, laughing at the near miss, and then almost collided with a woman stepping from the store.

"CHASE ANDREWS, you get back here! All three of you boys." They pedaled a few more yards, then thought better of it and returned to the woman, Miss Pansy Price, saleslady in fabric and notions. Her family had once owned the largest farm on the outskirts of the marsh and, although they were forced to sell out long ago, she continued her role as genteel landowner. Which wasn't easy living in a tiny apartment above the diner. Miss Pansy usually wore hats shaped like silk turbans, and this morning her headwear was pink, setting off red lipstick and splotches of rouge.

She scolded the boys. "I've a mind to tell y'all's mamas about this. Or better, yo' papas. Ridin' fast like that on the sidewalk, nearly runnin' me over. What ya got to say for yo'self, Chase?"

He had the sleekest bike—red seat and chrome handlebars, raised up. "We're sorry, Miss Pansy, we didn't see ya 'cause that girl over yonder got in the way." Chase, tanned with dark hair, pointed at Kya, who had stepped back and stood half inside a myrtle shrub.

"Never mind her. You cain't go blamin' yo' sins on somebody else, not even swamp trash. Now, you boys gotta do a good deed, make up fer this. There goes Miss Arial with her groceries, go help carry 'em to her truck. And put yo' shirttails in."

"Yes, ma'am," the boys said as they biked toward Miss Arial, who had taught them all second grade.

Kya knew that the parents of the dark-haired boy owned the Western Auto store, which was why he rode the snazziest bike. She'd seen him unloading big cardboard boxes of merchandise from the truck, packing it in, but she had never spoken a word to him or the others.

She waited a few minutes, then, head low again, walked toward the grocery. Inside the Piggly Wiggly, Kya studied the selection of grits and chose a one-pound bag of coarse ground yellow because a red tag hung from the top—a *special of the week*. Like Ma taught her. She fretted in the aisle until no other customers stood at the register, then walked up and faced the checkout lady, Mrs. Singletary, who asked, "Where's ya mama at?" Mrs. Singletary's hair was cut short, curled tight, and colored purple as an iris in sunlight.

"Doin' chores, ma'am."

"Well, ya got money for the grits, or don't ya?"

"Yes'm." Not knowing how to count the exact amount, she laid down the whole dollar.

Mrs. Singletary wondered if the child knew the difference in the coins, so as she placed the change into Kya's open palm she counted slowly, "Twenty-five, fifty, sixty, seventy, eighty, eighty-five and three pennies. 'Cause the grits cost twelve cents."

Kya felt sick to her stomach. Was she supposed to count something back? She stared to the puzzle of coins in her palm.

Mrs. Singletary seemed to soften. "Okay, then. Git on with ya."

Kya dashed from the store and walked as fast as she could toward the marsh track. Plenty of times, Ma had told her, "Never run in town or people'll think you stole something." But as soon as Kya reached the sandy track, she ran a good half mile. Then speed-walked the rest.

Back home, thinking she knew how to fix grits, she threw them into boiling water like Ma had done, but they lumped up all together in one big ball that burned on the bottom and stayed raw in the middle. So rubbery she could only eat a few bites, so she searched the garden again and found a few more turnip greens between the goldenrod. Then boiled them up and ate them all, slurping down the pot likker.

In a few days she got the hang of fixing grits, although no matter how hard she stirred, they lumped up some. The next week she bought backbones—marked with a red tag—and boiled them with grits and collard greens in a mush that tasted fine.

Kya had done the laundry plenty with Ma, so knew how to scrub clothes on the rub board under the yard spigot with bars of lye soap. Pa's overalls were so heavy wet she couldn't wring them out with her tiny hands, and couldn't reach the line to hang them, so draped them sopping over the palmetto fronds at the edge of the woods.

She and Pa did this two-step, living apart in the same shack, sometimes not seeing each other for days. Almost never speaking. She tidied up after herself and after him, like a serious little woman. She wasn't near enough of a cook to fix meals for him—he usually wasn't there anyway—but she made his bed, picked up, swept up, and washed the dishes most of the time. Not because she'd been told, but because it was the only way to keep the shack decent for Ma's return.

Ma had always said the autumn moon showed up for Kya's birthday. So even though she couldn't remember the date of her birth, one evening when the moon rose swollen and golden from the lagoon, Kya said to herself, "I reckon I'm seven." Pa never mentioned it; certainly there was no cake. He didn't say anything about her going to school either, and she, not knowing much about it, was too afraid to bring it up.

Surely Ma would come back for her birthday, so the morning after the harvest moon she put on the calico dress and stared down the lane. Kya willed Ma to be walking toward the shack, still in her alligator shoes and long skirt. When no one came, she got the pot of grits and walked through the woods to the seashore. Hands to her mouth, she held her head back and called, *"Kee-ow, kee-ow, kee-ow."* Specks of silver appeared in the sky from up and down the beach, from over the surf.

"Here they come. I can't count as high as that many gulls are," she said.

Crying and screeching, the birds swirled and dived, hovered near her face, and landed as she tossed grits to them. Finally, they quieted and stood about preening, and she sat on the sand, her legs folded to the side. One large gull settled onto the sand near Kya.

"It's my birthday," she told the bird.

3.

Chase

1969

The rotted legs of the old abandoned fire tower straddled the bog, which created its own tendrils of mist. Except for cawing crows, the hushed forest seemed to hold an expectant mood as the two boys, Benji Mason and Steve Long, both ten, both blond, started up the damp staircase on the morning of October 30, 1969.

"Fall ain't s'posed to be this hot," Steve called back to Benji.

"Yeah, and everythang quiet 'cept the crows."

Glancing down between the steps, Steve said, "Whoa. What's that?"

"Where?"

"See, there. Blue clothes, like somebody's lyin' in the mud."

Benji called out, "Hey, you! *Whatchadoin'*?"

"I see a face, but it ain't movin'."

Arms pumping, they ran back to the ground and pushed their way to the other side of the tower's base, greenish mud clinging to their boots. There lay a man, flat on his back, his left leg turned grotesquely forward from the knee. His eyes and mouth wide open.

"Jesus Christ!" Benji said.

"My God, it's Chase Andrews."

"We better git the sheriff."

"But we ain't s'posed to be out here."

"That don't matter now. And them crows'll be snooping 'round anytime now."

They swung their heads toward the cawing, as Steve said, "Maybe one of us oughta stay, keep them birds off him."

"Ya're crazy if you think I'm gonna stick 'round here by maself. And I'm bettin' a Injun-head you won't either."

With that, they grabbed their bikes, pedaled hard down the syrupy sand track back to Main, through town, and ran inside the low-slung building where Sheriff Ed Jackson sat at his desk in an office lit with single lightbulbs dangling on cords. Hefty and of medium height, he had reddish hair, his face and arms splotched with pale freckles, and sat thumbing through a *Sports Afield*.

Without knocking, the boys rushed through the open door.

"Sheriff . . ."

"Hey, Steve, Benji. You boys been to a fire?"

"We seen Chase Andrews flat out in the swamp under the fire tower. He looks dead. Ain't movin' one bit."

Ever since Barkley Cove had been settled in 1751, no lawman extended his jurisdiction beyond the saw grass. In the 1940s and '50s, a few sheriffs set hounds on some mainland convicts who'd escaped into the marsh, and the office still kept dogs just in case. But Jackson mostly ignored crimes committed in the swamp. Why interrupt rats killing rats?

But this was Chase. The sheriff stood and took his hat from the rack. "Show me."

Limbs of oak and wild holly screeched against the patrol truck as the sheriff maneuvered down the sandy track with Dr. Vern Murphy, lean and fit with graying hair, the town's only physician, sitting beside him. Each man swayed to the tune of the deep ruts, Vern's head almost banging against the window. Old friends about the same age, they fished together some and were often thrown onto the same case. Both silent now at the prospect of confirming whose body lay in the bog.

Steve and Benji sat in the truck bed with their bikes until the truck stopped.

"He's over there, Mr. Jackson. Behind them bushes."

Ed stepped from the truck. "You boys wait here." Then he and Dr. Murphy waded the mud to where Chase lay. The crows had flown off when the truck came, but other birds and insects whirred above. Insolent life thrumming on.

"It's Chase, all right. Sam and Patti Love won't survive this." The Andrewses had ordered every spark plug, balanced every account, strung every price tag at the Western Auto for their only child, Chase.

Squatting next to the body, listening for a heartbeat with his stethoscope, Vern declared him dead.

"How long ya reckon?" Ed asked.

"I'd say at least ten hours. The coroner'll know for sure."

"He must've climbed up last night, then. Fell from the top."

Vern examined Chase briefly without moving him, then stood next to Ed. Both men stared at Chase's eyes, still looking skyward from his bloated face, then glanced at his gaping mouth.

"How many times I've told folks in this town something like this was bound to happen," the sheriff said.

They had known Chase since he was born. Had watched his life ease from charming child to cute teen; star quarterback and town hot shot to working for his parents. Finally, handsome man wedding the prettiest girl. Now, he sprawled alone, less dignified than the slough. Death's crude pluck, as always, stealing the show.

Ed broke the silence. "Thing is, I can't figure why the others didn't run for help. They always come up here in a pack, or at least a couple of 'em, to make out." The sheriff and doctor exchanged brief but knowing nods that even though he was married, Chase might bring another woman to the tower. "Let's step back out of here. Get a good look at things," Ed said, as he lifted his feet, stepping higher than necessary. "You boys stay where you are; don't go making any more tracks."

Pointing to some footprints that led from the staircase, across the bog, to within eight feet of Chase, Ed asked them, "These your prints from this morning?"

"Yessir, that's as far as we went," Benji said. "Soon as we seen it was Chase, we backed up. You can see there where we backed up."

"Okay." Ed turned. "Vern, something's not right. There's no footprints near the body. If he was with his friends or whoever, once he fell, they would've run down here and stepped all around him, knelt next to him. To see if he was alive. Look how deep our tracks are in this mud, but there're no other fresh tracks. None going toward the stairs or away from the stairs, none around the body."

"Maybe he was by himself, then. That would explain everything."

"Well, I'll tell you one thing that doesn't explain. Where're *his* footprints? How did Chase Andrews walk down the path, cross this muck to the stairs so he could climb to the top, and not leave any footprints himself?"

4.

School

1952

A few days after her birthday, out alone barefooting in mud, Kya bent over, watching a tadpole getting its frog legs. Suddenly she stood. A car churned through deep sand near the end of their lane. No one ever drove here. Then the murmur of people talking—a man and a woman—drifted through the trees. Kya ran fast to the brush, where she could see who was coming but still have ways to escape. Like Jodie taught her.

A tall woman emerged from the car, unsteadily maneuvering in high heels just like Ma had done along the sandy lane. They must be the orphanage people come to get her.

I can outrun her for sure. She'd fall nose-first in them shoes. Kya stayed put and watched the woman step to the porch's screen door.

"Yoo-hoo, anybody home? Truant officer here. I've come to take Catherine Clark to school."

Now this was something. Kya sat mute. She was pretty sure she was supposed to go to school at six. Here they were, a year late.

She had no notion how to talk to kids, certainly not to a teacher, but she wanted to learn to read and what came after twenty-nine.

"Catherine, dear, if ya can hear me, please come on out. It's the law, hon; ya gotta go to school. But 'sides that, you'll like it, dear. Ya get a hot lunch every day for free. I think today they're havin' chicken pie with crust."

That was something else. Kya was very hungry. For breakfast she'd boiled grits with soda crackers stirred in because she didn't have any salt. One thing she already knew about life: you can't eat grits without salt. She'd eaten chicken pie only a few times in her life, but she could still see that golden crust, crunchy on the outside, soft inside. She could feel that full gravy taste, like it was round. It was her stomach acting on its own that made Kya stand up among the palmetto fronds.

"Hello, dear, I'm Mrs. Culpepper. You're all grown up and ready to go to school, aren't ya?"

"Yes'm," Kya said, head low.

"It's okay, you can go barefoot, other chillin do, but 'cause you're a li'l girl, you have to wear a skirt. Do you have a dress or a skirt, hon?"

"Yes'm."

"Okay then, let's go get ya dressed up."

Mrs. Culpepper followed Kya through the porch door, having to step over a row of bird nests Kya had lined up along the boards. In the bedroom Kya put on the only dress that fit, a plaid jumper with one shoulder strap held up with a safety pin.

"That's fine, dear, you look just fine."

Mrs. Culpepper held out her hand. Kya stared at it. She hadn't touched another person in weeks, hadn't touched a stranger her whole life. But she put her small hand in Mrs. Culpepper's and was led down the path to the Ford Crestliner driven by a silent man wearing a gray fedora. Sitting in the backseat, Kya didn't smile and didn't feel like a chick tucked under its mother's wing.

Barkley Cove had one school for whites. First grade through twelfth went to a brick two-story at the opposite end of Main from the sheriff's office. The black kids had their own school, a one-story cement block structure out near Colored Town.

When she was led into the school office, they found her name but no date of birth in the county birth records, so they put her in the second grade, even though she'd never been to school a day in her life. Anyhow, they said, the first grade was too crowded, and what difference would it make to marsh people who'd do a few months of school, maybe, then never be seen again. As the principal walked her down a wide hallway that echoed their footsteps, sweat popped out on her brow. He opened the door to a classroom and gave her a little push.

Plaid shirts, full skirts, shoes, lots of shoes, some bare feet, and eyes—all staring. She'd never seen so many people. Maybe a dozen. The teacher, the same Mrs. Arial those boys had helped, walked Kya to a desk near the back. She could put her things in the cubbyhole, she was told, but Kya didn't have any things.

The teacher walked back to the front and said, "Catherine, please stand and tell the class your full name."

Her stomach churned.

"Come now, dear, don't be shy."

Kya stood. "Miss Catherine Danielle Clark," she said, because that was what Ma once said was her whole name.

"Can you spell *dog* for us?"

Staring at the floor, Kya stood silent. Jodie and Ma had taught her some letters. But she'd never spelled a word aloud for anybody.

Nerves stirred in her stomach; still, she tried. *"G-o-d."*

Laughter let loose up and down the rows.

"Shh! Hush, y'all!" Mrs. Arial called out. "We never laugh, ya hear me, we never laugh at each other. Y'all know better'n that."

Kya sat down fast in her seat at the back of the room, trying to disappear like a bark beetle blending into the furrowed trunk of an oak. Yet nervous as she was, as the teacher continued the lesson, she leaned forward, waiting to learn what came after twenty-nine. So far all Miss Arial had talked about was something called phonics, and the students, their mouths shaped like O's, echoed her sounds of *ah, aa, o,* and *u,* all of them moaning like doves.

About eleven o'clock the warm-buttery smell of baking yeast rolls and pie pastry filled the halls and seeped into the room. Kya's stomach panged and fitted, and when the class finally formed a single file and marched into the cafeteria, her mouth was full of saliva. Copying the others, she picked up a tray, a green plastic plate, and flatware. A large window with a counter opened into the kitchen, and laid out before her was an enormous enamel pan of chicken pie crisscrossed with thick, crispy pastry, hot gravy bubbling up. A tall black woman, smiling and calling some of the kids by name, plopped a big helping of pie on her plate, then some pink-lady peas in butter and a yeast roll. She got banana pudding and her own small red-and-white carton of milk to put on her tray.

She turned into the seating area, where most of the tables were full of kids laughing and talking. She recognized Chase Andrews and his friends, who had nearly knocked her off the sidewalk with their bikes, so she turned her head away and sat at an empty table. Several times in quick succession, her eyes betrayed her and glanced at the boys, the only faces she knew. But they, like everyone else, ignored her.

Kya stared at the pie full of chicken, carrots, potatoes, and little peas. Golden brown pastry on top. Several girls, dressed in full skirts fluffed out wide with layers of crinolines, approached. One was tall, skinny, and blond, another round with chubby cheeks. Kya wondered how they could climb a tree or even get in a boat wearing those big skirts. Certainly couldn't wade for frogs; wouldn't even be able to see their own feet.

As they neared, Kya stared at her plate. What would she say if they sat next to her? But the girls passed her by, chirping like birds, and joined their friends at another table. For all the hunger in her stomach, she found her mouth had gone dry, making it difficult to swallow. So after eating only a few bites, she drank all the milk, stuffed as much pie as she could into the milk carton, carefully so nobody would see her do it, and wrapped it and the roll in her napkin.

The rest of the day, she never opened her mouth. Even when the teacher asked her a question, she sat mute. She reckoned she was supposed to learn from them, not them from her. *Why put maself up for being laughed at?* she thought.

At the last bell, she was told the bus would drop her three miles from her lane because the road was too sandy from there, and that she had to walk to the bus every morning. On the way home, as the bus swayed in deep ruts and passed stretches of cord grass, a chant rose from the front: "MISS Catherine Danielle Clark!" Tallskinnyblonde and Roundchubbycheeks, the girls at lunch, called out, "Where ya been, marsh hen? Where's yo' hat, swamp rat?"

The bus finally stopped at an unmarked intersection of tangled tracks way back in the woods. The driver cranked the door open, and Kya scooted out and ran for nearly half a mile, heaved for breath, then jogged all the way to their lane. She didn't stop at the shack but ran full out through the palmettos to the lagoon and down the trail that led through dense, sheltering oaks to the ocean. She broke out onto the barren beach, the sea opening its arms wide, the wind tearing loose her braided hair as she stopped at the tide line. She was as near to tears as she had been the whole day.

Above the roar of pounding waves, Kya called to the birds. The ocean sang bass, the gulls sang soprano. Shrieking and crying, they circled over the marsh and above the sand as she threw piecrust and yeast rolls onto the beach. Legs hanging down, heads twisting, they landed.

A few birds pecked gently between her toes, and she laughed from the tickling until tears streamed down her cheeks, and finally great, ragged sobs erupted from that tight place below her throat. When the carton was empty she didn't think she could stand the pain, so afraid they would leave her like everybody else. But the gulls squatted on the beach around her and went about their business of preening their gray extended wings. So she sat down too and wished she could gather them up and take them with her to the porch to sleep. She imagined them all packed in her bed, a fluffy bunch of warm, feathered bodies under the covers together.

Two days later she heard the Ford Crestliner churning in the sand and ran into the marsh, stepping heavily across sandbars, leaving footprints as plain as day, then tiptoeing into the water, leaving no tracks, doubling back, and taking off in a different direction. When she got to mud, she ran in circles, creating a confusion of clues. Then, when she reached hard ground, she whispered across it, jumping from grass clump to sticks, leaving no trace.

They came every two or three days for a few more weeks, the man in the fedora doing the search and chase, but he never even got close. Then one week no one came. There was only the cawing of crows. She dropped her hands to her sides, staring at the empty lane.

Kya never went back to school a day in her life. She returned to heron watching and shell collecting, where she reckoned she could learn something. "I can already coo like a dove," she told herself. "And lots better than them. Even with all them fine shoes."

One morning, a few weeks after her day at school, the sun glared white-hot as Kya climbed into her brothers' tree fort at the beach and searched for sailing ships hung with skull-and-crossbones flags. Proving that imagination grows in the loneliest of soils, she shouted, "Ho! Pirates ho!" Brandishing her sword, she jumped from the tree to attack. Suddenly pain shot through her right foot, racing like fire up her leg. Knees caving in, she fell on her side and shrieked. She saw a long rusty nail sticking deep in the bottom of her foot. "Pa!" she screamed. She tried to remember if he had come home last night. "HELP me, Pa," she cried out, but there was no answer. In one fast move, she reached down and yanked the nail out, screaming to cover the pain.

She moved her arms through the sand in nonsensical motions, whimpering. Finally, she sat up and looked at the bottom of her foot. There was almost no blood, just the tiny opening of a small, deep wound. Right then she remembered the lockjaw. Her stomach went tight and she felt cold. Jodie had told her about a boy who stepped on a rusty nail and didn't get a tetanus shot. His jaws jammed shut, clenched so tight he couldn't open his mouth. Then his spine cramped backward like a bow, but there was nothing anybody could do but stand there and watch him die from the contortions.

Jodie was very clear on one point: you had to get the shot within two days after stepping on a nail, or you were doomed. Kya had no idea how to get one of those shots.

"I gotta do sump'm. I'll lock up for sure waitin' for Pa." Sweat rolling down her face in beads, she hobbled across the beach, finally entering the cooler oaks around the shack.

Ma used to soak wounds in salt water and pack them with mud mixed with all kinds of potions. There was no salt in the kitchen, so Kya limped into the woods toward a brackish slipstream so salty at low tide, its edges glistened with brilliant white crystals. She sat on the ground, soaking her foot in the marsh's brine, all the while moving her mouth: open, close, open, close, mocking yawns, chewing motions, anything to keep it from jamming up. After nearly an hour, the tide receded enough for her to dig a hole in the black mud with her fingers, and she eased her foot gently into the silky earth. The air was cool here, and eagle cries gave her bearing.

By late afternoon she was very hungry, so went back to the shack. Pa's room was still empty, and he probably wouldn't be home for hours. Playing poker and drinking whiskey kept a man busy most of the night. There were no grits, but rummaging around, she found an old greasy tin of Crisco shortening, dipped up a tiny bit of the white fat, and spread it on a soda cracker. Nibbled at first, then ate five more.

She eased into her porch bed, listening for Pa's boat. The approaching night tore and darted and sleep came in bits, but she must have dropped off near morning for she woke with the sun fully on her face. Quickly she opened her mouth; it still worked. She shuffled back and forth from the brackish pool to the shack until, by tracking the sun, she knew two days had passed. She opened and closed her mouth. Maybe she had made it.

That night, tucking herself into the sheets of the floor mattress, her mud-caked foot wrapped in a rag, she wondered if she would wake up dead. No, she remembered, it wouldn't be that easy: her back would bow; her limbs twist.

A few minutes later, she felt a twinge in her lower back and sat up. "Oh no, oh no. Ma, Ma." The sensation in her back repeated itself and made her hush. "It's just an itch," she muttered. Finally, truly exhausted, she slept, not opening her eyes until doves murmured in the oak.

She walked to the pool twice a day for a week, living on saltines and Crisco, and Pa never came home the whole time. By the eighth day she could circle her foot without stiffness and the pain had retreated to the surface. She danced a little jig, favoring her foot, squealing, "I did it, I did it!"

The next morning, she headed for the beach to find more pirates.

"First thing I'm gonna do is boss my crew to pick up all them nails."

Every morning she woke early, still listening for the clatter of Ma's busy cooking. Ma's favorite breakfast had been scrambled eggs from her own hens, ripe red tomatoes sliced, and cornbread fritters made by pouring a mixture of cornmeal, water, and salt onto grease so hot the concoction bubbled up, the edges frying into crispy lace. Ma said you weren't really frying something unless you could hear it crackling from the next room, and all her life Kya had heard those fritters popping in grease when she woke. Smelled the blue, hot-corn smoke. But now the kitchen was silent, cold, and Kya slipped from her porch bed and stole to the lagoon.

Months passed, winter easing gently into place, as southern winters do. The sun, warm as a blanket, wrapped Kya's shoulders, coaxing her deeper into the marsh. Sometimes she heard night-sounds she didn't know or jumped from lightning too close, but whenever she stumbled, it was the land that caught her. Until at last, at some unclaimed moment, the heart-pain seeped away like water into sand. Still there, but deep. Kya laid her hand upon the breathing, wet earth, and the marsh became her mother.

5.

Investigation

1969

Overhead, cicadas squealed against a mean sun. All other life-forms cowered from the heat, emitting only a vacant hum from the undergrowth.

Wiping his brow, Sheriff Jackson said, "Vern, there's more to do here, but it doesn't feel right. Chase's wife and folks don't know he's passed."

"I'll go tell them, Ed," Dr. Vern Murphy replied.

"I appreciate that. Take my truck. Send the ambulance back for Chase, and Joe with my truck. But don't speak a word about this to anybody else. I don't want everybody in this town out here, and that's just what'll happen if you mention it."

Before moving, Vern stared for a long minute at Chase, as though he had overlooked something. As a doctor, he should fix this. Heavy swamp air stood behind them, waiting patiently for its turn.

Ed turned to the boys. "Y'all stay right here. I don't need anybody yapping about this in town, and don't put your hands on anything or make any more tracks in the mud."

"Yessir," Benji said. "Ya think somebody killed Chase, don't ya? 'Cause there's no footprints. Pushed him off, maybe?"

"I didn't say any such thing. This is standard police work. Now, you boys just keep out of the way and don't repeat anything you hear out here."

Deputy Joe Purdue, a small man with thick sideburns, showed up in the patrol truck in less than fifteen minutes.

"Just can't take it in. Chase dead. He was the best quarterback this town ever saw. This is plumb outta kilter."

"You got that right. Well, let's get to work."

"What ya got so far?"

Ed moved farther from the boys. "Well, obviously, on the surface, it looks like an accident: he fell from the tower and was killed. But so far I haven't found any of his footprints walking toward the steps or prints from anybody else either. Let's see if we can find any evidence that somebody covered 'em up."

The two lawmen combed the area for a full ten minutes. "You're right, not one print 'cept for the boys," Joe said.

"Yeah, and no signs of somebody brushing them out. I just don't get it. Let's move on. I'll work on this later," Ed said.

They took pictures of the body, of its position relative to the steps, close-ups of head wounds, the leg bent wrong. Joe made notes as Ed dictated. As they measured the distance from the body to the trail, they heard the sides of the ambulance scratching the thick bushes along the lane. The driver, an old black man who'd taken the wounded, ill, dying, and dead under his charge for decades, bowed his head in respect and whispered suggestions: "A'right den, his'n arms ain't gwine tuck in much, so cain't roll 'im onta the gunny; hafta lift 'im and he's gwine be heavy; Sheriff, sir, ya cradle Mr. Chase's head. Dat's good. My, my." By late morning, they'd loaded him, complete with clinging sludge, into the back.

Since Dr. Murphy had by now informed Chase's parents of his death, Ed told the boys they could go on home, and he and Joe started up the stairs, which switched to the top, narrowing at each level. As they climbed, the round corners of the world moved out farther and farther, the lush, rounded forests and watery marsh expanding to the very rims.

When they reached the last step, Jackson lifted his hands and pushed open an iron grate. After they climbed onto the platform, he eased it down again because it was part of the floor. Wooden planks, splintered and grayed with age, formed the center of the platform, but around the perimeter, the floor was a series of see-through square grates that could be opened and closed. As long as they were down you could walk on them safely, but if one was left open, you could fall to the earth sixty feet below.

"Hey, look at that." Ed pointed to the far side of the platform, where one of the grates stood open.

"What the hell?" Joe said as they walked to it. Peering down, they saw the perfect outline of Chase's misshapen form embedded in the mud. Yellowish goo and duckweed had splashed to the sides like a splatter painting.

"This doesn't figure," Ed said. "Sometimes folks forget to close the grate over the stairs. You know, on their way back down. We've found it open a few times, but the others are almost never left open."

"Why would Chase open this one in the first place? Why would anybody?"

"Unless somebody planned to push somebody else to their death," Ed said.

"Then why didn't they close it afterward?"

"Because if Chase had fallen through on his own, he couldn't have closed it. Had to be left open to look like an accident."

"Look at that support beam below the hole. It's all bashed in and splintered."

"Yeah, I see. Chase must've banged his head on it when he fell."

"I'll climb out there, look for blood or hair samples. Collect some splinters."

"Thanks, Joe. And take some close-ups. I'll go get a rope to spot you. We don't need two bodies in this muck in one day. And we have to take fingerprints off this grate, the grate by the stairs, the railing, the banisters. Everything anybody would've touched. And collect any hair samples, threads."

More than two hours later, they stretched their backs from the leaning and stooping. Ed said, "I'm not saying there was foul play. Way too early. But besides that, I can't think of anyone who'd want to kill Chase."

"Well, I'd say there'd be quite a list," the deputy said.

"Like who? What're you talking about?"

"C'mon, Ed. Ya know how Chase was. Tom-cattin', ruttin' 'round like a penned bull let out. 'Fore he was married, after he was married, with single girls, married women. I seen randy dogs at a bitch fest better behaved."

"C'mon, he wasn't that bad. Sure. He had a reputation as a ladies' man. But I don't see anybody in this town committin' murder over it."

"I'm just sayin' there's people didn't like him. Some jealous husband. It'd have to be somebody he knew. Somebody we all know. Not likely Chase'd climb up here with some stranger," Joe said.

"Unless he was up to his navel in debt with some out-of-towner. Something like that we didn't know about. And a man strong enough to push Chase Andrews. No small task."

Joe said, "I can already think of a few guys up to it."

6.

A Boat and a Boy

1952

One morning, Pa, shaved fresh and dressed in a wrinkled button-down shirt, came into the kitchen and said he was leaving on the Trailways bus for Asheville to discuss some issues with the army. He figured he had more disability due him and was off to see about it and wouldn't be back for three or four days. He'd never told Kya his business, where he was going, or when he was coming back, so, standing there in her too-short bib overalls, she stared up at him, mute.

"Ah b'leeve ya deaf and dumb as all git-out," he said, the porch door slapping behind him.

Kya watched him gimp along the path, left leg swinging to the side, then forward. Her fingers knotted. Maybe they were all going to leave her, one by one down this lane. When he reached the road and unexpectedly looked back, she threw her hand up and waved hard. A shot to keep him tethered. Pa lifted an arm in a quick, dismissive salutation. But it was something. It was more than Ma had done.

From there, she wandered to the lagoon, where early light caught the glimmer of hundreds of dragonfly wings. Oaks and thick brush encircled the water, darkening it cavelike, and she stopped as she eyed Pa's boat drifting there on the line. If she took it into the marsh and he found out, he'd take his belt to her. Or the paddle he kept by the porch door; the "welcome bat," Jodie had called it.

Perhaps a yearning to reach out yonder pulled her toward the boat—a bent-up, flat-bottomed metal skiff Pa used for fishing. She'd been out in it all her life, usually with Jodie. Sometimes he'd let her steer. She even knew the way through some of the intricate channels and estuaries that wandered through a patchwork of water and land, land and water, finally to the sea. Because even though the ocean was just beyond the trees surrounding the shack, the only way to get there by boat was to go in the opposite direction, inland, and wind through miles of the maze of waterways that eventually hooked back to the sea.

But, being only seven and a girl, she'd never taken the boat out by herself. It floated there, tied by a single cotton line to a log. Gray grunge, frayed fishing tackle, and half-crushed beer cans covered the boat floor. Stepping in, she said out loud, "Gotta check the gas like Jodie said, so Pa won't figure I took it." She poked a broken reed into the rusted tank. "'Nough for a short ride, I reckon."

Like any good robber, she looked around, then flicked the cotton line free of the log and poled forward with the lone paddle. The silent cloud of dragonflies parted before her.

Not able to resist, she pulled the starter rope and jerked back when the motor caught the first time, sputtering and burping white smoke. Grabbing the tiller, she turned the throttle too far, and the boat turned sharply, the engine screaming. She released the throttle, threw her hands up, and the boat eased to a drift, purring.

When in trouble, just let go. Go back to idle.

Accelerating now more gently, she steered around the old fallen cypress, *putt, putt, putt* beyond the piled sticks of the beaver lodge. Then, holding her breath, she steered toward the lagoon entrance, almost hidden by brambles. Ducking beneath the low-hanging limbs of giant trees, she churned slowly through thicket for more than a hundred yards, as easy turtles slid from water-logs. A floating mat of duckweed colored the water as green as the leafy ceiling, creating an emerald tunnel. Finally, the trees parted, and she glided into a place of wide sky and reaching grasses, and the sounds of cawing birds. The view a chick gets, she reckoned, when it finally breaks its shell.

Kya tooled along, a tiny speck of a girl in a boat, turning this way and that as endless estuaries branched and braided before her. *Keep left at all the turns going out,* Jodie had said. She barely touched the throttle, easing the boat through the current, keeping the noise low. As she broke around a stand of reeds, a whitetail doe with last spring's fawn stood lapping water. Their heads jerked up, slinging droplets through the air. Kya didn't stop or they would bolt, a lesson she'd learned from watching wild turkeys: if you act like a predator, they act like prey. Just ignore them, keep going slow. She drifted by, and the deer stood as still as a pine until Kya disappeared beyond the salt grass.

She entered a place with dark lagoons in a throat of oaks and remembered a channel on the far side that flowed to an enormous estuary. Several times she came upon dead ends, had to backtrack to take another turn. Keeping all these landmarks straight in her mind so she could get back. Finally the estuary lay ahead, water stretching so far it captured the whole sky and all the clouds within it.

The tide was going out, she knew by water lines along the creek shores. When it receded enough, any time from now, some channels would shallow up and she'd run aground, get stranded. She'd have to head back before then.

As she rounded a stand of tall grass, suddenly the ocean's face—gray, stern, and pulsing—frowned at her. Waves slammed one another, awash in their own white saliva, breaking apart on the shore with loud booms—energy searching for a beachhead. Then they flattened into quiet tongues of foam, waiting for the next surge.

The surf taunted her, daring her to breach the waves and enter the sea, but without Jodie, her courage failed. Time to turn around anyway. Thunderheads grew in the western sky, forming huge gray mushrooms pressing at the seams.

There'd been no other people, not even distant boats, so it was a surprise when she entered the large estuary again, and there, close against the marsh grass, was a boy fishing from another battered rig. Her course would take her only twenty feet from him. By now, she looked every bit the swamp child—hair blown into tangles, dusty cheeks streaked with wind-tears.

Neither low gas nor storm threat gave her the same edgy feeling as seeing another person, especially a boy. Ma had told her older sisters to watch out for them; if you look tempting, men turn into predators. Squishing her lips tight, she thought, *What am I gonna do? I gotta go right by him.*

From the corner of her eye, she saw he was thin, his golden curls stuffed under a red baseball cap. Much older than she, eleven, maybe twelve. Her face was grim as she approached, but he smiled at her, warm and open, and touched the brim of his hat like a gentleman greeting a fine lady in a gown and bonnet. She nodded slightly, then looked ahead, increasing the throttle and passing him by.

All she could think of now was getting back to familiar footing, but somewhere she must have turned wrong, for when she reached the second string of lagoons, she couldn't find the channel that led home. Round and round, near oak knees and myrtle thickets, she searched. A slow panic eased in. Now, the grass banks, sandbars, and bends all looked the same. She cut the engine and stood smack-dab in the middle

43

of the boat, balancing with feet spread wide, trying to see over the reeds, but couldn't. She sat. Lost. Low on gas. Storm coming.

Stealing Pa's words, she cussed her brother for leaving. "Damn ya, Jodie! Shit fire an' fall in. You just shit fire an' fall in it."

She whimpered once as the boat drifted in soft current. Clouds, gaining ground against the sun, moved weighted but silent overhead, pushing the sky and dragging shadows across the clear water. Could be a gale any minute. Worse, though: if she wandered too long, Pa would know she took the boat. She eased ahead; maybe she could find that boy.

Another few minutes of creek brought a bend and the large estuary ahead, and on the other side, the boy in his boat. Egrets took flight, a line of white flags against the mounting gray clouds. She anchored him hard with her eyes. Afraid to go near him, afraid not to. Finally, she turned across the estuary.

He looked up when she neared.

"Hey," he said.

"Hey." She looked beyond his shoulder into the reeds.

"Which way you headed, anyhow?" he asked. "Not out, I hope. That storm's comin'."

"No," she said, looking down at the water.

"You okay?"

Her throat tightened against a sob. She nodded but couldn't speak.

"You lost?"

She bobbed her head again. Wasn't going to cry like a girl.

"Well, then. I git lost all the time," he said, and smiled. "Hey, I know you. You're Jodie Clark's sister."

"I used ta be. He's gone."

"Well, you're still his . . ." But he let it drop.

"How'd you know me?" She threw a quick, direct look at his eyes.

44

"Oh, I've been fishin' with Jodie some. I saw you a couple a' times. You were just a little kid. You're Kya, right?"

Someone knew her name. She was taken aback. Felt anchored to something; released from something else.

"Yeah. You know my place? From here?"

"Reckon I do. It's 'bout time anyhow." He nodded at the clouds. "Follow me." He pulled his line, put tackle in the box, and started his outboard. As he headed across the estuary, he waved, and she followed. Cruising slowly, he went directly to the right channel, looked back to make sure she'd made the turn, and kept going. He did that at every bend to the oak lagoons. As he turned into the dark waterway toward home, she could see where she'd gone wrong, and would never make the mistake again.

He guided her—even after she waved that she knew her way— across her lagoon, up to the shore where the shack squatted in the woods. She motored up to the old waterlogged pine and tied up. He drifted back from her boat, bobbing in their contrary wakes.

"You okay now?"

"Yeah."

"Well, storm's comin', I better git."

She nodded, then remembered how Ma taught her. "Thank ya."

"All right, then. My name's Tate 'case ya see me again."

She didn't respond, so he said, "Bye now."

As he headed out, slow raindrops splattered the lagoon beach, and she said, "It's gonna rain bullfrogs; that boy'll get soaked through."

She stooped to the gas tank and stuck in her reed dipstick, cupping her hands around the rim, so rain wouldn't drop in. Maybe she couldn't count coins, but she knew for sure, you can't let water get in gas.

It's way low. Pa's gonna know. I gotta tote a can to the Sing Oil 'fore Pa gits back.

She knew the owner, Mr. Johnny Lane, always referred to her family as swamp trash, but dealing with him, the storms, and tides would be worth it, because all she could think of now was getting back into that space of grass and sky and water. Alone, she'd been scared, but that was already humming as excitement. There was something else, too. The calmness of the boy. She'd never known anybody to speak or move so steady. So sure and easy. Just being near him, and not even that close, had eased her tightness. For the first time since Ma and Jodie left, she breathed without pain; felt something other than the hurt. She needed this boat and that boy.

That same afternoon, holding his bike by the handlebars, Tate Walker strolled through town, nodding at Miss Pansy in the Five and Dime, and past the Western Auto to the tip of the town wharf. He scanned the sea for his dad's shrimp boat, *The Cherry Pie*, and spotted its bright red paint far out, the wide net-wings rocking with the swells. As it neared, escorted by its own cloud of gulls, he waved, and his father, a large man with mountain shoulders and thick red hair and a beard, threw his hand in the air. Scupper, as everyone in the village called him, tossed the line to Tate, who tied up, then jumped on board to help the crew unload the catch.

Scupper tousled Tate's hair. "How's it, son? Thanks for coming by."

Tate smiled, nodded. "Sure." They and the crew busied about, loading shrimp into crates, toting them to the wharf, calling out to one another about grabbing beers at the Dog-Gone, asking Tate about school. Taller by a hand than the other men, Scupper scooped up three wire crates at a time, carrying them across the plank, going back for more. His fists were bear-sized, knuckles chapped and split. In less than forty minutes the deck was hosed, nets tied, lines secured.

He told the crew he'd join them another day for beer; he had to do some tuning up before going home. In the wheelhouse, Scupper put a 78 record of Miliza Korjus on the player strapped to the counter and turned the volume up. He and Tate went below and squeezed into the engine hold, where Tate handed tools to his dad as he greased parts and tightened bolts by a dim lightbulb. All the while the soaring, sweet opera lifted higher into the sky.

Scupper's great-great-grandfather, emigrating from Scotland, had shipwrecked off the coast of North Carolina in the 1760s and was the only survivor. He swam to shore, landing on the Outer Banks, found a wife, and fathered thirteen children. Many could trace their roots back to that one Mr. Walker, but Scupper and Tate stayed mostly to themselves. Didn't join the Sunday picnic spreads of chicken salad and deviled eggs with their relatives often, not like they had when his mother and sister were still there.

Finally, in the graying dusk, Scupper slapped Tate on the shoulders. "All done. Let's get home, get supper on."

They walked up the wharf, down Main, and out a winding road to their house, a two-story with weathered cedar-shake siding, built in the 1800s. The white window trim had been painted fresh, and the lawn running almost to the sea was cut neat. But the azaleas and rosebushes next to the house sulked in weeds.

Pulling off yellow boots in the mudroom, Scupper asked, "You tired of burgers?"

"Never tired of burgers."

Tate stood at the kitchen counter, picking up globs of hamburger meat, forming patties, and placing them on a plate. His mother and sister, Carianne, both wearing baseball caps, grinned at him from a picture hanging next to the window. Carianne loved that Atlanta Crackers cap, had worn it everywhere.

He looked away from them, started slicing tomatoes, stirring baked beans. If not for him, they'd be here. His mother basting a chicken, Carianne cutting biscuits.

As usual Scupper got the burgers a bit black, but they were juicy inside and thick as a small city phone book. Both hungry, they ate in silence for a while, and then Scupper asked Tate about school.

"Biology's good; I like it, but we're doing poetry in English class. Can't say I like it much. We each gotta read one out loud. You used to recite some, but I don't remember them."

"I got the poem for you, son," Scupper said. "My favorite—'The Cremation of Sam McGee' by Robert Service. Used to read it out to y'all. Was your mama's favorite. She laughed every time I read it, never got tired of it."

Tate looked down at the mention of his mother, pushed his beans around.

Scupper went on. "Don't go thinking poetry's just for sissies. There's mushy love poems, for sure, but there's also funny ones, lots about nature, war even. Whole point of it—they make ya feel something." His dad had told him many times that the definition of a real man is one who cries without shame, reads poetry with his heart, feels opera in his soul, and does what's necessary to defend a woman. Scupper walked to the sitting room, calling back, "I used to know most of it by heart, but not anymore. But here it is, I'll read it to ya." He sat back down at the table and began reading. When he got to this segment:

> "And there sat Sam, looking cool and calm, in the heart of
> the furnace roar;
> And he wore a smile you could see a mile, and he said,
> 'Please close that door.

48

It's fine in here, but I greatly fear you'll let in the cold
    and storm—
Since I left Plumtree down in Tennessee, it's the first time
    I've been warm.'"

Scupper and Tate chuckled.

"Your mom always laughed at that."

They smiled, remembering. Just sat there a minute. Then Scupper said he'd wash up while Tate did his homework. In his room, scanning through the poetry book for one to read in class, Tate found a poem by Thomas Moore:

> . . . she's gone to the Lake of the Dismal Swamp,
> Where, all night long, by a fire-fly lamp,
> She paddles her white canoe.
>
> And her fire-fly lamp I soon shall see,
> And her paddle I soon shall hear;
> Long and loving our life shall be,
> And I'll hide the maid in a cypress tree,
> When the footstep of death is near.

The words made him think of Kya, Jodie's little sister. She'd seemed so small and alone in the marsh's big sweep. He imagined his own sister lost out there. His dad was right—poems made you feel something.

7

The Fishing Season

1952

That evening, after the fishing boy led her home through the marsh, Kya sat cross-legged on her porch bed. Mist from the downpour eased through the patched-up screen, touching her face. She thought about the boy. Kind yet strong, like Jodie. The only people she ever spoke to were Pa now and then and, even less often, the cash-register lady at the Piggly Wiggly, Mrs. Singletary, who had recently taken to teaching Kya the difference between quarters, nickels, and dimes—she already knew about pennies. But Mrs. Singletary could also get nosey.

"Dahlin', what's yo' name, anyhow? And why don't yo' ma come in anymore? Haven't seen 'er since the turnips put out."

"Ma's got lots of chores, so she sends me to the store."

"Yeah, dear, but ya never buy nears enough for yo' family."

"Ya know, ma'am, I gotta go. Ma needs these grits right away."

When possible, Kya avoided Mrs. Singletary, using the other checkout lady, who didn't show any interest except to say kids shouldn't come to the market barefoot. She thought of telling the lady she didn't plan to pick grapes with her toes. Who could afford grapes, anyhow?

More and more Kya didn't talk to anybody but the gulls. She wondered if she could strike some bargain with Pa to use his boat. Out in the marsh, she could collect feathers and shells and maybe see the boy sometimes. She'd never had a friend, but she could feel the use of it, the pull. They could boat around in the estuaries some, explore the fens. He might think of her as a little kid, but he knew his way around the marsh and might teach her.

Pa didn't have a car. He used the boat to fish, to go to town, to maneuver through the swamp to the Swamp Guinea, a weathered bar and poker joint connected to solid ground by a rickety boardwalk through cattails. Made of rough-cut clapboard under a tin roof, it rambled from one add-on to the next, the floor at different levels depending on how high the brick chicken-legs perched it above the swamp. When Pa went there or anywhere, he took the boat, only rarely walked, so why would he lend it to her?

But he'd let her brothers use it when he wasn't, probably because they caught fish for supper. She had no interest in fishing, but maybe she could trade something else, figuring that was the way to reach him. Cook maybe, do more around the house, until Ma came back.

The rain eased. A single drop, here then there, shook a leaf like the flick of a cat's ear. Kya hopped up, cleaned out the Frigidaire-cupboard, mopped the stained plywood kitchen floor, and scraped off months of caked-on grits from the woodstove burners. Early the next morning, she scrubbed Pa's sheets, reeking of sweat and whiskey, and draped them over the palmettos. She went through her brothers' room, not much bigger than a closet, dusting and sweeping. Dirty socks were piled in the back of the closet and yellowed comic books strewn next to the two soiled mattresses on the floor. She tried to see the boys' faces, the feet that went with the socks, but the details blurred. Even Jodie's face was fading; she'd see his eyes for an instant, then they'd slip away, closing.

The next morning, carrying a gallon can, she walked the sandy tracks to the Piggly and bought matches, backbone, and salt. Saved out two dimes. "Can't get milk, gotta get gas."

She stopped by the Sing Oil filling station just outside Barkley Cove, which stood in a grove of pines surrounded by rusted-out trucks and jalopy cars stacked on cement blocks.

Mr. Lane saw Kya coming. "Git on outta here, ya little beggar-hen. Marsh trash."

"I got cash money, Mr. Lane. I need gas and oil for Pa's boat motor." She held out two dimes, two nickels, and five pennies.

"Well, it ain't hardly worth ma trouble for such a piddly sum, but c'mon, give it here." He reached for the bent-up, square container.

She thanked Mr. Lane, who grunted again. The groceries and gas weighed more with every mile, and it took some time to get home. Finally in the shade of the lagoon, she emptied the can into the gas tank and scrubbed the boat with rags and wet sand for grist until the metal sides showed through the grime.

On the fourth day after Pa left, she started keeping a lookout. By late afternoon a cold dread set in and her breathing shallowed up. Here she was again, staring down the lane. Mean as he was, she needed him to come back. Finally, in the early evening, there he came, walking the sandy ruts. She ran to the kitchen and laid out a goulash of boiled mustard greens, backbone, and grits. She didn't know how to make gravy, so poured the backbone stock—floating with morsels of white fat—into an empty jelly jar. The plates were cracked and didn't match, but she had the fork on the left, the knife on the right like Ma taught her. Then she waited, flattened up against the Frigidaire like a roadkill stork.

He banged the front door open against the wall and walked through the sitting room to his bedroom in three strides, without calling her or looking in the kitchen. That was normal. She heard him putting his case on the floor, pulling out drawers. He'd notice the fresh bedding, the clean floor for sure. If not his eyes, his nose would catch the difference.

In a few minutes he stepped out, straight into the kitchen, and looked at the set table, at the steaming bowls of food. He saw her standing against the fridge, and they stared at each other like they'd never seen each other before.

"Ah swannee, girl, what's a' this? Looks like ya went an' got all growed up. Cookin' and all." He didn't smile, but his face was calm. He was unshaven, with dark unwashed hair hanging across his left temple. But he was sober; she knew the signs.

"Yessir. I fixed cornbread too, but it didn't come out."

"Well, ah thankee. That's a mighty good girl. Ah'm plumb wore out and hungry as a wallow-hog." He pulled out a chair and sat, so she did the same. In silence they filled their plates and picked stringy meat from the stingy backbones. He lifted a vertebra and sucked out the marrow, fatty juice glistening on his whiskered cheeks. Gnawed on those bones till they were slick as silk ribbons.

"This here's better'n a cold collard sandwich," he said.

"I wish the cornbread'd come out. Maybe shoulda put more soda in, less eggs." Kya couldn't believe she was talking on so, but couldn't stop herself. "Ma made it so good, but I guess I didn't pay enough mind to the details . . ." Then thought she shouldn't be talking about Ma, so hushed up.

Pa pushed his plate toward her. "'Nough for a dab more?"

"Yessir, there's aplenty."

"Oh, and tump some of that cornbread right in tha stew. Ah got a hankerin' for soppin' up the stock, and my bet is that bread's just fine, mushy like spoonbread."

She smiled to herself as she filled his plate. Who would've thought they'd find cornbread as a footing.

But now, after thinking about it, she worried that if she asked to use the boat, he would think she'd cooked and cleaned only for the favor, which was how it started out, but now seemed somehow different. She liked sitting down and eating like a family. Her need to talk to somebody felt urgent.

So she didn't mention using the boat by herself, instead asked, "Can I go out fishin' with ya sometime?"

He laughed hard, but it was kind. The first time he'd laughed since Ma and the others left. "So ya wanta go fishin'?"

"Yessir, I do."

"You're a girl," he said, looking at his plate, chewing backbone.

"Yessir, I'm your girl."

"Well, Ah might could take ya out sometime."

The next morning, as Kya careened down the sandy lane, her arms held straight out, she sputtered wet noises from her lips, spittle spraying. She would lift off and sail over the marsh, looking for nests, then rise and fly wing to wing with eagles. Her fingers became long feathers, splayed against the sky, gathering the wind beneath her. Then suddenly she was jerked back to Earth by Pa hollering to her from the boat. Her wings collapsed, stomach pitched; he must have figured out she'd used it. She could already feel the paddle on her bottom and the backs of her legs. She knew how to hide, wait until he was drunk, and he'd never find her. But she was too far down the lane, in full view, and there he

54

was standing with all his poles and rods, motioning for her to come. She walked over, quiet, scared. The fishing tackle was strewn about, a poke of corn likker tucked under his seat.

"Git in" was all he said as invitation. She started to express glee or gratitude, but his blank expression kept her quiet, as she stepped to the bow and sat on the metal seat facing forward. He pull-cranked and they headed up the channel, ducking the overgrowth as they cruised up and down the waterways, Kya memorizing broken trees and old stump signposts. He eased the motor down in a backwater and motioned for her to sit on the center seat.

"Go on now, scratch some worms from the can," he said, a hand-rolled cigarette hanging at the corner of his mouth. He taught her to snag the bait, to cast and reel. It seemed he contorted his body in odd postures to avoid brushing against her. They only talked fishing; never ventured to other subjects, neither smiled often, but on common ground they were steady. He drank some likker but then got busy and didn't drink more. At late day, the sun sighed, fading to the color of butter, and they may not have noticed, but their own shoulders finally rounded and their necks slacked.

Secretly Kya hoped not to catch a fish, but she felt a tug, jerked her line, and raised a thick bream, flashing silver and blue. Pa leaned out and snatched it in the net, then sat back, slapping his knee and yahooing like she'd never seen. She grinned wide and they looked into each other's eyes, closing a circuit.

Before Pa strung it up, the bream flopped around in the boat bottom and Kya had to watch a distant string of pelicans, study the cloud forms, anything but look into dying fish eyes staring at a world without water, wide mouth sucking worthless air. But what it cost her and what it cost that fish was worth it to have this little shred of family. Perhaps not for the fish, but still.

They went out in the boat again the next day, and in a dark lagoon, Kya spotted the soft breast feathers of a great horned owl floating on the surface. Each curled at both ends, so that they drifted around like tiny orange boats. She scooped them up and put them in her pocket. Later she found an abandoned hummingbird nest woven onto an out-stretched branch, and tucked it safely in the bow.

That evening, Pa cooked up a supper of fried fish—coated in corn-meal and black pepper—served with grits and greens. As Kya washed up after, Pa walked into the kitchen, carrying his old World War II–issue knapsack. Standing near the door, he flung it roughly onto one of the chairs. It slid to the floor with a thud, which made her jump and whirl around.

"Thought ya could use that fer yo' feathers, bird nests, and all that other stuff ya c'lect."

"Oh," Kya said. "Oh, thank ya." But he was already out the porch door. She picked up the frayed knapsack, made of canvas tough enough for a lifetime and covered in small pockets and secret compartments. Heavy-duty zips. She stared out the window. He had never given her anything.

Every warmish day of winter and every day of spring, Pa and Kya went out, far up and down the coast, trolling, casting, and reeling. Whether in estuary or creek, she scanned for that boy Tate in his boat, hoping to see him again. She thought about him sometimes, wanted to be his friend, but had no idea how to go about it or even how to find him. Then, just like that, one afternoon she and Pa came around a bend, and there he was fishing, almost in that same spot where she first saw him. Right off, he grinned and waved. Without thinking, she threw her hand up and waved back, almost smiling. Then dropped her hand just as quick when Pa looked at her, surprised.

"One a' Jodie's friends, before he left," she said.

"Ya gotta watch out for folks 'round here," he said. "Woods're full a' white trash. Pert near ever'body out here's a no-'count."

She nodded. Wanted to look back at the boy, but didn't. Then worried he would think her unfriendly.

Pa knew the marsh the way a hawk knows his meadow: how to hunt, how to hide, how to terrorize intruders. And Kya's wide-eyed questions spurred him to explain goose seasons, fish habits, how to read weather in the clouds and riptides in the waves.

Some days she packed a picnic supper in the knapsack and they ate crumbly cornbread, which she had almost mastered, with sliced onions, as the setting sun posed over the marsh. Occasionally, he forgot the bootleg and they drank tea from jelly jars.

"My folks weren't always po', ya know," Pa blurted out one day as they sat in oak shadows, casting lines across a brown lagoon buzzing with low-flying insects.

"They had land, rich land, raised tobaccy and cott'n and such. Over near Asheville. Yo' gramma on my side wore bonnets big as wagon wheels and long skirts. We lived in a house wif a verander that went a' the way around, two stories high. It wa' fine, mighty fine."

A gramma. Kya's lips parted. Somewhere, there was or had been a grandmother. Where was she now? Kya longed to ask what happened to everybody. But was afraid.

Pa continued on his own. "Then it all went wrong together. Ah was a young'un through most of it, so don't know, but there was the D'pression, cott'n weevils, Ah don't know what all, and it was gone. Only thang left was debts, lotsa debts."

With these sketchy details, Kya struggled to visualize his past. There was nothing of Ma's history. Pa would go into a rage if any of them talked about their lives before Kya was born. She knew her family had lived somewhere far away before the marsh, near her other grandparents, a place where Ma wore store-bought dresses with small pearly buttons, satin ribbons, and lace trim. After they moved into the shack, Ma kept the dresses in trunks, taking one out every few years and stripping it down for a work smock because there was no money for anything new. Now those fine clothes along with their story were gone, burned in the bonfire Pa started after Jodie left.

Kya and Pa cast some more, their lines swishing over soft yellow pollen floating on the still water, and she thought that was the end of it, but he added, "Someday Ah'll take ya to Asheville, show ya the land that was our'n, shoulda been your'n."

After a bit he jerked his line. "Looky here, hon, Ah got us a big un, big as Alabamee!"

Back in the shack they fried the fish and hush puppies "fat as goose aigs." Then she displayed her collections, carefully pinning the insects to pieces of cardboard and the feathers to the wall of the back bedroom in a soft, stirring collage. Later she lay in her bed on the porch listening to the pines. She closed her eyes, and then opened them wide. He had called her "hon."

8

Negative Data

1969

After finishing their morning's investigative work at the fire tower, Sheriff Ed Jackson and Deputy Joe Purdue escorted Chase's widow, Pearl, and his parents, Patti Love and Sam, to see him lying on a steel table under a sheet in a chilled lab at the clinic, which served as a morgue. To say good-bye. But it was too cold for any mother; unbearable for any wife. Both women had to be helped from the room.

Back at the sheriff's office, Joe said, "Well, that was as bad as it gets . . ."

"Yeah. Don't know how anybody gets through it."

"Sam didn't say a word. He never was a talker, but this'll do him in."

Saltwater marsh, some say, can eat a cement block for breakfast, and not even the sheriff's bunker-style office could keep it at bay. Watermarks, outlined with salt crystals, waved across the lower walls, and black mildew spread like blood vessels toward the ceiling. Tiny dark mushrooms hunkered in the corners.

The sheriff pulled a bottle from the bottom drawer of his desk and poured them both a double in coffee mugs. They sipped until the sun, as golden and syrupy as the bourbon, slipped into the sea.

Four days later, Joe, waving documents in the air, entered the sheriff's office. "I got the first of the lab reports."

"Let's have a look."

They sat on opposite sides of the sheriff's desk, scanning. Joe, now and then, swatted at a single housefly.

Ed read out loud, "Time of death between midnight and two A.M., October 29 to 30, 1969. Just what we thought."

After a minute of reading, he continued. "What we have is negative data."

"You got that right. There ain't a thing here, Sheriff."

"Except for the two boys going up to the third switchback, there're no fresh fingerprints on the railing, the grates, nothing. None from Chase or anybody else." Afternoon whiskers shadowed the sheriff's otherwise ruddy complexion.

"So somebody wiped 'em clean. Everything. If nothing else, why aren't his fingerprints on the railing, the grate?"

"Exactly. First we had no footprints—now no fingerprints. There's no evidence at all that he walked across the mud to the steps, walked up the steps, or opened the two grates at the top—the one above the stairs and the one he fell through. Or that anybody else did either. But negative data's still data. Somebody cleaned up real good or killed him somewhere else and moved his body to the tower."

"But if his body was hauled to the tower, there'd be tire tracks."

"Right, we need to go back out there, look for tread marks besides ours and the ambulance. May have overlooked something."

After a minute more of reading, Ed said, "Anyway, I'm confident now, this was no accident."

Joe said, "I agree, and not just anybody can wipe up tracks this good."

"I'm hungry. Let's go by the diner on the way out there."

"Well, get ready for an ambush. Everybody in town's pretty riled up. Chase Andrews's murder's the biggest thing's happened 'round here, maybe ever. Gossip's goin' up like smoke signals."

"Well, keep an ear out. We might pick up a tidbit or two. Most ne'er-do-wells can't keep their mouths shut."

A full bank of windows, framed by hurricane shutters, covered the front of the Barkley Cove Diner, which overlooked the harbor. Only the narrow street stood between the building, constructed in 1889, and the soggy steps of the village pier. Discarded shrimp baskets and wadded-up fishing nets lined the wall under the windows, and here and there, mollusk shells littered the sidewalk. Everywhere: seabird cries, seabird dung. The aroma of sausage and biscuits, boiled turnip greens, and fried chicken thankfully overtook the high smell of fish barrels lining the dock.

A mild bustle spilled out when the sheriff opened the door. Every booth—high-backed with red padded upholstery—was taken, as were most of the tables. Joe pointed to two empty stools at the soda fountain counter, and the two walked toward them.

On the way they heard Mr. Lane from the Sing Oil saying to his diesel mechanic, "I reckon it was Lamar Sands. Ya r'member, he caught his wife doin' a number wif Chase right on the deck of his fancy ski boat. There's motive, and Lamar's had other run-ins wif tha law."

"What run-ins?"

"He was wif that bunch that slit the sheriff's tars."

"They were just kids back then."

"Thar was sump'm else too, I just cain't r'member."

Behind the counter, owner-cook Jim Bo Sweeny darted from flipping crab cakes on the griddle to stirring a pot of creamed corn on the burner to poking chicken thighs in the deep fryer, then back again. Putting piled-high plates in front of customers in between. People said he could mix biscuit dough with one hand while filleting a catfish with the other. He offered up his famous specialty—grilled flounder stuffed with shrimp served on pimento-cheese grits—only a few times a year. No advertising needed; word got out.

As the sheriff and deputy wove among the tables toward the counter, they heard Miss Pansy Price of Kress's Five and Dime say to a friend, "It coulda been that woman lives out in the marsh. Crazy 'nough for the loony bin. I jus' bet she'd be up to this kinda thing . . ."

"What d'ya mean? What'd she have to do with anything?"

"Well, for a while thar, she was got herself involved wif . . ."

As the sheriff and deputy stepped up to the counter, Ed said, "Let's just order take-out po'boys and get out of here. We can't get dragged into all this."

9.

Jumpin'

1953

Sitting in the bow, Kya watched low fingers of fog reaching for their boat. At first, torn-off cloud bits streamed over their heads, then mist engulfed them in grayness, and there was only the *tick, tick, tick* of the quiet motor. Minutes later, small splotches of unexpected color formed as the weathered shape of the marina gas station eased into view, as though it and not them was moving. Pa motored in, bumping gently against the dock. She'd only been here once. The owner, an old black man, sprang up from his chair to help them—the reason everybody called him Jumpin'. His white sideburns and salt-and-pepper hair framed a wide, generous face and owl eyes. Tall and spare, he seemed to never stop talking, smiling, or throwing his head back, lips shut tight in his own brand of laugh. He didn't dress in overalls, like most workmen around, but wore an ironed blue button-down shirt, too-short dark trousers, and work boots. Not often, but now and then on the meanest summer days, a tattered straw hat.

His Gas and Bait teetered on its own wobbly wharf. A cable ran from the closest oak on shore, about forty feet across the backwater, and held on with all its might. Jumpin's great-grandpa had built the wharf and shack of cypress planks way back before anybody could remember, sometime before the Civil War.

Three generations had nailed bright metal signs—Nehi Grape Soda, Royal Crown Cola, Camel Filters, and twenty years' worth of North Carolina automobile license plates—all over the shack, and that burst of color could be seen from the sea through all but the thickest fog.

"Hello, Mister Jake. How ya doin'?"

"Well, Ah woke up on the right side of dirt," Pa answered.

Jumpin' laughed as if he'd never heard the worn-out phrase. "Ya got your li'l daughter with you an' all. That's mighty fine."

Pa nodded. Then, as an afterthought, "Yep, this here's ma daughter, Miz Kya Clark."

"Well, I'm mighty proud to know ya, Miss Kya."

Kya searched her bare toes but found no words.

Jumpin' wasn't bothered and kept talking about the good fishing lately. Then he asked Pa, "Fill 'er up then, Mister Jake?"

"Yeah, slam 'er right up to tha top."

The men talked weather, fishing, then more weather till the tank was full.

"Good day to y'all, now," he said, as he tossed off the line.

Pa cruised slowly back onto a bright sea—the sun taking less time to devour the fog than it took Jumpin' to fill a tank. They chugged around a piney peninsula for several miles to Barkley Cove, where Pa tied to the deeply etched beams of the town wharf. Fishermen busied about, packing fish, tying line.

"Ah reckon we can git us some rest'rant vittles," Pa said, and led her along the pier toward the Barkley Cove Diner. Kya had never eaten restaurant food; had never set foot inside. Her heart thumped as she brushed dried mud from her way-too-short overalls and patted down her tangled hair. As Pa opened the door, every customer paused mid-bite. A few men nodded faintly at Pa; the women frowned and turned their heads. One snorted, "Well, they prob'ly can't read the *shirt and shoes required.*"

Pa motioned for her to sit at a small table overlooking the wharf. She couldn't read the menu, but he told her most of it, and she ordered fried chicken, mashed potatoes, gravy, white acre peas, and biscuits fluffy as fresh-picked cotton. He had fried shrimp, cheese grits, fried "okree," and fried green tomatoes. The waitress put a whole dish of butter pats perched on ice cubes and a basket of cornbread and biscuits on their table, and all the sweet iced tea they could drink. Then they had black-berry cobbler with ice cream for dessert. So full, Kya thought she might get sick, but figured it'd be worth it.

As Pa stood at the cash register paying the bill, Kya stepped out onto the sidewalk, where the ripe smell of fishing boats hung over the bay. She held a greasy napkin wrapped around the leftover chicken and biscuits. Her overalls pockets were stuffed with packages of saltines, which the waitress had left right on the table for the taking.

"Hi." Kya heard a tiny voice behind her and turned to see a girl of about four years with blond ringlets looking up at her. She was dressed in a pale blue frock and reached out her hand. Kya stared at the little hand; it was puffy-soft and maybe the cleanest thing Kya had ever seen. Never scrubbed with lye soap, certainly no mussel mud beneath the nails. Then she looked into the girl's eyes, in which she herself was reflected as just another kid.

Kya shifted the napkin to her left hand and extended her right slowly toward the girl's.

"Hey there, get away!" Suddenly Mrs. Teresa White, wife of the Methodist preacher, rushed from the door of the Buster Brown Shoe Shop.

Barkley Cove served its religion hard-boiled and deep-fried. Tiny as it was, the village supported four churches, and those were just for the whites; the blacks had three more.

Of course, the pastors and preachers, and certainly their wives, enjoyed highly respected positions in the village, always dressing and behaving accordingly. Teresa White often wore pastel skirts and white blouses, matching pumps and purse.

Now she hurried toward her daughter and lifted her in her arms. Stepping away from Kya, she put the girl back on the sidewalk and squatted next to the child.

"Meryl Lynn, dahlin', don't go near that girl, ya hear me. She's dirty."

Kya watched the mother run her fingers through the curls; didn't miss how long they held each other's eyes.

A woman came out of the Piggly Wiggly and walked quickly up to them. "Ya all right, Teresa? What happened here? Was that girl botherin' Meryl Lynn?"

"I saw her in time. Thank you, Jenny. I wish those people wouldn't come to town. Look at her. Filthy. Plumb nasty. There's that stomach flu goin' around and I just know for a fact it came in with them. Last year they brought in that case of measles, and that's serious." Teresa walked away, clutching the child.

Just then Pa, carrying some beer in a brown paper bag, called behind her, "Whatcha doin'? C'mon, we gotta git outta here. Tide's goin' out." Kya turned and followed, and as they steered home to the marsh, she saw the curls and eyes of mother and child.

Pa still disappeared some, not coming back for several days, but not as often as before. And when he did show up, he didn't collapse in a stupor but ate a meal and talked some. One night they played gin rummy, he guffawing when she won, and she giggling with her hands over her mouth like a regular girl.

Each time Kya stepped off the porch, she looked down the lane, thinking that even though the wild wisteria was fading with late spring and her mother had left late the previous summer, she might see Ma walking home through the sand. Still in her fake alligator heels. Now that she and Pa were fishing and talking, maybe they could try again to be a family. Pa had beat all of them, mostly when he was drunk. He'd be all right for a few days at a time—they would eat chicken stew together; once they flew a kite on the beach. Then: drink, shout, hit. Details of some of the bouts were sharp in her mind. Once Pa shoved Ma into the kitchen wall, hitting her until she slumped to the floor. Kya, sobbing for him to quit, touched his arm. He grabbed Kya by the shoulders, shouted for her to pull down her jeans and underpants, and bent her over the kitchen table. In one smooth, practiced motion he slid the belt from his pants and whipped her. Of course, she remembered the hot pain slicing her bare bottom, but curiously, she recalled the jeans pooled around her skinny ankles in more vivid detail. And Ma crumpled into the corner by the cookstove, crying out. Kya didn't know what all the fighting was about.

But if Ma came back now, when Pa was acting decent, maybe they could start over. Kya never thought it would be Ma who left and Pa who stayed. But she knew her mother wouldn't leave her forever; if she was out there somewhere in the world, she'd come back. Kya could still see the full, red lips as Ma sang to the radio, and hear her words, "Now listen close to Mr. Orson Welles; he speaks proper like a gentleman. Don't ever say *ain't*, it isn't even a word."

Ma had painted the estuaries and sunsets in oils and watercolors so rich they seemed peeled from the earth. She had brought some art supplies with her and could buy bits and pieces at Kress's Five and Dime. Sometimes Ma had let Kya paint her own pictures on brown paper bags from the Piggly Wiggly.

In early September of that fishing summer, on one afternoon that paled with heat, Kya walked to the mailbox at the end of the lane. Leafing through the grocery ads, she stopped dead when she saw a blue envelope addressed in Ma's neat hand. A few sycamore leaves were turning the same shade of yellow as when she left. All that time without a trace and now a letter. Kya stared at it, held it to the light, ran her fingers across the slanted, perfect script. Her heart banged against her chest.

"Ma's alive. Living somewhere else. Why hasn't she come home?" She thought of tearing the letter open, but the only word she could read for sure was her name, and it was not on the envelope.

She ran to the shack, but Pa had motored somewhere in the boat. So she propped the letter against the saltshaker on the table where he'd see it. As she boiled black-eyed peas with onions, she kept an eye on the letter lest it disappear.

Every few seconds, she ducked to the kitchen window to listen for the boat's *whirr*. Then suddenly Pa was limp-walking up the steps. All courage left her, and she dashed past him, hollering that she was going to the outhouse; supper would be ready soon. She stood inside the smelly latrine, her heart running races to her stomach. Balancing on the wooden bench, she watched through the quarter-moon slit in the door, not knowing exactly what she expected.

Then the porch door slammed, and she saw Pa walking fast toward the lagoon. He went straight to the boat, a poke in his hand, and motored away. She ran back to the house, into the kitchen, but the letter was gone. She flung open his dresser drawers, rummaged through his closet, searching. "It's mine, too! It's mine as much as yours." Back in the kitchen, she looked in the trash can and found the letter's ashes, still fringed in blue. With a spoon she dipped them up and laid them on the table, a little pile of black and blue remains. She picked, bit by bit, through the garbage; maybe some words had drifted to the bottom. But there was nothing but traces of cinder clinging to onionskin.

She sat at the table, the peas still singing in the pot, and stared at the little mound. "Ma touched these. Maybe Pa'll tell me what she wrote. Don't be stupid—that's as likely as snow fallin' in the swamp."

Even the postmark was gone. Now she'd never know where Ma was. She put the ashes in a little bottle and kept it in her cigar box next to her bed.

Pa didn't come home that night or the next day, and when he finally did, it was the old drunk who staggered through the door. When she mounted the courage to ask about the letter, he barked, "It ain't none a' yo' bidness." And then, "She ain't comin' back, so ya can just forget 'bout that." Carrying a poke, he shuffled toward the boat.

"That isn't true," Kya hollered at his back, her fists bunched at her sides. She watched him leaving, then shouted at the empty lagoon, *"Ain't isn't even a word!"*

Later she would wonder if she should have opened the letter on her own, not even shown it to Pa. Then she could have saved the words to read someday, and he'd have been better off not knowing them.

Pa never took her fishing again. Those warm days were just a thrown-in season. Low clouds parting, the sun splashing her world briefly, then closing up dark and tight-fisted again.

Kya couldn't remember how to pray. Was it how you held your hands or how hard you squinted your eyes that mattered? "Maybe if I pray, Ma and Jodie will come home. Even with all the shouting and fussing, that life was better than this lumpy-grits."

She sang mis-snippets of hymns—"and He walks with me when dew is still on the roses"—all she remembered from the little white church where Ma had taken her a few times. Their last visit had been Easter Sunday before Ma left, but all Kya remembered about the holiday was shouting and blood, somebody falling, she and Ma running, so she dropped the memory altogether.

Kya looked through the trees at Ma's corn and turnip patch, all weeds now. Certainly there were no roses.

"Just forget it. No god's gonna come to this garden."

10.

Just Grass in the Wind

1969

Sand keeps secrets better than mud. The sheriff parked his rig at the beginning of the fire tower lane so they wouldn't drive over any evidence of someone driving the night of the alleged murder. But as they walked along the track, looking for vehicle treads other than their own, sand grains shifted into formless dimples with every step.

Then, at the mud holes and swampy areas near the tower, a profusion of detailed stories revealed themselves: a raccoon with her four young had trailed in and out of the muck; a snail had woven a lacy pattern interrupted by the arrival of a bear; and a small turtle had lain in the cool mud, its belly forming a smooth shallow bowl.

"Clear as a picture, but besides our rigs, not a thing man-made."

"I dunno," Joe said. "See this straight edge, then a little triangle. That could be a tread."

"No, I think that's a bit of turkey print, where a deer stepped on top, made it look geometrical like that."

After another quarter hour, the sheriff said, "Let's hike out to that little bay. See if somebody boated over here instead of coming by truck." Pushing pungent myrtle from their faces, they walked to the tiny inlet. The damp sand revealed prints of crabs, herons, and pipers, but no humans.

"Well, but look at this." Joe pointed to a large pattern of disturbed sand crystals that fanned into an almost perfect half circle. "Could be the imprint of a round-bowed boat that was pulled on shore."

"No. See where the wind blew this broken grass stalk back and forth through the sand. Drawing this half circle. That's just grass in the wind."

They stood looking around. The rest of the small half-moon beach was covered in a thick layer of broken shells, a jumble of crustacean parts, and crab claws. Shells the best secret-keepers of all.

11.

Croker Sacks Full

1956

In the winter of 1956, when Kya was ten, Pa came hobbling to the shack less and less often. Weeks passed with no whiskey bottle on the floor, no body sprawled on the bed, no Monday money. She kept expecting to see him limping through the trees, toting his poke. One full moon, then another had passed since she'd seen him.

Sycamore and hickories stretched naked limbs against a dull sky, and the relentless wind sucked any joy the winter sun might have spread across the bleakness. A useless, drying wind in a sea-land that couldn't dry.

Sitting on the front steps, she thought about it. A poker-game fight could have ended with him beat up and dumped in the swamp on a cold, rainy night. Or maybe he just got fall-down drunk, wandered off into the woods, and fell face-first in the backwater bog.

"I guess he's gone for good."

She bit her lips until her mouth turned white. It wasn't like the pain when Ma left—in fact, she struggled to mourn him at all. But being completely alone was a feeling so vast it echoed, and the authorities were sure to find out and take her away. She'd have to pretend, even to Jumpin', that Pa was still around.

And there would be no Monday money. She'd stretched the last few dollars for weeks, surviving on grits, boiled mussels, and the occasional remnant egg from the rangy hens. The only remaining supplies were a few matches, a nubbin of soap, and a handful of grits. A fistful of Blue Tips wouldn't make a winter. Without them she couldn't boil the grits, which she fixed for herself, the gulls, and the chickens.

"I don't know how to do life without grits."

At least, she thought, wherever Pa had disappeared to this time, he had gone on foot. Kya had the boat.

Of course, she'd have to find another way to get food, but for right now she pushed the thought to a far corner of her mind. After a supper of boiled mussels, which she had learned to smash into a paste and spread on soda crackers, she thumbed through Ma's beloved books, play-reading the fairy tales. Even at ten she still couldn't read.

Then the kerosene light flickered, faded, and died. One minute there was a soft circle of a world, and then darkness. She made an *oh* sound. Pa had always bought the kerosene and filled the lamp, so she hadn't thought much about it. Until it was dark.

She sat for a few seconds, trying to squeeze light from the leftovers, but there was almost nothing. Then the rounded hump of the Frigidaire and the window frame began to take shape in the dimness, so she touched her fingers along the countertop until she found a candle stub. Lighting it would take a match and there were only five left. But darkness was a right-now thing.

Swish. She struck the match, lit the candle, and the blackness retreated to the corners. But she'd seen enough of it to know she had to have light, and kerosene cost money. She opened her mouth in a shallow pant. "Maybe I oughta walk to town and turn myself in to the authorities. At least they'd give me food and send me to school."

But after thinking a minute she said, "No, I cain't leave the gulls, the heron, the shack. The marsh is all the family I got."

Sitting in the last of the candlelight, she had an idea.

Earlier than usual, she got up the next morning when the tide was low, pulled on her overalls, and slipped out with a bucket, claw knife, and empty tow bags. Squatting in mud, she collected mussels along the sloughs like Ma had taught her, and in four hours of crouching and kneeling had two croker sacks full.

The slow sun pulled from the sea as she motored through dense fog up to Jumpin's Gas and Bait. He stood as she neared.

"Hello, Miss Kya, ya wantin' some gas?"

She tucked her head. Hadn't spoken a word to anyone since her last trip to the Piggly Wiggly, and her speech was slipping some. "Maybe gas. But that depends. I hear tell you buy mussels, and I got some here. Can you pay me cash money and some gas throwed in?" She pointed to the bags.

"Yessiree, you sho' do. They fresh?"

"I dug 'em 'fore dawn. Just now."

"Well, then. I can give ya fifty cent for one bag, a full tank for the other."

Kya smiled slightly. Real money she made herself. "Thank ya" was all she said.

As Jumpin' filled the tank, Kya walked into his tiny store there on the wharf. She'd never paid it much mind because she shopped at the Piggly, but now she saw that besides bait and tobacco, he sold matches, lard, soap, sardines, Vienna sausages, grits, soda crackers, toilet paper, and kerosene. About everything she needed in the world was right here. Lined up on the counter were five one-gallon jars filled with penny candy—Red Hots, jawbreakers, and Sugar Daddys. It seemed like more candy than would be in the world.

With the mussel money she bought matches, a candle, and grits. Kerosene and soap would have to wait for another croker full. It took all her might not to buy a Sugar Daddy instead of the candle.

"How many bags you buy a week?" she asked.

"Well now, we striking up a bidness deal?" he asked as he laughed in his particular way—mouth closed, head thrown back. "I buy 'bout forty pounds ever' two-three days. But mind, others bring 'em in, too. If ya bring 'em in, and I already got some, well, you'd be out. It's first come, first serve. No other way of doing it."

"Okay. Thank you, that'd be fine. Bye, Jumpin'." Then she added, "Oh, by the way, my pa sends his regards to ya."

"That so, well then. Ya do the same from me, if ya please. Bye yourself, Miss Kya." He smiled big as she motored away. She almost smiled herself. Buying her own gas and groceries surely made her a grown-up. Later, at the shack when she unpacked the tiny pile of supplies, she saw a yellow-and-red surprise at the bottom of the bag. Not too grown-up for a Sugar Daddy Jumpin' had dropped inside.

To stay ahead of the other pickers, Kya slipped down to the marsh by candle or moon—her shadow wavering around on the glistening sand— and gathered mussels deep in the night. She added oysters to her catch and sometimes slept near gullies under the stars to get to Jumpin's by first light. The mussel money turned out to be more reliable than the Monday money ever had, and she usually managed to beat out other pickers.

She stopped going to the Piggly, where Mrs. Singletary always asked why she wasn't in school. Sooner or later they'd grab her, drag her in. She got by with her supplies from Jumpin's and had more mussels than she could eat. They weren't that bad tossed into the grits, mashed up beyond recognition. They didn't have eyes to look at her like the fish did.

12.

Pennies and Grits

1956

For weeks after Pa left, Kya would look up when ravens cawed; maybe they'd seen him swing-stepping through the woods. At any strange sound in the wind, she cocked her head, listening for somebody. Anybody. Even a mad dash from the truant lady would be good sport.

Mostly she looked for the fishing boy. A few times over the years, she'd seen him in the distance, but hadn't spoken to him since she was seven, three years ago when he showed her the way home through the marsh. He was the only soul she knew in the world besides Jumpin' and a few salesladies. Wherever she glided through the waterways, she scanned for him.

One morning, as she motored into a cord grass estuary, she saw his boat tucked in the reeds. Tate wore a different baseball cap and was taller now, but even from more than fifty yards, she recognized the blond curls. Kya idled down, maneuvered quietly into long grass, and peered out at him. Working her lips, she thought of cruising over, maybe asking if he had caught any fish. That seemed to be what Pa and anybody else in the marsh said when they came across somebody: "Anythang bitin'? Had any nibbles?"

But she only stared, didn't move. She felt a strong pull toward him and a strong push away, the result being stuck firmly in this spot. Finally, she eased toward home, her heart pushing against her ribs.

Every time she saw him it was the same: watching him as she did the herons.

She still collected feathers and shells, but left them, salty and sandy, strewn around the brick-'n'-board steps. She dallied some of each day while dishes piled up in the sink, and why wash overalls that got muddied up again? Long ago she'd taken to wearing the old throwaway overalls from gone-away siblings. Her shirts full of holes. She had no more shoes at all.

One evening Kya slipped the pink-and-green flowery sundress, the one Ma had worn to church, from the wire hanger. For years now she had fingered this beauty—the only dress Pa didn't burn—had touched the little pink flowers. There was a stain across the front, a faded brown splotch under the shoulder straps, blood maybe. But it was faint now, scrubbed out like other bad memories.

Kya pulled the dress over her head, down her thin frame. The hem came almost to her toes; that wouldn't do. She pulled it off, hung it up to wait for another few years. It'd be a shame to cut it up, wear it to dig mussels.

A few days later Kya took the boat over to Point Beach, an apron of white sand several miles south of Jumpin's. Time, waves, and winds had modeled it into an elongated tip, which collected more shells than other beaches, and she had found rare ones there. After securing her boat at the southern end, she strolled north, searching. Suddenly distant voices—shrill and excited—drifted on the air.

Instantly, she ran across the beach toward the woods, where an oak, more than eighty feet from one side to the other, stood knee-deep in tropical ferns. Hiding behind the tree, she watched a band of kids strolling down the sand, now and then dashing around in the waves, kicking up sea spray. One boy ran ahead; another threw a football. Against the white sand, their bright madras shorts looked like colorful birds and marked the changing season. Summer was walking toward her down the beach.

As they moved closer, she flattened herself against the oak and peered around. Five girls and four boys, a bit older than she, maybe twelve. She recognized Chase Andrews throwing the ball to those boys he was always with.

The girls—Tallskinnyblonde, Ponytailfreckleface, Shortblackhair, Alwayswearspearls, and Roundchubbycheeks—hung back in a little covey, walking slower, chattering and giggling. Their voices lifted up to Kya like chimes. She was too young to care much about the boys; her eyes fixed on the troop of girls. Together they squatted to watch a crab skittering sideways across the sand. Laughing, they leaned against one another's shoulders until they flopped on the sand in a bundle.

Kya bit her bottom lip as she watched. Wondering how it would feel to be among them. Their joy created an aura almost visible against the deepening sky. Ma had said women need one another more than they need men, but she never told her how to get inside the pride. Easily, she slipped deeper into the forest and watched from behind the giant ferns until the kids wandered back down the beach, until they were little spots on the sand, the way they came.

Dawn smoldered beneath gray clouds as Kya pulled up to Jumpin's wharf. He walked out of the little shop shaking his head.

"I'm sorry as can be, Miss Kya," he said. "But they beatcha to it. I got my week's quota of mussels, cain't buy no mo'."

She cut the engine and the boat banged against a piling. This was the second week she'd been beat out. Her money was gone and she couldn't buy a single thing. Down to pennies and grits.

"Miss Kya, ya gotta find some udder ways to bring cash in. Ya can't git all yo' coons up one tree."

Back at her place, she sat pondering on the brick 'n' boards, and came up with another idea. She fished for eight hours straight, then soaked her catch of twenty in saltwater brine through the night. At daybreak she lined them up on the shelves of Pa's old smokehouse—the size and shape of an outhouse—built a fire in the pit, and poked green sticks into the flames like he'd done. Blue-gray smoke billowed and puffed up the chimney and through every crack in the walls. The whole shack huffing.

The next day she motored to Jumpin's and, still standing in her boat, held up her bucket. In all it was a pitiful display of small bream and carp, falling apart at the seams. "Ya buy smoked fish, Jumpin'? I got some here."

"Well, I declare, ya sho' did, Miss Kya. Tell ya what: I'll take 'em on consignment like. If I sell 'em, ya get the money; if I don't, ya get 'em back like they is. That do?"

"Okay, thanks, Jumpin'."

That evening Jumpin' walked down the sandy track to Colored Town—a cluster of shacks and lean-tos, and even a few real houses squatting about on backwater bogs and mud sloughs. The scattered encampment was in deep woods, back from the sea, with no breeze, and "more skeeters than the whole state of Jawja."

After about three miles he could smell the smoke from cookfires drifting through the pines and hear the chatter of some of his grandchillin. There were no roads in Colored Town, just trails leading off through the woods this way and that to different family dwellings. His was a real house he and his pa had built with pine lumber and a raw-wood fence around the hardpan dirt yard, which Mabel, his good-sized wife, swept clean as a whistle just like a floor. No snake could slink within thirty yards of the steps without being spotted by her hoe.

She came out of the house to meet him with a smile, as she often did, and he handed her the pail with Kya's smoked fish.

"What's this?" she asked. "Looks like sump'm even dogs wouldn't drag in."

"It's that girl again. Miss Kya brung 'em. Sometimes she ain't the first one with mussels, so she's gone to smokin' fish. Wants me to sell 'em."

"Lawd, we gotta do something 'bout that child. Ain't nobody gonna buy them fish; I can cook 'em up in stew. Our church can come up wif some clothes, other things for her. We'll tell 'er there's some family that'll trade jumpers for carpies. What size is she?"

"Ya askin' me? Skinny. All's I know is she's skinny as a tick on a flagpole. I 'spect she'll be there first thing in the mornin'. She's plumb broke."

After eating a breakfast of warmed-up mussels-in-grits, Kya motored over to Jumpin's to see if any money'd come in from the smoked fish. In all these years it had just been him there or customers, but as she approached slowly she saw a large black woman sweeping the wharf like it was a kitchen floor. Jumpin' was sitting in his chair, leaning back against the store wall doing figures in his ledger. Seeing her, he jumped up, waved.

"G'mornin'," she called quietly, drifting expertly up to the dock.

"Hiya, Miss Kya. Got somebody here for ya to meet. This here's ma wife, Mabel." Mabel walked up and stood next to Jumpin', so that when Kya stepped onto the wharf, they were close.

Mabel reached out and took Kya's hand, held it gently in hers, and said, "It's mighty fine to meet ya, Miss Kya. Jumpin's told me what a fine girl ya are. One a' de best oryster pickers."

In spite of hoeing her garden, cooking half of every day, and scrubbing and mending for whites, Mabel's hand was supple. Kya kept her fingers in that velvet glove but didn't know what to say, so stood quiet.

"Now, Miss Kya, we got a family who'll trade clothes and other stuff ya need for yo' smoked fish."

Kya nodded. Smiled at her feet. Then asked, "What about gas for ma boat?"

Mabel turned question eyes at Jumpin'.

"Well now," he said, "I'll give ya some today 'cause I know you're short. But ya keep bringin' in mussels and such when ya can."

Mabel said in her big voice, "Lawd, child, let's don't worry none about the details. Now let me look atcha. I gotta calculate yo' size to tell 'em." She led her into the tiny shop. "Let's sit right here, and ya tell me what clothes and what-all else ya need."

After they discussed the list, Mabel traced Kya's feet on a piece of brown paper bag, then said, "Well, come back tomorrer and there'll be a stack here for ya."

"I'm much obliged, Mabel." Then, her voice low, said, "There's something else. I found these old packages of seeds, but I don't know about gardenin'."

"Well now." Mabel leaned back and laughed deep in her generous bosom. "I can sure do a garden." She went over every step in great detail, then reached into some cans on the shelf and brought out squash, tomato, and pumpkin seeds. She folded each kind into some paper and drew a picture of the vegetable on the outside. Kya didn't know if Mabel did this because she couldn't write or because she knew Kya couldn't read, but it worked fine for both of them.

She thanked them as she stepped into her boat.

"I'm glad to help ya, Miss Kya. Now come back tomorrer for yo' things," Mabel said.

That very afternoon, Kya started hoeing the rows where Ma's garden used to be. The hoe made clunking sounds as it moved down the rows, releasing earthy smells and uprooting pinkish worms. Then a different *clink* sounded, and Kya bent to uncover one of Ma's old metal-and-plastic barrettes. She swiped it gently against her overalls until all the grit fell clear. As if reflected in the cheap artifact, Ma's red mouth and dark eyes were clearer than they'd been in years. Kya looked around; surely Ma was walking up the lane even now, come to help turn this earth. Finally home. Such stillness was rare; even the crows were quiet, and she could hear her own breathing.

Sweeping up bunches of her hair, she pinned the barrette above her left ear. Maybe Ma was never coming home. Maybe some dreams should just fade away. She lifted the hoe and clobbered a chunk of hard clay into smithereens.

When Kya motored up to Jumpin's wharf the next morning, he was alone. Perhaps the large form of his wife and her fine ideas had been an illusion. But there, sitting on the wharf, were two boxes of goods that Jumpin' was pointing to, a wide grin on his face.

"G'mornin', Miss Kya. This here's for ya."

Kya jumped onto the wharf and stared at the overflowing crates.

"Go on, then," Jumpin' said. "It's all your'n."

Gently she pulled out overalls, jeans, and real blouses, not just T-shirts. A pair of navy blue lace-up Keds and some Buster Brown two-tone saddle shoes, polished brown and white so many times they glowed. Kya held up a white blouse with a lace collar and a blue satin bow at the neck. Her mouth opened a little bit.

The other box had matches, grits, a tub of oleo, dried beans, and a whole quart of homemade lard. On top, wrapped in newspaper, were fresh turnips and greens, rutabagas, and okra.

"Jumpin'," she said softly, "this is more than those fish woulda cost. This could be a month's fish."

"Well now, what'a folks gonna do with old clothes layin' 'round the house? If they got these things extra, and ya need 'em, and ya got fish, and they need fish, then that's the deal. Ya gotta take 'em now, 'cause I ain't got room for that junk 'round here."

Kya knew that was true. Jumpin' had no extra space, so she'd be doing him a favor to take them off his wharf.

"I'll take 'em, then. But you tell 'em thank you, will you? And I'll smoke more fish and bring it in soon as I can."

"Okay then, Miss Kya. That'll be fine. Ya bring in fish when ya git 'em."

Kya chugged back into the sea. Once she rounded the peninsula, out of sight of Jumpin's, she idled down, dug in the box, and pulled out the blouse with the lace collar. She put it on right over her scratchy bib overalls with patched knees, and tied the little satin ribbon into a bow at her neck. Then, one hand on the tiller, the other on lace, she glided across ocean and estuaries toward home.

13.

Feathers

1960

Lanky yet brawny for fourteen, Kya stood on an afternoon beach, flinging crumbs to gulls. Still couldn't count them; still couldn't read. No longer did she daydream of winging with eagles; perhaps when you have to paw your supper from mud, imagination flattens to that of adulthood. Ma's sundress fit snugly across her breasts and fell just below her knees; she reckoned she had caught up, and then some. She walked back to the shack, got a pole and line, and went straight to fishing from a thicket on the far side of her lagoon.

Just as she cast, a stick snapped behind her. She jerked her head around, searching. A footfall in brush. Not a bear, whose large paws squished in debris, but a solid *clunk* in the brambles. Then the crows cawed. Crows can't keep secrets any better than mud; once they see something curious in the forest they have to tell everybody. Those who listen are rewarded: either warned of predators or alerted to food. Kya knew something was up.

She pulled in the line, wrapped it around the pole even as she pushed silently through the brush with her shoulders. Stopped again, listened.

A dark clearing—one of her favorite places—spread cavernlike under five oaks so dense only hazy streams of sunlight filtered through the canopy, striking lush patches of trillium and white violets. Her eyes scanned the clearing but saw no one.

Then a shape slunk through a thicket beyond, and her eyes swung there. It stopped. Her heart pumped harder. She hunkered down, stoop-running fast and quiet into the undergrowth on the edge of the clearing. Looking back through the branches, she saw an older boy walking fast through the woods, his head moving to and fro. He stopped as he saw her.

Kya ducked behind a thorn bush, then squeezed into a rabbit run that twisted through brambles thick as a fort wall. Still bent, she scrambled, scratching her arms on prickly scrub. Paused again, listening. Hid there in burning heat, her throat racking from thirst. After ten minutes, no one came, so she crept to a spring that pooled in moss, and drank like a deer. She wondered who that boy was and why he'd come. That was the thing about going to Jumpin's—people saw her there. Like the underbelly of a porcupine, she was exposed.

Finally, between dusk and dark, that time when the shadows were unsure, she walked back toward the shack by way of the oak clearing.

"'Cause of him sneaking 'round, I didn't catch any fish ta smoke."

In the center of the clearing was a rotted-down stump, so carpeted in moss it looked like an old man hiding under a cape. Kya approached it, then stopped. Lodged in the stump and sticking straight up was a thin black feather about five or six inches long. To most it would have looked ordinary, maybe a crow's wing feather. But she knew it was extraordinary for it was the "eyebrow" of a great blue heron, the feather that bows gracefully above the eye, extending back beyond her elegant head. One of the most exquisite fragments of the coastal marsh, right here. She had never found one but knew instantly what it was, having squatted eye to eye with herons all her life.

A great blue heron is the color of gray mist reflecting in blue water. And like mist, she can fade into the backdrop, all of her disappearing except the concentric circles of her lock-and-load eyes. She is a patient, solitary hunter, standing alone as long as it takes to snatch her prey. Or, eyeing her catch, she will stride forward one slow step at a time, like a predacious bridesmaid. And yet, on rare occasions she hunts on the wing, darting and diving sharply, swordlike beak in the lead.

"How'd it get stuck straight up in the stump?" Whispering, Kya looked around. "That boy must've put it here. He could be watchin' me right now." She stood still, heart pounding again. Backing away, she left the feather and ran to the shack and locked the screen door, which she seldom did since it offered scant protection.

Yet as soon as dawn crept between the trees, she felt a strong pull toward the feather, at least to look at it again. At sunrise she ran to the clearing, looked around carefully, then walked to the stump and lifted the feather. It was sleek, almost velvety. Back at the shack, she found a special place for it in the center of her collection—from tiny hummingbird feathers to large eagle tails—that winged across the wall. She wondered why a boy would bring her a feather.

The next morning, Kya wanted to rush to the stump to see if another one had been left, but she made herself wait. She must not run into the boy. Finally, in late morning she walked to the clearing, approaching slowly, listening. She didn't hear or see anybody, so she stepped forward, and a rare, brief smile lit her face when she saw a thin white feather stuck into the top of the stump. It reached from her fingertips to her elbow, and curved gracefully to a slender point. She lifted it and laughed out loud. A magnificent tail feather of a tropicbird. She'd never seen these seabirds because they didn't occur in this region, but on rare occasions they were blown over land on hurricane wings.

Kya's heart filled with wonder that someone had such a collection of rare feathers that he could spare this one.

Since she couldn't read Ma's old guidebook, she didn't know the names for most of the birds or insects, so made up her own. And even though she couldn't write, Kya had found a way to label her specimens. Her talent had matured and now she could draw, paint, and sketch anything. Using chalks or watercolors from the Five and Dime, she sketched the birds, insects, or shells on grocery bags and attached them to her samples.

That night she splurged and lit two candles and set them in saucers on the kitchen table so she could see all the colors of the white; so she could paint the tropicbird feather.

For more than a week there was no feather on the stump. Kya went by several times a day, cautiously peeping through ferns, but saw nothing. She sat in the cabin in midday, something she rarely did.

"Shoulda soaked beans for supper. Now it's too late." She walked through the kitchen, rummaging through the cupboard, drumming her fingers on the table. Thought of painting, but didn't. Walked again to the stump.

Even from some distance she could see a long, striped tail feather of a wild turkey. It caught her up. Turkeys had been one of her favorites. She'd watched as many as twelve chicks tuck themselves under the mother's wings even as the hen walked along, a few tumbling out of the back, then scrambling to catch up.

But about a year ago, as Kya strolled through a stand of pines, she'd heard a high-pitched shriek. A flock of fifteen wild turkeys—mostly hens, a few toms and jakes—rushed about, pecking what looked like an oily rag crumpled in the dirt. Dust stirred from their feet and shrouded the woods, drifting up through branches, caught there. As Kya had crept closer, she saw it was a hen turkey on the ground, and the birds of her own flock were pecking and toe-scratching her neck and head. Somehow she'd managed to get her wings so tangled with briars, her feathers stuck out at strange angles and she could no longer fly. Jodie had said that if a bird becomes different from the others—disfigured or wounded—it is more likely to attract a predator, so the rest of the flock will kill it, which is better than drawing in an eagle, who might take one of them in the bargain.

A large female clawed at the bedraggled hen with her large, horny feet, then pinned her to the ground as another female jabbed at her naked neck and head. The hen squealed, looked around with wild eyes at her own flock assaulting her.

Kya ran into the clearing, throwing her arms around. "Hey, what ya doing? Git outta here. Stop it!" The flurry of wings kicked up more dust as the turkeys scattered into brush, two of them flying heavy into an oak. But Kya was too late. The hen, her eyes wide open, lay limp. Blood ran from her wrinkled neck, bent crooked on the dirt.

"Shoo, go on!" Kya chased the last of the large birds until they shuffled away, their business complete. She knelt next to the dead hen and covered the bird's eye with a sycamore leaf.

That night after watching the turkeys, she ate a supper of leftover cornbread and beans, then lay on her porch bed, watching the moon touch the lagoon. Suddenly, she heard voices in the woods coming toward the shack. They sounded nervous, squeaky. Boys, not men. She sat straight up. There was no back door. It was get out now or still be sitting on the bed when they came. Quick as a mouse, she slipped to the door, but just then candles appeared, moving up and down, their light jiggling in halos. Too late to run.

The voices got louder. "Here we come, Marsh Girl!"

"Hey—ya in thar? Miss Missin' Link!"

"Show us yo' teeth! Show us yo' swamp grass!" Peals of laughter.

She ducked lower behind the half wall of the porch as the footsteps moved closer. The flames flickered madly, then went out altogether as five boys, maybe thirteen or fourteen years old, ran across the yard. All talking stopped as they galloped full speed to the porch and tagged the door with their palms, making slapping sounds.

Every smack a stab in the turkey hen's heart.

Against the wall, Kya wanted to whimper but held her breath. They could break through the door easy. One hard yank, and they'd be in.

But they backed down the steps, ran into the trees again, hooting and hollering with relief that they had survived the Marsh Girl, the Wolf Child, the girl who couldn't spell *dog*. Their words and laughter carried back to her through the forest as they disappeared into the night, back to safety. She watched the relit candles, bobbing through the trees. Then sat staring into the stone-quiet darkness. Shamed.

Kya thought of that day and night whenever she saw wild turkeys, but she was thrilled to see the tail feather on the stump. Just to know the game was still on.

14.

Red Fibers

1969

Muggy heat blurred the morning into a haze of no sea, no sky. Joe walked out of the sheriff's building and met Ed getting out of the patrol truck. "C'mon over here, Sheriff. Got more from the lab on the Chase Andrews case. Hot as a boar's breath inside." He led the way to a large oak, its ancient roots punching through the bare dirt like fists. The sheriff followed, crunching acorns, and they stood in the shade, faces to the sea breeze.

He read out loud. "'Bruising on the body, interior injuries, consistent with an extensive fall.' He did bang the back of his head on that beam—the blood and hair samples matched his—which caused severe bruising and damage to the posterior lobe but didn't kill him.

"There you have it; he died where we found him, had not been moved. The blood and hair on the crossbeam prove it. 'Cause of death: sudden impact on occipital and parietal lobe of the posterior cerebral cortex, severed spine'—from falling off the tower."

"So somebody did destroy all the foot- and fingerprints. Anything else?"

"Listen to this. They found lots of foreign fibers on his jacket. Red wool fibers that didn't come from any of his clothes. Sample included." The sheriff shook a small plastic bag.

Both men peered at the fuzzy red threads flattened against the plastic like spider webbing.

"Wool, it says. Could be a sweater, scarf, hat," Joe said.

"Shirt, skirt, socks, cape. Hell, it could be anything. And we have to find it."

15.

The Game

1960

The next noon, hands on her cheeks, Kya approached the stump slowly, almost in prayer. But no feather on the stump. Her lips pinched.

"A' course. I gotta leave something for him."

Her pocket brought a tail feather from an immature bald eagle she'd found that morning. Only someone who knew birds well would know this splotchy, tatty feather was eagle. A three-year-old, not yet crowned. Not as precious as the tail feather of the tropicbird, but still a dear thing. She laid it carefully on the stump with a little rock on top, pinned from the wind.

That night, arms folded under her head, she lay on her porch bed, a slight smile on her face. Her family had abandoned her to survive a swamp, but here was someone who came on his own, leaving gifts for her in the forest. Uncertainty lingered, but the more she thought about it, the less likely it seemed the boy meant her harm. It didn't fit that anyone who liked birds would be mean.

The next morning, she sprang from bed and went about doing what Ma had called a "deep clean." At Ma's dresser, Kya meant only to cull the remnants of the drawers, but as she picked up her mother's brass-and-steel scissors—the finger holes curled and shaped with intricate patterns of lilies—she suddenly pulled back her hair, not trimmed since Ma left more than seven years ago, and cut off eight inches. Now it fell just below her shoulders. She looked at herself in the mirror, tossed her head a bit, smiled. Scrubbed her fingernails and brushed her hair till it shone.

Replacing the brush and scissors, she looked down among some of Ma's old cosmetics. The liquid foundation and rouge had dried and cracked, but the shelf life of lipstick must be decades because when she opened a tube, it looked fresh. For the first time, never having played dress-up as a little girl, she put some on her lips. Smacked, then smiled again in the mirror. Thought she looked a bit pretty. Not like Ma, but pleasing enough. She giggled, then wiped it off. Just before closing the drawer, she saw a bottle of dried-up Revlon fingernail polish—Barely Pink.

Kya lifted the little jar, remembering how Ma had walked back from town one day with this bottle of fingernail polish, of all things. Ma said it would look real good with their olive skin. She lined up Kya and her two older sisters in a row on the faded sofa, told them to stick out their bare feet, and painted all those toes and then their fingernails. Then she did her own, and they laughed and had a fine time flouncing around the yard, flashing their pink nails. Pa was off somewhere, but the boat was moored at the lagoon. Ma came up with the idea of all the girls going out in the boat, something they had never done.

They climbed into the old skiff, still cavorting like they were tipsy. It took a few pulls to get the outboard cranked, but finally it jumped to, and off they went, Ma steering across the lagoon and into the narrow channel that led to the marsh. They breezed along the waterways, but Ma didn't know all that much about it, and when they went into a shallow lagoon, they got stuck in gummy black mud, thick as tar. They poled this way and that but couldn't budge. There was nothing left to do but climb over the side, skirts and all, sinking in the muck up to their knees.

Ma hollering, "Now don't turn it over, girls, don't turn it over," they hauled on the boat until it was free, squealing at one another's muddy faces. It took some doing to get back in, flopping over the side like so many landed fish. And, instead of sitting on the seats, the four of them squinched up on the bottom of the boat all in a line, holding their feet to the sky, wiggling their toes, their pink nails gleaming through the mud.

Lying there Ma said, "You all listen now, this is a real lesson in life. Yes, we got stuck, but what'd we girls do? We made it fun, we laughed. That's what sisters and girlfriends are all about. Sticking together even in the mud, 'specially in mud."

Ma hadn't bought any polish remover, so when it began to peel and chip, they had faded, patchy pink nails on all their fingers and toes, reminding them of the good time they'd had, and that real-life lesson.

Looking at the old bottle, Kya tried to see her sisters' faces. And said out loud, "Where're you now, Ma? Why didn't you stick?"

As soon as she reached the oak clearing the next afternoon, Kya saw bright, unnatural colors against the muted greens and browns of the forest. On the stump was a small red-and-white milk carton and next to it another feather. It seemed the boy had upped the ante. She walked over and picked up the feather first.

Silver and soft, it was from the crest of a night heron, one of the most beautiful of the marsh. Then she looked inside the milk carton. Rolled up tight were some packages of seeds—turnips, carrots, and green beans—and, at the bottom of the carton, wrapped in brown paper, a spark plug for her boat engine. She smiled again and turned a little circle. She had learned how to live without most things, but now and then she needed a spark plug. Jumpin' had taught her a few minor engine repairs, but every part meant a walk to town and cash money.

And yet here was an extra spark plug, to be set aside until needed. A surplus. Her heart filled up. The same feeling as having a full tank of gas or seeing the sunset under a paint-brushed sky. She stood absolutely still, trying to take it in, what it meant. She had watched male birds wooing females by bringing them gifts. But she was pretty young for nesting.

At the bottom of the carton was a note. She unfolded it and looked at the words, written carefully in simple script that a child could read. Kya knew the time of the tides in her heart, could find her way home by the stars, knew every feather of an eagle, but even at fourteen, couldn't read these words.

She had forgotten to bring anything to leave. Her pockets yielded only ordinary feathers, shells, and seedpods, so she hurried back to the shack and stood in front of her feather-wall, window-shopping. The most graceful were the tail feathers from a tundra swan. She took one from the wall to leave at the stump next time she passed.

As evening fell, she took her blanket and slept in the marsh, close to a gully full of moon and mussels, and had two tow bags filled by dawn. Gas money. They were too heavy to tote, so she dragged the first one back toward the lagoon. Even though it wasn't the shortest route, she went by way of the oak clearing to leave the swan feather. She walked into the trees without looking, and there, leaning against the stump, was the feather boy. She recognized him as Tate, who had shown her the way home through the marsh when she was a little girl. Tate, who, for years, she had watched from a distance without the courage to go near. Of course, he was taller and older, probably eighteen. His golden hair stuck out from his cap in all manner of curls and loose bits, and his face was tan, pleasing. He was calm, smiled wide, his whole face beaming. But it was his eyes that caught her up; they were golden brown with flecks of green, and fixed on hers the way heron eyes catch a minnow.

She halted, shaken by the sudden break in the unwritten rules. That was the fun of it, a game where they didn't have to talk or even be seen. Heat rose in her face.

"Hey, Kya. Please . . . don't . . . run. It's . . . just me . . . Tate," he said very quietly, slowly, like she was dumb or something. That was probably what the townspeople said of her, that she barely spoke human.

Tate couldn't help staring. She must be thirteen or fourteen, he thought. But even at that age, she had the most striking face he'd ever seen. Her large eyes nearly black, her nose slender over shapely lips, painted her in an exotic light. She was tall, thin, giving her a fragile, lithesome look as though molded wild by the wind. Yet young, strapping muscles showed through with quiet power.

Her impulse, as always, was to run. But there was another sensation. A fullness she hadn't felt for years. As if something warm had been poured inside her heart. She thought of the feathers, the spark plug, and the seeds. All of it might end if she ran. Without speaking, she lifted her hand and held the elegant swan feather toward him. Slowly, as though she might spring like a startled fawn, he walked over and studied it in her hand. She watched in silence, looking only at the feather, not his face, nowhere near her eyes.

"Tundra swan, right? Incredible, Kya. Thank you," he said. He was much taller and bent slightly as he took it from her. Of course, this was the time for her to thank him for his gifts, but she stood silent, wishing he would go, wishing they could stick to their game.

Trying to fill the silence, he continued. "My dad's the one who taught me birds."

Finally she looked up at him and said, "I can't read yo' note."

"Well, sure, since you don't go to school. I forgot. All it said was, I saw you a couple of times when I was fishing, and it got me thinking that maybe you could use the seeds and the spark plug. I had extra and thought it might save you a trip to town. I figured you'd like the feathers."

Kya hung her head and said, "Thank you for them; that was mighty fine of you."

Tate noticed that while her face and body showed early inklings and foothills of womanhood, her mannerisms and turns of phrase were somewhat childlike, in contrast to the village girls whose mannerisms—overdoing their makeup, cussing, and smoking—outranked their foothills.

"You're welcome. Well, I better be going, getting late. I'll drop by now and then, if that's okay."

Kya didn't say a word to that. The game must be over. As soon as he realized she wasn't going to speak again, he nodded to her, touched his hat, and turned to go. But just as he ducked his head to step into the brambles, he looked back at her.

"You know, I could teach you to read."

16.

Reading

1960

For days, Tate didn't return for the reading lessons. Before the feather game, loneliness had become a natural appendage to Kya, like an arm. Now it grew roots inside her and pressed against her chest.

Late one afternoon, she struck out in her boat. "I cain't just sit 'round waitin'."

Instead of docking at Jumpin's, where she'd be seen, she stashed her rig in a small cove just south and, carrying a croker sack, walked down the shaded path toward Colored Town. A soft rain had fallen most of the day, and now as the sun neared the horizon, the forest formed its own fog that drifted through succulent glades. She'd never gone to Colored Town, but knew where it was and figured she could find Jumpin' and Mabel's place once she got there.

She wore jeans and a pink blouse from Mabel. In the croker sack were two pint jars of real runny blackberry jam she'd made herself to return Jumpin' and Mabel's kindness. A need to be with someone, a chance to talk with a woman friend urged her toward them. If Jumpin' wasn't home yet, maybe she could sit down with Mabel and visit a spell.

Then, nearing a bend in the road, Kya heard voices coming toward her. She stopped, listened carefully. Quickly she stepped off the path into the woods and hid behind a myrtle thicket. A minute later, two white boys, dressed in raggedy bib overalls, came around the bend, toting fishing tackle and a string of catfish long as her arm. She froze behind the thicket and waited.

One of the boys pointed down the lane. "Lookee up thar."

"Ain't we lucky. Here comes a nigger walkin' to Nigger Town." Kya looked down the path, and there, walking home for the evening, was Jumpin'. Quite close, he had surely heard the boys, but he simply dropped his head, stepped into the woods to give them a berth, and moved on.

What's the matter with 'im, why don't he do sump'm? Kya raged to herself. She knew *nigger* was a real bad word—she knew by the way Pa had used it like a cussword. Jumpin' could have knocked the boys' heads together, taught them a lesson. But he walked on fast.

"Jest an ol' nigger walkin' to town. Watch out, nigger-boy, don't fall down," they taunted Jumpin', who kept his eyes on his toes. One of the boys reached down, picked up a stone, and slung it at Jumpin's back. It hit just under his shoulder blade with a thud. He lurched over a bit, kept walking. The boys laughed as he disappeared around the bend, then they picked up more rocks and followed him.

Kya stalked through brush until she was ahead of them, her eyes glued on their caps bobbing above the branches. She crouched at a spot where thick bushes grew next to the lane, where in seconds they would pass within a foot of her. Jumpin' was up ahead, out of sight. She twisted the cloth bag with the jam so that it was wrung tight and knotted against the jars. As the boys drew even with the thicket, she swung the heavy bag and whacked the closest one hard across the back of his head. He pitched forward and fell on his face. Hollering and screeching, she rushed the other boy, ready to bash his head too, but he took off. She slipped about fifty yards into the trees and watched until the first boy stood, holding his head and cussing.

Toting the bag of jam jars, she turned back toward her boat and motored home. Thought she'd probably never go viztin' again.

The next day, when the sound of Tate's motor chugged through the channel, Kya ran to the lagoon and stood in the bushes, watching him step out of his boat, holding a rucksack. Looking around, he called out to her, and she stepped slowly forward dressed in jeans that fit and a white blouse with mismatched buttons.

"Hey, Kya. Sorry I couldn't get here sooner. Had to help my dad, but we'll get you reading in no time."

"Hey, Tate."

"Let's sit here." He pointed to an oak knee in deep shade of the lagoon. From the rucksack he pulled out a thin, faded book of the alphabet and a lined writing pad. With a careful slow hand, he formed the letters between the lines, *a A, b B*, asking her to do the same, patient with her tongue-between-lips effort. As she wrote, he said the letters out loud. Softly, slowly.

She remembered some of the letters from Jodie and Ma but didn't know much at all about putting them into proper words.

After only minutes, he said, "See, you can already write a word."

"What d'ya mean?"

"*C-a-b.* You can write the word *cab.*"

"What's *cab?*" she asked. He knew not to laugh.

"Don't worry if you don't know it. Let's keep going. Soon you'll write a word you know."

Later he said, "You'll have to work lots more on the alphabet. It'll take a little while to get it, but you can already read a bit. I'll show you." He didn't have a grammar reader, so her first book was his dad's copy of Aldo Leopold's *A Sand County Almanac*. He pointed to the opening sentence and asked her to read it back to him. The first word was *There* and she had to go back to the alphabet and practice the sound of each letter, but he was patient, explaining the special sound of *th*, and when she finally said it, she threw her arms up and laughed. Beaming, he watched her.

Slowly, she unraveled each word of the sentence: "'There are some who can live without wild things, and some who cannot.'"

"Oh," she said. "Oh."

"You can read, Kya. There will never be a time again when you can't read."

"It ain't just that." She spoke almost in a whisper. "I wadn't aware that words could hold so much. I didn't know a sentence could be so full."

He smiled. "That's a very good sentence. Not all words hold that much."

Over the coming days, sitting on the oak knee in shade or the shore in sun, Tate taught her how to read the words, which sang of the geese and cranes, real all around them. "What if there be no more goose music?"

In between helping his dad or pitching baseball with his friends, he came to Kya's place several times a week and, now, no matter what she was doing—weeding the garden, feeding the chickens, searching for shells—she listened for the sound of his boat humming up the channel.

On the beach one day, reading about what chickadees eat for lunch, she asked him, "You live with yo' family in Barkley Cove?"

"I live with my dad. Yes, in Barkley."

Kya didn't ask if he had more family, now gone. His ma must have left him, too. Part of her longed to touch his hand, a strange wanting, but her fingers wouldn't do it. Instead she memorized the bluish veins on the inside of his wrist, as intricate as those sketched on the wings of wasps.

At night, sitting at the kitchen table, she went over the lessons by kerosene lamp, its soft light seeping through the shack windows and touching the lower branches of the oaks. The only light for miles and miles of blackness except for the soft glow of fireflies.

Carefully, she wrote and said each word over and over. Tate said long words were simply little ones strung together—so she wasn't afraid of them, went straight to learning *Pleistocene* along with *sat*. Learning to read was the most fun she'd ever had. But she couldn't figure why Tate had offered to teach po' white trash like her, why he'd come in the first place, bringing exquisite feathers. But she didn't ask, afraid it might get him thinking on it, send him away.

Now at last Kya could label all her precious specimens. She took each feather, insect, shell, or flower, looked up how to spell the name in Ma's books, and wrote it carefully on her brown-paper-bag painting.

. . .

"What comes after twenty-nine?" she asked Tate one day.

He looked at her. She knew more about tides and snow geese, eagles and stars than most ever would, yet she couldn't count to thirty. He didn't want to shame her, so didn't show surprise. She was awfully good at reading eyes.

"Thirty," he said simply. "Here, I'll show you the numbers and we'll do some basic arithmetic. It's easy. I'll bring you some books about it."

She went around reading everything—the directions on the grits bag, Tate's notes, and the stories from her fairy-tale books she had pretended to read for years. Then one night she made a little *oh* sound, and took the old Bible from the shelf. Sitting at the table, she turned the thin pages carefully to the one with the family names. She found her own at the very bottom. There it was, her birthday: *Miss Catherine Danielle Clark, October 10, 1945*. Then, going back up the list, she read the real names of her brothers and sisters:

Master Jeremy Andrew Clark, January 2, 1939. "Jeremy," she said out loud. "Jodie, I sure never thought a' you as Master Jeremy."

Miss Amanda Margaret Clark, May 17, 1937. Kya touched the name with her fingers. Repeated it several times.

She read on. *Master Napier Murphy Clark, April 4, 1936*. Kya spoke softly, "Murph, ya name was Napier."

At the top, the oldest, *Miss Mary Helen Clark, September 19, 1934*. She rubbed her fingers over the names again, which brought faces before her eyes. They blurred, but she could see them all squeezed around the table eating stew, passing cornbread, even laughing some. She was ashamed that she had forgotten their names, but now that she'd found them, she would never let them go again.

Above the list of children she read: *Mister Jackson Henry Clark married Miss Julienne Maria Jacques, June 12, 1933*. Not until that moment had she known her parents' proper names.

She sat there for a few minutes with the Bible open on the table. Her family before her.

Time ensures children never know their parents young. Kya would never see the handsome Jake swagger into an Asheville soda fountain in early 1930, where he spotted Maria Jacques, a beauty with black curls and red lips, visiting from New Orleans. Over a milkshake he told her his family owned a plantation and that after high school he'd study to be a lawyer and live in a columned mansion.

But when the Depression deepened, the bank auctioned the land out from under the Clarks' feet, and his father took Jake from school. They moved down the road to a small pine cabin that once, not so long ago really, had been occupied by slaves. Jake worked the tobacco fields, stacking leaves with black men and women, babies strapped on their backs with colorful shawls.

One night two years later, without saying good-bye, Jake left before dawn, taking with him as many fine clothes and family treasures—including his great-grandfather's gold pocket watch and his grandmother's diamond ring—as he could carry. He hitchhiked to New Orleans and found Maria living with her family in an elegant home near the waterfront. They were descendants of a French merchant, owners of a shoe factory.

Jake pawned the heirlooms and entertained her in fine restaurants hung with red velvet curtains, telling her that he would buy her that columned mansion. As he knelt under a magnolia tree, she agreed to marry him, and they wed in 1933 in a small church ceremony, her family standing silent.

By now, the money was gone, so he accepted a job from his

father-in-law in the shoe factory. Jake assumed he would be made manager, but Mr. Jacques, a man not easily taken in, insisted Jake learn the business from the bottom up like any other employee. So Jake labored at cutting out soles.

He and Maria lived in a small garage apartment furnished with a few grand pieces from her dowry mixed with flea-market tables and chairs. He enrolled in night classes to finish high school but usually skipped out to play poker and, stinking of whiskey, came home late to his new wife. After only three weeks, the teacher dropped him from the classes.

Maria begged him to stop drinking, to show enthusiasm for his job so that her father would promote him. But the babies started coming and the drinking never stopped. Between 1934 and 1940 they had four children, and Jake was promoted only once.

The war with Germany was an equalizer. Boiled down to the same uniform-hue as everyone else, he could hide his shame, once again play proud. But one night, sitting in a muddy foxhole in France, someone shouted that their sergeant was shot and sprawled bleeding twenty yards away. Mere boys, they should have been sitting in a dugout waiting to bat, nervous about some fastball. Still, they jumped at once, scrambling to save the wounded man—all but one.

Jake hunched in a corner, too scared to move, but a mortar exploded yellow-white just beyond the hole, shattering the bones of his left leg into fragments. When the soldiers tumbled back into the trench, dragging the sergeant, they assumed Jake had been hit while helping the others rescue their comrade. He was declared a hero. No one would ever know. Except Jake.

With a medal and a medical discharge, he was sent home. Determined not to work again in the shoe factory, Jake stayed only a few nights in New Orleans. With Maria standing by silently, he sold all her fine furniture and silver, then packed his family onto the train and moved them to North Carolina. He discovered from an old friend that his mother and father had died, clearing the way for his plan.

He'd convinced Maria that living in a cabin his father had built as a fishing retreat on the coast of North Carolina would be a new start. There would be no rent and Jake could finish high school. He bought a small fishing boat in Barkley Cove and motored through miles of marsh waterways with his family and all their possessions piled around them—a few fine hatboxes perched on top. When they finally broke into the lagoon, where the ratty shack with rusted-out screens hunkered under the oaks, Maria clutched her youngest child, Jodie, fighting tears.

Pa assured her, "Don't ya worry none. I'll get this fixed up in no time."

But Jake never improved the shack or finished high school. Soon after they arrived, he took up drinking and poker at the Swamp Guinea, trying to leave that foxhole in a shot glass.

Maria did what she could to make a home. She bought sheets from rummage sales for the floor mattresses and a stand-alone tin bathtub; she washed the laundry under the yard spigot, and figured out on her own how to plant a garden, how to keep chickens.

Soon after they arrived, dressed in their best, she hiked the children to Barkley Cove to register them in school. Jake, however, scoffed at the notion of education, and more days than not, told Murph and Jodie to skip school and bring in squirrels or fish for supper.

Jake took Maria for only one moonlit boat ride, the result of which was their last child, a daughter named Catherine Danielle; later nicknamed Kya because, when first asked, that's what she said her name was.

Now and then, when sober, Jake dreamed again of completing school, making a better life for them all, but the shadow of the foxhole would move across his mind. Once sure and cocky, handsome and fit, he could no longer wear the man he had become and he'd take a swig from his poke. Blending in with the fighting, drinking, cussing renegades of the marsh was the easiest thing Jake ever did.

17.

Crossing the Threshold

1960

One day during the reading summer when she motored to Jumpin's, he said, "Now, Miss Kya, there's sump'm else. Some men been pokin' 'round, askin' 'bout ya."

She looked right at him instead of off to the side. "Who, what d'they want?"

"I b'lieve they're from the Sochul Services. They askin' all kinds of questions. Is yo' pa still 'round, where ya ma is, if ya goin' to school this fall. An when ya come here; they 'specially wanta know what times ya come here."

"What'd you tell 'em, Jumpin'?"

"Well, I done ma best to put 'em off ya. Told 'em ya pa just fine, out fishin's all." He laughed, threw his head back. "Then I told 'em I neva know when ya boat in here. Now, don't ya worry none, Miss Kya. Jumpin'll send 'em on a snipe hunt if they come again."

"Thank ya." After filling her tank, Kya headed straight home. She'd have to be on guard more now, maybe find a place in the marsh where she could hide out some until they gave up on her.

Late that afternoon, as Tate pulled up to the shore, the hull crunching softly on sand, she said, "Can we meet somewheres else, 'sides here?"

"Hey, Kya, good to see you." Tate greeted her, still sitting at the tiller.

"What d'ya think?"

"It's *besides*, not *'sides*, and it's polite to greet people before asking a favor."

"You say *'sides* sometimes," she said, almost smiling.

"Yeah, we all got magnolia mouth, being from the North Carolina sticks, but we have to try."

"Good afternoon, Mr. Tate," she said, making a little curtsy. He caught a glimpse of the spunk and sass somewhere inside. "Now, can we meet somewhere besides here? Please."

"Sure, I guess, but why?"

"Jumpin' said the Social Services are lookin' for me. I'm scared they'll pull me in like a trout, put me in a foster home or sump'm."

"Well, we better hide way out there where the crawdads sing. I pity any foster parents who take you on." Tate's whole face smiled.

"What d'ya mean, where the crawdads sing? Ma used to say that." Kya remembered Ma always encouraging her to explore the marsh: "Go as far as you can—way out yonder where the crawdads sing."

"Just means far in the bush where critters are wild, still behaving like critters. Now, you got any ideas where we can meet?"

"There's a place I found one time, an old fallin'-down cabin. Once you know the turnoff, ya can get there by boat; I can walk there from here."

"Okay then, get in. Show me this time; next time we'll meet there."

"If I'm out there I'll leave a little pile of rocks right here by the tyin'-up log." Kya pointed to a spot on the lagoon beach. "Otherwise, I'm 'round here somewhere and will come out when I hear yo' motor."

They puttered slowly through the marsh, then planed off south through open sea, away from town. She bounced along in the bow, wind-tears streaming across her cheeks and tickling cool in her ears. When they reached a small cove, she guided him up a narrow freshwater creek hung low with brambles. Several times the creek seemed to peter out, but Kya motioned that it was okay to go on, and they crashed through more brush.

Finally they broke into a wide meadow where the stream ran by an old one-room log cabin, collapsed on one end. The logs had buckled, some lying around the ground like pick-up sticks. The roof, still sitting on the half wall, sloped down from high end to low like a lopsided hat. Tate pulled the boat up onto the mud and they silently walked to the open door.

Inside was dark and reeked of rat urine. "Well, I hope you don't plan on living here—the whole thing could collapse on your head." Tate pushed at the wall. It seemed sturdy enough.

"It's just a hideout. I can stash some food 'case I have to go on the run awhile."

Tate turned and looked at her as their eyes adjusted to the dark.

"Kya, you ever thought of just going back to school? It wouldn't kill you, and they might leave you alone if you did."

"They must've figured out I'm alone, and if I go, they'll grab me, put me in a home. Anyway, I'm too old for school now. Where would they put me, first grade?" Her eyes widened at the notion of sitting in a tiny chair, surrounded by little kids who could pronounce words, count to fifty.

"What, so you plan to live alone in the marsh forever?"

"Better than going to a foster home. Pa used to say he'd farm us out to one if we were bad. Told us they're mean."

"No, they're not. Not always. Most of them are nice people who like kids," he said.

"You sayin' you'd go to a foster home 'fore you'd live in the marsh?" she asked, chin jutted out, hand on her hip.

He was silent a minute. "Well, bring some blankets out, matches in case it gets cold. Maybe some tins of sardines. They last forever. But don't keep fresh food; it'll bring the bears in."

"I ain't scared of bears."

"I'm not scared of bears."

For the rest of the summer Kya and Tate did the reading lessons at the tumbledown cabin. By mid-August they had read through *A Sand County Almanac*, and although she couldn't read every word, she got most of it. Aldo Leopold taught her that floodplains are living extensions of the rivers, which will claim them back any time they choose. Anyone living on a floodplain is just waiting in the river's wings. She learned where the geese go in winter, and the meaning of their music. His soft words, sounding almost like poetry, taught her that soil is packed with life and one of the most precious riches on Earth; that draining wetlands dries the land for miles beyond, killing plants and animals along with the water. Some of the seeds lie dormant in the desiccated earth for decades, waiting, and when the water finally comes home again, they burst through the soil, unfolding their faces. Wonders and real-life knowledge she would've never learned in school. Truths everyone should know, yet somehow, even though they lay exposed all around, seemed to lie in secret like the seeds.

They met at the log cabin several times a week, but she slept most nights in her shack or on the beach with the gulls. She had to collect firewood before winter, so made a mission of it, toting loads from near and far and stacking them somewhat neatly between two pines. The turnips in her garden barely poked their heads above the goldenrod; still she had more vegetables than she and the deer could eat. She harvested the last of the late-summer crop and stored the squash and beets in the cool shade of the brick-'n'-board steps.

But all the while, she kept her ears out for the lugging sounds of an automobile, filled with men come to take her away. Sometimes the listening was tiresome and creepy, so she'd walk to the log cabin and sleep the night on the dirt floor, wrapped in her spare blanket. She timed her mussel collecting and fish smoking so that Tate could take them to Jumpin's and bring back her supplies. Keeping her underbelly less exposed.

"Remember when you read your first sentence, you said that some words hold a lot?" Tate said one day, sitting on the creek bank.

"Yeah, I remember, why?"

"Well, especially poems. The words in poems do more than say things. They stir up emotions. Even make you laugh."

"Ma used to read poems, but I don't remember any."

"Listen to this; it's by Edward Lear." He took out a folded envelope and read,

> "Then Mr. Daddy Long-legs
> And Mr. Floppy Fly
> Rushed downward to the foamy sea
> With one sponge-taneous cry;

And there they found a little boat,
Whose sails were pink and gray;
And off they sailed among the waves,
Far, and far away."

Smiling, she said, "It makes a rhythm like waves hitting the beach."

After that she went into a poem-writing phase, making them up as she boated through the marsh or looked for shells—simple verses, singsong and silly. "There's a mama blue jay lifting from a branch; I'd fly too, if I had a chance." They made her laugh out loud; filled up a few lonely minutes of a long, lonely day.

One late afternoon, reading at the kitchen table, she remembered Ma's book of poetry and scrounged until she found it. The volume so worn, the covers had long since gone, the pages held together by two frayed rubber bands. Kya carefully took them off and thumbed through the pages, reading Ma's notes in the margins. At the end was a list of page numbers of Ma's favorites.

Kya turned to one by James Wright:

Suddenly lost and cold,
I knew the yard lay bare,
I longed to touch and hold
My child, my talking child,
Laughing or tame or wild . . .

Trees and the sun were gone,
Everything gone but us.
His mother sang in the house,
And kept our supper warm,

And loved us, God knows how,
The wide earth darkened so.

And this one by Galway Kinnell.

I did care. . . .
I did say everything I thought
In the mildest words I knew. And now, . . .
I have to say I am relieved it is over:
At the end I could feel only pity
For that urge toward more life.
. . . Goodbye.

Kya touched the words as if they were a message, as though Ma had underlined them specifically so her daughter would read them someday by this dim kerosene flame and understand. It wasn't much, not a handwritten note tucked in the back of a sock drawer, but it was something. She sensed that the words clinched a powerful meaning, but she couldn't shake it free. If she ever became a poet, she'd make the message clear.

After Tate started his senior year in September, he couldn't come to Kya's place as often, but when he did, he brought her discarded textbooks from school. He didn't say a word about the biology books being too advanced for her, so she plowed through chapters she wouldn't have seen for four years in school. "Don't worry," he'd say, "you'll get a little more every time you read it." And that was true.

As the days grew shorter, again they met near her shack because there wasn't enough daylight to get to the reading cabin. They had always studied outside, but when a crazed wind blew one morning, Kya built up the fire in the woodstove. No one had crossed the shack's threshold since Pa disappeared more than four years ago, and to ask anybody inside would seem unthinkable. Anyone but Tate.

"Wanta sit in the kitchen by the stove?" she said when he dragged his rig onto the lagoon shore.

"Sure," he said, knowing not to make a big deal of the invitation.

As soon as he stepped inside the porch, he took nearly twenty minutes to explore and exclaim over her feathers and shells and bones and nests. When they finally settled at the table, she pulled her chair close to his, their arms and elbows nearly touching. Just to feel him near.

With Tate so busy helping his dad, the days dragged slow from nose to tail. Late one evening she took her first novel, *Rebecca* by Daphne du Maurier, from Ma's bookshelf and read about love. After a while she closed the book and walked to the closet. She slipped on Ma's sundress and swished around the room, flipping the skirt about, whirling in front of the mirror. Her mane and hips swaying, she imagined Tate asking her to dance. His hand on her waist. As if she were Mrs. de Winter.

Abruptly she caught herself and bent over, giggling. Then stood very still.

"Come on up here, child," Mabel sang out one afternoon. "I got ya some things." Jumpin' usually brought the boxes of goods for Kya, but when Mabel showed up, there was usually something special.

"Go on then, pick up yo' stuff. I'll fill yo' tank," Jumpin' said, so Kya hopped onto the wharf.

"Look here, Miss Kya," Mabel said, as she lifted a peach-colored dress with a layer of chiffon over the flowered skirt, the most beautiful piece of clothing Kya had ever seen, prettier than Ma's sundress. "This dress is fit for a princess like you." She held it in front of Kya, who touched it and smiled. Then, facing away from Jumpin', Mabel leaned over at the middle with some effort and lifted a white bra from the box.

Kya felt heat all over.

"Now, Miss Kya, don't be shy, hon. Ya be needin' this 'bout now. And, child, if there's ever anything ya need to talk to me about, anything ya don't understand, ya let ol' Mabel know. Ya heah?"

"Yes'm. Thank you, Mabel." Kya tucked the bra deep in the box, under some jeans and T-shirts, a bag of black-eyed peas, and a jar of put-up peaches.

A few weeks later, watching pelicans float and feed in the sea, her boat riding up and down waves, Kya's stomach suddenly cramped up. She'd never been seasick, and this felt different from any pain she'd ever had. She pulled her boat ashore at Point Beach and sat on the sand, legs folded to one side like a wing. The pain sharpened, and she grimaced, made a little moan. She must have the runs coming.

Suddenly she heard the purr of a motor and saw Tate's rig cutting through the white-capped surf. He turned inland the instant he saw her and made for shore. She spat out some of Pa's cussing. She always liked seeing Tate, but not when she might have to run to the oak woods any second with diarrhea. After dragging his boat next to hers, he plopped down on the sand beside her.

"Hey, Kya. What're you doing? I was just going out to your place."

"Hey, Tate. It's good to see you." She tried to sound normal, but her stomach twisted tightly.

"What's wrong?" he asked.

"What do you mean?"

"You don't look good. What's wrong?"

"I think I'm sick. My stomach's cramping real hard."

"Oh." Tate looked out over the sea. Dug his bare toes in the sand.

"Maybe you should go," she said, head down.

"Maybe I should stay till you're better. Suppose you can't get yourself home?"

"I might have to go to the woods. I might be sick."

"Maybe. But I don't think that's going to help," he said quietly.

"What do you mean? You don't know what's wrong with me."

"Does this feel different from other stomachaches?"

"Yes."

"You're almost fifteen, right?"

"Yes. What's that got to do with it?"

He was quiet a minute. Shuffled his feet, digging his toes deeper in the sand. Looking away from her, he said, "It might be, you know, what happens to girls your age. Remember, a few months ago I brought you a pamphlet about it. It was with those biology books." Tate glanced at her briefly, his face blazing, and looked away again.

Kya dropped her eyes as her whole body blushed. Of course, there'd been no Ma to tell her, but indeed a school booklet Tate had brought explained some. Now her time had come, and here she was sitting on the beach becoming a woman right in front of a boy. Shame and panic filled her. What was she supposed to do? What exactly would happen? How much blood would there be? She imagined it leaking into the sand around her. She sat silent as a sharp pain racked her middle.

"Can you get yourself home?" he asked, still not looking at her.

"I think so."

"It'll be okay, Kya. Every girl goes through this just fine. You go on home. I'll follow way back to make sure you get there."

"You don't have to."

"Don't worry about me. Now get going." He stood and walked to his boat, not looking at her. He motored out and waited quite far offshore until she headed up coast toward her channel. So far back he was just a speck, he followed until she reached her lagoon. Standing on the bank, she waved briefly to him, her face down, not meeting his eyes.

Just as she had figured out most things, Kya figured out how to become a woman on her own. But the next morning at first light, she boated over to Jumpin's. A pale sun seemed suspended in thick fog as she approached his wharf and looked for Mabel, knowing there was little chance she'd be there. Sure enough, only Jumpin' walked out to greet her.

"Hi, Miss Kya. Ya needin' gas a'ready?"

Still sitting in the boat, Kya answered quietly, "I need to see Mabel."

"I'm sorry as can be, child, Mabel ain't here today. Can I help ya?"

Head down low, she said, "I need to see Mabel bad. Soon."

"Well then." Jumpin' looked across the small bay out to sea and saw no more boats coming in. Anybody needing gas at any time of day and every day including Christmas could count on Jumpin' being here—he hadn't missed a single day in fifty years, except when their baby angel, Daisy, died. He couldn't leave his post. "Ya hang on there, Miss Kya, I gonna run up the lane a ways, get some chillin to fetch Mabel. Any boat come in, ya tell 'em I'll be right back."

"I will. Thank you."

Jumpin' hurried up the wharf and disappeared as Kya waited, glancing out in the bay every few seconds, dreading another boat coming in. But in no time he was back, saying some kids had gone to get Mabel; Kya should "just wait a spell."

Jumpin' busied himself unpacking packets of chewing tobacco on the shelves and generally doing around. Kya stayed in her boat. Finally Mabel hurried across the boards, which shook with her swing as if a small piano were being pushed down the wharf. Carrying a paper bag, she didn't bellow out a greeting, as she would have otherwise, but stood on the wharf above Kya and said quietly, "Mornin', Miss Kya, what's all this 'bout, child? What's wrong, hon?"

Kya dropped her head more, mumbled something Mabel couldn't hear.

"Can ya get out of that boat, or should I get in there with ya?"

Kya didn't answer, so Mabel, almost two hundred pounds' worth, stepped one foot, then the other into the small boat, which complained by bumping against the piling. She sat down on the center bench, facing Kya at the stern.

"Now, child, tell me what's wrong."

The two leaned their heads together, Kya whispering, and then Mabel pulled Kya right over to her full bosom, hugging and rocking her. Kya was rigid at first, not accustomed to yielding to hugs, but this didn't discourage Mabel, and finally Kya went limp and slumped against the comfort of those pillows. After a while, Mabel leaned back and opened the brown paper bag.

"Well, I figured what's wrong, so I brought ya some things." And there, sitting in the boat at Jumpin's wharf, Mabel explained the details to Kya.

"Now, Miss Kya, this ain't nothin' to be 'shamed of. It ain't no curse, like folks say; this here's the startin' of all life, and only a woman can do it. You're a woman now, baby."

When Kya heard Tate's boat the next afternoon, she hid in thick brambles and watched him. For anyone to know her at all seemed strange enough, but now he knew about the most personal and private occurrence of her life. Her cheeks burned at the thought of it. She would hide until he left.

As he pulled onto the lagoon shore and stepped out of the boat, he carried a white box tied up with string. "Yo! Kya, where are you?" he called. "I brought petite cakes from Parker's."

Kya had not tasted anything like cake for years. Tate lifted some books out of the boat, so Kya moseyed out of the bushes behind him.

"Oh, there you are. Look at this." He opened the box, and there, arranged neatly, were little cakes, each only an inch square, covered in vanilla icing with a tiny pink rose perched on the top. "Come on, dig in."

Kya lifted one and, still not looking at Tate, bit into it. Then pushed the rest of it into her mouth. Licked her fingers.

"Here." Tate set the box next to their oak. "Have all you want. Let's get started. I brought a new book." And that was that. They went into the lessons, never uttering a word about the other thing.

Autumn was coming; the evergreens might not have noticed, but the sycamores did. They flashed thousands of golden leaves across slate-gray skies. Late one afternoon, after the lesson, Tate lingering when he should have left, he and Kya sat on a log in the woods. She finally asked the question she'd wanted to ask for months. "Tate, I appreciate your teaching me to read and all those things you gave me. But why'd you do it? Don't you have a girlfriend or somebody like that?"

"Nah—well, sometimes I do. I had one, but not now. I like being out here in the quiet and I like the way you're so interested in the marsh, Kya. Most people don't pay it any attention except to fish. They think it's wasteland that should be drained and developed. People don't understand that most sea creatures—including the very ones they eat—need the marsh."

He didn't mention how he felt sorry for her being alone, that he knew how the kids had treated her for years; how the villagers called her the Marsh Girl and made up stories about her. Sneaking out to her shack, running through the dark and tagging it, had become a regular tradition, an initiation for boys becoming men. What did that say about men? Some of them were already making bets about who would be the first to get her cherry. Things that infuriated and worried him.

But that wasn't the main reason he'd left feathers for Kya in the forest, or why he kept coming to see her. The other words Tate didn't say were his feelings for her that seemed tangled up between the sweet love for a lost sister and the fiery love for a girl. He couldn't come close to sorting it out himself, but he'd never been hit by a stronger wave. A power of emotions as painful as pleasurable.

Poking a grass stalk down an ant hole, she finally asked, "Where's your ma?"

A breeze wandered through the trees, gently shaking branches. Tate didn't answer.

"You don't have to say nothing," she said.

"Anything."

"You don't have to say anything."

"My mother and little sister died in a car wreck over in Asheville. My sister's name was Carianne."

"Oh. I'm so sorry, Tate. I bet your ma was real nice and pretty."

"Yes. Both of them were." He spoke to the ground, between his knees. "I've never talked about it before. To anybody."

Me neither, Kya thought. Out loud she said, "My ma walked off one day and didn't come back. The mama deer always come back."

"Well, at least you can hope she does. Mine won't come back for sure."

They were silent a moment, then Tate continued. "I think . . ." But he stopped, looked away.

Kya looked at him, but he stared at the ground. Quiet.

She said, "What? You think what? You can say anything to me."

Still he said nothing. From a patience born from knowing, she waited.

Finally, very softly he said, "I think they went to Asheville to buy my birthday present. There was this certain bike I wanted, had to have it. The Western Auto didn't carry them, so I think they went to Asheville to buy that bike for me."

"That doesn't make it your fault," she said.

"I know, but it feels like my fault," Tate said. "I don't even remember what kind of bike it was."

Kya leaned closer to him, not enough to touch. But she felt a sensation—almost like the space between their shoulders had shifted. She wondered if Tate felt it. She wanted to lean in closer, just enough so their arms would gently brush together. To touch. And wondered if Tate would notice.

And just at that second, the wind picked up, and thousands upon thousands of yellow sycamore leaves broke from their life support and streamed across the sky. Autumn leaves don't fall; they fly. They take their time and wander on this, their only chance to soar. Reflecting sunlight, they swirled and sailed and fluttered on the wind drafts.

Tate sprang from the log and called to her, "See how many leaves you can catch before they hit the ground!" Kya jumped up, and the two of them leapt and skipped through curtains of falling leaves, reaching their arms wide, snatching them before they fell to the earth. Laughing, Tate dived toward a leaf only inches from the ground, caught it, and rolled over, holding his trophy in the air. Kya threw her hands up, releasing all the leaves she had rescued back into the wind. As she ran back through them, they caught like gold in her hair.

Then, as she whirled around, she bumped into Tate, who had stood, and they froze, staring into each other's eyes. They stopped laughing. He took her shoulders, hesitated an instant, then kissed her lips, as the leaves rained and danced around them as silently as snow.

She knew nothing about kissing and held her head and lips stiff. They broke away and looked at each other, wondering where that had come from and what to do next. He lifted a leaf gently from her hair and dropped it to the ground. Her heart beat wildly. Of all the ragged loves she'd known from wayward family, none had felt like this.

"Am I your girlfriend now?" she asked.

He smiled. "Do you want to be?"

"Yes."

"You might be too young," he said.

"But I know feathers. I bet the other girls don't know feathers."

"All right, then." And he kissed her again. This time she tilted her head to the side and her lips softened. And for the first time in her life, her heart was full.

18.

White Canoe

1960

Now, every new word began with a squeal, every sentence a race. Tate grabbing Kya, the two of them tumbling, half childlike, half not, through sourweed, red with autumn.

"Be serious a second," he said. "The only way to get multiplication tables is to memorize them." He wrote *12 × 12 = 144* in the sand, but she ran past him, dived into the breaking surf, down to the calm, and swam until he followed into a place where gray-blue light beams slanted through the quiet and highlighted their forms. Sleek as porpoises. Later, sandy and salty, they rolled across the beach, arms tight around each other as if they were one.

The next afternoon he motored into her lagoon but stayed in his boat after beaching. A large basket covered in a red-checkered cloth sat at his feet.

"What's that? What'd you bring?" she asked.

"A surprise. Go on, get in."

They flowed through the slow-moving channels into the sea, then south to a tiny half-moon bay. After wrist-flicking the blanket onto the sand, he placed the covered basket on it, and as they sat, he lifted the cloth.

"Happy birthday, Kya," he said. "You're fifteen." A two-tiered bakery cake, tall as a hatbox and decorated with shells of pink icing, rose from the basket. Her name scripted on top. Presents, wrapped in colorful paper and tied with bows, surrounded the cake.

She stared, flabbergasted, her mouth open. No one had wished her happy birthday since Ma left. No one had ever given her a store-bought cake with her name on it. She'd never had presents in real wrapping paper with ribbons.

"How'd you know my birthday?" Having no calendar, she had no idea it was today.

"I read it in your Bible."

While she pleaded for him not to cut through her name, he sliced enormous pieces of cake and plopped them on paper plates. Staring into each other's eyes, they broke off bites and stuffed them in their mouths. Smacking loudly. Licking fingers. Laughing through icing-smeared grins. Eating cake the way it should be eaten, the way everybody wants to eat it.

"Want to open your presents?" He smiled.

The first: a small magnifying glass, "so you can see the fine details of insect wings." Second: a plastic clasp, painted silver and decorated with a rhinestone seagull, "for your hair." Somewhat awkwardly, he pulled some locks behind her ear and clipped the barrette in place. She touched it. More beautiful than Ma's.

The last present was in a larger box, and Kya opened it to find ten jars of oil paint, tins of watercolors, and different-sized brushes: "for your paintings."

Kya picked up each color, each brush. "I can get more when you need them. Even canvas, from Sea Oaks."

She dipped her head. "Thank you, Tate."

"Easy does it. Go slow, now," Scupper called out as Tate, surrounded by fishing nets, oil rags, and preening pelicans, powered the winch. The bow of *The Cherry Pie* bobbled on the cradle, gave a shudder, then glided onto the underwater rails at Pete's Boat Yard, the lopsided pier and rusted-out boathouse, the only haul-out in Barkley Cove.

"Okay, good, she's on. Bring her out." Tate eased more power to the winch, and the boat crawled up the track and into dry dock. They secured her in cables and set about scraping blotchy barnacles from her hull as crystal-sharp arias of Miliza Korjus rose from the record player. They'd have to apply primer, then the annual coat of red paint. Tate's mother had chosen the color, and Scupper would never change it. Once in a while Scupper stopped scraping and waved his large arms to the music's sinuous shape.

Now, early winter, Scupper paid Tate adult wages to work for him after school and on weekends, but Tate couldn't get out to Kya's as much. He didn't mention this to his dad; he'd never mentioned anything about Kya to his dad.

They hacked at barnacles until dark, until even Scupper's arms burned. "I'm too tired to cook, and I reckon you are, too. Let's grab some grub at the diner on the way home."

Nodding at everyone, there not being one person they didn't know, they sat at a corner table. Both ordered the special: chicken-fried steak, mash and gravy, turnips, and coleslaw. Biscuits. Pecan pie with ice cream. At the next table, a family of four joined hands and lowered their heads as the father said a blessing out loud. At "Amen" they kissed the air, squeezed hands, and passed the cornbread.

Scupper said, "Now, son, I know this job's keeping ya from things. That's the way it is, but you didn't go to the homecoming dance or anything last fall, and I don't want you to miss all of it, this being your last year. There's that big dance at the pavilion coming up. You asking a girl?"

"Nah. I might go, not sure. But there's nobody I want to ask."

"There's not one single girl in school you'd go with?"

"Nope."

"Well then." Scupper leaned back as the waitress put down his plate of food. "Thank you, Betty. You sure heaped it up good." Betty moved around and set down Tate's plate, piled even higher.

"Y'all eat up now," she said. "Thar's more where this come from. The special's all-you-can-eat." She smiled at Tate before walking with an extra hip-swing back to the kitchen.

Tate said, "The girls at school are silly. All they talk about is hair-dos and high heels."

"Well now, that's what girls do. Sometimes you gotta take things as they are."

"Maybe."

"Now, son, I don't pay much mind to idle talk, never have done. But there's a regular riptide of gossip saying you've got something going with that girl in the marsh." Tate threw up his hands. "Now hold on, hold on," Scupper continued. "I don't believe all the stories about her; she's probably nice. But take a care, son. You don't want to go starting a family too early. You get my meaning, don't you?"

Keeping his voice low, Tate hissed, "First you say you don't believe those stories about her, then you say I shouldn't start a family, showing you do believe she's that kind of girl. Well, let me tell you something, she's not. She's more pure and innocent than any of those girls you'd have me go to the dance with. Oh man, some of the girls in this town, well, let's just say they hunt in packs, take no prisoners. And yes, I've been going out to see Kya some. You know why? I'm teaching her how to read because people in this town are so mean to her she couldn't even go to school."

"That's fine, Tate. That's good of you. But please understand it's my job to say things like this. It may not be pleasant and all for us to talk about, but parents have to warn their kids about things. That's my job, so don't get huffy about it."

"I know," Tate mumbled while buttering a biscuit. Feeling very huffy.

"Come on now. Let's get another helping, then some of that pecan pie."

After the pie came, Scupper said, "Well, since we've talked about things we never mention, I might as well say something else on my mind."

Tate rolled his eyes at his pie.

Scupper continued. "I want you to know, son, how proud I am of you. All on your own, you've studied the marsh life, done real well at school, applied for college to get a degree in science. And got accepted. I'm just not the kind to speak on such things much. But I'm mighty proud of you, son. All right?"

"Yeah. All right."

Later in his room, Tate recited from his favorite poem:
"Oh when shall I see the dusky Lake,
And the white canoe of my dear?"

. . .

Around the work, as best he could, Tate got out to Kya's, but could never stay long. Sometimes boating forty minutes for a ten-minute beach walk, holding hands. Kissing a lot. Not wasting a minute. Boating back. He wanted to touch her breasts; would kill just to look at them. Lying awake at night, he thought of her thighs, how soft, yet firm, they must be. To think beyond her thighs sent him roiling in the sheets. But she was so young and timid. If he did things wrong, it might affect her somehow, then he'd be worse than the boys who only talked about snagging her. His desire to protect her was as strong as the other. Sometimes.

On every trip to Kya's, Tate took school or library books, especially on marsh creatures and biology. Her progress was startling. She could read anything now, he said, and once you can read anything you can learn everything. It was up to her. "Nobody's come close to filling their brains," he said. "We're all like giraffes not using their necks to reach the higher leaves."

Alone for hours, by the light of the lantern, Kya read how plants and animals change over time to adjust to the ever-shifting earth; how some cells divide and specialize into lungs or hearts, while others remain uncommitted as stem cells in case they're needed later. Birds sing mostly at dawn because the cool, moist air of morning carries their songs and their meanings much farther. All her life, she'd seen these marvels at eye level, so nature's ways came easily to her.

Within all the worlds of biology, she searched for an explanation of why a mother would leave her offspring.

131

One cold day, long after all the sycamore leaves had fallen, Tate stepped out of his boat with a present wrapped in red-and-green paper.

"I don't have anything for you," she said, as he held the present out for her. "I didn't know it's Christmas."

"It's not." He smiled. "Not by a long shot," he lied. "Come on, it's not much."

Carefully she took the paper off to find a secondhand Webster's dictionary. "Oh, Tate, thank you."

"Look inside," he said. Tucked in the *P* section was a pelican feather, forget-me-not blossoms pressed between two pages of the *F*s, a dried mushroom under *M*. So many treasures were stashed among the pages, the book would not completely close.

"I'll try to come back the day after Christmas. Maybe I can bring a turkey dinner." He kissed her good-bye. After he left, she swore out loud. Her first chance since Ma left to give a gift to someone she loved, and she'd missed it.

A few days later, shivering in the sleeveless, peach-colored chiffon dress, she waited for Tate on the lagoon shore. Pacing, she clutched her present for him—a head tuft from a male cardinal—wrapped in the paper he had used. As soon as he stepped out of his boat, she stuck the present into his hands, insisting he open it there, so he did. "Thank you, Kya. I don't have one."

Her Christmas complete.

"Now let's get you inside. You must be freezing in that dress." The kitchen was warm from the woodstove, but still he suggested she change into a sweater and jeans.

Working together they heated the food he'd brought: turkey,

132

cornbread dressing, cranberry sauce, sweet potato casserole, and pumpkin pie—all leftovers from Christmas dinner at the diner with his dad. Kya had made biscuits, and they ate at the kitchen table, which she had decorated with wild holly and seashells.

"I'll wash up," she said, as she poured hot water from the woodstove into the basin.

"I'll help you." And he came up behind her and put his arms around her waist. She leaned her head back against his chest, eyes closed. Slowly his fingers moved under her sweater, across her sleek stomach, toward her breasts. As usual, she wore no bra, and his fingers circled her nipples. His touch lingered there, but a sensation spread down her body as though his hands had moved between her legs. A hollowness that urgently needed filling pulsed through her. But she didn't know what to do, what to say, so pushed back.

"It's okay," he said. And just held her there. Both of them breathing deep.

The sun, still shy and submissive to winter, peeped in now and then between days of mean wind and bitter rain. Then one afternoon, just like that, spring elbowed her way in for good. The day warmed, and the sky shone as if polished. Kya spoke quietly, as she and Tate walked along the grassy bank of a deep creek, overhung with tall sweetgum trees. Suddenly he grabbed her hand, shushing her. Her eyes followed his to the water's edge, where a bullfrog, six inches wide, hunkered under foliage. A common enough sight, except this frog was completely and brilliantly white.

Tate and Kya grinned at each other and watched until he disappeared in one silent, big-legged leap. Still, they were quiet as they backed away into the brush another five yards. Kya put her hands over her mouth and giggled. Bounced away from him in a girlish jig in a body not quite so girlish.

Tate watched her for a second, no longer thinking about frogs. He stepped toward her purposely. His expression stopped her in front of a broad oak. He took her shoulders and pushed her firmly against the tree. Holding her arms along her sides, he kissed her, his groin pushing against hers. Since Christmas they had kissed and explored slowly; not like this. He had always taken the lead but had watched her questioningly for signs to desist; not like now.

He pulled away, the deep golden-brown layers of his eyes boring into hers. Slowly he unbuttoned her shirt and pulled it off, exposing her breasts. He took his time to examine them with his eyes and fingers, circling her nipples. Then he unzipped her shorts and pulled them down, until they dropped to the ground. Almost naked for the first time in front of him, she panted and moved her hands to cover herself. Gently he moved her hands away and took his time looking at her body. Her groin throbbed as if all her blood had surged there. He stepped out of his shorts and, still staring at her, pushed his erection against her.

When she turned away in shyness, he lifted her chin and said, "Look at me. Look me in the eyes, Kya."

"Tate, Tate." She reached out, trying to kiss him, but he held her back, forcing only her eyes to take him in. She didn't know raw nakedness could bring such want. He whispered his hands against her inner thighs, and instinctively she stepped each foot to the side slightly. His fingers moved between her legs and slowly massaged parts of her she never knew existed. She threw her head back and whimpered.

Abruptly, he pushed away from her and stepped back. "God, Kya, I'm sorry. I'm sorry."

"Tate, please, I want to."

"Not like this, Kya."

"Why not? Why not like this?"

She reached for his shoulders and tried to pull him back to her.

"Why not?" she said again.

He picked up her clothes and dressed her. Not touching her where she wanted, where parts of her body still pounded. Then he lifted her and carried her to the creek bank. Put her down, and sat beside her.

"Kya, I want you more than anything. I want you forever. But you're too young. You're only fifteen."

"So what? You're only four years older. It's not like you're suddenly mister know-it-all adult."

"Yes, but I can't get pregnant. And I can't be damaged as easily by this. I won't do it, Kya, because I love you." Love. There was nothing about the word she understood.

"You still think I'm a little girl," she whined.

"Kya, you're sounding more and more like a little girl every second." But he smiled as he said it, and pulled her closer.

"When, then, if not now? When can we?"

"Just not yet."

They were quiet for a moment, and then she asked, "How did you know what to do?" Head down, shy again.

"The same way you did."

One afternoon in May as they walked from the lagoon, he said, "You know, I'm going away soon. To college."

He had spoken of going to Chapel Hill, but Kya had pushed it from her mind, knowing at least they had summer.

"When? Not now."

"Not long. A few weeks."

"But why? I thought college started in the fall."

"I got accepted for a job in a biology lab on campus. I can't pass that up. So I'm starting summer quarter."

Of all the people who left her, only Jodie had said good-bye. Everyone else had walked away forever, but this didn't feel any better. Her chest burned.

"I'll come back as much as I can. It's not that far, really. Less than a day by bus."

She sat quiet. Finally she said, "Why do you have to go, Tate? Why can't you stay here, shrimp like your dad?"

"Kya, you know why. I just can't do that. I want to study the marsh, be a research biologist." They had reached the beach and sat on the sand.

"Then what? There're no jobs like that here. You'll never come home again."

"Yes, I will. I won't leave you, Kya. I promise. I'll come back to you."

She jumped to her feet, startling the plovers, who flew up, squawking. She ran from the beach into the woods. Tate ran after her, but as soon as he reached the trees, he stopped, looked around. She had already lost him.

But just in case she stood in earshot, he called out, "Kya, you can't run from every whipstitch. Sometimes you have to discuss things. Face things." Then with less patience, "Damn it, Kya. Damn it to hell!"

A week later, Kya heard Tate's boat whirring across her lagoon and hid behind a bush. As he eased through the channel, the heron lifted on slow silver wings. Some part of her wanted to run, but she stepped onto the shore, waiting.

"Hey," he said. For once he didn't wear a cap, and his wild blond curls wafted about his tanned face. It seemed that in the last few months, his shoulders had widened into those of a man.

"Hey."

He stepped from the boat, took her hand, and led her to the reading-log, where they sat.

"Turns out I'm leaving sooner than I thought. I'm skipping the graduation ceremonies so I can start my job. Kya, I've come to say good-bye." Even his voice seemed manlike, ready for a more serious world.

She didn't answer, but sat looking away from him. Her throat pulled in tight. He placed two bags of school and library rejects, mostly science books, at her feet.

She wasn't sure she could speak. She wanted him to take her again to the place of the white frog. In case he never came back, she wanted him to take her there now.

"I'm going to miss you, Kya. Every day, all day."

"You might forget me. When you get busy with all that college stuff and see all those pretty girls."

"I'll never forget you. Ever. You take care of the marsh till I get back, you hear? And be careful."

"I will."

"I mean it now, Kya. Watch out for folks; don't let strangers get near you."

"I think I can hide or outrun anybody."

"Yes, I believe you can. I'll come home in about a month, I promise. For the Fourth of July. I'll be back before you know it."

She didn't answer, and he stood, jammed his hands into his jeans pockets. She stood next to him, but they both looked away, into the trees.

He took her shoulders and kissed her for a long time.

"Good-bye, Kya." For a moment she looked somewhere over his shoulder and then into his eyes. A chasm she knew to its greatest depths.

"Good-bye, Tate."

Without another word, he got in his boat and motored across the lagoon. Just before entering the thick brambles of the channel, he turned and waved. She lifted her hand high above her head, and then touched it to her heart.

19.

Something Going On

1969

The morning after reading the second lab report, the eighth day since finding Chase Andrews's body in the swamp, Deputy Purdue pushed open the door to the sheriff's office with his foot and stepped inside. He carried two paper cups of coffee and a bag of hot donuts—just pulled from the fryer.

"Oh man, the smell of Parker's," Ed said as Joe placed the goods on the desk. Each man dug an enormous donut from the brown paper bag splotched with grease stains. Smacked loudly, licked glazed fingers.

Speaking over each other, both men announced, "Well, I got something."

"Go ahead," Ed said.

"I got it from several sources that Chase had something goin' on in the marsh."

"Going on? What do you mean?"

"Not sure, but some guys at the Dog-Gone say 'bout four years ago he started goin' out to the marsh a lot by himself, was real secretive about it. He'd still go fishin' or boatin' with his friends, but made a lot of trips alone. I was thinkin' maybe he got himself mixed up with some potheads or worse. Got over his head with some nasty drug thug. Ya lie down with dogs, ya get up with fleas. Or in this case, not get up at all."

"I don't know. He was such an athlete; hard to picture him getting mixed up in drugs," the sheriff said.

"Former athlete. And anyhow, lots of 'em get tangled up in drugs. When the grand days of hero dry up, they gotta get a high from somewheres else. Or maybe he had a woman out there."

"I just don't know of any ladies out there that'd be his type. He only hung out with the so-called Barkley elite. Not trash."

"Well, if he thought of himself as slummin', maybe that's why he was so quiet about it."

"True," the sheriff said. "Anyway, whatever he had going on out there, it opens up a whole new side of his life we didn't know about. Let's do some snooping, see what he was up to."

"Ya said you got something, too?"

"Not sure what. Chase's mother called, said she had something important to tell us about the case. Something to do with a shell necklace he wore all the time. She's sure it's a clue. Wants to come in here to tell us about it."

"When's she coming?"

"This afternoon, pretty soon."

"It'd be nice to have a real clue. Beats walkin' around looking for some guy wearin' a red wool sweater with a motive attached. We gotta admit, if this was a murder, it was a clever one. The marsh chewed up and swallowed all the evidence, if there was any. Do we have time for lunch before Patti Love gets here?"

"Sure. And the special's fried pork chops. Blackberry pie."

20.

July 4

1961

Dressed in the now too-short peach chiffon, Kya walked barefoot to the lagoon on July 4 and sat on the reading-log. Cruel heat shrugged off the last wisps of fog, and a dense humidity she could barely breathe filled the air. Now and then she knelt to the lagoon and splashed cool water on her neck, all the while listening for the hum of Tate's boat. She didn't mind waiting; she read the books he'd given her.

The day dragged itself by minutes, the sun getting stuck in the middle. The log hardened, so she settled on the ground, her back against a tree. Finally, hungry, she rushed back to the shack for a leftover sausage and biscuit. Ate fast, afraid he would come while she quit her post.

The muggy afternoon rallied mosquitoes. No boat; no Tate. At dusk, she stood straight and still and silent as a stork, staring at the empty-quiet channel. Breathing hurt. Stepping out of the dress, she eased into the water and swam in the dark coolness, the water sliding over her skin, releasing heat from her core. She pulled from the lagoon and sat on a mossy patch of the bank, nude until she dried, until the moon slipped beneath the earth. Then, carrying her clothes, walked inside.

She waited the next day. Each hour warmed until noon, blistered after midday, throbbed past sunset. Later, the moon threw hope across the water, but that died, too. Another sunrise, another white-hot noon. Sunset again. All hope gone to neutral. Her eyes shifted listlessly, and though she listened for Tate's boat, she was no longer coiled.

The lagoon smelled of life and death at once, an organic jumbling of promise and decay. Frogs croaked. Dully she watched fireflies scribbling across the night. She never collected lightning bugs in bottles; you learn a lot more about something when it's not in a jar. Jodie had taught her that the female firefly flickers the light under her tail to signal to the male that she's ready to mate. Each species of firefly has its own language of flashes. As Kya watched, some females signed *dot, dot, dot, dash,* flying a zigzag dance, while others flashed *dash, dash, dot* in a different dance pattern. The males, of course, knew the signals of their species and flew only to those females. Then, as Jodie had put it, they rubbed their bottoms together like most things did, so they could produce young.

Suddenly Kya sat up and paid attention: one of the females had changed her code. First she flashed the proper sequence of dashes and dots, attracting a male of her species, and they mated. Then she flickered a different signal, and a male of a different species flew to her. Reading her message, the second male was convinced he'd found a willing female of his own kind and hovered above her to mate. But suddenly the female firefly reached up, grabbed him with her mouth, and ate him, chewing all six legs and both wings.

Kya watched others. The females got what they wanted—first a mate, then a meal—just by changing their signals.

Kya knew judgment had no place here. Evil was not in play, just life pulsing on, even at the expense of some of the players. Biology sees right and wrong as the same color in different light.

She waited another hour for Tate, and finally walked toward the shack.

The next morning, swearing at the shreds of cruel hope, she went back to the lagoon. Sitting at the water's edge, she listened for the sound of a boat chugging down the channel or across the distant estuaries.

At noon she stood and screamed, "TATE, TATE, NO, NO." Then dropped to her knees, her face against the mud. She felt a strong pull out from under her. A tide she knew well.

21.

Coop

1961

Hot wind rattled the palmetto fronds like small dry bones. For three days after giving up on Tate, Kya didn't get out of bed. Drugged by despair and heat, she tossed in clothes and sheets damp from sweat, her skin sticky. She sent her toes on missions to scout for cool spots between the sheets, but they found none.

She didn't note the time of moonrise or when a great horned owl took a diurnal dive at a blue jay. From bed, she heard the marsh beyond in the lifting of blackbird wings, but didn't go to it. She hurt from the crying songs of the gulls above the beach, calling to her. But for the first time in her life, did not go to them. She hoped the pain from ignoring them would displace the tear in her heart. It did not.

Listless, she wondered what she had done to send everyone away. Her own ma. Her sisters. Her whole family. Jodie. And now Tate. Her most poignant memories were unknown dates of family members disappearing down the lane. The last of a white scarf trailing through the leaves. A pile of socks left on a floor mattress.

Tate and life and love had been the same thing. Now there was no Tate.

"Why, Tate, why?" She mumbled into the sheets, "You were supposed to be different. To stay. You said you loved me, but there is no such thing. There is no one on Earth you can count on." From somewhere very deep, she made herself a promise never to trust or love anyone again.

She'd always found the muscle and heart to pull herself from the mire, to take the next step, no matter how shaky. But where had all that grit brought her? She drifted in and out of thin sleep.

Suddenly, the sun—full, bright, and glaring—struck her face. Never in her life had she slept until midday. She heard a soft rustling sound and, raising herself onto her elbows, saw a raven-sized Cooper's hawk standing on the other side of the screen door, peering in. For the first time in days, an interest stirred in her. She roused herself as the hawk took wing.

Finally, she made a mush of hot water and grits and headed to the beach to feed the gulls. When she broke onto the beach, all of them swirled and dived in flurries, and she dropped to her knees and tossed the food on the sand. As they crowded around her, she felt their feathers brushing her arms and thighs, and threw her head back, smiling with them. Even as tears streamed her cheeks.

For a month after July 4, Kya did not leave her place, did not go into the marsh or to Jumpin's for gas or supplies. She lived on dried fish, mussels, oysters. Grits and greens.

When all her shelves were empty, she finally motored to Jumpin's for supplies but didn't chat with him as usual. Did her business and left him standing, staring after her. Needing people ended in hurt.

A few mornings later, the Cooper's hawk was back on her steps, peering at her through the screen. *How odd*, she thought, cocking her head at him. "Hey, Coop."

With a little hop, he lifted, made a flyby, then soared high into the clouds. Watching him, at last, Kya said to herself, "I have to get back into the marsh," and she took the boat out, easing along the channels and slipstreams, searching for bird nests, feathers, or shells for the first time since Tate abandoned her. Even so, she couldn't avoid thoughts of him. The intellectual fascinations or the pretty girls of Chapel Hill had drawn him in. She couldn't imagine college women, but whatever form they took would be better than a tangled-haired, barefoot mussel-monger who lived in a shack.

By the end of August, her life once more found its footing: boat, collect, paint. Months passed. She only went to Jumpin's when low supplies demanded, but spoke very little to him.

Her collections matured, categorized methodically by order, genus, and species; by age according to bone wear; by size in millimeters of feathers; or by the most fragile hues of greens. The science and art entwined in each other's strengths: the colors, the light, the species, the life; weaving a masterpiece of knowledge and beauty that filled every corner of her shack. Her world. She grew with them—the trunk of the vine—alone, but holding all the wonders together.

But just as her collection grew, so did her loneliness. A pain as large as her heart lived in her chest. Nothing eased it. Not the gulls, not a splendid sunset, not the rarest of shells.

Months turned into a year.

The lonely became larger than she could hold. She wished for some-one's voice, presence, touch, but wished more to protect her heart.

Months passed into another year. Then another.

PART 2

The Swamp

22.

Same Tide

1965

Nineteen years old, legs longer, eyes larger and seemingly blacker, Kya sat on Point Beach, watching sand crabs bury themselves backward into the swash. Suddenly, from the south, she heard voices and jumped to her feet. The group of kids—now young adults—she'd watched occasionally through the years ambled toward her, tossing a football, running and kicking the surf. Anxious they would see her, she loped to the trees, sand tearing from her heels, and hid behind the broad trunk of an oak tree. Knowing how odd this made her.

Not much has changed, she thought, *them laughing, me holing up like a sand crab.* A wild thing ashamed of her own freakish ways.

Tallskinnyblonde, Ponytailfreckleface, Alwayswearspearls, and Roundchubbycheeks romped the beach, tangled in laughs and hugs. On her rare trips to the village, she'd heard their slurs. "Yeah, the Marsh Girl gits her clothes from colored people; has to trade mussels for grits."

Yet after all these years, they were still a group of friends. That was something. Silly-looking on the outside, yes, but as Mabel had said several times, they were a sure troop. "Ya need some girlfriends, hon, 'cause they're furever. Without a vow. A clutch of women's the most tender, most tough place on Earth."

Kya found herself laughing softly with them as they kicked salt water on one another. Then, shrieking, they rushed as one into the deeper surf. Kya's smile faded when they pulled themselves out of the water and into their traditional group hug.

Their squeals made Kya's silence even louder. Their togetherness tugged at her loneliness, but she knew being labeled as marsh trash kept her behind the oak tree.

Her eyes shifted to the tallest guy. Wearing khaki shorts and no shirt, he threw the football. Kya watched the cords of muscles bunching on his back. His tan shoulders. She knew he was Chase Andrews, and over the years, ever since he nearly ran her over on his bicycle, she'd seen him with these friends on the beach, walking into the diner for milk shakes, or at Jumpin's buying gas.

Now, as the group came closer, she watched only him. When another tossed the ball, he ran to catch it and came close to her tree, his bare feet digging in the hot sand. As he raised his arm to throw, he happened to glance back and caught Kya's eyes. After passing the ball, without giving any sign to the others, he turned and held her gaze. His hair was black, like hers, but his eyes were pale blue, his face strong, striking. A shadow-smile formed on his lips. Then he walked back to the others, shoulders relaxed, sure.

But he had noticed her. Had held her eyes. Her breath froze as a heat flowed through her.

She tracked them, mostly him, down the shore. Her mind looking one way, her desire the other. Her body watched Chase Andrews, not her heart.

The next day she returned—same tide, different time, but no one was there, just noisy sandpipers and wave-riding sand crabs.

She tried to force herself to avoid that beach and stick to the marsh, searching for bird nests and feathers. Stay safe, feeding grits to gulls. Life had made her an expert at mashing feelings into a storable size.

But loneliness has a compass of its own. And she went back to the beach to look for him the next day. And the next.

Late one afternoon, after watching for Chase Andrews, Kya walks from her shack and lies back on a sliver of beach, slick from the last wave. She stretches her arms over her head, brushing them against the wet sand, and extends her legs, toes pointed. Eyes closed, she rolls slowly toward the sea. Her hips and arms leave slight indentions in the glistening sand, brightening and then dimming as she moves. Rolling nearer the waves, she senses the ocean's roar through the length of her body and feels the question: *When will the sea touch me? Where will it touch me first?*

The foamy surge rushes the shore, reaching toward her. Tingling with expectancy, she breathes deep. Turns more and more slowly. With each revolution, just before her face sweeps the sand, she lifts her head gently and takes in the sun-salt smell. *I am close, very close. It is coming. When will I feel it?*

A fever builds. The sand wetter beneath her, the rumble of surf louder. Even slower, by inches she moves, waiting for the touch. Soon, soon. Almost feeling it before it comes.

She wants to open her eyes to peek, to see how much longer. But she resists, squinting her lids even tighter, the sky bright behind them, giving no hints.

Suddenly she shrieks as the power rushes beneath her, fondles her thighs, between her legs, flows along her back, swirling under her head, pulling her hair in inky strands. She rolls faster into the deepening wave, against streaming shells and ocean bits, the water embracing her. Pushing against the sea's strong body, she is grasped, held. Not alone.

Kya sits up and opens her eyes to the ocean foaming around her in soft white patterns, always changing.

Since Chase had glanced at her on the beach, she'd already gone to Jumpin's wharf twice in one week. Not admitting to herself that she hoped to see Chase there. Being noticed by someone had lit a social cord. And now, she asked Jumpin', "How's Mabel doing, anyway? Are any of your grandkids home?" like the old days. Jumpin' noticed the change, knew better than to comment. "Yessiree, got fou' wif us right now. House full up wif giggles and I don't know whut all."

But a few mornings later when Kya motored to the wharf, Jumpin' was nowhere to be seen. Brown pelicans, hunched up on posts, eyed her as though they were minding shop. Kya smiled at them.

A touch on her shoulder made her jump.

"Hi." She turned to see Chase standing behind her. She dropped her smile.

"I'm Chase Andrews." His eyes, ice-pack blue, pierced her own. He seemed completely comfortable to stare into her.

She said nothing, but shifted her weight.

"I've seen ya around some. Ya know, over the years, in the marsh. What's yo' name?" For a moment he thought she wasn't going to speak; maybe she was dumb or spoke a primal language, like some said. A less self-assured man might have walked away.

"Kya." Obviously, he didn't remember their sidewalk-bicycle encounter or know her in any way except as the Marsh Girl.

"Kya—that's different. But nice. You wanta go for a picnic? In my boat, this Sunday."

She looked past him, taking time to evaluate his words, but couldn't see them to an end. Here was a chance to be with someone.

Finally she said, "Okay." He told her to meet him at the oak peninsula north of Point Beach at noon. Then he stepped into his blue-and-white ski boat, metal bits gleaming from every possible surface, and accelerated away.

She turned at the sound of more footsteps. Jumpin' scurried up the dock. "Hi, Miss Kya. Sorry, I been totin' empty crates over yonder. Fill 'er up?"

Kya nodded.

On the way home, she cut the motor and drifted, the shore in sight. Leaning against the old knapsack, watching the sky, she recited poetry by heart, as she did sometimes. One of her favorites was John Masefield's "Sea Fever":

> . . . all I ask is a windy day with the white clouds flying,
> And the flung spray and the blown spume, and the
>   sea-gulls crying.

Kya recalled a poem written by a lesser-known poet, Amanda Hamilton, published recently in the local newspaper she'd bought at the Piggly Wiggly:

> Trapped inside,
> Love is a caged beast,
> Eating its own flesh.

> Love must be free to wander,
> To land upon its chosen shore
> And breathe.

The words made her think of Tate, and her breathing stopped. All he'd needed was to find something better and he was gone. Didn't even come to say good-bye.

Kya didn't know, but Tate had come back to see her.

The day before he was to bus home that Fourth of July, Dr. Blum, the professor who'd hired him, walked into the protozoology lab and asked Tate if he'd like to join a group of renowned ecologists for a bird-ing expedition over the weekend.

"I've noticed your interest in ornithology and wondered if you'd like to come. I only have room for one student, and I thought of you."

"Yes, absolutely. I'll be there." After Dr. Blum left, Tate stood there, alone, amid lab tables, microscopes, and the hum of the autoclave, wondering how he'd folded so fast. How quickly he'd jumped to im-press his professor. The pride of being singled out, the only student invited.

His next chance to go home—and only for one night—had been fifteen days later. He was frantic to apologize to Kya, who would un-derstand after she learned of Dr. Blum's invitation.

He'd cut throttle as he left the sea and turned into the channel, where logs were lined with the glistening backs of sunbathing turtles. Almost halfway, he spotted her boat carefully hidden in tall cord grass. In-stantly, he slowed and saw her up ahead, kneeling on a wide sandbar, apparently fascinated by some small crustacean.

Her head low to the ground, she hadn't seen him or heard his slow-moving boat. He quietly turned his skiff into reeds, out of view. He'd known for years that she sometimes spied on him, peeping through needle brush. On impulse, he would do the same.

Barefoot, dressed in cutoff jeans and a white T-shirt, she stood up, stretching her arms high. Showcasing her wasp-thin waist. She knelt again and scooped sand in her hands, sifting it through her fingers, examining organisms left squiggling in her palm. He smiled at the young biologist, absorbed, oblivious. He imagined her standing at the back of the birding group, trying not to be noticed but being the first to spot and identify every bird. Shyly and softly, she would have listed the precise species of grasses woven into each nest, or the age in days of a female fledgling based on the emerging colors of her wing-tips. Exquisite minutiae beyond any guidebook or knowledge of the esteemed ecology group. The smallest specifics on which a species spins. The essence.

Suddenly Tate startled as Kya sprang to her feet, sand spilling from her fingers, and looked upstream, away from Tate. He could barely hear the low churn of an outboard motor coming their way, probably a fisherman or marsh dweller headed to town. A purring sound, common and calm as doves. But Kya grabbed the knapsack, sprinted across the sandbar, and scrambled into tall grass. Squatting low to the ground and snatching glances to see if the boat had come into view, she duck-walked toward her boat. Knees lifting nearly to her chin. She was closer to Tate now, and he saw her eyes, dark and crazed. When she reached her boat, she hunkered beside its girth, head low.

The fisherman—a merry-faced, hatted old man—puttered into view, saw neither Kya nor Tate, and disappeared beyond the bend. But she remained frozen, listening until the motor whined away, then stood, dabbing her brow. Continued to look in the direction of the boat as a deer eyes the empty brush of a departed panther.

On some level he knew she behaved this way, but since the feather game, had not witnessed the raw, unpeeled core. How tormented, isolated, and strange.

He'd been at college less than two months but had already stepped directly into the world he wanted, analyzing the stunning symmetry of the DNA molecule as if he'd crawled inside a glistening cathedral of coiling atoms and climbed the winding, acidic rungs of the helix. Seeing that all life depends on this precise and intricate code transcribed on fragile, organic slivers, which would perish instantly in a slightly warmer or colder world. At last, surrounded by enormous questions and people as curious as he to find the answers, drawing him toward his goal of research biologist in his own lab, interacting with other scientists.

Kya's mind could easily live there, but she could not. Breathing hard, he stared at his decision hiding there in cord grass: Kya or everything else.

"Kya, Kya, I just can't do this," he whispered. "I'm sorry."

After she moved away, he got into his boat and motored back toward the ocean. Swearing at the coward inside who would not tell her good-bye.

23.

The Shell

1965

The night after seeing Chase Andrews on Jumpin's wharf, Kya sat at her kitchen table in the easy flicker of lantern light. She'd started cooking again, and she nibbled on a supper of buttermilk biscuits, turnips, and pinto beans, reading while she ate. But thoughts of the picnic-date with Chase the next day unraveled every sentence.

Kya stood and walked into the night, into the creamy light of a three-quarter moon. The marsh's soft air fell silklike around her shoulders. The moonlight chose an unexpected path through the pines, laying shadows about in rhymes. She strolled like a sleepwalker as the moon pulled herself naked from the waters and climbed limb by limb through the oaks. The slick mud of the lagoon shore glowed in the intense light, and hundreds of fireflies dotted the woods. Wearing a secondhand white dress with a flowing skirt and waving her arms slowly about, Kya waltzed to the music of katydids and leopard frogs. She slid her hands along her sides and up her neck. Then moved them along her thighs as she held Chase Andrews's face in her eyes. She wanted him to touch her this way. Her breathing deepened. No one had ever looked at her as he did. Not even Tate.

She danced among the pale wings of mayflies, fluttering above the bright moon-mud.

The next morning, she rounded the peninsula and saw Chase in his boat, just offshore. Here in daylight, reality drifted ahead, waiting, and her throat dried. Steering onto the beach, she stepped out and pulled her boat in, the hull crunching against the sand.

Chase drifted up alongside. "Hi."

Looking over her shoulder, she nodded. He stepped out of his boat and held out his hand to her—long tanned fingers, an open palm. She hesitated; touching someone meant giving part of herself away, a piece she never got back.

Even so, she placed her hand lightly in his. He steadied her as she stepped into the stern and sat on the cushioned bench. A warm, fine day beamed down, and Kya, wearing denim cutoffs and a white cotton blouse—an outfit she'd copied from the others—looked normal. He sat next to her, and she felt his sleeve slide gently across her arm.

Chase eased the boat toward the ocean. The open water tossed the boat more than the quiet marsh, and she knew the pitching motion of the sea would brush her arm against his. That anticipation of touch kept her eyes straight ahead, but she did not move away.

Finally, a larger wave rose and dipped, and his arm, solid and warm, caressed hers. Jarring away, then touching again with every rise and drop. And when a swell surged beneath them, his thigh brushed against hers and her breathing stopped.

As they headed south along the coast, theirs the only boat in this remoteness, he accelerated. Ten minutes on, several miles of white beach stretched along the tide line, protected from the rest of the world by a rounded, thick forest. Up ahead, Point Beach unfolded into the water like a brilliant white fan.

Chase had not said a word since his greeting; she had not spoken at all. He glided the boat onto shore and tucked the picnic basket in the boat's shadow on the sand.

"Wanta walk?" he asked.

"Yes."

They strolled along the water, each small wave rushing their ankles in little eddies and then sucking at their feet as it was pulled back into the sea.

He didn't hold her hand, but now and then, in natural movement, their fingers brushed. Occasionally they knelt to examine a shell or a strand of transparent seaweed spiraled into art. Chase's blue eyes were playful; he smiled easily. His skin was dark tan like hers. Together they were tall, elegant, similar.

Kya knew Chase had chosen not to go to college but to work for his dad. He was a standout in town, the tom turkey. And somewhere within, she worried she was also a piece of beach art, a curiosity to be turned over in his hands, then tossed back on the sand. But she walked on. She'd given love a chance; now she wanted simply to fill the empty spaces. Ease the loneliness while walling off her heart.

After a half mile he faced her and bowed low, sweeping his arm in an exaggerated invitation for them to sit on the sand, against a driftwood log. They dug their feet into the white crystals and leaned back.

From his pocket Chase pulled out a harmonica.

"Oh," she said, "you play." The words felt rough on her tongue.

"Not very good. But when I got an audience leanin' against driftwood on the beach . . ." Closing his eyes, he played "Shenandoah," his palm fluttering on the instrument like a bird trapped against glass. It was a lovely, plaintive sound, like a note from a faraway home. Then, abruptly, he stopped midsong and picked up a shell slightly larger than a nickel, creamy white with bright splotches of red and purple.

"Hey, look at this," he said.

"Oh, it's an ornate scallop, *Pecten ornatus*," Kya said. "I only see them rarely. There are many of that genus here, but this particular species usually inhabits regions south of this latitude because these waters are too cool for them."

He stared at her. Of all the gossip, no one ever mentioned that the Marsh Girl, the girl who couldn't spell *dog*, knew the Latin names of shells, where they occurred—and why, forchristsake.

"I don't know about that," he said, "but look here, it's twisted." The little wings flaring on either side of the hinge were crooked, and there was a perfect little hole at the base. He turned it over in his palm. "Here, you keep it. You're the shell girl."

"Thanks." She slid it into her pocket.

He played a few more songs, ending with a stampede of "Dixie," and then they walked back to the wicker picnic basket and sat on a plaid blanket eating cold fried chicken, salt-cured ham and biscuits, and potato salad. Sweet and dill pickles. Slices of four-layer cake with half-inch-thick caramel icing. All homemade, wrapped in wax paper. He opened two bottles of Royal Crown Cola and poured them into Dixie cups—her first drink of soda pop in her life. The generous spread was incredible to her, with the neatly arranged cloth napkins, plastic plates and forks. Even minuscule pewter salt and pepper shakers. His mother must have packed it, she thought, not knowing he was meeting the Marsh Girl.

They talked softly of sea things—pelicans gliding and sandpipers prancing—no touching, little laughing. As Kya pointed out a jagged cord of pelicans, he nodded and maneuvered closer to her, so their shoulders brushed lightly. When she looked at him, he lifted her chin with his hand and kissed her. He touched her neck lightly, then feathered his fingers over her blouse toward her breast. Kissing and holding her, more firmly now, he leaned back until they were lying on the blanket. Slowly he moved until he was on top of her, pushed his groin between her legs, and in one movement pulled up her blouse. She jerked her head away and squirmed out from under him, her blacker-than-night eyes blazing. Tugged her top down.

"Easy, easy. It's okay."

She lay there—hair strewn across the sand, face flushed, red mouth slightly parted—stunning. Carefully, he reached up to touch her face, but fast as a cat, she sprang away, and stood.

Kya breathed hard. Last night, dancing alone on the lagoon shore, swaying about with the moon and mayflies, she'd imagined she was ready. Thought she knew all about mating from watching doves. No one had ever told her about sex, and her only experience with foreplay had been with Tate. But she knew the details from her biology books and had seen more creatures copulating—and it wasn't merely "rubbing their bottoms together" like Jodie had said—than most people ever would.

But this was too abrupt—picnic, then mate the Marsh Girl. Even male birds woo the females for a while, flashing brilliant feathers, building bowers, staging magnificent dances and love songs. Yes, Chase had laid out a banquet, but she was worth more than fried chicken. And "Dixie" didn't count as a love song. She should've known it would be like this. Only time male mammals hover is when they're in the rut.

The silence grew as they stared at each other, broken only by the sound of their breathing and the breakers beyond. Chase sat up and reached for her arm, but she jerked it away.

"I'm sorry. It's okay," he said as he stood. True, he'd come here to snag her, to be the first, but watching those eyes firing, he was entranced.

He tried again. "C'mon, Kya. I said I'm sorry. Let's just forget it. I'll take you back to yo' boat."

At that she turned and walked across the sand toward the woods. Her long body swaying.

"What're ya doin'? You can't walk back from here. It's miles."

But she was already in the trees, and ran a crow-route, first inland, then across the peninsula, toward her boat. The area was new to her, but blackbirds guided her across the inland marsh. She didn't slow for bogs or gullies, splashed right through creeks, jumped logs.

Finally, she bent over and, heaving, fell to her knees. Cussing worn-out words. As long as she ranted, sobs couldn't surface. But nothing could stop the burning shame and sharp sadness. A simple hope of being with someone, of actually being wanted, of being touched, had drawn her in. But these hurried groping hands were only a *taking*, not a *sharing* or *giving*.

She listened for sounds of him coming after her, not sure whether she wanted him to break through the brush and hold her, begging for forgiveness, or not. Raging again at that. Then, spent, she stood and walked the rest of the way to her boat.

24.

The Fire Tower

1965

Thunderheads piled and pushed against the horizon as Kya motored into the afternoon sea. She hadn't seen Chase since their beach picnic ten days ago, but still felt the shape and firmness of his body pinning hers against the sand.

No other boats were in sight as she steered toward an inlet south of Point Beach, where she had once seen unusual butterflies—so powerfully white they might have been albino. But forty yards out, she suddenly released the throttle when she saw Chase's friends packing picnic baskets and bright towels into their boats. Kya turned quickly to speed away but, against a strong pull, turned back and searched for him. She knew that no part of this yearning made sense. Illogical behavior to fill an emptiness would not fulfill much more. How much do you trade to defeat lonesomeness?

And there, near the spot where he kissed her, she saw him walking with fishing rods toward his boat. Behind him, Alwayswearspearls carried a cooler.

Suddenly, Chase turned his head and looked directly at her drifting in her boat. She didn't turn away but stared back at him. As always shyness won, so she broke eye contact, sped off, and steered into a shadowy cove. She'd wait until their little navy left before going to the beach herself.

Ten minutes later, she motored back into the sea and, up ahead, saw Chase alone in his boat, bobbing waves. Waiting.

The old longing swelled. He was still interested in her. True, he'd come on too strong at the picnic, but he'd stopped when she brushed him away. Had apologized. Perhaps she should give him another chance.

He motioned her over and called, "Hi, Kya."

She didn't go toward him, but not away either. He motored closer.

"Kya, I'm sorry 'bout the other day. Okay? C'mon, I wanta show you the fire tower."

She said nothing, still drifting his way, knowing it was weakness.

"Look, if you've never climbed the tower, it's a great way to see the marsh. Follow me."

She increased throttle and turned her boat toward his, all the while scanning the sea to make sure his friends were out of sight.

Chase motioned her north past Barkley Cove—the village serene and colorful in the distance—and landed on the beach of a small bay tucked in deep forest. After securing the boats, he led her down an overgrown path of wax myrtle and prickly holly. She'd never been to this watery and rooty forest, because it stood on the other side of the village and was too close to people. As they walked, thin runnels of backwater seeped under the brush—slinky reminders that the sea owned this land.

Then a true swamp settled deep with its low-earth smell and fusty air. Sudden, subtle, and silent all at once, it stretched into the mouth of the dark receding forest.

Kya saw the weathered wooden platform of the abandoned fire tower above the canopy, and a few minutes later, they arrived at its straddle-legged base, made of rough-cut poles. Black mud oozed around the legs and under the tower, and damp rot ate its way along the beams. Stairs switched to the top, the structure narrowing at each level.

After crossing the sludge, they started the climb, Chase leading. By the fifth switchback, the rounded oak forests tumbled west as far as they could see. In every other direction, slipstreams, lagoons, creeks, and estuaries wove through brilliant green grass to the sea. Kya had never been this high above the marsh. Now all the pieces lay beneath her, and she saw her friend's full face for the first time.

When they reached the last step, Chase pushed open the iron grate covering the stairwell. After they climbed onto the platform, he eased it down again. Before stepping on it, Kya tested it by tapping it with her toes. Chase laughed lightly. "It's fine, don't worry." He led her to the railing, where they looked over the marshland. Two red-tailed hawks, the wind whistling through their wings, soared by at eye level, their heads cocked in surprise to see a young man and woman standing in their airspace.

Chase turned to her and said, "Thanks for comin', Kya. For giving me another chance to say I'm sorry 'bout the other day. I was way outta line and it won't happen again."

She said nothing. Parts of her wanted to kiss him now, to feel his strength against her.

Reaching into her jeans pocket, she said, "I made a necklace with the shell you found. You don't have to wear it if you don't want to." She'd strung the shell on the rawhide the night before, thinking to herself she would wear it, but knowing all along she hoped to see Chase again and would give it to him if she had the chance. But even her wistful daydream had not envisioned them standing together on top of the fire tower overlooking the world. A summit.

"Thank ya, Kya," he said. He looked at it, and then he put it on over his head, fingering the shell as it rested against his throat. "'Course I'll wear it."

He said nothing trite like *I'll wear it forever, till the day I die.*

"Take me to your house," Chase said. Kya imagined the shack hunkered under oaks, its gray boards stained with blood from the rusting roof. The screens more holes than mesh. A place of patches.

"It's far," is all she said.

"Kya, I don't care how far or what it's like. C'mon, let's go."

This chance of acceptance might go away if she said no.

"All right." They climbed down the tower, and he led her back to the bay, motioning for her to lead the way in her boat. She cruised south to the maze of estuaries and ducked her head as she slipped into her channel, overhung with green. His boat was almost too big to fit in the jungle growth, certainly too blue and white, but it squeezed through, limbs screeching along the hull.

When her lagoon opened before them, the delicate details of every mossy branch and brilliant leaf reflected in the clear dark water. Dragonflies and snowy egrets lifted briefly at his strange boat, then resettled gracefully on silent wings. Kya tied up as Chase motored up to the shore. The great blue heron, having long ago accepted those less wild, stood stork-still only feet away.

Her laundry of faded overalls and T-shirts hung tatty on the line, and so many turnips had spread into the forests, it was difficult to tell where the garden ended and the wilderness began.

Looking at the patched screen porch, he asked, "How long ya lived out here by yourself?"

"I don't know exactly when Pa left. But about ten years, I think."

"That's neat. Livin' out here with no parents to tell ya what to do."

Kya didn't respond except to say, "There's nothing to see inside." But he was already walking up the brick-'n'-board steps. The first things he saw were her collections lining homemade shelves. A collage of the shimmering life just beyond the screen.

"You did all this?" he said.

"Yes."

He looked at some butterflies briefly but quickly lost interest. Thought, *Why keep stuff you can see right outside your door?*

Her little mattress on the porch floor had a cover as worn as an old bathrobe, but it was made up neat. A few steps took them through the tiny sitting room, with its sagging sofa, and then he peeped into the back bedroom, where feathers in every color, shape, and size winged across the walls.

She motioned him into the kitchen, wondering what she could offer him. For sure she had no Coca-Cola or iced tea, no cookies or even cold biscuits. The leftover cornbread sat on the stovetop next to a pot of black-eyed peas, shelled and ready to boil for supper. Not one thing for a guest.

Out of habit she stuck a few pieces of wood into the stove's firebox. Stoking it just so with the poker; flames jumping to instantly.

"That's it," she said, keeping her back to him, as she pumped the hand crank and filled the dented-in kettle—a picture of the 1920s propped up here in the 1960s. No running water, no electricity, no bathroom. The tin bathtub, its rim bent and rusted, stood in the corner of the kitchen, the stand-alone pie chest held leftovers covered neatly with tea towels, and the humped refrigerator gaped open, a flyswatter in its mouth. Chase had never seen anything like it.

He cranked the pump, watched the water come out into the enamel basin that served as the sink. Touched the wood stacked neatly against the stove. The only lights were a few kerosene lanterns, their chimneys smoked gray.

Chase was her first visitor since Tate, who had seemed as natural and accepting as other marsh creatures. With Chase, she felt exposed, as if someone were filleting her like a fish. Shame welled up inside. She kept her back to him but felt him move around the room, followed by the familiar creaks of the floor. Then he came up behind her, turned her gently, and embraced her lightly. He put his lips against her hair, and she could feel his breath near her ear.

"Kya, nobody I know could've lived out here alone like this. Most kids, even the guys, would've been too scared."

She thought he was going to kiss her, but he dropped his arms and walked to the table.

"What do you want with me?" she asked. "Tell me the truth."

"Look, I'm not gonna lie. You're gorgeous, free, wild as a dang gale. The other day, I wanted to get as close as I could. Who wouldn't? But that ain't right. I shouldn't've come on like that. I just wanta be with ya, okay? Get to know each other."

"Then what?"

"We'll just find out how we feel. I won't do anything unless ya want me to. How's that?"

"That's fine."

"Ya said you had a beach. Let's go to the beach."

She cut off pieces of the leftover cornbread for the gulls and walked ahead of him down the path until it opened wide to the bright sand and sea. As she let out her soft cry, the gulls appeared and circled above and around her shoulders. The large male, Big Red, landed and walked back and forth across her feet.

Chase stood a little distance away, watching as Kya disappeared into the spiraling birds. He hadn't planned on feeling anything for this strange and feral barefoot girl, but watching her swirl across the sand, birds at her fingertips, he was intrigued by her self-reliance as well as her beauty. He'd never known anyone like Kya; a curiosity as well as desire stirred in him. When she came back to where he stood, he asked if he could come again the next day, promised he would not even hold her hand, that he just wanted to be near her. She simply nodded. The first hope in her heart since Tate left.

25.

A Visit from Patti Love

1969

A light knock sounded on the door of the sheriff's office. Joe and Ed looked up as Patti Love Andrews, Chase's mother, appeared shadowy and fractured through the frosted glass. Still, they could recognize her in a black dress and hat. Graying brown hair in a tidy bun. An appropriately dull shade of lipstick.

Both men stood, and Ed opened the door, "Patti Love, hello. Come on in. Sit down. Can I offer you some coffee?"

She glanced at the half-empty mugs, lip-drips running down the rims. "No, thank you, Ed." She sat in the chair Joe pulled up. "Do you have any leads yet? Any more information since the lab report?"

"No. No, we don't. We're going over everything with a fine-tooth comb, and you and Sam'll be the first to know if we come up with anything."

"But it wasn't an accident, Ed. Right? I know it wasn't an accident. Chase woulda never just fallen off the tower by himself. You know what an athlete he was. And smart."

"We agree there's evidence enough to suspect foul play. But it's an ongoing investigation and nothing definite yet. Now, you said you had something to tell us?"

"Yes, and I think it's important." Patti Love looked from Ed to Joe and back to Ed. "There was a shell necklace that Chase wore all the time. Had for years. I know he was wearin' it the night he went to the tower. Sam and I had him over for dinner, remember I told you that—Pearl couldn't come; it was her bridge night—and he had on the necklace right before he went out to the tower. And then after he . . . well, when we saw him at the clinic, he didn't have the necklace on. I assumed the coroner had taken it off him, so I didn't mention it then, and with the funeral and all, I had forgotten about it. Then, the other day I drove over to Sea Oaks and asked the coroner if I could see Chase's things, his personal effects. You know, they had kept them for the lab work, but I wanted to hold them, just to feel what he wore that last night. So they let me sit at a table and go through them, and, Sheriff, that shell necklace wasn't there. I asked the coroner if he had taken it off, and he said no, he had not. He said he never saw any necklace at all."

"That's very curious," Ed said. "What was it strung with? Maybe it came off when he fell."

"It was a single shell hung on a piece of rawhide that was just long enough to go over his head. It wasn't loose and was tied in a knot. I just don't see how it could've flung off."

"I agree. Rawhide's tough and makes a mean knot," Ed said. "Why did he wear it all the time? Did somebody special make it for him? Give it to him?"

Patti Love sat silent, looking off to the side of the sheriff's desk. She dreaded saying more because she'd never admitted that her son had been involved with marsh trash. Of course, there had been village rumors that Chase and the Marsh Girl had been involved for more than a year before his marriage. And Patti Love suspected even after, but when friends had asked about the stories, she'd always denied them. But now it was different. Now she had to speak out because she just knew that wench had something to do with his death.

"Yes, I know who made the necklace for Chase. It was that woman who boats around in that old rattletrap boat; has for years. She made it and gave it to him when they were seeing each other for a while."

"You talking about the Marsh Girl?" the sheriff asked.

Joe spoke up. "You seen her lately? She's not a girl anymore, probably mid-twenties and a real looker."

"The Clark woman? Just trying to be clear," Ed asked. Brows bunched.

Patti Love said, "I don't know her name. Or even if she has one. People do call her the Marsh Girl. You know, she sold mussels to Jumpin' for years."

"Right. We're talking about the same person. Go ahead."

"Well, I was shocked when the coroner said Chase didn't have on the necklace. And then it occurred to me that she's the only one who'd have any interest in taking it. Chase had broken off their relationship and married Pearl. She couldn't have him, so maybe she killed him and took the necklace from his neck."

Patti Love trembled slightly, then caught her breath.

"I see. Well, this is very important, Patti Love, and worth pursuing. But let's not get ahead of ourselves," Ed said. "You're sure she gave it to him?"

"Yes, I'm sure. I know because Chase didn't want to tell me, but he finally did."

"Do you know anything else about the necklace or their relationship?"

"Not much at all. I don't even know for sure how long they saw each other. Probably nobody does. He was very sneaky about it. Like I said, he didn't tell me for months. Then after he told me, I never knew whether he was going out in his boat with his other friends or with her."

"Well, we'll look into it. I promise you that."

"Thank you. I'm sure this is a clue." She rose to leave, and Ed opened the door for her.

"Come back anytime you want to talk, Patti Love."

"Bye, Ed, Joe."

After closing the door, Ed sat again, and Joe asked, "Well, what d'ya think?"

"If somebody took the necklace off Chase at the tower, that would at least put them at the scene, and I can see somebody from the marsh being involved in this thing. They got their own laws. But I just don't know if a woman could've pushed a big guy like Chase through that hole."

"She coulda lured him up there, opened the grate before he got there, then when he came toward her in the dark, she coulda pushed him in before he even saw her," Joe said.

"Seems possible. Not easy, but possible. It's not much of a lead. The *absence* of a shell necklace," the sheriff said.

"At this point it's our only lead. 'Cept for the *absence* of prints and some mysterious red fibers."

"Right."

"But what I can't figure," Joe said, "is why she'd bother to take the necklace off him? Okay, as the woman wronged, she was hell-bent on killin' him. Even that's a stretch for motive, but why take the necklace when it could connect her smack-dab to the crime?"

"You know how it is. Seems like there's something in every murder case that doesn't make sense. People mess up. Maybe she was shocked and furious that he still wore the necklace, and after committing murder, it didn't seem like a big deal to snatch it off his neck. She wouldn't have known anybody could link the necklace to her. Your sources said Chase had something going on out there. Maybe, like you said earlier, it wasn't drugs at all, but a woman. This woman."

Joe said, "'Nother kind of drug."

"And marsh folks know how to cover prints because they snare, track, trap, and such. Well, it won't hurt to go out there and have a talk with her. Ask her where she was that night. We can question her about the necklace and see if it shakes her up a bit."

Joe asked, "You know how ta get ta her place?"

"Not sure by boat, but I think I can find it in the truck. Down that real windy road that goes way past a long chain of lagoons. A while back, I had to make house calls to see her father a few times. Nasty piece of work, that one."

"When we going?"

"Crack of day, see if we can get there before she takes off. Tomorrow. But first, we better go out to the tower and search really good for that necklace. Maybe it's been there all along."

"I don't see how. We've searched all over that place, looking for tracks, treads, clues."

"Still, we gotta do it. Let's go."

Later, after combing through the muck under the tower with rakes and fingers, they declared no shell necklace present.

Pale light seeped under a low, heavy dawn as Ed and Joe drove down the marsh track, hoping to get to the Marsh Girl's place before she boated off somewhere. They took several wrong turns and ended up at dead ends or at some ramshackle dwelling. At one shack somebody yelled, "Sheriff!" and mostly naked bodies took off in all directions, charging through brambles. "Damn potheads," the sheriff said. "At least the moonshiners kept their clothes on."

But finally they came to the long lane that led to Kya's shack. "This is it," Ed said.

He turned his outsized pickup onto the track and cruised quietly toward the dwelling, easing to a stop fifty feet from the door. Both men got out without a sound. Ed knocked on the wooden frame of the screen door. "Hello! Anybody home?" Silence followed, so he tried again. They waited two to three minutes. "Let's have a look 'round back, see if her boat's there."

"Nope. Looks like that log's where she ties up. She's a'ready gone. Dag-nabit," Joe said.

"Yep, heard us coming. She can probably hear a rabbit sleeping."

The next time they went before dawn, parked way down the road, and found her boat tied to its log. Still no one answered the door.

Joe whispered, "I get this feelin' she's right here watchin' us. Don't you? She's squattin' right here in the damn palmettos. Purt' near. I just know it." His head swung, eyes scanning the brambles.

"Well, this isn't going to work. If we come up with anything else we can get a warrant. Let's get outta here."

26.

The Boat Ashore

1965

The first week they were together, Chase pulled into Kya's lagoon almost every day after his work at the Western Auto, and they explored remote oak-lined channels. On Saturday morning, he took her on an expedition far up the coast to a place she'd never been because it was too far for her little boat. Here—instead of the estuaries and enormous sweeps of grass as in her marsh—clear water flowed as far as she could see through a bright and open cypress forest. Brilliant white herons and storks stood among water lilies and floating plants so green they seemed to glow. Hunched up on cypress knees as large as easy chairs, they ate pimento-cheese sandwiches and potato chips, grinning as geese glided just below their toes.

Like most people, Chase knew the marsh as a thing to be used, to boat and fish, or drain for farming, so Kya's knowledge of its critters, currents, and cattails intrigued him. But he scoffed at her soft touch, cruising at slow speeds, drifting silently past deer, whispering near birds' nests. He had no interest in learning the shells or feathers himself and questioned her when she scribbled notes in her journal or collected specimens.

"Why're you painting grass?" he asked one day in her kitchen.

"I'm painting their flowers."

He laughed. "Grass doesn't have flowers."

"Of course they do. See these blossoms. They're tiny, but beautiful. Each grass species has a different flower or inflorescence."

"What're ya gonna do with all this stuff anyway?"

"I'm keeping records so I can learn about the marsh."

"All ya need to know is when and where the fish bite, and I can tell ya that," he said.

She laughed for his sake, something she'd never done. Giving away another piece of herself just to have someone else.

That afternoon, after Chase left, Kya motored into the marsh alone. But did not feel alone. She accelerated slightly faster than usual, her long hair trailing in the wind, a slight smile brushed on her lips. Just knowing she would see him again soon, be with someone, lifted her to a new place.

Then, rounding a bend of tall grass, up ahead she saw Tate. He was quite far, maybe forty yards, and had not heard her boat. Instantly, she dropped throttle and killed the engine. Grabbed the oar and rowed backward into the grass.

"Home from college, I guess," she whispered. She'd seen him a few times over the years, but never this close. But now there he was, his untamed hair struggling with another red cap. Tanned face.

Tate wore high-top waders and strode through a lagoon, scooping up water samples in tiny vials. Not old jelly jars as when they were barefoot kids but petite tubes clinking in a special carrying rack. Professorial. Out of her league.

She didn't row away, but watched him awhile, thinking that every girl probably remembers her first love. She let out a long breath, then rowed back the way she came.

The next day, as Chase and Kya cruised north along the coast, four porpoises moved into their wake and followed them. It was a gray-sky day, and fingers of fog flirted with the waves. Chase switched off the engine, and as the boat drifted, he took out his harmonica and played the old song "Michael Row the Boat Ashore," a yearning and melodic tune sung by slaves in the 1860s as they rowed boats to the mainland from the Sea Islands of South Carolina. Ma used to sing it while scrubbing, and Kya sort of remembered the words. As if inspired by the music, the porpoises swam closer and circled the boat, their keen eyes fixing on Kya's. Then, two of them eased up against the hull, and she bowed her face only inches from theirs, and sang softly:

> "Sister, help to trim dat boat, hallelujah
> Brudder lend a helpin' hand, hallelujah.
> Ma fadder gone to unknown land, hallelujah.
> Michael, row the boat ashore, hallelujah.
>
> "Jordan's river is deep and wide,
> Meet my mother on the other side, hallelujah.
> Jordan's river is chilly and cold
> Chills the body but not the soul, hallelujah."

The porpoises stared at Kya for a few more seconds and then slipped backward into the sea.

Over the next few weeks, Chase and Kya spent evenings lazing with the gulls on her beach, lying back on sand still warm from the sun. Chase didn't take her into town, to the picture show or sock hops; it was the two of them, the marsh, the sea, and the sky. He didn't kiss her, only held her hand or put his arm lightly around her shoulders in the coolness.

Then one night he stayed late into the dark, and they sat on the beach under the stars by a small fire, shoulders touching, a blanket around them. The flames threw light across their faces and dark across the shore behind them, as campfires do. Looking into her eyes, he asked, "Is it okay if I kiss you now?" She nodded, so he leaned down and kissed her softly at first, and then like a man.

They lay back on the blanket, and she wiggled in as close to him as she could get. Feeling his strong body. He held her tight with both of his arms, but only touched her shoulders with his hands. Nothing more. She breathed deep, breathed in the warmth, the scents of him and the sea, the togetherness.

Only a few days later, Tate, still home from graduate school, raced his boat toward Kya's marsh channel, the first time he'd done so in five years. He still couldn't explain to himself why he'd never gone back to her before now. Mostly he'd been a coward, ashamed. Finally, he was going to find her, tell her he'd never stopped loving her and beg her to forgive him.

Those four years at university, he'd convinced himself that Kya could not fit in the academic world he sought. All through undergraduate, he'd tried to forget her; after all, there were plenty of female distractions at Chapel Hill. He even had a few long-term relationships, but no one compared. What he'd learned right after DNA, isotopes, and protozoans was that he couldn't breathe without her. True, Kya couldn't live in the university world he had sought, but now he could live in hers.

He had it all figured out. His professor had said Tate could finish graduate school in the next three years because he'd been conducting his research for his PhD dissertation all through undergraduate and it was nearly complete. Then, recently Tate learned that a federal research lab was to be built near Sea Oaks, and that he would have an excellent chance of being hired as a full-time research scientist. No one on Earth was better qualified: he'd been studying the local marsh most of his life, and soon he would have the PhD to back it up. In just a few short years, he could live here in the marsh with Kya and work at the lab. Marry Kya. If she would have him.

Now, as he bounced across waves toward her channel, suddenly Kya's boat zoomed south, perpendicular to his course. Letting go of the tiller, he threw both arms above his head, waving frantically to get her attention. Shouted out her name. But she was looking east. Tate glanced in that direction and saw Chase's ski boat veering toward her. Tate idled back, watching as Kya and Chase spun around each other in the blue-gray waves, in ever-smaller circles like eagles courting in the sky. Their wakes crazed and swirling.

Tate stared as they met and touched fingers across the churning water. He'd heard the rumors from his old friends in Barkley Cove but hoped they weren't true. He understood why Kya would fall for such a man, handsome, no doubt romantic, whizzing her around in his fancy boat, taking her on fancy picnics. She wouldn't know anything of his life in town—dating and courting other young women in Barkley, even Sea Oaks.

And, Tate thought, *who am I to say anything? I didn't treat her any better. I broke a promise, didn't even have the guts to break up with her.*

He dipped his head, then stole another glance just in time to see Chase lean over to kiss her. *Kya, Kya,* he thought. *How could I have left you?* Slowly, he accelerated and turned back toward the town harbor to help his dad crate and carry the catch.

A few days later, never knowing when Chase might come, Kya once again found herself listening for the sound of his boat. Just as she had for Tate. So whether pulling weeds, chopping stove wood, or collecting mussels, she'd tilt her head just so to catch the sound. "Squint yo' ears," Jodie used to say.

Tired of being weighted down by hope, she threw three days' worth of biscuits, cold backstrap, and sardines in her knapsack and walked out to the old falling-down log cabin; the "reading cabin," as she thought of it. Out here, in the real remote, she was free to wander, collect at will, read the words, read the wild. Not waiting for the sounds of someone was a release. And a strength.

In a scrub-oak thicket, just around the bend from the cabin, she found the tiny neck feather of a red-throated loon and laughed out loud. Had wanted this feather for as long as she could remember, and here it was a stone's throw downstream.

Mostly she came to read. After Tate left her those years ago, she no longer had access to books, so one morning she'd motored beyond Point Beach and another ten miles to Sea Oaks, a slightly larger and much swankier town than Barkley Cove. Jumpin' had said anyone could borrow books from the library there. She'd doubted if that was true for someone who lived in a swamp, but she had been determined to find out.

She'd tied up at the town wharf and crossed the tree-lined square overlooking the sea. As she walked toward the library, no one looked at her, whispered behind her back, or shooed her away from a window display. Here, she was not the Marsh Girl.

She handed Mrs. Hines, the librarian, a list of college textbooks. "Could you please help me find *The Principles of Organic Chemistry* by Geissman, *Invertebrate Zoology of the Coastal Marsh* by Jones, and *Fundamentals of Ecology* by Odum . . ." She'd seen these titles referenced in the last of the books Tate had given before he left her for college.

"Oh, my. I see. We'll have to get a library loan from the University of North Carolina at Chapel Hill for these books."

So now, sitting outside the old cabin, she picked up a scientific digest. One article on reproductive strategies was titled "Sneaky Fuckers." Kya laughed.

As is well known, the article began, in nature, usually the males with the most prominent secondary sexual characteristics, such as the biggest antlers, deepest voices, broadest chests, and superior knowledge secure the best territories because they have fended off weaker males. The females choose to mate with these imposing alphas and are thereby inseminated with the best DNA around, which is passed on to the female's offspring—one of the most powerful phenomena in the adaptation and continuance of life. Plus, the females get the best territory for their young.

However, some stunted males, not strong, adorned, or smart enough to hold good territories, possess bags of tricks to fool the females. They parade their smaller forms around in pumped-up postures or shout frequently—even if in shrill voices. By relying on pretense and false signals, they manage to grab a copulation here or there. Pint-sized male bullfrogs, the author wrote, hunker down in the grass and hide near an alpha male who is croaking with great gusto to call in mates. When several females are attracted to his strong vocals at the same time, and the alpha is busy copulating with one, the weaker male leaps in and mates one of the others. The imposter males were referred to as "sneaky fuckers."

Kya remembered, those many years ago, Ma warning her older sisters about young men who overrevved their rusted-out pickups or drove jalopies around with radios blaring. "Unworthy boys make a lot of noise," Ma had said.

She read a consolation for females. Nature is audacious enough to ensure that the males who send out dishonest signals or go from one female to the next almost always end up alone.

Another article delved into the wild rivalries between sperm. Across most life-forms, males compete to inseminate females. Male lions occasionally fight to the death; rival bull elephants lock tusks and demolish the ground beneath their feet as they tear at each other's flesh. Though very ritualized, the conflicts can still end in mutilations.

To avoid such injuries, inseminators of some species compete in less violent, more creative methods. Insects, the most imaginative. The penis of the male damselfly is equipped with a small scoop, which removes sperm ejected by a previous opponent before he supplies his own.

Kya dropped the journal on her lap, her mind drifting with the clouds. Some female insects eat their mates, overstressed mammal mothers abandon their young, many males design risky or shifty ways to outsperm their competitors. Nothing seemed too indecorous as long as the tick and the tock of life carried on. She knew this was not a dark side to Nature, just inventive ways to endure against all odds. Surely for humans there was more.

After finding Kya gone three days in a row, Chase started asking if he could come on a certain day, at a given time to see her at her shack or this or that beach, and always arrived on time. From far off she would see his brightly colored boat—like vivid feathers of a male bird's breeding plumage—floating on the waves and know he'd come just for her.

Kya started to picture him taking her on a picnic with his friends. All of them laughing, running into the waves, kicking the surf. Him lifting her, swirling around. Then sitting with the others sharing sandwiches and drinks from coolers. Bit by bit, pictures of marriage and children formed in spite of her resistance. *Probably some biological urge to push me into reproducing,* she told herself. But why couldn't she have loved ones like everybody else? Why not?

Yet every time she tried to ask when he would introduce her to his friends and parents, the words stuck to her tongue.

Drifting offshore, on a hot day a few months after they met, he said it was perfect for a swim. "I won't look," he said. "Take off your clothes and jump in, then I will." She stood in front of him, balancing in the boat, but as she pulled her T-shirt over her head, he didn't turn away. He reached out and ran his fingers lightly across her firm breasts. She didn't stop him. Pulling her closer, he unzipped her shorts and slipped them easily from her slender hips. Then he took off his shirt and shorts and pushed her down gently onto the towels.

Kneeling at her feet, without saying a word, he ran his fingers like a whisper along her left ankle up to the inside of her knee, slowly along the inside of her thigh. She raised her body toward his hand. His fingers lingered at the top of her thigh, rubbed over her panties, then moved across her belly, light as a thought. She sensed his fingers moving up her stomach toward her breasts and twisted her body away from him. Firmly, he pushed her flat and slid his fingers to her breast, slowly outlining the nipple with one finger. He looked at her, unsmiling, as he moved his hand down and pulled at the top of her panties. She wanted him, all of him, and her body pushed against his. But seconds later, she put her hand on his.

"C'mon, Kya," he said. "Please. We've waited forever. I've been pretty patient, don't ya think?"

"Chase, you promised."

"Damn it, Kya. What're we waiting for?" He sat up. "Surely, I showed ya I care for you. Why not?"

Sitting up, she pulled down her T-shirt. "What happens next? How do I know you won't leave me?"

"How does anybody ever know? But, Kya, I'm not going anywhere. I'm falling in love with you. I want to be with you all the time. What else can I do to show you?"

He had never mentioned love. Kya searched his eyes for truth but found only a hard stare. Unreadable. She didn't know exactly how she felt about Chase, but she was no longer lonely. That seemed enough.

"Soon, okay?"

He pulled her close to him. "It's okay. C'mere." He held her and they lay under the sun, drifting on the sea, the *slosh, slosh, slosh* of the waves beneath them.

Day drained away and night settled heavily, the village lights dancing here and there on the distant shore. Stars twinkling above their world of sea and sky.

Chase said, "I wonder what makes stars twinkle."

"Disturbance in the atmosphere. You know, like high atmospheric winds."

"That so?"

"I'm sure you know that most stars are too far away for us to see. We see only their light, which can be distorted by the atmosphere. But, of course, the stars are not stationary, but moving very fast."

Kya knew from reading Albert Einstein's books that time is no more fixed than the stars. Time speeds and bends around planets and suns, is different in the mountains than in the valleys, and is part of the same fabric as space, which curves and swells as does the sea. Objects, whether planets or apples, fall or orbit, not because of a gravitational energy, but because they plummet into the silky folds of spacetime— like into the ripples on a pond—created by those of higher mass.

But Kya said none of this. Unfortunately, gravity holds no sway on human thought, and the high school text still taught that apples fall to the ground because of a powerful force from the Earth.

"Oh, guess what," Chase said. "They've asked me to help coach the high school football team."

She smiled at him.

Then thought, *Like everything else in the universe, we tumble toward those of higher mass.*

The next morning, on a rare trip to the Piggly Wiggly to buy personal items Jumpin' didn't carry, Kya stepped out of the grocery and nearly bumped right into Chase's parents—Sam and Patti Love. They knew who she was—everyone did.

She'd seen them in town occasionally through the years, mostly from a distance. Sam could be seen behind the counter in the Western Auto, dealing with customers, opening the cash register. Kya remembered how when she was a girl, he shooed her away from the window as though she might frighten away real customers. Patti Love didn't work full time at the store, allowing time for her to hurry along the street, handing out pamphlets for the Annual Quilting Contest or the Blue-Crab Queen Festival. Always dressed in a fine outfit with high-heel pumps, pocketbook, and hat, in matching colors demanded by the southern season. No matter the subject, she managed to mention Chase as being the best quarterback the town had ever seen.

Kya smiled shyly, looking right into Patti Love's eyes, hoping they would speak to her in some personal way and introduce themselves. Maybe acknowledge her as Chase's girl. But they halted abruptly, said nothing, and sidestepped around her—making a wider berth than necessary. Moved on.

The evening after bumping into them, Kya and Chase drifted in her boat under an oak so huge its knees jutted over the water, creating little grottoes for otters and ducks. Keeping her voice low, partly so she wouldn't disturb the mallards and partly in fear, Kya told Chase about seeing his parents and asked if she would meet them soon.

Chase sat silent, making her stomach lump up.

Finally he said, "'Course you will. Soon, I promise." But he didn't look at her when he said it.

"They know about me, right? About us?" she asked.

"A' course."

The boat must have drifted too close to the oak, because right then a great horned owl, plump and cushy as a down pillow, dropped from the tree on reaching wings, then stroked slow and easy across the lagoon, his breast feathers reflecting soft patterns on the water.

Chase reached out and took Kya's hand, wringing the doubt from her fingers.

For weeks, sunsets and moonrises followed Chase and Kya's easy movements through the marsh. But each time she resisted his advances, he stopped. Images of does or turkey hens alone with their demanding young, the males long gone to other females, weighed solid in her mind.

Lying around near naked in the boat was as far as it went, no matter what the townspeople said. Although Chase and Kya kept to themselves, the town was small and people saw them together in his boat or on the beaches. The shrimpers didn't miss much on the seas. There was talk. Tittle-tattle.

27

Out Hog Mountain Road

1966

The shack stood silent against the early stir of blackbird wings, as an earnest winter fog formed along the ground, bunching up against the walls like large wisps of cotton. Using several weeks of mussel money, Kya had bought special groceries and fried slices of molasses ham, stirred redeye gravy, and served them with sour-cream biscuits and blackberry jam. Chase drank instant Maxwell House; she, hot Tetley tea. They'd been together nearly a year, though neither spoke of that. Chase said how lucky he was that his father owned the Western Auto: "This way we'll have a nice house when we get married. I'm gonna build you a two-story on the beach with a wraparound veranda. Or whatever kinda house you want, Kya."

Kya could barely breathe. He wanted her in his life. Not just a hint, but something like a proposal. She would belong to someone. Be part of a family. She sat straighter in her chair.

He continued. "I don't think we should live right in town. That'd be too much of a jump for you. But we could build a place on tha outskirts. Ya know, close to the marsh."

Lately, a few vague thoughts of marriage to Chase had formed in her mind, but she had not dared dwell on them. But here he was saying it out loud. Kya's breath was shallow, her mind disbelieving and sorting details all at the same time. *I can do this*, she thought. *If we live away from people it could work.*

Then, head low, she asked, "What about your parents? Have you told them?"

"Kya, ya gotta understand something 'bout my folks. They love me. If I say you're my choice, that'll be that. They'll just fall in love with ya when they get to know ya."

She chewed on her lips. Wanting to believe.

"I'll build a studio for all yo' stuff," he continued. "With big windows so ya can see the details of all those dad-burned feathers."

She didn't know if she felt about Chase the way a wife should, but in this moment her heart soared with something like love. No more digging mussels.

She reached out and touched the shell necklace under his throat.

"Oh, by the way," Chase said. "I have to drive over to Asheville in a few days to buy goods for the store. I was thinkin', why don't ya come with me?"

Eyes downcast, she'd said, "But that's a large town. There'd be lots of people. And I don't have the right clothes, or don't even know what the right clothes are, and . . ."

"Kya, Kya. Listen. You'd be with me. I know everything. We don't have to go anywhere fancy. You'd see a lot of North Carolina just driving over—the Piedmont, the Great Smoky Mountains, forchristsake. Then when we got there, we could just go to a drive-in for burgers. You can wear what you have on. You don't have to talk to one soul if you don't want to. I'll take care of everything. I've been lots of times. Even to Atlanta. Asheville's nothing. Look, if we're gonna get married, ya might as well start gettin' out in tha world a bit. Spread those long wings of yours."

She nodded. If nothing else, to see the mountains.

He continued. "It's a two-day job, so we'll have to stay overnight. In a casual place. You know, a small motel. It's okay, because we're adults."

"Oh," was all she said. Then whispered, "I see."

Kya had never driven up the road a piece, so, a few days later, as she and Chase rode west out of Barkley in his pickup, she stared out the window, holding on to the seat with both hands. The road wound through miles of saw grass and palmettos, leaving the sea in the rear window.

For more than an hour, the familiar reaches of grass and waterways slipped by the truck's window. Kya identified marsh wrens and egrets, comforted by the sameness, like she hadn't left home but brought it with her.

Then abruptly, at a line drawn across the earth, the marsh meadows ended, and dusty ground—hacked raw, fenced into squares, and furrowed into rows—spread before them. Fields of paraplegic snags stood in felled forests. Poles, strung with wires, trudged toward the horizon. Of course, she knew coastal marsh didn't cover the globe, but she'd never been beyond it. What had people done to the land? Every house, the same shoebox shape, squatted on sheared lawn. A flock of pink flamingos fed across a yard, but when Kya whirled in surprise, she saw they were plastic. The deer, cement. The only ducks flew painted on mailboxes.

"They're incredible, huh?" Chase said.

"What?"

"The houses. You've never seen anything like 'em, huh?"

"No, I haven't."

Hours later, out on the flatlands of the Piedmont, she saw the Appalachians sketched in gentle blue lines along the horizon. As they neared, peaks rose around them and forested mountains flowed softly into the distance as far as Kya could see.

Clouds lazed in the folded arms of the hills, then billowed up and drifted away. Some tendrils twisted into tight spirals and traced the warmer ravines, behaving like mist tracking the dank fens of the marsh. The same game of physics playing on a different field of biology.

Kya was of the low country, a land of horizons, where the sun set and the moon rose on time. But here, where the topography was a jumble, the sun balanced along the summits, setting behind a ridge one moment and then popping up again when Chase's truck ascended the next rise. In the mountains, she noticed, the time of sunset depended on where you stood on the hill.

She wondered where her grandpa's land was. Maybe her kin had kept pigs in a weather-grayed barn like the one she saw in a meadow, creek running by. A family that should have been hers once toiled, laughed, and cried in this landscape. Some would still be here, scattered through the county. Anonymous.

The road became a four-lane highway, and Kya held on tight as Chase's truck sped within feet of other fast-moving vehicles. He turned onto a curving roadway that rose magically into the air and led them toward the town. "A cloverleaf exit," he said proudly.

Enormous buildings, eight and ten stories high, stood against the outline of the mountains. Scores of cars scuttled like sand crabs, and there were so many people on the sidewalks, Kya pushed her face to the window, searching their faces, thinking surely Ma and Pa must be among them. One boy, tanned and dark-haired, running down the sidewalk, looked like Jodie, and she spun around to watch him. Her brother would be grown now, of course, but she tracked the boy until they turned a corner.

On the other side of town, Chase booked them into a motel out Hog Mountain Road, a single-story row of brown rooms, lit up by neon lights the shape of palm trees, of all things.

After Chase unlocked their door, she stepped into a room that seemed clean enough but reeked of Pine-Sol and was furnished in America cheap: fake-panel walls, sagging bed with a nickel vibrator machine, and a black-and-white TV secured to the table with an impossibly large chain and padlock. The bedspreads were lime green, the carpet orange shag. Kya's mind went back to all the places they had lain together—in crystal sand by tidal pools, in moonlit drifting boats. Here, the bed loomed as the centerpiece, but the room didn't look like love.

She stood knowingly near the door. "It's not great," he said, putting his duffel bag on the chair.

He walked toward her. "It's time, don't you agree, Kya? It's time."

Of course, it had been his plan. But she was ready. Her body had been longing for months and, after the talk of marriage, her mind gave in. She nodded.

He came toward her slowly and unbuttoned her blouse, then turned her gently around and unfastened her bra. Traced his fingers across her breasts. An excited heat flowed from her breasts to her thighs. As he pulled her down onto the bed in the glow of the red and green neon lights filtering through thin curtains, she closed her eyes. Before, during all those almost-times, when she had stopped him, his wandering fingers had taken on a magical touch, bringing parts of her to life, causing her body to arch toward him, to long and want. But now, with permission finally granted, an urgency gripped him and he seemed to bypass her needs and push his way. She cried out against a sharp tear-ing, thinking something was wrong.

"It's okay. It'll be better now," he said with great authority. But it didn't get much better, and soon he fell to her side, grinning.

As he passed into sleep, she watched the blinking lights of the *Va-cancy* sign.

Several weeks later, after finishing a breakfast of fried eggs and ham-grits at Kya's shack, she and Chase sat at her kitchen table. She was wrapped snugly in a blanket after lovemaking, which had improved only slightly since their first attempt at the motel. Each time left her wanting, but she didn't have the faintest notion how to broach such a subject. And anyway, she didn't know how she was supposed to feel. Maybe this was normal.

Chase stood from the table and, lifting her chin with his fingers, kissed her, saying, "Well, I won't be out much in the next few days with Christmas comin' up and all. There's lots of events and stuff, and some relatives comin' in."

Kya looked up at him and said, "I was hoping maybe I could . . . you know, go to some of the parties and things. At least maybe Christmas dinner with your family."

Chase sat back down in his chair. "Kya, look, I've been wantin' to talk ta ya 'bout this. I wanta ask ya to the Elks Club dance and stuff like that, but I know how shy you are, how ya don't ever do stuff in town. I know you'd be miserable. You wouldn't know anybody, ya don't have the right clothes. Do ya even know how to dance? None a' those things are what you do. You understand that, right?"

Looking at the floor, she said, "Yes, and all that's true. But, well, I have to start fitting in with some of your life. Spread my wings, like you said. I guess I have to get the right clothes, meet some of your friends." She raised her head. "You could teach me to dance."

"Well sure, an' I will. But I think of you and me as what we have out here. I love our time here together, just you and me. To tell you the truth, I'm gittin' kinda tired a' those stupid dances. Been the same fer years. High school gym. Old folks, young folks all together. Same dumb music. I'm ready to move on. You know, when we're married, we won't do stuff like that anyway, so why drag ya into it now? Don't make any sense. Okay?"

She looked back at the floor, so he lifted her chin again and held her eyes with his own. Then, grinning big, he said, "And, man, as far as having Christmas dinner wif ma family. Ma ancient aunts come in from Florida. Never stop talkin'. I wouldn't wish that on anybody. 'Specially you. Believe me, you ain't missin' a thing."

She was silent.

"Really, Kya, I wantcha to be okay with this. What we have out here is the most special thing anybody could hope for. All that other stuff"—he swiped his hands through the air—"is just stupid."

He reached over and pulled her into his lap, and she rested her head on his shoulder.

"This is where it's at, Kya. Not that other stuff." And he kissed her, warm and tender. Then stood. "Okay. Gotta go."

Kya spent Christmas alone with the gulls, as she had every year since Ma left.

Two days after Christmas, Chase still hadn't come. Breaking her self-promise to never wait for anyone again, Kya paced the shore of the lagoon, her hair woven into a French braid, mouth painted with Ma's old lipstick.

The marsh beyond lay in its winter cloak of browns and grays. Miles of spent grasses, having dispersed their seeds, bowed their heads to the water in surrender. The wind whipped and tore, rattling the coarse stems in a noisy chorus. Kya yanked her hair down and wiped her lips with the back of her hand.

The morning of the fourth day, she sat alone in the kitchen pushing biscuits and eggs around her plate. "For all his talk of '*this being where it's at*,' where is he now?" she spat. In her mind, she saw Chase playing touch football with friends or dancing at parties. "Those stupid things he's getting tired of."

Finally the sound of his boat. She sprang from the table, banged the door shut, and ran from the shack to the lagoon, as the boat chugged into view. But it wasn't Chase's ski boat or Chase, but a young man with yellow-gold hair, cut shorter but still barely contained under a ski cap. It was the old fishing rig, and there, standing, even as the boat moved forward, was Tate, grown into a man. Face no longer boyish, but handsome, mature. His eyes formed a question, his lips a shy smile.

Her first thought was to run. But her mind screamed, *NO! This is my lagoon; I always run. Not this time.* Her next thought was to pick up a rock, and she hurled it at his face from twenty feet. He ducked quickly, the stone whizzing by his forehead.

"Shit, Kya! What the hell? Wait," he said as she picked up another rock and took aim. He put his hands over his face. "Kya, for God's sake, stop. Please. Can't we talk?"

The rock hit him hard on the shoulder.

"GET OUT OF MY LAGOON! YOU LOW-DOWN DIRTY CREEP! HOW'S THAT FOR TALK!" The screaming fishwife looked frantically for another rock.

"Kya, listen to me. I know you're with Chase now. I respect that. I just want to talk with you. Please, Kya."

"Why should I talk with you? I never want to see you again EVER!" She picked up a handful of smaller stones and slung them at his face.

He jerked to the side, bent forward, and grabbed the gunwale as his boat ran aground.

"I SAID, GET OUT OF HERE!" Still yelling but softer, she said, "Yes, I am with someone else now."

Tate steadied himself after the jolt of hitting the shore, and then sat on the bow seat of his boat. "Kya, please, there're things you should know about him." Tate had not planned on having a conversation about Chase. None of this surprise visit to see Kya was going as he'd imagined.

"What are you talking about? You have no right to talk to me about my private life." She had walked up to within five feet of him and spat her words.

Firmly he said, "I know I don't, but I'm doing it anyway."

At this, Kya turned to leave, but Tate talked louder at her back. "You don't live in town. You don't know that Chase goes out with other women. Just the other night I watched him drive away after a party with a blonde in his pickup. He's not good enough for you."

She whirled around. "Oh, really! YOU are the one who left me, who didn't come back when you promised, who never came back. You are the one who never wrote to explain why or even if you were alive or dead. You didn't have the nerve to break up with me. You were not man enough to face me. Just disappeared. CHICKEN SHIT ASSHOLE. You come floating in here after all these years . . . You're worse than he is. He might not be perfect, but you're worse by a long shot." She stopped abruptly, staring at him.

Palms open, he pleaded, "You're right about me, Kya. Everything you said is true. I was a chicken shit. And I had no right to bring up Chase. It's none of my business. And I'll never bother you again. I just

197

need to apologize and explain things. I've been sorry for years, Kya, please."

She hung like a sail where the wind just went out. Tate was more than her first love: he shared her devotion to the marsh, had taught her to read, and was the only connection, however small, to her vanished family. He was a page of time, a clipping pasted in a scrapbook because it was all she had. Her heart pounded as the fury dissipated.

"Look at you—so beautiful. A woman. You doing okay? Still selling mussels?" He was astonished at how she had changed, her features more refined yet haunting, her cheekbones sharp, lips full.

"Yes. Yes."

"Here, I brought you something." From an envelope he handed her a tiny red cheek feather from a northern flicker. She thought of tossing it on the ground, but she'd never found this feather; why shouldn't she keep it? She tucked it in her pocket and didn't thank him.

Talking fast, he said, "Kya, leaving you was not only wrong, it was the worst thing I have done or ever will do in my life. I have regretted it for years and will always regret it. I think of you every day. For the rest of my life, I'll be sorry I left you. I truly thought that you wouldn't be able to leave the marsh and live in the other world, so I didn't see how we could stay together. But that was wrong, and it was bullshit that I didn't come back and talk to you about it. I knew how many times you'd been left before. I didn't want to know how badly I hurt you. I was not man enough. Just like you said." He finished and watched her.

Finally she said, "What do you want now, Tate?"

"If only you could, some way, forgive me." He breathed in and waited.

Kya looked at her toes. Why should the injured, the still bleeding, bear the onus of forgiveness? She didn't answer.

"I just had to tell you, Kya."

When still she said nothing, he continued. "I'm in graduate school, zoology. Protozoology mostly. You would love it."

She couldn't imagine it, and looked back over the lagoon to see if Chase was coming. Tate didn't miss this; he'd guessed right off she was out here waiting for Chase.

Just last week Tate had watched Chase, in his white dinner jacket, at the Christmas gala, dancing with different women. The dance, like most Barkley Cove events, had been held at the high school gymnasium. As "Wooly Bully" struggled from a too-small hi-fi set up under the basketball hoop, Chase whirled a brunette. When "Mr. Tambourine Man" began, he left the dance floor and the brunette, and shared pulls of Wild Turkey from his Tar Heels flask with other former jocks. Tate was close by chatting with two of his old high school teachers and heard Chase say, "Yeah, she's wild as a she-fox in a snare. Just what you'd expect from a marsh minx. Worth every bit a' the gas money."

Tate had to force himself to walk away.

A cold wind whipped up and rippled across the lagoon. Expecting Chase, Kya had run out in her jeans and light sweater. She folded her arms tightly around herself.

"You're freezing; let's go inside." Tate motioned toward the shack, where smoke puffed from the rusty stovepipe.

"Tate, I think you should leave now." She threw several quick glances at the channel. What if Chase arrived with Tate here?

"Kya, please, just for a few minutes. I really want to see your collections again."

As answer, she turned and ran to the shack, and Tate followed her. Inside the porch, he stopped short. Her collections had grown from a child's hobby to a natural history museum of the marsh. He lifted a scallop shell, labeled with a watercolor of the beach where it was found, plus insets showing the creature eating smaller creatures of the sea. For each specimen—hundreds, maybe thousands of them—it was the same. He had seen some of them before, as a boy, but now as a doctoral candidate in zoology, he saw them as a scientist.

He turned to her, still standing in the doorway. "Kya, these are wonderful, beautifully detailed. You could publish these. This could be a book—lots of books."

"No, no. They're just for me. They help me learn, is all."

"Kya, listen to me. You know better than anybody that the reference books for this area are almost nonexistent. With these notations, technical data, and splendid drawings, these are the books everyone's been waiting for." It was true. Ma's old guidebooks to the shells, plants, birds, and mammals of the area were the only ones printed, and they were pitifully inaccurate, with only simple black-and-white pictures and sketchy information on each entry.

"If I can take a few samples, I'll find out about a publisher, see what they say."

She stared, not knowing how to see this. Would she have to go somewhere, meet people? Tate didn't miss the questions in her eyes.

"You wouldn't have to leave home. You could mail your samples to a publisher. It would bring some money in. Probably not a huge amount, but maybe you wouldn't have to dig mussels the rest of your life."

Still, Kya didn't say anything. Once again Tate was nudging her to care for herself, not just offering to care for her. It seemed that all her life, he had been there. Then gone.

"Give it a try, Kya. What can it hurt?"

She finally agreed that he could take some samples, and he chose a selection of soft watercolors of shells and the great blue heron because of her detailed sketches of the bird in each season, and a delicate oil of the curved eyebrow feather.

Tate lifted the painting of the feather—a profusion of hundreds of the thinnest brushstrokes of rich colors culminating into a deep black so reflective it seemed sunlight was touching the canvas. The detail of a slight tear in the shaft was so distinctive that both Tate and Kya realized at the same second that this was a painting of the very first feather he'd gifted her in the forest. They looked up from the feather into each other's eyes. She turned away from him. Forcing herself not to feel. She would not be drawn back to someone she couldn't trust.

He stepped up to her and touched her shoulder. Tried gently to turn her around. "Kya, I'm so sorry about leaving you. Please, can't you forgive me?"

Finally, she turned and looked at him. "I don't know how to, Tate. I could never believe you again. Please, Tate, you have to go now."

"I know. Thank you for listening to me, for giving me this chance to apologize." He waited for a beat, but she said no more. At least he was leaving with something. The hope for a publisher was a reason to contact her again.

"Good-bye, Kya." She didn't answer. He stared at her, and she looked into his eyes but then turned away. He walked out the door toward his boat.

She waited until he was gone, then sat on the damp, cold sand of the lagoon waiting for Chase. Speaking out loud, she repeated the words she'd said to Tate. "Chase may not be perfect, but you're worse."

But as she stared deep into the dark waters, Tate's words about Chase—*"drive away after a party with a blonde in his pickup"*—wouldn't leave her mind.

Chase didn't come until a week after Christmas. Pulling into the lagoon, he said he could stay all night, ring in the New Year together. Arm in arm, they walked to the shack, where the same fog, it seemed, draped across the roof. After lovemaking, they cuddled in blankets around the stove. The dense air couldn't hold another molecule of moisture, so when the kettle boiled, heavy droplets swelled on the cool windowpanes.

Chase slipped the harmonica from his pocket and, pressing it along his lips, played the wistful tune "Molly Malone." "Now her ghost wheels her barrow through the streets broad and narrow, singing cockles and mussels, alive, alive-o."

It seemed to Kya that when Chase played these melancholy tunes was when he most had a soul.

28.

The Shrimper

1969

At beer time the Dog-Gone served up better gossip than the diner. The sheriff and Joe stepped inside the elongated, jam-packed beer hall and up to the bar, made from a single longleaf pine, which extended down the left side of the room, seemingly out of sight into the dim. Locals—all men, since women weren't allowed—bunched up to the bar or sat at scattered tables. The two barkeeps roasted hot dogs; fried shrimp, oysters, and hush puppies; stirred grits; poured beers and bourbon. The only light emitted from various flashing beer signs, giving off an amber glow, like campfires licking whiskered faces. The *clonk*s and *clink*s of billiard balls sounded from the back quarter.

Ed and Joe eased into a midbar cluster of fishermen, and as soon as they ordered Millers and fried oysters, the questions began: Anything new? How come there's no fingerprints; that part true? Ya guys thoughta ol' man Hanson? He's crazy as a loon, be just like sump'm he'd do, climb the tower, push off whoever comes along. This 'un got ya bumfuzzled, ain't it?

Joe facing one way, Ed the other, they rode the buzz. Answering, listening, nodding. Then through the hubbub, the sheriff's ear caught the corner of an even voice, a balanced tone, and turned to face Hal Miller, shrimper crew for Tim O'Neal.

"Can I talk with ya a minute, Sheriff? Alone?"

Ed backed away from the bar. "Sure can, Hal, come with me." He led him to a small table next to the wall, and they sat. "Need a refill on that beer?"

"No, fine fer now. Thank ya, though."

"Something on your mind, Hal?"

"Yeah, sure is. Gotta git her out, too. Been drivin' me a bit ditty."

"Let's have it."

"Oh man." Hal shook his head. "I don't know. May be nothing, either that, or I shoulda told ya sooner. I been haunted by what I seen."

"Just tell me, Hal. Together, we'll sort out if it's important or not."

"Well, it's about the Chase Andrews thing. It was the very night he died, well, I was crewing for Tim, and we were comin' into the bay late, way past midnight, and me and Allen Hunt seen that woman, the one people call the Marsh Girl, motoring just outta the bay."

"Is that so? How long after midnight?"

"Must'a been 'bout one forty-five in the mornin'."

"Where was she motoring?"

"Well, that's the thing, Sheriff. She was headed right toward the fire tower. If she stayed her course, she woulda landed at that little bay out from the tower."

Ed breathed out. "Yeah, Hal. That's important info. Very important. Can you be sure it was her?"

"Well, Allen and I talked about it at the time and were pretty sure it was her. I mean, we both thought the same thing. Wondered what the hell she was doin' out that late, cruisin' along with no lights on. Lucky we seen her, might've run her over. Then we just forgot about it.

It was only later I put two and two together and realized it was the same night Chase died at the tower. Well, then I reckoned I better speak up."

"Did anybody else on the boat see her?"

"Well, I don't know 'bout that. Others were about, fer sure, we were headin' in. All hands up. But I never talked to the others 'bout it. Ya know, just no reason to at the time. And haven't asked 'em since."

"I understand. Hal, you did the right thing to tell me. It's your duty to speak up like this. Don't worry about anything. All you can do is tell me what you saw. I'll ask you and Allen in to make a statement. Can I buy you that beer now?"

"No, I think I'll just go on home. G'night."

"Good night. Thanks again." As soon as Hal stood, Ed waved for Joe, who had been glancing over every few seconds to read the sheriff's face. They gave Hal a minute to clear the room with good-byes, then stepped onto the street.

Ed told Joe what Hal had witnessed.

"Man," Joe said, "that just about does it. Don't you think?"

"I think the judge may issue a warrant on this. Not sure, and I'd like to be sure before I ask. With a warrant we can search her place for any trace of red fibers that match those found on Chase's clothes. We gotta find out her story for that night."

29.

Seaweed

Through the winter, Chase came to Kya's shack often, usually spending one night each weekend. Even on cold, damp days, they glided through misty thickets, her collecting, him playing whimsical tunes on his harmonica. The notes floated with the fog, dissipating into the darker reaches of the lowland forests, and seemed somehow to be absorbed and memorized by the marsh because whenever Kya passed those channels again, she heard his music.

One morning in early March, Kya eased alone through the sea toward the village, the sky in a frumpy sweater of gray clouds. Chase's birthday was in two days, and she was headed to the Piggly to buy ingredients for a special supper—featuring her first caramel cake. Had pictured setting the candlelit cake in front of him at the table—an event that hadn't happened in the kitchen since Ma left. Several times recently he'd said he was saving money for their house. She reckoned she'd better learn to bake.

After securing her boat, as she walked along the dock toward the single file of shops, she saw Chase standing at the end talking with friends. His arms draped the shoulders of a slim, blond girl. Kya's mind strained to make sense of this, even as her legs kept moving on their own. She'd never approached him when he was with others or in town, but short of jumping into the sea, there was no way to avoid them.

Chase and his friends turned at once to look at her, and in the same instant, he dropped his arm from the girl. Kya was dressed in white cutoff denims, setting off her long legs. A black braid fell over each breast. The group stopped talking and stared. Knowing she couldn't run up to him burned her heart with the wrongness of things.

As she reached the end of the wharf, where they stood, he said, "Oh, Kya, hi."

Looking from him to them, she said, "Hi, Chase."

She heard him saying, "Kya, you remember Brian, and Tim, Pearl, Tina." He rattled off a few more names until his voice faded. Turning toward Kya, he said, "And this is Kya Clark."

Of course, she didn't remember them; she'd never been introduced to them. Only knew them as Tallskinnyblonde and the rest. She felt like seaweed dragged on a line but managed to smile and say hello. This was the opportunity for which she'd waited. Here she was standing among the friends she wanted to join. Her mind fought for words, something clever to say that might interest them. Finally, two of them greeted her coolly and turned abruptly away, the others following quickly like a school of minnows finning down the street.

"Well, so here we are," Chase said.

"I don't want to interrupt anything. I've just come for supplies, then back home."

"You're not interrupting. I just ran into them. I'll be out on Sunday, like I said."

Chase shifted his feet, fingered the shell necklace.

"I'll see you then," she said, but he'd already turned to catch the others. She hurried toward the market, stepping around a family of mallard ducks waddling down Main Street, their bright feet surprisingly orange against the dull pavement. In the Piggly Wiggly, pushing the vision of Chase and the girl from her head, she rounded the end of the bread aisle and saw the truant lady, Mrs. Culpepper, only four feet away. They stood there like a rabbit and a coyote caught together in a yard fence. Kya was now taller than the woman and much more educated, though neither would have thought of that. After all the running, she wanted to bolt, but stood her ground and returned Mrs. Culpepper's stare. The woman nodded slightly, then moved on.

Kya found the picnic items—cheese, French bread, and cake ingredients—costing all the money she'd managed to save for the occasion. But it seemed someone else's hand lifted the items and put them into the cart. All she could see was Chase's arm resting on the girl's shoulder. She bought a local newspaper because the headlines mentioned a marine laboratory that was to open up the coast nearby.

Once out of the store, head down, she scurried like a robber-ferret to the pier. Back at the shack, she sat down at the kitchen table to read the article about the new lab. Sure enough, a swanky scientific facility was being developed twenty miles south of Barkley Cove near Sea Oaks. Scientists would study the ecology of the marsh, which contributed to the survival of almost half of sea life in one way or another, and . . .

Kya turned the page to continue the story, and there loomed a large picture of Chase and a girl above an engagement announcement: *Andrews-Stone.* Bunches of words jumped out, then sobs, and finally ragged heaves. She stood, looking at the paper from a distance. Picked it up again to see—surely she had imagined it. There they were, their faces close together, smiling. The girl, Pearl Stone, beautiful, rich-looking, with a pearl necklace and lace blouse. The one his arm had been around. *Alwayswearspearls.*

Touching the wall, Kya made her way to the porch and fell on the bed, hands over her opened mouth. Then she heard a motor. Abruptly, she sat up, looked toward the lagoon, and saw Chase pulling his boat onto the shore.

Quick as a mouse escaping a lidless box, she slipped out the porch door before he saw her and ran into the woods, away from the lagoon. Squatting behind palmettos, she watched as he went into the shack, calling her. He would see the article spread open on the table. In a few minutes, he came out again and walked toward the beach, figuring he would find her there.

She didn't budge, even when he came back, still shouting her name. Not until he motored away did she emerge from the brambles. Moving sluggishly, she got food for the gulls and followed the sun to the beach. A strong ocean breeze pushed up the path, so that when she emerged on the beach, at least she had the wind to lean on. She called the gulls and flung large bits of French bread into the air. Then swore louder and meaner than the wind.

30.

The Rips

1967

From the beach, Kya ran to her rig and roared full throttle into the sea, headed straight for the rips. Holding her head back, she screamed, "You mean, SHIT . . . SUMBITCH!" Sloppy and confused waves jerked the bow sideways, pulling against the tiller. As always, the ocean seemed angrier than the marsh. Deeper, it had more to say.

Long ago, Kya'd learned how to read ordinary currents and riptides; how to ride them out or break away by cutting perpendicular to their course. But she'd never headed straight into the deeper currents, some of them stirred by the Gulf Stream, which gushes four billion cubic feet of water every second, more power than all the land rivers on Earth combined—all streaming just beyond North Carolina's outstretched arms. The surge produces cruel backcurrents, fisted eddies, and reverse circulations that swirl with coastal riptides, birthing one of the nastiest snake pits of the planet's seas. Kya had avoided these areas all her life, but not now. Today she aimed straight for their throats, anything to outrun the pain, the anger.

Roiling water pushed toward her, rising under the bow and yanking the boat starboard. It heaved heavily, then righted. She was pulled into a furious rip, which carried her a quarter faster. Turning out of it seemed too risky, so she fought to steer with the current, watching for sandbars, which formed ever-shifting barriers beneath the surface. One glancing touch could flip her.

Waves broke over her back, drenching her hair. Fast-moving, dark clouds streamed just above her head, blocking the sunlight and obscuring the signs of eddies and turbulence. Sucking the day's heat.

Still, fear eluded her, even as she longed to feel terrified, anything to dislodge the blade jammed against her heart.

Suddenly the dark tumbling waters of the current shifted, and the small rig spun starboard, rearing on its side. The force slammed her onto the bottom of the boat, seawater sloshing over her. Stunned, she sat in the water, bracing for another wave.

Of course, she was nowhere near the actual Gulf Stream. This was the training camp, the mere playing fields for the serious sea. But to her, she had ventured into the mean and meant to ride it out. Win something. Kill the pain.

Having lost all sense of symmetry and pattern, slate-colored waves broke from every angle. She dragged herself back into her seat and took the tiller but didn't know where to steer. Land slung as a distant line, surfacing only now and then between whitecaps. Just when she glimpsed solid earth, the boat spun or tilted and she lost sight of it. She'd been so sure about riding the current, but it had grown muscular, hauling her farther into the furious, darkening sea. The clouds bunched and settled low, blocking the sun. Wet through, she shivered as her energy drained, making it difficult to steer. She'd brought no foul-weather gear, no food, no water.

Finally the fear came. From a place deeper than the sea. Fear from knowing she would be alone again. Probably always. A life sentence.

Ugly gasping noises passed from her throat as the boat skewed and rolled broadside. Tipping dangerously with each wave.

By now six inches of foamy water covered the floor of the boat, burning her bare feet with its cold. How quickly the sea and clouds defeated the spring heat. Folding one arm over her chest, she tried to warm herself as she steered weakly with the other hand, not fighting the water, just moving with it.

At last, the waters calmed, and although the current swept her along to its own purpose, the ocean no longer thrashed and churned. Up ahead she saw a small, elongated sandbar, maybe a hundred feet long, glistening with sea and wet shells. Fighting the strong underflow, and just at the right second, Kya jerked the tiller and turned out of the current. She steered around to the leeward side of the bar and, in the stiller waters, beached as gently as a first kiss. She stepped onto the narrow slip and sank to the sand. Lay back and felt the solid land against her.

She knew it wasn't Chase she mourned, but a life defined by rejections. As the sky and clouds struggled overhead, she said out loud, "I have to do life alone. But I knew this. I've known a long time that people don't stay."

It hadn't been a coincidence that Chase slyly mentioned marriage as bait, immediately bedded her, then dropped her for someone else. She knew from her studies that males go from one female to the next, so why had she fallen for this man? His fancy ski boat was the same as the pumped-up neck and outsized antlers of a buck deer in rut: appendages to ward off other males and attract one female after another. Yet she had fallen for the same ruse as Ma: *leapfrogging sneaky fuckers.* What lies had Pa told her; to what expensive restaurants had he taken her before his money gave out and he brought her home to his real territory—a swamp shack? Perhaps love is best left as a fallow field.

Speaking out loud, she recited an Amanda Hamilton poem:

"I must let go now.

Let you go.

Love is too often

The answer for staying.

Too seldom the reason

For going.

I drop the line

And watch you drift away.

"All along

You thought

The fiery current

Of your lover's breast

Pulled you to the deep.

But it was my heart-tide

Releasing you

To float adrift

With seaweed."

The weak sun found space between the heavy-bottomed clouds and touched the sandbar. Kya looked around. The current, the grand sweep of the sea, and this sand had conspired as a delicate catch-net, because all around her lay the most astonishing collection of shells she'd ever seen. The angle of the bar and its gentle flow gathered the shells on the leeward side and laid them gently upon the sand without breaking them. She spotted several rare ones and many of her favorites, intact and pearly. Still glistening.

Moving among them, she chose the most precious and stashed them in a pile. She flipped the boat, drained the water, and lined the shells carefully along the bottom seam. Now she planned her trip back by standing tall and studying the waters. She read the sea and, having learned from the shells, would embark from the leeward side and head straight for land from here. Avoiding the strongest current altogether.

As she pushed off, she knew no one would ever see this sandbar again. The elements had created a brief and shifting smile of sand, angled just so. The next tide, the next current would design another sandbar, and another, but never this one. Not the one who caught her. The one who told her a thing or two.

Later, wandering her beach, she recited her favorite Amanda Hamilton poem.

> "Fading moon, follow
> My footsteps
> Through light unbroken
> By land shadows,
> And share my senses
> That feel the cool
> Shoulders of silence.
>
> "Only you know
> How one side of a moment
> Is stretched by loneliness
> For miles
> To the other edge,
> And how much sky
> Is in one breath

When time slides backward
From the sand."

If anyone understood loneliness, the moon would.

Drifting back to the predictable cycles of tadpoles and the ballet of fireflies, Kya burrowed deeper into the wordless wilderness. Nature seemed the only stone that would not slip midstream.

31.

A Book

1968

The rusted-out mailbox, mounted on a pole Pa cut, stood at the end of the road that had no name. Kya's only mail was bulk postings sent to all residents. She had no bills to pay, no girlfriends or old aunts to send silly-sweet notes. Except for that one letter from Ma years ago, her mail was a neutral thing, and sometimes she wouldn't empty the box for weeks.

But in her twenty-second year, more than a year after Chase and Pearl announced their engagement, she walked the sandy lane, blistering with heat, to the mailbox every day and looked inside. Finally one morning, she found a bulky manila envelope and slid the contents—an advance copy of *The Sea Shells of the Eastern Seaboard*, by Catherine Danielle Clark—into her hands. She breathed in, no one to show it to.

Sitting on her beach, she looked at every page. When Kya had written to the publisher after Tate's initial contact and submitted more drawings, they sent her a contract by return mail. Because all her paintings and text for each shell sample had been completed for years, her editor, Mr. Robert Foster, wrote to her that the book would be published in record time and that her second on birds would follow soon after. He included an advance payment of five thousand dollars. Pa would have tripped over his gimpy leg and spilled his poke.

Now in her hands, the final copy—every brushstroke, every carefully thought-out color, every word of the natural histories, printed in a book. There were also drawings of the creatures who live inside— how they eat, how they move, how they mate—because people forget about creatures who live in shells.

She touched the pages and remembered each shell and the story of finding it, where it lay on the beach, the season, the sunrise. A family album.

Over the coming months, up and down the coasts of North Carolina, South Carolina, Georgia, Virginia, Florida, and New England, gift shops and bookstores put her book in their windows or on display tables. The royalty checks would come in every six months, they said, and might be several thousand dollars each.

Sitting at the kitchen table, she drafted a letter of thanks to Tate, but as she read it over, her heart paused. A note did not seem enough. Because of his kindness, her love of the marsh could now be her life's work. Her life. Every feather, shell, or insect she collected could be shared with others, and no longer would she have to dig through mud for her supper. Might not have to eat grits every day.

Jumpin' had told her Tate was working as an ecologist at the new institute and laboratory near Sea Oaks, which had assigned him a spiffed-up research boat. At times, she'd seen him in the distance, but steered clear.

She added a postscript to the note: "If you're near my place sometime, stop by. I'd like to give you a copy of the book," and addressed it to him at the lab.

The next week she hired a fix-it man, Jerry, who put in running water, a water heater, and a full bathroom with a claw-foot tub in the back bedroom. He set a sink in a cabinet topped with tiles and installed a flush toilet. Electricity was brought in, and Jerry put in a range and new refrigerator. Kya insisted on keeping the old woodstove, firewood piled next to it, because it heated the shack, but mostly because it had baked a thousand biscuits from her mother's heart. What if Ma came back and her stove was gone? He made kitchen cabinets of heart pine, hung a new front door, a new screen on the porch, and made shelves for her specimens from floor to ceiling. She ordered a sofa, chairs, beds, mattresses, and rugs from Sears, Roebuck but kept the old kitchen table. And now she had a real closet to store a few mementos—a little scrap-closet of her fallen-away family.

As before, the shack stood unpainted on the outside, the weathered pine boards and tin roof rich in gray and rust colors, brushed by Spanish moss from the overhanging oak. Less rickety, but still woven into the weft of the marsh. Kya continued sleeping on the porch, except in the coldest of winter. But now she had a bed.

One morning, Jumpin' told Kya developers were coming to the area with big plans to drain the "murky swamp" and build hotels. Now and then, over the last year she'd seen large machines cutting entire stands of oaks in a week, then digging channels to dry the marsh. When finished, they moved on to new spots, leaving tracks of thirst and hardpan behind. Apparently, they had not read Aldo Leopold's book.

A poem by Amanda Hamilton said it clearly.

Child to child
Eye to eye
We grew as one,
Sharing souls.
Wing by wing,
Leaf by leaf
You left this world,
You died before the child.
My friend, the Wild.

Kya didn't know if her family owned the land or just squatted it, as had most marsh people for four centuries. Over the years, searching for clues of Ma's whereabouts, she'd read every scrap of paper in the shack and had never seen anything like a deed.

As soon as she got home from Jumpin's, she wrapped the old Bible in a cloth and took it to the Barkley Cove courthouse. The county clerk, a white-haired man with an enormous forehead and tiny shoulders, brought out a large leather volume of records, some maps, and a few aerial photographs, which he spread on the counter. Running her finger across the map, Kya pointed out her lagoon and outlined the rough boundaries of what she thought of as her land. The clerk checked the reference number and searched for the deed in an old wooden filing cabinet.

"Yep, here et is," he said. "It were surveyed proper and bought up in 1897 by a Mr. Napier Clark."

"That's my grandpa," Kya said. She thumbed through the thin pages of the Bible, and there, in the records of births and deaths, was one Napier Murphy Clark. Such a grand name. The same as her brother's. She told the clerk her pa was dead, which he probably was.

"It's ne'er been sold. So, yessiree bobtail, I reckon it b'longs to you.

219

But I'm afred to tell ya, there're some back taxes, Miz Clark, and to keep the land you gotta pay 'em. In fact, ma'am, the way the law reads, whoever comes along and pays off them back taxes owns the land even if they don't got no deed."

"How much?" Kya had not opened a bank account, and all the cash she owned after the improvements to her house, some three thousand dollars, was right in her knapsack. But they must be talking forty years of back taxes—thousands and thousands of dollars.

"Well, let's lookee here. It's listed as 'waste-land cateegory,' so the taxes fer most of them years was about five dollars. Let's see here, I gotta calc'late it." He stepped over to a fat and clunky adding machine, punched in numbers, and, after every entry, pulled back the crank handle, which made a churning sound as if it were actually summing up.

"Looks like it'll be 'bout eight hundr'd dollars total—put the land free and clear."

Kya walked out of the courthouse with a full deed in her name for three hundred ten acres of lush lagoons, sparkling marsh, oak forests, and a long private beach on the North Carolina coastline. "Wasteland *cateegory*. Murky swamp."

Pulling back into her lagoon at dusk, she had a talk with the heron. "It's all right. That spot's your'n!"

The next noon there was a note from Tate in her mailbox, which seemed strange and somehow formal since he'd only ever left messages for her on the feather stump. He thanked her for the invitation to stop by her place for a copy of her book and added that he'd be there that very afternoon.

Carrying one of the six copies of her new book the publishers had given her, she waited on the old reading-log. In about twenty minutes she heard the sound of Tate's old boat chugging up the channel and stood. As he eased into view from the undergrowth, they waved and smiled softly. Both guarded. The last time he'd pulled in here, she'd hurled rocks in his face.

After tying up, Tate stepped up to her. "Kya, your book is a wonder." He leaned slightly forward, as if to hug her, but the hardened rinds of her heart held her back.

Instead she handed him the book. "Here, Tate. This is for you."

"Thank you, Kya," he said as he opened it and paged through. He didn't mention that, of course, he'd already bought one at the Sea Oaks Bookshelf and marveled at every page. "Nothing like this has ever been published. I'm sure this is just a beginning for you."

She simply bowed her head and smiled slightly.

Then, turning to the title page, he said, "Oh, you haven't signed it. You have to inscribe it for me. Please."

She jerked her head up at him. Had not thought of that. What words could she possibly write to Tate?

He took a pen from his jeans pocket and handed it to her.

She took it and, after a few seconds, wrote:

To the Feather Boy

Thank you

From the Marsh Girl

Tate read the words, then turned away, staring far across the marsh because he couldn't hold her. Finally, he lifted her hand and squeezed it.

"Thank you, Kya."

"It was you, Tate," she said, and then thought, *It was always you*. One side of her heart longing, the other shielding.

He stood for a minute, and when she didn't say more, he turned to go. But as he got into his boat, he said, "Kya, when you see me out in the marsh, please don't hide in the grass like a spotted fawn. Just call out to me and we can do some exploring together. Okay?"

"All right."

"Thanks again for the book."

"Good-bye, Tate." She watched until he disappeared in the thicket and then said, "I could have at least invited him in for tea. That wouldn't hurt anything. I could be his friend." Then with rare pride she thought of her book. "I could be his colleague."

An hour after Tate left, Kya motored to Jumpin's wharf, another copy of her book tucked in her knapsack. As she approached, she saw him leaning against the wall of his weathered shop. He stood and waved to her, but she did not wave back. Knowing something was different, he waited silently as she tied up. She stepped up to him, lifted his hand, and put the book in his palm. At first he didn't understand, but she pointed to her name and said, "I'm okay now, Jumpin'. Thank you, and thank Mabel for all you did for me."

He stared at her. In another time and place, an old black man and a young white woman might have hugged. But not there, not then. She covered his hand with hers, turned, and motored away. It was the first time she'd seen him speechless. She kept on buying gas and supplies from him but never accepted a handout from them again. And each time she came to his wharf, she saw her book propped up in the tiny window for all to see. As a father would have shown it.

32.

Alibi

1969

Low dark clouds raced over a steel sea toward Barkley Cove. The wind hit first, rattling windows and hurling waves over the wharf. Boats, tied to the dock, bobbed up and down like toys, as men in yellow slickers tied this line or that, securing. Then sideways rain slammed the village, obscuring everything except the odd yellow form moving about in the grayness.

The wind whistled through the sheriff's window, and he raised his voice. "So, Joe, you had something to tell me?"

"Sure do. I found out where Miss Clark will claim she was the night Chase died."

"What? Did you finally catch up to her?"

"Ya kiddin'? She's slipperier'n a damn eel. Gets gone ever' time I get near. So I drove over to Jumpin's marina this morning to see if he knew when she'd be coming next. Like everybody else she hasta go there for gas, so I figured I'd catch her up sooner or later. You won't believe what I found out."

"Let's have it."

"I got two reliable sources say she was outta town that night."

"What? Who? She never goes out of town, and even if she did, who'd know about it?"

"Ya remember Tate Walker? Dr. Walker now. Works out at the new ecology lab."

"Yeah, I know him. His dad's a shrimper. Scupper Walker."

"Well, Tate says he knew Kya—he calls her Kya—quite well when they were younger."

"Oh?"

"Not like that. They were just kids. He taught her to read, 'parently."

"He tell you this himself?"

"Yep. He was there at Jumpin's. I was askin' Jumpin' if he knew where or how I could ask the Marsh Girl some questions. He said he didn't know from one minute to the next when he'd see her."

"Jumpin's always been good to her. Doubt if he'll tell us much."

"Well, I asked him if, by any chance, he knew what she was doin' the night Chase died. And he said that as a matter of fact he did, that she'd come to his place the second mornin' after Chase died, and that he was the very one who told her he was dead. He said she'd been in Greenville for two nights, including the night Chase died."

"Greenville?"

"That's what he said, and then Tate, who'd been standin' there all that time, he piped in and said, yeah, she'd been in Greenville, that he was the one who told her how to buy the bus ticket."

"Well, that is some news," Sheriff Jackson said. "And very convenient that they were both standing there with the same story. Why would she go over to Greenville?"

"Tate said that a publishing company—ya know, she's gone and written a book on shells and one of seabirds—well, they paid her expenses to go over there and meet 'em."

"Hard to imagine fancy publishing people wanting to meet her. I guess it'll be pretty easy to check out. What'd Tate say about teaching her to read?"

"I asked him how he knew her. He said he useta go out near her place to fish, and when he found out she couldn't read, he taught her."

"Um. That so?"

Joe said, "Anyway, this changes everything. She does have an alibi. A good one. I'd say being in Greenville's a pretty good alibi."

"Yeah. On the surface. You know what they say about good alibis. And we got that shrimper saying he saw her boating directly toward the fire tower the very night Chase fell off it."

"He could've been wrong. It was dark. No moon until after two A.M. Maybe she was in Greenville, and he saw somebody else out there in a boat looks like hers."

"Well, like I said, this supposed trip to Greenville should be easy to check out."

The storm abated into a whine and drizzle; still, instead of walking to the diner, the two lawmen sent a runner for a takeout of chicken 'n' dumplings, butter beans, summer squash casserole, cane syrup, and biscuits.

Right after lunch, a knock sounded on the sheriff's door. Miss Pansy Price opened it and stepped inside. Joe and Ed stood. Her turban hat glistened a rose color.

"Afternoon, Miss Pansy." Both nodded.

"Good afternoon, Ed. Joe. May I have a seat? I won't take long. I believe I have important information concerning the case."

"Yes, of course. Sit down, please." The two men sat as soon as Miss Pansy settled like a fair-sized hen into the chair, tucking feathers here and there, her pocketbook perching on her lap like a prized egg. The sheriff, continuing, couldn't resist. "And what case would that be, Miss Pansy?"

"Oh, for heaven's sake, Ed. You know what case. Who murdered Chase Andrews. That case."

"We don't know if he was murdered, Miss Pansy. All right? Now, what do you have for us?"

"As you know, I'm employed at Kress's." She never lowered her standing by referring to the entire name: Kress's Five and Dime. She waited for the sheriff to acknowledge her comment with a nod—even though they all knew she'd worked there since she sold toy soldiers to him as a boy—and then continued. "I believe the Marsh Girl is a suspect. Is that correct?"

"Who told you that?"

"Oh, lots of people are convinced, but Patti Love's the main source."

"I see."

"Well, from Kress's me and some other employees saw the Marsh Girl get on and off the bus on days that woulda put her out of town the night Chase died. I can testify to those dates and times."

"That so?" Joe and Ed exchanged glances. "What are the dates and times?"

Miss Pansy sat straighter in her chair. "She left on the 2:30 P.M. bus on October 28 and returned at 1:16 on the thirtieth."

"You said others saw her, too?"

"Yes. I can get a list if you like."

"That won't be necessary. We'll come over to the Five and Dime if we want statements. Thank you, Miss Pansy." The sheriff stood, so Miss Pansy and Ed did as well.

She moved toward the door. "Well, thank you for your time. As you said, you know where to find me."

They said good-byes.

Joe sat back down. "Well, there it is. Confirms what Tate and Jumpin' said. She was in Greenville that night, or leastwise, she got on a bus and went somewheres."

The sheriff blew out a long breath. "Appears so. But I reckon if somebody can bus over to Greenville by day, they can bus back here at night. Do their business. Bus back to Greenville. Nobody the wiser."

"I guess. Seems a bit of a stretch."

"Go get the bus schedules. We'll see if the times work out. If a return trip is possible in one night."

Before Joe stepped out, Ed continued. "Could be she wanted to be seen out there in broad daylight getting on and off of buses. When you think about it, she had to do something out of the ordinary for an alibi. To claim that she'd been alone in her shack the night Chase died, as she usually is, would be no alibi at all. Zip. So she planned up something that lots of people would see her do. Making a great alibi right in front of all those folks on Main Street. Brilliant."

"Well yeah, that's a good point. Anyhow, we don't have to play gumshoe anymore. We can set right here drinkin' coffee and let the ladies of this town waltz in and outta here with all the goods. I'll go get the bus schedules."

Joe returned fifteen minutes later.

"Well, you're right," he said. "See here, it would be possible to bus from Greenville to Barkley Cove and then back again all in one night. Easy, really."

"Yeah, plenty of time between the two buses to push somebody off the fire tower. I say we get a warrant."

33.

The Scar

1968

In the winter of 1968, Kya sat at her kitchen table one morning, sweeping orange and pink watercolors across paper, creating the plump form of a mushroom. She had finished her book on seabirds and now worked on a guide to mushrooms. Already had plans for another on butterflies and moths.

Black-eyed peas, red onions, and salt ham boiled in the old dented pot on the woodstove, which she still preferred to the new range. Especially in winter. The tin roof sang under a light rain. Then, suddenly the sounds of a truck laboring through sand came down her lane. Rumbling louder than the roof. Panic rising, she stepped to the window and saw a red pickup maneuvering the muddy ruts.

Kya's first thought was to run, but the truck was already pulling up to the porch. Hunched down below the windowsill, she watched a man in a gray-green military uniform step out. He just stood there, truck door ajar, looking through the woods, down the path toward the lagoon. Then, closing the door softly, he jogged through the rain to the porch door and knocked.

She cussed. He was probably lost, would ask directions and go on, but she didn't want to deal with him. She could hide here in the kitchen, hope he went away. But she heard him call. "Yo! Anybody home? Hello!"

Annoyed yet curious, she walked through the newly furnished sitting room to the porch. The stranger, tall with dark hair, stood on the front step holding the screen door open, five feet from her. His uniform seemed stiff enough to stand on its own, as if it were holding him together. The breast of his jacket was covered with colorful rectangular medals. But most eye-catching of all was a jagged red scar that cut his face in half from his left ear to the top of his lips. Kya gasped.

In an instant she returned to the Easter Sunday about six months before Ma left for good. Singing "Rock of Ages," she and Ma walked arm in arm through the sitting room to the kitchen and gathered up the brilliantly colored eggs they had painted the night before. The other kids were out fishing, so she and Ma had time to hide the eggs, then get the chicken and biscuits into the oven. The brothers and sisters were too old to hunt for treats, but they would run around searching, pretending not to find them, then holding each discovered treasure high in the air, laughing.

Ma and Kya were leaving the kitchen with their baskets of eggs and chocolate bunnies from the Five and Dime, just as Pa rounded the corner from the hall.

Yanking Kya's Easter bonnet from her head and waving it around, he screamed at Ma, "Whar ya git the money for these fancy thangs? Bonnets and shiny leather shoes? Them prissy eggs and chocolate bunnies? Say. Whar?"

"Come on, Jake, please hush. It's Easter; this is for the kids."

He shoved Ma backward. "Ya out whoring, that's what. That how you git the money? Tell me *now*." He grabbed Ma by the arms and shook her so hard her face seemed to rattle around her eyes, which stayed very still and wide open. Eggs tumbled from the basket and rolled in wobbly pastels across the floor.

"Pa, please, stop!" Kya cried out, then sobbed.

He lifted his hand and slapped Kya hard across the cheek. "Shut up, ya prissy-pot crybaby! Git that silly-looking dress and fancy shoes off ya. Them's whorin' clothes."

She ducked down, holding her face, chasing after Ma's hand-painted eggs.

"I'm talkin' to ya, woman! Whar ya gettin' yo' money?" He lifted the iron fire poker from the corner and moved toward Ma.

Kya screamed as loud as she could and grabbed at Pa's arm as he slammed the poker across Ma's chest. Blood popped out on the flowery sundress like red polka dots. Then a big body moved down the hall and Kya looked up to see Jodie tackle Pa from behind, sending them both sprawling across the floor. Her brother got between Ma and Pa and hollered for Kya and Ma to run, and they did. But before she turned, Kya saw Pa raise the poker and whack Jodie across the face, his jaw twisting grossly, blood spewing. The scene played out in her mind now in a flash. Her brother crumbling onto the floor, lying among purple-pink eggs and chocolate bunnies. She and Ma running through palmettos, hiding in brush. Her dress bloody, Ma kept saying it was fine, the eggs wouldn't break, and they could still cook the chicken. Kya didn't understand why they stayed hidden there—she was sure her brother was dying, needed their help, but she was too afraid to move. They waited for a long time and then snuck back, looking through the windows to make sure Pa was gone.

Jodie lay cold on the floor, blood pooled around him, and Kya cried that he was dead. But Ma roused him and moved him to the sofa, where she stitched up his face with her sewing needle. When all was quiet,

Kya snatched her bonnet from the floor and ran fast through the woods and threw it with all her might into the saw grass.

Now she looked into the eyes of the stranger standing on her porch and said, "Jodie."

He smiled, the scar going crooked, and replied, "Kya, I hoped you'd be here." They stared, each searching for the other in older eyes. Jodie couldn't know he had been with her all these years, that scores of times he had shown her the way through the marsh, taught her over and over about herons and fireflies. More than anyone else, she had wanted to see Jodie or Ma again. Her heart had erased the scar and all the pain in that package. No wonder her mind buried the scene; no wonder Ma had left. Hit by a poker across the chest. Kya saw those rubbed-out stains on the flowered sundress as blood again.

He wanted to hug her, fold her into his arms, but as he moved toward her, she hung her head low to the side in profound shyness and backed up. So he simply stepped onto the porch.

"Come in," she said, and led him into the small living room chockfull with her specimens.

"Oh," he said. "Yes, then. I saw your book, Kya. I didn't know for sure if it was you, but yes, now I can see it was. It's amazing." He walked around looking at her collections, also examining the room with its new furniture, glancing down the halls to the bedrooms. Not wanting to snoop, but taking it all in.

"Do you want coffee, tea?" She didn't know if he'd come for a visit or to stay. What did he want after all these years?

"Coffee would be great. Thank you."

In the kitchen, he recognized the old woodstove next to the new gas range and refrigerator. He ran his hand over the old kitchen table, which she had kept as it was. With all its peeling-paint history. She poured the coffee in mugs, and they sat.

"You're a soldier, then."

"Two tours in 'Nam. I'm staying in the army for a few more months. They've been good to me. Paid for my college degree—mechanical engineering, Georgia Tech. Least I can do is stay in a while."

Georgia wasn't all that far away—he could have visited sooner. But he was here now.

"You all left," she said. "Pa stayed a while after you, but then he went, too. I don't know where, don't know if he's alive or not."

"You've been here by yourself since then?"

"Yes."

"Kya, I shouldn't have left you with that monster. I've ached, felt terrible about it for years. I was a coward, a stupid coward. These damned medals don't mean a thing." He swiped at his chest. "I left you, a little girl, alone to survive in a swamp with a madman. I don't expect you to forgive me, ever."

"Jodie, it's okay. You were just a kid yourself. What could you do?"

"I could've come back when I was older. At first it was day-to-day survival on the back streets of Atlanta." He sneered. "I left here with seventy-five cents in my pocket. Stole it from the money Pa left in the kitchen; took it knowing it would leave you short. I scraped by on odd jobs till the army took me in. After training, it was straight to war. When I got home, so much time had passed, I figured you were long gone, run away yourself. That's the reason I didn't write; I think I signed up to go back as a kind of self-punishment. What I deserved for leaving you. Then after I graduated from Tech, a couple of months ago, I saw your book in a shop. Catherine Danielle Clark. My heart just broke and leapt for joy all at once. I had to find you—figured I'd start here and track you down."

"Well, here we are then." She smiled for the first time. His eyes were the same as they had been. Faces change with life's toll, but eyes remain a window to what was, and she could see him there. "Jodie, I'm so sorry you worried about leaving me. Not once did I blame you. We were the victims, not the guilty."

He smiled. "Thank you, Kya." Tears welled, and they both looked away.

She hesitated, then said, "This may be hard to believe, but for a while Pa was good to me. He drank less, taught me to fish, and we went out in the boat a lot, all over the marsh. But then, of course, he went back to drinking and left me to fend for myself."

Jodie nodded. "Yeah, I saw that side of him a few times, but he always went back to the bottle. He told me once it had something to do with the war. I've been to war myself and seen things that could drive a man to drink. But he shouldn't have taken it out on his wife, his own kids."

"What about Ma, the others?" she asked. "Did you ever hear from them, know where they went?"

"I don't know a thing about Murph, Mandy, or Missy. I wouldn't know them if I passed them in the street. By now I 'spose they've scattered with the wind. But Ma, well, Kya, that's another reason I wanted to find you. There is some news of her."

"Some news? What? Tell me." Chills flowed from Kya's arms to her fingertips.

"Kya, it's not good. I only found out last week. Ma died two years ago."

She bent at the waist, holding her face in her hands. Soft groans came from her throat. Jodie tried to hold her, but she moved away from him.

Jodie continued. "Ma had a sister, Rosemary, who tried to track us down through the Red Cross when Ma died, but they couldn't find us. Then a couple of months ago they found me through the army and put me in touch with Rosemary."

In hoarse tones Kya mumbled, "Ma was alive until two years ago. I've been waiting all these years for her to walk down the lane." She stood and held on to the sink. "Why didn't she come back? Why didn't somebody tell me where she was? And now it's too late."

Jodie went to her, and even though she tried to turn away, he put his arms around her. "I'm sorry, Kya. Come sit down. I'll tell you what Rosemary said."

He waited for her, then said, "Ma was ill from a major breakdown when she left us and went to New Orleans—that's where she grew up. She was mentally and physically ill. I remember New Orleans a little bit. I guess I was five when we left. All I remember is a nice house, big windows overlooking a garden. But once we moved here, Pa wouldn't let any of us talk about New Orleans, our grandparents, or any of it. So it was all wiped away."

Kya nodded. "I never knew."

Jodie continued. "Rosemary said their parents had been against Ma's marriage to Pa from the start, but Ma went off to North Carolina with her husband, not a penny to their names. Eventually Ma began writing to Rosemary and told her of her circumstances—living in a swamp shack with a drunk man who beat her and her children. Then one day, years later, Ma showed up. She had on those fake alligator heels that she cherished. Hadn't bathed or combed her hair in days.

"For months Ma was mute, didn't speak one word. She stayed in her old room in her parents' home, barely eating. Of course, they had doctors come out, but no one could help her. Ma's father contacted the sheriff in Barkley Cove to ask if Ma's children were all right, but his office said they didn't even try to keep track of the marsh people."

Kya sniffed now and then.

"Finally, almost a year later, Ma became hysterical and told Rosemary she remembered she had left her children. Rosemary helped her write a letter to Pa asking if she could come get us and bring us to live with her in New Orleans. He wrote back that if she returned or contacted any of us, he would beat us unrecognizable. She knew he was capable of such a thing."

The letter in the blue envelope. Ma had asked for her, for all of them. Ma had wanted to see her. But the outcome of the letter had been vastly different. The words had enraged Pa and sent him back to drinking, and then Kya had lost him as well. She didn't mention to Jodie that she still kept the letter's ashes in a little jar.

"Rosemary said Ma never made friends, never dined with the family or interacted with anybody. She allowed herself no life, no pleasure. After a while, she started talking more, and all she talked about was her children. Rosemary said Ma loved us all her life but was frozen in some horrible place of believing that we'd be harmed if she returned and abandoned if she didn't. She didn't leave us to have a fling; she'd been driven to madness and barely knew she'd left."

Kya asked, "How did she die?"

"She had leukemia. Rosemary said it was possibly treatable, but she refused all medication. She just became weaker and weaker, and slipped away two years ago. Rosemary said she died much as she had lived. In darkness, in silence."

Jodie and Kya sat still. Kya thought of the poem by Galway Kinnell that Ma had underlined in her book:

> I have to say I am relieved it is over:
> At the end I could feel only pity
> For that urge toward more life.
> . . . Goodbye.

Jodie stood. "Come with me, Kya, I want to show you something." He led her outside to his pickup and they climbed into the back.

Carefully, he removed a tarp and opened a large cardboard box, and one by one, pulled out and unwrapped oil paintings. He stood them up around the bed of the truck. One was of three young girls—Kya and her sisters—squatting by the lagoon, watching dragonflies. Another of Jodie and their brother holding up a string of fish.

"I brought them in case you were still here. Rosemary sent these to me. She said that for years, day and night, Ma painted us."

One painting showed all five children as if they were watching the artist. Kya stared into the eyes of her sisters and brothers, looking back at her.

In a whisper, she asked, "Who's who?"

"What?"

"There were never any photographs. I don't know them. Who's who?"

"Oh." He couldn't breathe, then finally said, "Well, this is Missy, the oldest. Then Murph. Mandy. Of course, this little cutie is me. And that's you."

He gave her time, then said, "Look at this one."

Before him was an astonishingly colorful oil of two children squatting in swirls of green grass and wild flowers. The girl was only a toddler, perhaps three years old, her straight black hair falling over her shoulders. The boy, a bit older, with golden curls, pointed to a monarch butterfly, its black-and-yellow wings spread across a daisy. His hand was on the girl's arm.

"I think that's Tate Walker," Jodie said. "And you."

"I think you're right. It looks like him. Why would Ma paint Tate?"

"He used to come around quite a bit, fish with me. He was always showing you insects and stuff."

"Why don't I remember that?"

"You were very young. One afternoon Tate boated into our lagoon, where Pa was pulling on his poke, really drunk. You were wading and Pa was supposed to be watching you. Suddenly, for no reason at all, Pa grabbed you by your arms and shook you so hard your head was thrown back. Then he dropped you in the mud and started laughing. Tate jumped out of the boat and ran up to you. He was only seven or eight years old, but he shouted at Pa. Of course, Pa smacked him and screamed at him to get off his land, never come back or he'd shoot him. By this time we'd all run down to see what was happening. Even with Pa ranting and raving, Tate picked you up and handed you to Ma. He made sure you were all right before he left. We still went fishing some after that, but he never came back to our place again."

Not until he led me home that first time I took the boat into the marsh, Kya thought. She looked at the painting—so pastel, so peaceful. Somehow Ma's mind had pulled beauty from lunacy. Anyone looking at these portraits would think they portrayed the happiest of families, living on a seashore, playing in sunshine.

Jodie and Kya sat on the rim of the truck bed, still looking quietly at the paintings.

He continued. "Ma was isolated and alone. Under those circumstances people behave differently."

Kya made a soft groan. "Please don't talk to me about isolation. No one has to tell me how it changes a person. I have lived it. I am isolation," Kya whispered with a slight edge. "I forgive Ma for leaving. But I don't understand why she didn't come back—why she abandoned me. You probably don't remember, but after she walked away, you told me that a she-fox will sometimes leave her kits if she's starving or under some other extreme stress. The kits die—as they probably would have anyway—but the vixen lives to breed again when conditions are better, when she can raise a new litter to maturity.

"I've read a lot about this since. In nature—out yonder where the crawdads sing—these ruthless-seeming behaviors actually increase the mother's number of young over her lifetime, and thus her genes for abandoning offspring in times of stress are passed on to the next generation. And on and on. It happens in humans, too. Some behaviors that seem harsh to us now ensured the survival of early man in whatever swamp he was in at the time. Without them, we wouldn't be here. We still store those instincts in our genes, and they express themselves when certain circumstances prevail. Some parts of us will always be what we were, what we had to be to survive—way back yonder.

"Maybe some primitive urge—some ancient genes, not appropriate anymore—drove Ma to leave us because of the stress, the horror and real danger of living with Pa. That doesn't make it right; she *should have chosen to stay*. But knowing that these tendencies are in our biological blueprints might help one forgive even a failed mother. That may explain her leaving, but I still don't see why she didn't come back. Why she didn't even write to me. She could've written letter after letter, year after year, until one finally got to me."

"I guess some things can't be explained, only forgiven or not. I don't know the answer. Maybe there isn't one. I'm sorry to bring you this bad news."

"I've had no family, no news of family for most of my life. Now within a few minutes I've found a brother and lost my mother."

"I'm so sorry, Kya."

"Don't be. Actually, I lost Ma years ago, and now you're back, Jodie. I can't tell you how much I wanted to see you again. This is one of the happiest and yet saddest days of my life." She touched his arm with her fingers, and he already knew her enough to know this was rare.

They walked back into the shack, and he looked around at the new things, the freshly painted walls, the handcrafted kitchen cabinets.

"How'd you manage, Kya? Before your book, how'd you get money, food?"

"Oh, that's a long boring story. Mostly I sold mussels, oysters, and smoked fish to Jumpin'."

Jodie threw his head back and laughed out loud. "Jumpin'! I haven't thought about him for years. Is he still around?"

Kya didn't laugh. "Jumpin' has been my best friend, for years my only friend. My only family unless you count herring gulls."

Jodie turned serious. "Didn't you have friends in school?"

"I only went to school one day in my life," she chuckled. "The kids laughed at me, so I never went back. Spent weeks outsmarting the truant officers. Which, after all the things you'd taught me, wasn't very hard."

He looked astonished. "How did you learn to read? To write your book?"

"Actually, it was Tate Walker who taught me to read."

"You ever see him anymore?"

"Now and then." She stood, faced the stove. "More coffee?"

Jodie felt the lonely life hanging in her kitchen. It was there in the tiny supply of onions in the vegetable basket, the single plate drying in the rack, the cornbread wrapped carefully in a tea towel, the way an old widow might do it.

"I've had plenty, thanks. But what about a ride around the marsh?" he asked.

"Of course. You won't believe it, I have a new motor but still use that same old boat."

The sun had broken up the clouds and shone bright and warm for a winter day. As she steered them through narrow channels and glassy estuaries, he exclaimed at a remembered snag, the same as it had been, and a beaver lodge still piled in the exact spot. They laughed when they came to the lagoon where Ma, Kya, and their sisters had grounded the boat in mud.

Back at the shack, she put together a picnic, which they ate on the beach with the gulls.

"I was so young when they all left," she said. "Tell me about the others." So he told her stories of their older brother, Murph, who carried her around on his shoulders through the woods.

"You used to laugh the whole time. He would jog and turn circles with you way up there. And one time you laughed so hard you wet your pants right on his neck."

"Oh no! I didn't." Kya leaned back, laughing.

"Yes, you did. He squealed some, but he kept on going, ran right into the lagoon until he was underwater, and you still riding his shoulders. We were all watching—Ma, Missy, Mandy, and me—and laughed till we cried. Ma had to sit right down on the ground, she was laughing so hard."

Her mind invented pictures to go with the stories. Family scraps and shreds Kya never thought she'd have.

Jodie continued. "It was Missy who started feeding the gulls."

"What? Really! I thought I started it on my own, after everybody left."

"No, she fed the gulls every day she could get away with it. She gave them all names. She called one Big Red, I remember that. You know, after that red spot on their bills."

"It's not the same bird, of course—I've gone through a few generations of Big Reds myself. But there, the one on the left, that's Big Red today." She tried to connect with the sister who had given her the gulls, but all she could see was the face in the painting. Which was more than she'd had before.

The red spot on a herring gull's bill, Kya knew, was more than decoration. Only when the chicks pecked at the spot with their bills would the parent release the captured food for them. If the red spot was obscured so that the chicks didn't tap it, the parent wouldn't feed them and they would die. Even in nature, parenthood is a thinner line than one might think.

They sat for a moment, then Kya said, "I just don't remember much about it at all."

"You're lucky, then. Just keep it that way."

They sat there like that, quietly. Not remembering.

She cooked a southern supper as Ma would have: black-eyed peas with red onions, fried ham, cornbread with cracklin', butter beans cooked in butter and milk. Blackberry cobbler with hard cream with some bourbon Jodie brought. As they ate, he told her he would like to stay a few days, if that was okay, and she said he was welcome as long as he liked.

"This is your land now, Kya. You earned it. I'm stationed at Fort Benning for a while yet, so I can't stay long. After that I'll probably get a job in Atlanta so we can stay in touch; I'd like to see you as often as I can get up here. Knowing you're okay is all I ever wanted in my life."

"I'd like that, Jodie. Please come whenever you can."

The next evening, as they sat on the beach, wave tips tickling their bare toes, Kya chatted in unusual fashion, and Tate seemed to be in every paragraph. There was the time he showed her the way home when she, as a little girl, was lost in the marsh. Or the first poem Tate read to her. She talked about the feather game and how he taught her to read, how he was a scientist at the lab now. He was her first love, but he had dropped her when he went to college, left her waiting on the lagoon shore. So it had ended.

"How long ago was that?" Jodie asked.

"About seven years, I guess. When he first went to Chapel Hill."

"Did you ever see him again?"

"He came back to apologize; said he still loved me. He was the one who suggested I publish reference books. It's nice to see him now and then in the marsh, but I'd never get involved again. He can't be trusted."

"Kya, that was seven years ago. He was just a boy, first time away from home, hundreds of pretty girls around. If he came back and apologized and says he loves you, maybe you should cut him a little slack."

"Most men go from one female to the next. The unworthy ones strut about, pulling you in with falsehoods. Which is probably why Ma fell for a man like Pa. Tate wasn't the only guy who left me. Chase Andrews even talked to me about marriage, but he married someone else. Didn't even tell me; I read it in the paper."

"I'm so sorry. I am, but, Kya, it's not just guys who are unfaithful. I've been duped, dropped, run over a few times myself. Let's face it, a lot of times love doesn't work out. Yet even when it fails, it connects you to others and, in the end, that is all you have, *the connections*. Look at us; you and I have each other now, and just think, if I have kids and you have kids, well, that's a whole new string of connections. And on it goes. Kya, if you love Tate, take a chance."

Kya thought of Ma's painting of Tate and herself as children, their heads close together, surrounded by pastel flowers and butterflies. Maybe a message from Ma after all.

On the third morning of Jodie's visit, they unpacked Ma's paintings— all but one, which Jodie kept—and hung some on the walls. The shack took on a different light, as though more windows had opened up. She stood back and stared at them—a miracle to have some of Ma's paintings back on the walls. Pulled from the fire.

Then Kya walked Jodie out to his pickup and gave him a bag lunch she'd made for his trip. They both looked through the trees, down the lane, everywhere except into each other's eyes.

Finally he said, "I better get going, but here's my address and phone number," as he held out a scrap of notepaper. She stopped breathing, and with her left hand held herself steady on the truck as she took the paper with her right. Such a simple thing: the address of a brother on a slip of paper. Such an astonishing thing: a family she could find. A number she could call and he would answer. She choked on her own throat as he pulled her to him, and finally, after a lifetime, she sagged against him and wept.

"I never thought I'd see you again. I thought you were gone forever."

"I'll always be here, I promise. Whenever I move, I'll send my new address. If you ever need me, you write or call, you hear?"

"I will. And come back for a visit whenever you can."

"Kya, go find Tate. He's a good man."

He waved from the truck window all the way down the lane, as she watched, crying and laughing all at once. And when he turned onto the track, she could see his red pickup through the holes of the forest where a white scarf had once trailed away, his long arm waving until he was gone.

34.

Search the Shack

1969

Well, again she's not here," Joe said, knocking on the frame of Kya's screen door. Ed stood on the brick-'n'-board steps, cupping his hands on the mesh to see inside. Enormous limbs of the oak, hung with long strands of Spanish moss, cast shadows on the weathered boards and pointy roof of the shack. Only gray patches of sky blinked through the late November morning.

"Of course she's not here. It doesn't matter; we have a search warrant. Just go on in, bet it isn't locked."

Joe opened the door, calling out, "Anybody home? Sheriff here." Inside, they stared at the shelves of her menagerie.

"Ed, lookit all this stuff. It keeps goin' in the next room yonder, and on down the hall. Looks like she's a bit off her rocker. Crazy as a three-eyed rat."

"Maybe, but apparently she's quite an expert on the marsh. You know she published those books. Let's get busy. Okay, here're the things to look for." The sheriff read out loud from a short list. "Articles of red-wool clothing that might match the red fibers found on Chase's jacket. A diary, calendar, or notes, something that might mention places and times of her whereabouts; the shell necklace; or stubs from those night buses. And let's not mess up her stuff. No reason to do that. We can look under, around everything; don't need to ruin any of this."

"Yeah, I hear ya. Almost like a shrine in here. Half a' me's impressed, the other half's got the heebie-jeebies."

"It's going to be tedious, that's for sure," the sheriff said as he carefully looked behind a row of bird nests. "I'll start back in her bedroom."

The men worked silently, pushing clothes around in drawers, poking in closet corners, shifting jars of snakeskins and sharks' teeth in search of evidence.

After ten minutes, Joe called, "Come look at this."

As Ed entered the porch, Joe said, "Did ya know that female birds only got one ovary?"

"What're ya talking about?"

"See. These drawings and notes show that female birds only got one ovary."

"Dang it, Joe. We're not here for a biology lesson. Get back to work."

"Wait a second. Look here. This is a male peacock feather, and the note says that over eons of time, the males' feathers got larger and larger to attract females, till the point the males can barely lift off the ground. Can't hardly fly anymore."

"Are you finished? We have a job to do."

"Well, it's very interesting."

Ed walked from the room. "Get to work, man."

Ten minutes later, Joe called out again. As Ed walked out of the small bedroom, toward the sitting room, he said, "Let me guess. You found a stuffed mouse with three eyes."

There was no reply, but when Ed walked into the room, Joe held up a red wool hat.

"Where'd you find that?"

"Right here, hangin' on this row of hooks with these coats, other hats, and stuff."

"In the open like that?"

"Right here like I said."

From his pocket, Ed pulled out the plastic bag containing the red fibers taken from Chase's denim jacket the night he died and held it against the red hat.

"They look exactly the same. Same color, same size and thickness," Joe said as both men studied the hat and sample.

"They do. Both of them have fuzzy beige wool mixed in with the red."

"Man, this could be it."

"We'll have to send the hat to the lab, of course. But if these fibers match, we'll bring her in for questioning. Bag and label the hat."

After four hours of searching, the men met in the kitchen.

Stretching his back, Ed said, "I reckon if there's anything else, we would've found it by now. We can always come back. Call it a day."

Maneuvering the ruts back to town, Joe said, "Seems like if she's guilty of this thing, she woulda hidden the red cap. Not just hung it in the open like that."

"She probably had no idea fibers would fall off the hat onto his jacket. Or that the lab could identify them. She just wouldn't know something like that."

"Well, she might not a' known that, but I bet she knows a bunch. Those male peacocks struttin' around, competin' so much for sex, they can't hardly fly. I ain't sure what it all means, but it adds up to some-thing."

35

The Compass

1969

One July afternoon in 1969, more than seven months after Jodie's visit, *The Eastern Seacoast Birds* by Catherine Danielle Clark—her second book, a volume of stark detail and beauty—appeared in her mailbox. She ran her fingers over the striking jacket—her painting of a herring gull. Smiling, she said, "Hey, Big Red, you made it to the cover."

Carrying the new book, Kya walked silently to the shady oak clearing near her shack, searching for mushrooms. The moist duff felt cool on her feet as she neared a cluster of intensely yellow toadstools. Midstride, she halted. There, sitting on the old feather stump, was a small milk carton, red and white, just like the one from so long ago. Unexpectedly, she laughed out loud.

Inside the carton, wrapped in tissue paper, was an old army-issue compass in a brass case, tarnished green-gray with age. She breathed in at the sight of it. She had never needed a compass because the directions seemed obvious to her. But on cloudy days, when the sun was elusive, the compass would guide her.

A folded note read: *Dearest Kya, This compass was my grandpa's from the First World War. He gave it to me when I was little, but I've never used it, and I thought maybe you would get the best out of it. Love, Tate. P.S. I'm glad you can read this note!*

Kya read the words *Dearest* and *Love* again. Tate. The golden-haired boy in the boat, guiding her home before a storm, gifting her feathers on a weathered stump, teaching her to read; the tender teen-ager steering her through her first cycle as a woman and arousing her first sexual desires as a female; the young scientist encouraging her to publish her books.

Despite gifting him the shell book, she had continued to hide in the undergrowth when she saw him in the marsh, rowing away unseen. The dishonest signals of fireflies, all she knew of love.

Even Jodie had said she should give Tate another chance. But every time she thought of him or saw him, her heart jumped from the old love to the pain of abandonment. She wished it would settle on one side or the other.

Several mornings later, she slipped through the estuaries in an early fog, the compass tucked in her knapsack, though she would not likely need it. She planned to search for rare wild flowers on a wooded tongue of sand that jutted into the sea, but part of her scanned the waterways for Tate's boat.

The fog turned stubborn and lingered, twisting its tendrils around tree snags and low-lying limbs. The air was still; even the birds were quiet as she eased forward through the channel. Nearby, a *clonk, clonk* sounded as a slow-moving oar tapped a gunwale, and then a boat emerged ghoul-like from the haze.

Colors, which had been muted by the dimness, formed into shapes as they moved into the light. Golden hair beneath a red cap. As if coming in from a dream, Tate stood in the stern of his old fishing boat poling through the channel. Kya cut her engine and rowed backward into a thicket to watch him pass. Always backward to watch him pass.

At sundown, calmer, heart back in place, Kya stood on the beach, and recited:

> "Sunsets are never simple.
> Twilight is refracted and reflected
> But never true.
> Eventide is a disguise
> Covering tracks,
> Covering lies.
>
> "We don't care
> That dusk deceives.
> We see brilliant colors,
> And never learn
> The sun has dropped
> Beneath the earth
> By the time we see the burn.
>
> "Sunsets are in disguise,
> Covering truths, covering lies.
>
> *"A.H."*

36

To Trap a Fox

1969

Joe walked through the opened door of the sheriff's office. "Okay, got the report."

"Let's have a look."

Both men scanned quickly to the last page. Ed said, "That's it. A perfect match. Fibers from her hat were on Chase's jacket as he lay dead." The sheriff slapped the report across his wrist, then continued. "Let's review what we have here. Number one, the shrimper will testify that he saw Miss Clark boating toward the fire tower just before Chase fell to his death. His colleague will back him up. Two, Patti Love said Miss Clark made the shell necklace for Chase, and it disappeared the night he died. Three, fibers from her hat were on his jacket. Four, motive: the woman wronged. And an alibi we can refute. That should do it."

"A better motive might help," Joe said. "Being jilted doesn't seem like enough."

"It's not like we're finished with the investigation, but we have enough to bring her in for questioning. Probably enough to charge her. We'll see how it goes once we get her here."

"Well, that's the problem, isn't it? How? She's outrun everybody for years. Truant officers, census takers, *you name it*, she's outwit 'em all. Includin' us. We go out there chasin' her through swamp grass, we'll make fools of ourselves."

"I'm not afraid of that. Just because nobody else could catch her doesn't mean we can't. But that wouldn't be the smartest way of doing it. I say we set a trap."

"Oh yeah. Well," the deputy said, "I know a thing or two 'bout trappin'. And when you go to trap a fox, it's usually the trap that gets foxed. It's not like we have surprise on our side. We been out there knockin' on her door enough to scare off a brown bear. What about the hounds? That'd be a sure thing."

The sheriff was silent a few seconds. "I don't know. Maybe I'm getting old and soft at the grand ol' age of fifty-one. But running down a woman with hounds for questioning doesn't seem right. It's fine for escaped convicts, people already convicted of some crime. But, like everybody else, she's innocent until proven guilty, and I can't see setting hounds on a female suspect. Maybe as a last resort, but not yet."

"Okay. What kinda trap?"

"That's what we gotta figure out."

On December 15, as Ed and Joe discussed options of how to bring Kya in, someone knocked on the door. The large form of a man loomed behind the frosted glass.

"Come on in," the sheriff called.

As the man stepped inside, Ed said, "Well, hello, Rodney. What can we do for you?"

Rodney Horn, a retired mechanic, spent most of his days fishing with his pal Denny Smith. The villagers knew him as quiet and settled, always in bib overalls. Never missed church, but wore his overalls there as well, with a nice fresh shirt ironed and starched stiff as a plank by his wife, Elsie.

Rodney took off his felt hat and held it in front of his belly. Ed offered him a chair, but Rodney shook his head. "This won't take long," he said. "Just something might be rel'vant to the Chase Andrews thing."

"What ya got?" Joe asked.

"Well, it was a while back, now. Me and Denny were out fishin' on August 30, this year, and we seen something out at Cypress Cove. Think it might be of interest to ya."

"Go ahead," the sheriff said. "But please sit down, Rodney. We'd all feel more comfortable if you sat."

Rodney took the chair offered and, for the next five minutes, told them his story. After he left, Ed and Joe looked at each other.

Joe said, "Well, now we've got motive."

"Let's get her in here."

37.

Gray Sharks

1969

Just days before Christmas and earlier in the morning than usual, Kya motored slowly and quietly toward Jumpin's. Ever since the sheriff or his deputy had been sneaking out to her place, trying to catch her at home—failed efforts she'd observed from the palmettos—she'd bought her gas and supplies before first light, when only fishermen were about. Now, low clouds scudded just above a sloshing sea, and to the east, a squall—twisted tightly like a whip—threatened from the horizon. She'd have to finish at Jumpin's quickly and get home before it hit. From a quarter of a mile out, she saw his wharf billowed in with fog. She slowed even more and looked around for other boats in the soggy quiet.

Finally, at about forty yards out, she could see Jumpin's form in the old chair leaning against the wall. She waved. He did not. He did not stand. He shook his head slightly, just a whisper. She let go of the throttle.

She waved again. Jumpin' stared at her, but did not move.

Jerking the stick, she turned abruptly back toward the sea. But coming in from the fog was a large boat, the sheriff at the helm. Another couple of boats, flanking. And just behind them, the squall.

Gunning her engine, she threaded the needle between the oncoming rigs, her boat banging whitecaps as she raced for the open sea. She wanted to cut back toward the marsh, but the sheriff was too close; he'd catch her before she got there.

The sea no longer swelled in symmetrical waves but tossed in confusion. The water grew meaner as the edge of the storm engulfed her. In seconds it released a torrent. She was soaked through, long strands of hair stringing across her face. She turned into the wind to keep from capsizing, but the sea pushed over the bow.

Knowing their boats were faster, she hunched forward into the ragged wind. Maybe she could lose them in this soup or dive into the sea and make a swim for it. Her mind raced through the details of jumping in, which seemed her best chance. This close to shore, there'd be a backwash or rip, which would zip her along underwater, much faster than they'd think she could swim. Popping up to breathe now and then, she could get to land and sneak out on a brushy shore.

Behind her their motors raced louder than the storm. Getting closer. How could she simply stop? She'd never given up. She had to jump now. But suddenly, like gray sharks they massed around her, pulling close. One of the boats whipped in front of her, and she rammed its side. Thrown back against the outboard, her neck jerked. The sheriff reached out and grabbed her gunwale, all of them wallowing in the churning wakes. Two men swung into her boat as the deputy said, "Miss Catherine Clark, you're under arrest for the murder of Mr. Chase Andrews. Ya have the right to remain silent . . ."

She didn't hear the rest of it. No one hears the rest of it.

38.

Sunday Justice

1970

Kya's eyes blinked shut against sharp light that poured from overhead lamps and windows as tall as the ceiling. For two months she'd lived in dimness, and now, opening her eyes again, caught a soft edge of the marsh outside. Rounded oaks sheltering shrub-sized ferns and winter holly. She tried to hold the vital green a second longer but was led by firm hands toward a long table and chairs where her attorney, Tom Milton, sat. Her wrists were cuffed in front, forcing her hands into an awkward prayer pose. Dressed in black slacks and a plain white blouse, with a single braid falling between her shoulder blades, she didn't turn her head to look at the spectators. Still, she felt the heat and rustle of people knotted into the courtroom for her murder trial. Could sense people's shoulders and heads waggling to catch a glimpse of her. To see her in handcuffs. A smell of sweat, old smoke, and cheap perfume increased her nausea. Coughing noises ceased but the hubbub rose as she neared her seat—all distant sounds to her, because mostly she heard the sickness of her own jagged breathing. She stared at the floorboards—highly polished heart pine—while the cuffs were removed, and then sat heavy into the chair. It was 9:30 A.M. on February 25, 1970.

Tom leaned close to her and whispered that everything would be all right. She said nothing but searched his eyes for sincerity, anything to hang on. Not that she believed him, but for the first time ever, she had to put herself in the charge of another. Rather tall for seventy-one years, he wore his thick white hair and frumpy linen suits with the accidental if clichéd grace of a country statesman. He moved gently and spoke quietly behind a pleasant smile that lived on his face.

Judge Sims had appointed a young attorney for Miss Clark, since she had taken no action to do so herself, but when Tom Milton heard of this, he came out of retirement and requested to represent her pro bono. Like everyone else, he had heard stories about the Marsh Girl, and over the years had seen her occasionally, either drifting sleekly through waterways as part of the current or scurrying from the grocery like a coon from a rubbish bin.

When he first visited Kya in jail two months ago, he'd been led into a small dark room, where she sat at a table. She had not looked up at him. Tom had introduced himself, saying he would represent her, but she didn't speak or raise her eyes. He had an overpowering urge to reach out and pat her hand, but something—maybe her upright posture or the way she stared, vacant-eyed—shielded her from touch. Moving his head at different angles—trying to capture her eyes—he explained the court procedures, what she should expect, and then asked her some questions. But she never answered, never moved, and never looked at him. As they led her from the room, she turned her head and glimpsed through a small window where she could see the sky. Seabirds shrieked over the town harbor, and Kya seemed to be watching their songs.

On his next visit Tom reached into a brown paper bag and slid a glossy coffee-table book toward her. Titled *The Rarest Shells of the World*, it opened to life-sized oil paintings of shells from the most distant shores on Earth. Her mouth partly open, she turned slowly through the pages, nodding at particular specimens. He gave her time. Then, once again he spoke to her, and this time she looked into his eyes. With easy patience, he explained the court procedures and even drew a picture of the courtroom, showing the jury box, the judge's bench, where the attorneys and she would sit. Then he added stick figures of the bailiff, the judge, and the recorder and explained their roles.

As on the first meeting, he tried to explain the evidence against her and to ask about her whereabouts on the night Chase died, but she pulled back into her shell at any mention of details. Later, when he stood to leave, she slid the book back across the table, but he said, "No, I brought it for you. It's yours."

She bit her lips and blinked.

And now in the courtroom for the first time, he tried to distract her from the bustle behind them by pointing out the features of the courtroom in the drawing. But diversion was useless. By 9:45 A.M. the gallery overflowed with villagers filling every pew and buzzed with high-pitched comments about the evidence, the death penalty. A small balcony at the rear seated twenty more, and though not marked, everybody understood colored people were restricted to the balcony. Today, it was filled mostly with whites, with only a few blacks, this being a white case through and through. Sectioned off near the front sat a few journalists from the *Atlanta Constitution* and the *Raleigh Herald*. People who couldn't find seats bunched along the back wall and along the sides by the tall windows. Fidgeting, muttering, gossiping. The Marsh Girl put up for murder; it didn't get any better than this. Sunday Justice, the courthouse cat—his back black, his face white with a black mask around green eyes—stretched out in a puddle of sunlight in one of the deep windowsills. A courthouse fixture for years, he cleared the basement of rats and the courtroom of mice, earning his place.

Because Barkley Cove was the first village settled in this torn and marshy stretch of the North Carolina coast, the Crown had declared it the county seat and built the original courthouse in 1754. Later, even though other towns such as Sea Oaks became more populated and developed, Barkley Cove remained the official hub for county government.

Lightning struck the original courthouse in 1912, burning much of the wooden structure to ashes. Rebuilt the next year on the same square at the end of Main Street, it was a brick two-story with twelve-foot windows trimmed in granite. By the 1960s, wild grasses and palmettos, and even a few cattails, had moved in from the marsh and taken over the once-groomed grounds. A lily-choked lagoon flooded in spring and, over the years, had eaten part of the sidewalk.

In contrast, the courtroom itself, designed to replicate the original, was imposing. The elevated judge's bench, made of dark mahogany with a colorful inlay of the state's seal, stood under multiple flags, including the Confederate. The half wall of the jury box, also of mahogany, was trimmed in red cedar, and the windows that lined one side of the room framed the sea.

As the officials entered the courtroom, Tom pointed to the stick figures in his drawing and explained who they were. "That's the bailiff, Hank Jones," he said as a lanky man of sixty with a hairline that receded past his ears, making his head almost exactly half bald and half not, walked to the front of the room. He wore a gray uniform and a wide belt, hung with a radio, a flashlight, an impressive set of keys, and a holstered Colt six-shooter.

Mr. Jones called out to the crowd. "Sorry, folks, but y'all know the fire marshal's rules. If ya don't have a seat, ya gotta leave."

"That's Miss Henrietta Jones, the bailiff's daughter, the court recorder," Tom explained as a young woman, as tall and thin as her father, walked in quietly and sat at a desk near the judge's bench. Already seated, the prosecuting attorney, Mr. Eric Chastain, unpacked note pads from his briefcase. Eric, a broad-chested, redheaded man of nearly six feet, dressed in blue suits and wide bright ties purchased at Sears, Roebuck in Asheville.

Bailiff Jones called, "All rise. This court is in session. The Honorable Judge Harold Sims presiding." Sudden silence fell. The chamber door opened and Judge Sims entered and nodded for everyone to sit, and asked both the prosecuting and defense attorneys to approach the bench. A large-boned man with a round face and bold white sideburns, he lived in Sea Oaks but had officiated over Barkley Cove cases for nine years. He was generally considered to be a no-nonsense, levelheaded, and fair arbitrator. His voice boomed across the room.

"Mr. Milton, your motion to relocate this trial to another county on the grounds that Miss Clark cannot get a fair trial due to prejudices against her in this community is denied. I accept that she has lived in unusual circumstances and been subjected to some prejudice, but I see no evidence that she has endured more prejudices than many people on trial in small towns all across this nation. And some large towns, for that matter. We will proceed here and now." Nods of approval eased through the room as the attorneys returned to their seats.

He continued. "Catherine Danielle Clark of Barkley County, North

Carolina, you are charged with murder in the first degree of Chase Lawrence Andrews, formerly of Barkley Cove. First-degree murder is defined as a premeditated act and, in such cases, the state is allowed to seek the death penalty. The prosecutor has announced that they will do so if you are found guilty." The room murmured.

Tom seemed to have inched slightly closer to Kya, and she didn't deny herself that comfort.

"We will begin the jury selection." Judge Sims turned toward the first two rows filled with potential jurors. As he read off a list of rules and conditions, Sunday Justice jumped down from the windowsill with a thud and, in one fluid motion, leapt onto the judge's bench. Absent-mindedly, Judge Sims stroked the cat's head as he continued.

"In capital cases, the State of North Carolina allows a juror to be excused if he or she does not believe in the death penalty. Please raise your hand if you will not or cannot impose the death sentence if a guilty verdict is delivered." No hands were raised.

"Death penalty" was all Kya heard.

The judge continued. "Another legitimate reason to be excused from the jury is if you have now or had in the past such a close relationship with either Miss Clark or Mr. Andrews that you cannot be objective in this case. Please let me know now if you feel this is true."

From the middle of the second row, Mrs. Sally Culpepper lifted her hand and stated her name. Her gray hair was pulled back severely in a tiny knot, and her hat, suit, and shoes bore the same dull brown.

"All right, Sally, tell me what's on your mind," the judge said.

"As you know, I was the truant officer for Barkley County for nearly twenty-five years. Miss Clark was one of my cases, and so I had some dealings with her, or tried to."

Kya couldn't see Mrs. Culpepper or anyone in the main gallery unless she turned around, which of course she'd never do. But she remembered clearly the last time Mrs. Culpepper sat in the car while the man in the fedora tried to chase her down. Kya had been as easy on the old man as she could, taking off noisily through brambles to give him a clue, then circling back and hiding in some bushes next to the car. But Fedora ran in the opposite direction toward the beach.

Crouching there, Kya shook a holly branch against the car door, and Mrs. Culpepper looked out the window directly into her eyes. She thought at the time that the truant lady smiled slightly. In any case, she made no attempt to give her away when Fedora returned, cussing up a streak, then driving down the road for good.

Now, Mrs. Culpepper said to the judge, "Well, since I had dealings with her, I don't know if that means I should be excused."

Judge Sims said, "Thank you, Sally. Some of you may have dealt with Miss Clark in the shops or in official ways, as in Mrs. Culpepper's case, the truant officer. The point is: can you listen to the testimony given here and decide whether she's guilty or innocent based on the evidence, not on past experience or feelings?"

"Yessir, I'm sure I can do that. Your Honor."

"Thank you, Sally, you can stay."

By 11:30 seven women and five men sat in the jury box. From there Kya could see them and stole glances at their faces. Most of them she recognized from the village, though she knew few of the names. Mrs. Culpepper sat squarely in the middle and gave slight comfort to Kya. But next to her sat Teresa White, blond wife of the Methodist preacher, who years ago had rushed from the shoe shop to whisk her daughter away from Kya as she stood on the curb after having lunch in the diner with Pa—that one and only time. Mrs. White, who had told her daughter that Kya was dirty, now sat on the jury.

Judge Sims called for a lunch recess until 1:00 P.M. The diner would bring over tuna fish, chicken salad, and ham sandwiches for the jurors, who would eat in the deliberation room. To be fair to the town's two eating establishments, the Dog-Gone Beer Hall would deliver hot dogs, chili, and shrimp po'boys on alternative days. They always brought something for the cat, too. Sunday Justice preferred the po'boys.

39.

Chase by Chance

1969

A fog was lifting from an August morning in 1969 as Kya motored to a remote peninsula the locals called Cypress Cove, where she had once seen rare toadstools. August was late for mushrooms, but Cypress Cove was cool and moist, so perhaps she could find the rare species again. More than a month had passed since Tate had left the compass for her on the feather stump, and though she'd seen him in the marsh, she hadn't ventured close enough to thank him for the gift. Neither had she used the compass, though it was tucked safely in one of the many pockets of her knapsack.

Moss-draped trees hugged the bank, and their low-hanging limbs formed a cave close to the shore through which she glided, searching the thickets for small orange mushrooms on slender stalks. And finally she saw them, bold and brilliant, clinging to the sides of an old stump, and, after beaching her boat, sat cross-legged in the cove, drawing them.

Suddenly she heard footsteps on the duff and then a voice: "Well, look who's here. My Marsh Girl." Whirling around, standing at the same time, she stood face-to-face with Chase.

"Hello, Kya," he said. She looked around. How had he gotten here? She'd heard no boat. He read her question. "I was fishing, saw ya pass, so landed over yonder on the other side."

"Please just go," she said, stuffing her pencils and pad in the knapsack.

But he put his hand on her arm. "C'mon, Kya. I'm sorry about how things turned out." He leaned in, wisps of breakfast bourbon on his breath.

"Don't touch me!"

"Hey, I said I'm sorry. Ya knew we couldn't get married. Ya never coulda lived near town. But I always cared about ya; I stayed by ya."

"Stayed by me! What does that mean? Leave me alone." Kya tucked the knapsack under her arm and walked toward the boat, but he grabbed her arm, holding hard.

"Kya, there'll never be anybody else like ya, never. And I know ya love me." She ripped her arm from his hands.

"You're wrong! I'm not sure I ever loved you. But you talked to *me* about marriage, remember? You talked about building a house for you and me. Instead I found out about *your* engagement *to somebody else* in the newspaper. Why'd you do that? Why, Chase!"

"C'mon, Kya. It was impossible. Ya must've known it wouldn't work. What's wrong with how things were? Let's go back to what we had." He reached for her shoulders and pulled her toward him.

"Let go of me!" She twisted, tried to yank away, but he gripped her with both hands, hurting her arms. He put his mouth on hers and kissed her. She threw her arms up, knocking his hands away. She pulled her head back, hissing, "Don't you dare."

"There's my lynx. Wilder than ever." Grabbing her shoulders, he clipped the back of her knees with one of his legs and pushed her to the ground. Her head bounced hard on the dirt. "I know ya want me," he said, leering.

"No, stop!" she screamed. Kneeling, he jammed his knee in her stomach, knocking the breath from her, as he unzipped his jeans and pulled them down.

She reared up, pushing him with both hands. Suddenly he slugged her face with his right fist. A sick popping sound rang out inside her head. Her neck snapped back, and her body was thrown backward onto the ground. Just like Pa hitting Ma. Her mind blanked for seconds against a pounding pain; then she twisted and turned, trying to squirm out from under him, but he was too strong. Holding both her arms over her head with one hand, he unzipped her shorts and ripped down her panties as she kicked at him. She screamed, but there was no one to hear. Kicking at the ground, she struggled to free herself, but he grabbed her waist and flipped her over onto her stomach. Shoved her throbbing face into the dirt, then reached under her belly and pulled her pelvis up to him as he knelt behind.

"I'm not lettin' ya go this time. Like it or not, you're mine."

Finding strength from somewhere primal, she pushed against the ground with her knees and arms and reared up, at the same time swinging her elbow back across his jaw. As his head swung to the side, she struck him wildly with her fists until he lost his balance and sprawled backward onto the dirt. Then, taking aim, she kicked him in his groin, square and solid.

He bent double and rolled on his side, holding his testicles and writhing. For good measure, she kicked him in the back, knowing exactly where his kidneys lay. Several times. Hard.

Pulling up her shorts, she grabbed the knapsack and ran to her boat. Snapping the starter rope, she looked back as he rose to his hands and knees, moaning. She cussed until the motor cranked. Expecting him to chase after her any second, she turned the tiller sharply and accelerated away from the bank just as he stood. Her hands shaking, she zipped up her pants and held her body tight with one arm. Wild-eyed, she looked out to sea and saw another fishing rig nearby, two men staring at her.

40

Cypress Cove

1970

After lunch, Judge Sims asked the prosecutor, "Eric, are you ready to call your first witness?"

"We are, Your Honor." In former murder cases, Eric usually called the coroner first because his testimony introduced material evidence such as the murder weapon, time and place of death, and crime scene photographs, all of which made sharp impressions on the jurors. But in this case, there was no murder weapon, no fingerprints or footprints, so Eric intended to begin with motive.

"Your Honor, the People call Mr. Rodney Horn."

Everyone in court watched Rodney Horn step onto the witness stand and swear to tell the truth. Kya recognized his face even though she'd seen it for only a few seconds. She turned away. A retired mechanic, he was one of them, spending most of his days fishin', huntin', or playin' poker at the Swamp Guinea. Could hold his likker like a rain barrel. Today, as ever, he wore his denim bib overalls with a clean plaid shirt, starched so stiff the collar stood at attention. He held his fishing cap in his left hand as he was sworn in with the right, then sat down in the witness box, hat on his knee.

Eric stepped casually to the witness stand. "Good morning, Rodney."

"Mornin', Eric."

"Now, Rodney, I believe you were fishing with a friend near Cypress Cove on the morning of August 30, 1969? Is that correct?"

"That's 'xactly right. Me and Denny were out there fishin'. Been there since dawn."

"For the record, that would be Denny Smith?"

"Yeah, me 'n' Denny."

"All right. I would like you to tell the court what you saw that morning."

"Well, like I said, we been there since dawn, and it was near 'leven I reckon, and hadn't had a nibble for some time, so we was 'bout to pull our lines and head out, when we heard a commotion in the trees over on the point. In the woods."

"What kind of commotion?"

"Well, there was voices, kinda muffled at first, then louder. A man and a woman. But we couldn't see 'em, just heard them like they was fussin'."

"Then what happened?"

"Well, the woman started hollerin', so we motored over to get a better look. See if she was in trouble."

"And what did you see?"

"Well, by the time we got closer, we seen the woman was standin' next to the man and was kicking him right in the . . ." Rodney looked at the judge.

Judge Sims said, "Where did she kick him? You can say it."

"She kicked him right in the balls and he slumped over on his side, moanin' and groanin'. Then she kicked him again and again in his back. Mad as a mule chewin' bumblebees."

"Did you recognize the woman? Is she in the courtroom today?"

"Yeah, we knew 'er all right. It's that 'un there, the defendant. The one folks call the Marsh Girl."

Judge Sims leaned toward the witness. "Mr. Horn, the defendant's name is Miss Clark. Do not refer to her by any other name."

"A'right, then. It was Miss Clark we seen."

Eric continued. "Did you recognize the man she was kicking?"

"Well, we couldn't see him then 'cause he was writhin' and wigglin' around on the ground. But a few minutes later he stood up and it was Chase Andrews, the quarterback a few years back."

"And then what happened?"

"She came stumblin' out toward her boat, and well, she was part-way undressed. Her shorts 'round her ankles and her knickers 'round her knees. She was tryin' to pull up her shorts and run at the same time. The whole time shoutin' at him. She went to her boat, jumped in, and zoomed away, still pullin' at her pants. When she passed us by, she looked at us right in the eyes. That's how I know 'xactly who it was."

"You said she was shouting at him the entire time she was running toward her boat. Did you hear exactly what she said?"

"Yeah, we could hear her plain as day by then 'cause we were pretty close."

"Please tell the court what you heard her shout."

"She was screamin', 'Leave me alone, you bastard! You bother me again, I'll kill ya!'"

A loud murmur shot through the courtroom and didn't stop. Judge Sims banged his gavel. "That's it. That'll do it."

Eric said to his witness, "That will be all, thank you, Rodney. No further questions. Your witness."

Tom brushed past Eric and stepped to the witness stand.

"Now, Rodney, you testified that at first, when you heard those muffled but loud voices, you couldn't see what was going on between Miss Clark and Mr. Andrews. Is that correct?"

"That's right. We couldn't see 'em till we moved up some."

"And you said the woman, who you later identified as Miss Clark, was hollering as if she was in trouble. Correct?"

"Yeah."

"You didn't see any kissing or any sexual behavior between two consenting adults. You heard a woman shouting like she was being attacked, as if she was in trouble. Isn't that correct?"

"Yeah."

"So, isn't it possible that when Miss Clark kicked Mr. Andrews she was defending herself—a woman alone in the woods—against a very strong, athletic man? A former quarterback, who had attacked her?"

"Yeah, I reckon that's possible."

"No further questions."

"Redirect?"

"Yes, Your Honor," Eric said, standing at the prosecution table.

"So, Rodney, no matter whether certain behavior was consensual or not between the two of them, is it accurate to say that the defendant, Miss Clark, was extremely mad at the deceased, Chase Andrews?"

"Yeah, plenty mad."

"Mad enough to scream that if he bothered her again, she would kill him. Isn't that correct?"

"Yeah, that's how it was."

"No further questions, Your Honor."

41.

A Small Herd

1969

Kya's hands fumbled at the tiller as she looked back to see if Chase was following in his boat from Cypress Cove. She motored fast to her lagoon and limp-ran to the shack on swelling knees. In the kitchen, she dropped to the floor, crying, touching her swollen eye and spitting grit from her mouth. Then listened for sounds of him coming.

She had seen the shell necklace. He still wore it. How could that be?

"You're mine," he'd said. He'd be mad as hell that she kicked him and he'd come for her. He might come today. Or wait for night.

She couldn't tell anybody. Jumpin' would insist they call in the sheriff, but the law would never believe the Marsh Girl over Chase Andrews. She wasn't sure what the two fishermen had seen, but they'd never defend her. They'd say she had it coming because, before Chase left her, she'd been seen smooching with him for years, behaving unladylike. *Actin' the ho*, they'd say.

Outside, the wind howled from the sea and she worried that she'd never hear his motor coming, so, moving slowly from the pain, she packed biscuits, cheese, and nuts in her knapsack and, head low against a manic gale, hurried through cord grass along channels toward the reading cabin. The walk took forty-five minutes, and at every sound her sore and stiff body flinched and her head jerked to the side, scanning the undergrowth. Finally, the old log structure, up to its knees in tall grasses and clinging to the creek bank, whispered into view. Here the wind was calmer. The soft meadow quiet. She'd never told Chase about her hideout, but he might have known about it. She wasn't sure.

The packrat smell was gone. After the ecology lab hired Tate, he and Scupper fixed up the old cabin so he could stay overnight on some of his expeditions. They had shored up the walls, straightened the roof, and brought in basic furniture—a small quilt-covered bed, a cookstove, a table and chair. Pots and pans hung from the rafters. Then, out-of-place and plastic covered, a microscope sat on a folding table. In the corner, an old metal trunk stored tins of baked beans, sardines. Nothing to bring the bears in.

But inside, she felt trapped, unable to see if Chase was coming, so she sat on the edge of the creek, searching the grassy water land with her right eye. The left was swollen shut.

Downstream a herd of five female deer ignored her and wandered along the water's edge nibbling leaves. If only she could join in, belong to them. Kya knew it wasn't so much that the herd would be incomplete without one of its deer, but that each deer would be incomplete without her herd. One lifted her head, dark eyes searching north into the trees, stomping her right front foot, then the left. The others looked up, then whistled in alarm. Instantly, Kya's good eye probed the forest for signs of Chase or some other predator. But all was quiet. Perhaps the breeze had startled them. They stopped stomping but slowly moved away into the tall grass, leaving Kya alone and uneasy.

She scanned the meadow again for intruders, but the listening and searching sucked all her energy, so she went back into the cabin. Dug sweaty cheese from her bag. Then slumped on the floor and ate mindlessly, touching her bruised cheek. Her face, arms, and legs were cut and smeared with bloody grit. Knees scratched and throbbing. She sobbed, fighting shame, suddenly spitting the cheese out in a chunky, wet spray.

She'd brought this on herself. Consorting unchaperoned. A natural wanting had led her unmarried to a cheap motel, but still unsatisfied. Sex under flashing neon lights, marked only by blood smudged across the sheets like animal tracks.

Chase had probably bragged about their doings to everyone. No wonder people shunned her—she was unfit, disgusting.

As the half moon appeared between fast-moving clouds, she searched through the small window for manlike forms, hunched and sneaking. Finally she crawled into Tate's bed and slept under his quilt. Waking often, listening for footsteps, then pulling the soft fabric closely around her face.

More crumbling cheese for breakfast. Her face darkened to green-purple now, eye swollen like a boiled egg, neck stove-up. Parts of her upper lip twisted grotesquely. Like Ma, monstrous, afraid to go home. In sudden clarity Kya saw what Ma had endured and why she left. "Ma, Ma," she whispered. "I see. Finally I understand why you had to leave and never come back. I'm sorry I didn't know, that I couldn't help you." Kya dropped her head and sobbed. Then jerked her head up and said, "I will never live like that—a life wondering when and where the next fist will fall."

She hiked home that afternoon, but even though she was hungry and needed supplies, she didn't go to Jumpin's. Chase might see her there. Besides, she didn't want anyone, especially Jumpin', to see her battered face.

After a simple meal of hard bread and smoked fish, she sat on the edge of her porch bed, staring through the screen. Just at that moment she noticed a female praying mantis stalking along a branch near her face. The insect was plucking moths with her articulated forelegs, then chewing them up, their wings still flapping in her mouth. A male mantis, head high and proud as a pony, paraded along to court her. She appeared interested, her antennae flailing about like wands. His embrace might have been tight or tender, Kya couldn't tell, but while he probed about with his copulatory organ to fertilize her eggs, the female turned back her long, elegant neck and bit off his head. He was so busy humping, he didn't notice. His neck stump waved about as he continued his business, and she nibbled on his thorax, and then his wings. Finally, his last foreleg protruded from her mouth as his headless, heartless lower body copulated in perfect rhyme.

Female fireflies draw in strange males with dishonest signals and eat them; mantis females devour their own mates. Female insects, Kya thought, know how to deal with their lovers.

After a few days, she boated into the marsh, exploring areas Chase wouldn't know, but was jumpy and alert, making it difficult to paint. Her eye was still puffed around a thin slit, and the bruise had leached its nauseated colors across half her face. Much of her body throbbed with pain. At the chirp of a chipmunk she whirled around, listened keenly to the caws of crows—a language before words were, when communication was simple and clear—and wherever she went, mapped an escape route in her mind.

42.

A Cell

1970

Murky shafts of light streamed through the tiny window of Kya's cell. She stared at dust motes, dancing silently in one direction as though following some dreamy leader. When they hit the shadows, they vanished. Without the sun they were nothing.

She pulled the wooden crate, her only table, under the window, which was seven feet above the floor. Dressed in a gray jumpsuit with *COUNTY INMATE* printed on the back, she stood on the crate and stared at the sea, just visible beyond the thick glass and bars. Whitecaps slapped and spat, and pelicans, heads turning for fish, flew low over the waves. If she stretched her neck far to the right she could see the dense crown of the marsh's edge. Yesterday she had seen an eagle dive and twist toward a fish.

The county jail consisted of six twelve-by-twelve cells in a cement-block, one-story building behind the sheriff's office at the edge of town. The cells were in a row down the length of the building—only on one side, so inmates couldn't see one another. Three of the walls were damp cement blocks; the fourth was made of bars including the locked door.

Each cell had a wooden bed with a bumpy cotton mattress, a feather pillow, sheets, one gray wool blanket, a sink, and a wooden-crate table, plus a toilet. Over the sink was not a mirror but a picture of Jesus, framed there by the Ladies' Baptist Auxiliary. The only allowance made for her, the first female inmate—other than overnighters—in years, was a gray plastic curtain that could be pulled around the sink and toilet.

For two months before the trial, she'd been held in this cell without bail because of her failed attempt to escape the sheriff in her boat. Kya wondered who started using the word *cell* instead of *cage*. There must have been a moment in time when humanity demanded this shift. Self-scratched red webbing streaked her arms. For untracked minutes, sitting on her bed, she studied strands of her hair, plucking them like feathers. As the gulls do.

Standing on the crate, craning her neck toward the marsh, she recalled an Amanda Hamilton poem:

Broken Gull of Brandon Beach

Winged soul, you danced the skies,
And startled dawn with shrilling cries.
You followed sails and braved the sea,
Then caught the wind back to me.

You broke your wing; it dragged the land
And etched your mark upon the sand.
When feathers break, you cannot fly,
But who decides the time to die?

. . .

You disappeared, I know not where.
But your wing-marks still linger there.
A broken heart cannot fly,
But who decides the time to die?

Even though the inmates couldn't see one another, the only other occupants—two men at the far end of the row—spent much of each day and evening jabbering. Both were doing thirty days for starting a fight, which ended in broken bar mirrors and a few bones, over who could spit the farthest at the Dog-Gone Beer Hall. Mostly they lay on their beds, calling to each other from their adjoining cells, sounding like drum squatters. Much of the banter was gossip they'd heard about Kya's case from their visitors. Especially her odds of getting the death penalty, which had not been issued in the county for twenty years, and never to a woman.

Kya heard every word. Being dead didn't bother her; they couldn't scare her with threats of ending this shadow life. But the process of being killed by another's hand, planned out and set to schedule, was so unthinkable it stopped her breath.

Sleep avoided her, slinking around the edges, then darting away. Her mind would plunge along deep walls of sudden slumber—an instant of bliss—then her body would shudder her awake.

She stepped down from the crate and sat on the bed, knees tucked under her chin. They'd brought her here after court, so it might be six by now. Only one hour passed. Or maybe not even that.

43.

A Microscope

1969

In early September, more than a week after Chase attacked her, she walked down her beach. The wind ripped at a letter in her hand, so she held it against her breasts. Her editor had invited her to meet him in Greenville, writing that he understood she didn't come to town often, but he wanted to meet her, and the publisher would pay her expenses.

The day stood clear and hot, so she motored into the marsh. At the end of a narrow estuary, she rounded a grassy bend and saw Tate squatting on a wide sandbar, dipping up water samples in little vials. His cruiser–cum–research vessel was tied to a log and drifted across the channel, blocking it. She heaved on the tiller. Some of the swelling and bruising on her face had diminished, but ugly green and purple splotches still circled her eye. She panicked. She could not let Tate see her battered face and tried to turn her boat around quickly.

But he looked up and waved. "Pull in, Kya. I've got a new microscope to show you."

This had the same effect as the truant officer calling to her about chicken pie. She slowed but didn't answer.

"Come on. You won't believe this magnification. You can see the pseudopods on the amoebas."

She'd never seen an amoeba, certainly not its body parts. And seeing Tate again brought a peace, a calmness. Deciding that she could keep her bruised face turned away from him, she beached her boat and walked through the shallow water toward his. She wore cutoff jeans and a white T-shirt, her hair free. Standing at the top of the stern ladder, he held out his hand and she took it, looking away from him.

The cruiser's soft beige blended into the marsh, and Kya had never seen anything as fine as the teak deck and brass helm. "Come on down," he said, stepping below into the cabin. She scanned the captain's desk, the small kitchen outfitted better than her own, and the living area that had been converted into an onboard laboratory with multiple microscopes and racks of vials. Other instruments hummed and blinked.

Tate fiddled with the largest microscope and adjusted the slide.

"Here, just a minute." He touched a drop of marsh water onto the slide, covered it with another, and focused the eyepiece. He stood. "Have a look."

Kya leaned over gently, as if to kiss a baby. The microscope's light reflected in her dark pupils, and she drew in a breath as a Mardi Gras of costumed players pirouetted and careened into view. Unimaginable headdresses adorned astonishing bodies so eager for more life, they frolicked as though caught in a circus tent, not a single bead of water.

She put her hand on her heart. "I had no idea there were so many and so beautiful," she said, still looking.

He identified some odd species, then stepped back, watching her. *She feels the pulse of life*, he thought, *because there are no layers between her and her planet.*

He showed her more slides.

She whispered, "It's like never having seen the stars, then suddenly seeing them."

"Would you like some coffee?" he asked softly.

She raised her head. "No, no, thank you." Then she backed away from the microscope, moving toward the galley. Awkwardly, keeping her brown-green eye turned away.

Tate was accustomed to Kya being guarded, but her behavior seemed more distant and stranger than ever. Continuously keeping her head turned at an angle.

"Come on, Kya. Just have a cup of coffee." He'd already moved into the kitchenette and poured water into a machine that dripped out a strong brew. She stood by the ladder to the deck above, and he handed her a mug, motioning for her to go up. He invited her to sit on the cushioned bench, but she stood at the stern. Catlike, she knew the exit. The brilliant white sandbar curved away from them under sheltering oaks.

"Kya . . ." He started to ask a question, but when she faced him, he saw the fading bruise on her cheek.

"What happened to your face?" He walked toward her, reaching to touch her cheek. She turned away.

"Nothing. I ran into a door in the middle of the night." He knew that wasn't true by the way she flung her hand to her face. Someone had hit her. Had it been Chase? Was she still seeing him even though he was married? Tate worked his jaw. Kya moved to put her mug down, as if she were going.

He forced calm. "Have you started a new book?"

"I'm almost finished with the one on mushrooms. My editor's coming to Greenville sometime at the end of October and wants me to meet him there. But I'm not sure."

"You should go. It'd be good to meet him. There's a bus from

Barkley every day, one at night, too. It doesn't take long. An hour and twenty minutes maybe, something like that."

"I don't know where to buy a ticket."

"The driver'll know everything. Just show up at the bus stop on Main; he'll tell you what you need to do. I think Jumpin' has the schedule tacked up in his store." He almost mentioned that he had ridden the bus many times from Chapel Hill, but thought it better not to remind her of those days, of her waiting on a July beach.

They were quiet for a while, sipping their coffee, listening to a pair of hawks whistling along the walls of a tall cloud.

He hesitated to offer more coffee, knowing she would leave if he did. So he asked about her mushroom book, explained the protozoans he studied. Any bait to keep her.

The afternoon light softened and a cool wind picked up. Putting the mug down again, she said, "I have to go."

"I was thinking of opening some wine. Would you like some?"

"No, thanks."

"Wait a second before you go," Tate said as he went below to the galley and returned with a bag of leftover bread and biscuits. "Please give my regards to the gulls."

"Thanks." She climbed down the ladder.

As she walked toward her boat, he called out, "Kya, it's gotten cooler, don't you want a jacket or something?"

"No. I'm fine."

"Here, at least take my cap," and he tossed a red ski cap toward her. She caught it and slung it back to him. He threw it again, farther, and she jogged across the sandbar, leaned low and scooped it up. Laughing, she jumped into her boat, cranked the motor, and, as she boated near him, pitched the hat back into his boat. He grinned and she giggled. Then they stopped laughing and simply looked at each other as they lobbed the cap back and forth until she motored around the bend. She sat down hard on the stern seat and put her hand over her mouth. "No," she said out loud. "I cannot fall for him again. I will not get hurt all over again."

Tate stayed at the stern. Clenching his fists at the image of someone hitting her.

She hugged the coastline just beyond the surf, heading south. On this route she would pass her beach before reaching the channel that led through the marsh to her shack. Usually she didn't stop at her beach, but motored through the maze of waterways to her lagoon, and then walked to the shore.

But as she passed by, the gulls spotted her and swarmed the boat. Big Red landed on the bow, bobbing his head. She laughed. "Okay then, you win." Breaking through the surf, she beached her boat behind tall sea oats and stood at the shoreline tossing the crumbs Tate had given her.

As the sun spread gold and pink across the water, she sat on the sand while the gulls settled around her. Suddenly she heard a motor and saw Chase's ski boat racing toward her channel. He could not see her boat behind the sea oats, but she was in plain sight on the open sand. Instantly she lay flat, turning her head to the side, so she could watch him. He stood at the helm, hair blowing back, face in an ugly scowl. But he didn't look in her direction as he turned into the channel toward her shack.

When he was out of sight, she sat up. If she hadn't beached here with the gulls, he would have caught her at home. She'd learned over and over from Pa: these men had to have the last punch. Kya had left Chase sprawled on the dirt. The two old fishermen had probably seen her flatten him. As Pa would have it, Kya had to be taught a lesson.

As soon as he discovered she wasn't at the shack, he'd walk here to her beach. She ran to her boat, throttled up, and headed back toward Tate. But she didn't want to tell Tate what Chase had done to her; shame overwhelmed reason. She slowed down and drifted on swells as the sun disappeared. She had to hide and wait for Chase to leave. If she didn't see him go, she wouldn't know when it was safe to motor home.

She turned into the channel, panicked that he could roar in her direction at any second. Her motor just above idle, so she could hear his boat, she eased into a backwater thicket of overhanging trees and brush. She reversed deeper into the undergrowth, pushing limbs aside until layers of leaves and the falling night hid her.

Breathing hard, she listened. Finally she heard his engine screaming across the soft evening air. She ducked lower as he approached, suddenly worried that the tip of her boat was visible. The sound came very close, and in seconds his boat zoomed by. She sat there for nearly thirty minutes until it was truly dark, then cruised home by starlight.

She took her bedding to the beach and sat with the gulls. They paid her no mind, preening outstretched wings before settling down on the sand like feathered stones. As they chortled softly and tucked their heads for the night, she lay as close to them as she could get. But even among their soft cooing and ruffling, Kya couldn't sleep. Mostly she tossed from one side to the other, sitting up each time the wind mimicked footfalls.

Dawn surf roared on a slapping wind that stung her cheeks. She sat up among the birds, who wandered nearby, stretching and kick-scratching. Big Red—eyes wide, neck cocked—seemed to have found something most interesting in his underwing, an act that would normally have made Kya laugh. But the birds brought her no cheer.

She walked to the water's edge. Chase would not let this go. Being isolated was one thing; living in fear, quite another.

She imagined taking one step after the other into the churning sea, sinking into the stillness beneath the waves, strands of her hair suspending like black watercolor into the pale blue sea, her long fingers and arms drifting up toward the backlit blaze of the surface. Dreams of escape—even through death—always lift toward the light. The dangling, shiny prize of peace just out of grasp until finally her body descends to the bottom and settles in murky quiet. Safe.

Who decides the time to die?

44.

Cell Mate

1970

Kya stood in the middle of her cell. Here she was in jail. If those she'd loved, including Jodie and Tate, hadn't left her, she wouldn't be here. Leaning on someone leaves you on the ground.

Before being arrested, she'd caught glimpses of a path back to Tate: an opening of her heart. Love lingering closer to the surface. But when he'd come to visit her in jail on several occasions, she had refused to see him. She wasn't sure why jail had closed her heart even tighter. Why she hadn't embraced the comfort he could give her in this place. It seemed that now, Kya being more vulnerable than ever, was reason to trust others even less. Standing in the most fragile place of her life, she turned to the only net she knew—herself.

Being thrown behind bars with no bail made clear how alone she was. The sheriff's offer of a phone call starkly reminded her: there was no one to call. The only phone number she knew in the world was Jodie's, and how could she call her brother and say she was in jail accused of murder? After all those years, how could she bother him with her troubles? And maybe shame played a part.

They had abandoned her to survive and defend herself. So here she was, by herself.

Once more she lifted the wondrous shell book Tom Milton had given her, by far her most treasured volume. Some biology texts were stacked on the floor, which the guard said Tate had brought, but she couldn't hold the words in place. Sentences wandered off in several directions, circling back to the beginning. Shell pictures were easier.

Footsteps clanked on the cheap tile floor and Jacob, a small black man who served as guard, appeared in front of her door. He held a large brown-paper package. "Sorry to bother ya, Miz Clark, but ya got a viz'tor. Ya gotta come with me."

"Who is it?"

"It's yo' lawya, Mr. Milton." Metal-to-metal *clanks* sounded, as Jacob unlocked her door and handed her the package. "An' this here's from Jumpin'." She laid the parcel on the bed and followed Jacob down the hall and into a room—even smaller than her cell. Tom Milton rose from his chair as she entered. Kya nodded at him and then looked out the window, where an enormous cumulus cloud with peach-colored cheeks puffed itself up.

"Good evening, Kya."

"Mr. Milton."

"Kya, please call me Tom. And what's wrong with your arm? Have you hurt yourself?"

She jerked her hand, covering the webs she'd scratched on her arms. "Just mosquito bites, I think."

"I'll talk to the sheriff; you shouldn't have mosquitoes in your—room."

Head down, she said, "Please, no, it's okay. I'm not worried about insects."

"All right, of course, I won't do anything you don't want. Kya, I came to talk about your options."

"What options?"

"I'll explain. It's hard to know at this point how the jury is leaning. The prosecution has a good case. It's not solid by any means, but considering how people in this town are prejudiced, you have to be prepared that it won't be easy for us to win. But there's the option of a plea bargain. Do you know what I'm referring to?"

"Not exactly."

"You have pleaded not guilty to first-degree murder. If we lose, you lose big: life in prison or, as you know, they are seeking the death penalty. Your option is to plead guilty to a lesser charge, say, manslaughter. If you were willing to say, yes, you did go to the tower that night, you did meet Chase there, you had a disagreement, and in a horrible accident he stepped backward through the grate, the trial might end immediately, you wouldn't have to go through any more of this drama, and we could negotiate with the prosecution over a sentence. Since you've never been charged with anything before, they'd probably sentence you to ten years, and you could be out in, say, six years. I know that sounds bad, but it's better than spending life in prison or the other."

"No, I won't say anything that implies guilt. I will not go to prison."

"Kya, I understand, but please take some time to think about it. You don't want to live your entire life in jail, nor do you want—the other."

Kya looked out the window again. "I don't need to think about it. I won't stay in jail."

"Well, we don't have to decide now. We have some time. Let's see how it goes. Before I leave, is there anything you want to discuss with me?"

"Please get me out of here. One way or—the other."

"I'll do my best to get you out, Kya. But don't give up. And please help me. Like I've mentioned before, you need to be engaged, look at the jurors now and then . . ."

But Kya had turned to leave.

Jacob led her back to the cell, where she picked up the package from Jumpin'—unwrapped by the warden and taped up haphazardly again. She opened it, saving and folding the paper. Inside was a basket with some tiny vials of paint, a brush, paper, and a paper bag of Mabel's corn muffins. The basket was lined with a nest of pine straw, some oak leaves, a few shells, and long strands of cattails. Kya sniffed deeply. Pinched her lips. Jumpin'. Mabel.

The sun had set; no dust motes to follow.

Later Jacob cleared away her supper tray. "I declare, Miz Clark, ya didn't eat much a'tall. Them poke chops and greens as good as dey git." She smiled lightly at him, then listened as his steps clomped to the end of the hall. She waited to hear the thick metal door shut with heavy finality.

Then something moved on the hall floor, just outside the bars. Her eyes swung there. Sunday Justice sat on his haunches staring at her dark eyes with his green ones.

Her heart raced. Locked up alone all these weeks, and now this creature could step wizardlike between the bars. Be with her. Sunday Justice broke the stare and looked down the hall, toward the inmates' talk. Kya was terrified that he would leave her and walk to them. But he looked back at her, blinked in obligatory boredom, and squeezed easily between the bars. Inside.

Kya breathed out. Whispered, "Please stay."

Taking his time, he sniffed his way around the cell, researching the damp cement walls, the exposed pipes, and the sink, all the while compelled to ignore her. A small crack in the wall was the most interesting to him. She knew because he flicked his thoughts on his tail. He ended his tour next to the small bed. Then, just like that, he jumped onto her lap and circled, his large white paws finding soft purchase on her thighs. Kya sat frozen, her arms slightly raised, so as not to interfere with his maneuvering. Finally, he settled as though he had nested here every night of his life. He looked at her. Gently she touched his head, then scratched his neck. A loud purr erupted like a current. She closed her eyes at such easy acceptance. A deep pause in a lifetime of longing.

Afraid to move, she sat stiff until her leg cramped, then shifted slightly to stretch her muscles. Sunday Justice, without opening his eyes, slid off her lap and curled up next to her side. She lay down fully clothed, and they both nestled in. She watched him sleep, then followed. Not falling toward a jolt, but a drifting, finally, into an empty calm.

Once during the night, she opened her eyes and watched him sleeping on his back, forepaws stretched one way, hind paws the other. But when she awoke at dawn, he was gone. A moan struggled against the strength of her throat.

Later, Jacob stood outside her cell, holding the breakfast tray with one hand, unlocking the door with the other. "Gotcha yo' oatmeal, Miz Clark."

She took the tray, saying, "Jacob, the black and white cat that sleeps in the courtroom. He was here last night."

"Oh, sorry as can be. That's Sundee Justice. Sometimes he slips in wif me and I don't see 'im 'cause of carryin' the suppa trays. I end up closin' 'im in with y'all." Kind enough not to say *locking*.

"It's fine. I liked having him here. Please, will you let him in whenever you see him after supper? Or anytime."

He looked at her with soft eyes. "'Course I can. I'll do that, Miz Clark; I sho' will. Can see he'd be mighty good comp'ny."

"Thank you, Jacob."

That evening, Jacob returned. "Here's yo' food now, Miz Clark. Fried chicken, mashed taters wif gravy from the diner. Hope ya can eat sump'm tonight, now."

Kya stood, looking around his feet. She took the tray. "Thank you, Jacob. Have you seen the cat?"

"Nome. Not a'tall. But I'll keep an eye out."

Kya nodded. She sat on the bed, the only place to sit, and stared at the plate. Here in jail was better food than she had seen all her life. She poked around the chicken, pushed the butter beans. Having found food, her stomach was lost.

Then, the sound of the lock turning, the heavy metal door swinging.

At the end of the hall she heard Jacob say, "Thar ya go, then, Mista Sundee Justice."

Without breathing, Kya stared at the floor outside her cell and within a few seconds Sunday Justice stepped into view. His markings were surprisingly stark and soft at the same time. No hesitation this time, he stepped into her cell and walked up to her. She put the plate on the floor and he ate the chicken—pulled the drumstick right onto the floor—then lapped up the gravy. Skipped the butter beans. She smiled through it all, then wiped the floor clean with tissue.

He jumped on her bed, and a sweet sleep wrapped them together.

Jacob stood outside her door the next day. "Miz Clark, ya got anotha viz'ter."

"Who is it?"

"It's Mr. Tate again. He's done come sev'ral times now, Miz Clark, either brings sump'm or asks to see ya. Won't ya see him today, Miz Clark? It's Saderdee, no court, nothin' to do in here the livelong day."

"All right, Jacob."

Jacob led her to the same dingy room where she had met Tom Milton. As she stepped through the door, Tate rose from his chair and walked quickly toward her. He smiled lightly, but his eyes revealed the sadness from seeing her here.

"Kya, you look good. I've been so worried. Thank you for seeing me. Sit down." They sat opposite each other while Jacob stood in the corner reading a newspaper with considerate concentration.

"Hello, Tate. Thanks for the books you brought." She acted calm, but her heart pulled into pieces.

"What else can I do for you?"

"Maybe you could feed the gulls if you're out my way."

He smiled. "Yes, I've been feeding them. Every other day or so." He made it sound easygoing but had driven or boated to her place every dawn and dusk to feed them.

"Thank you."

"I was in court, Kya, sitting right behind you. You never turned around, so I didn't know if you knew that. But I'll be there every day."

She looked out of the window.

"Tom Milton's very good, Kya. Probably the best lawyer in this part of the state. He'll get you out of here. Just hang on."

When again she didn't speak, he continued. "And as soon as you're out of here, we'll get back to exploring lagoons like in the old days."

"Tate, please, you have to forget me."

"I have never and will never forget you, Kya."

"You know I'm different. I don't fit with other people. I cannot be part of your world. Please, can't you understand, I'm afraid to be close with anybody ever again. I can't."

"I don't blame you, Kya, but . . ."

"Tate, listen to me. For years I longed to be with people. I really believed that someone would stay with me, that I would actually have friends and a family. Be part of a group. But no one stayed. Not you or one member of my family. Now I've finally learned how to deal with that and how to protect myself. But I can't talk about this now. I appreciate your coming to see me in here, I do. And maybe someday we can be friends, but I can't think about what comes next. Not in here."

"Okay. I understand. Really, I do."

After a short silence, he continued. "The great horns are already calling."

She nodded, almost smiled.

"Oh, and yesterday when I was at your place, you won't believe it, but a male Cooper's hawk landed right on your front steps."

Finally a smile as she thought of the Coop. One of her many private memories. "Yes, I believe it."

Ten minutes later, Jacob said their time was up and Tate had to leave. Kya thanked him again for coming.

"I'll keep feeding the gulls, Kya. And I'll bring you some books."

She shook her head and followed Jacob.

45.

Red Cap

1970

On Monday morning, after Tate's visit, when Kya was led into the courtroom by the bailiff, she kept her eyes away from the spectators, as she had before, and looked deep into the shadowy trees outside. But she heard a familiar sound, maybe a soft cough, and turned her head. There in the first row of seats, sitting with Tate, were Jumpin' and Mabel, who wore her church bonnet decked out with silk roses. Folks had made a stir when they walked in with Tate and sat downstairs in the "white area." But when the bailiff reported this to Judge Sims, still in his chambers, the judge told him to announce that anybody of any color or creed could sit anywhere they wanted in his courtroom, and if somebody didn't like it, they were free to leave. In fact, he'd make sure they did.

On seeing Jumpin' and Mabel, Kya felt a smidge of strength, and her back straightened slightly.

The next witness for the prosecution, Dr. Steward Cone, the coroner, had graying hair cut very short and wore glasses that sat too far down his nose, a habit that forced him to tilt his head back to see through the lenses. As he answered Eric's questions, Kya's mind wandered to the gulls. These long months in jail, she had pined for them, yet all along, Tate had been feeding them. They had not been abandoned. She thought of Big Red, how he always walked across her toes when she threw crumbs to them.

The coroner tossed his head back to adjust his glasses, the gesture bringing Kya back to the courtroom.

"So to recap, you've testified that Chase Andrews died between midnight and two o'clock on the night of October 29 or the morning of the thirtieth, 1969. The cause of death was extensive injuries to the brain and spinal cord due to a fall through an open grate of the fire tower, sixty-three feet to the ground. As he fell, he hit the back of his head on a support beam, a fact confirmed by blood and hair samples taken from the beam. Is all that correct according to your expert opinion?"

"Yes."

"Now, Dr. Cone, why would an intelligent and fit young man like Chase Andrews step through an open grate and fall to his death? To rule out one possibility, was there alcohol or any other substance in his blood that could have impaired his judgment?"

"No, there was not."

"Evidence presented previously demonstrates that Chase Andrews hit the back of his head on that support beam, not his forehead." Eric stood in front of the jury and took a large step. "But when I step forward, my head ends up slightly ahead of my body. Were I to step into a hole here in front of me, the momentum and the weight of my head would pitch me forward. Correct? Chase Andrews would have hit his forehead on the beam, not the back of his skull, if he was stepping forward. So isn't it true, Dr. Cone, that the evidence suggests that Chase was going backward when he fell?"

"Yes, the evidence would support that conclusion."

"So we can also conclude that if Chase Andrews was standing with his back to the opened grate and was pushed by someone, he would have fallen backward, not forward?" Before Tom could object, Eric said very quickly, "I'm not asking you to state that this is conclusive evidence that Chase was pushed backward to his death. I am simply making it clear that if someone pushed Chase backward through the hole, the wounds to his head from the beam would have coincided with those actually found. Is that correct?"

"Yes."

"All right. Dr. Cone, when you examined Chase Andrews in the clinic, the morning of October 30, was he wearing a shell necklace?"

"No."

To suppress the rising nausea, Kya focused on Sunday Justice grooming himself on a windowsill. Pretzeled into an impossible position, one leg straight in the air, he licked the inside tip of his tail. His own bath seemed to absorb and entertain him entirely.

A few minutes later, the prosecutor was asking, "Is it correct that Chase Andrews wore a denim jacket the night he died?"

"Yes, that is correct."

"And according to your official report, Dr. Cone, did you not find red wool fibers on his jacket? Fibers that were not from any piece of clothing he was wearing?"

"Yes."

Eric held up a clear plastic bag containing bits of red wool. "Are these the red fibers that were found on Chase Andrews's jacket?"

"Yes."

Eric lifted a larger bag from his desk. "And isn't it true that the red wool fibers found on Chase's jacket matched those on this red cap?" He handed it to the witness.

"Yes. These are my labeled samples, and the fibers from the cap and jacket matched exactly."

"Where was this cap found?"

"The sheriff found the cap in Miss Clark's residence." This was not generally known, and murmurs rippled through the crowd.

"Was there any evidence that she had ever worn the cap?"

"Yes. Strands of Miss Clark's hair were found in the cap."

Watching Sunday Justice in court got Kya thinking about how her family had never had a pet. Not one dog or cat. The only thing close was the female skunk—a silky, slinky, and sassy creature—who lived under the shack. Ma called her Chanel.

After a few near misses, they'd all gotten to know one another, and Chanel became very polite, only flashing her armament when the kids got too rowdy. She'd come and go, sometimes within feet of whoever was coming up or down the brick 'n' boards.

Every spring she'd escort her little kits on forays into the oak woods and along the slipstreams. Them scurrying behind, running into and over one another in black-and-white confusions.

Pa, of course, was always threatening to get rid of her, but Jodie, showing maturity far beyond his father's, deadpanned, "Another one'll just move in, and I always reckoned it's better the skunk ya know than the skunk ya don't know." She smiled now, thinking of Jodie. Then caught herself.

"So, Dr. Cone, on the night Chase Andrews died, the night he fell backward through an open grate—a posture consistent with being pushed by someone—fibers on his jacket came from a red cap found at Miss Clark's residence. And there were strands of Miss Clark's hair in the cap."

"Yes."

"Thank you, Dr. Cone. I have no further questions."

Tom Milton looked briefly at Kya, who watched the sky. The room leaned physically toward the prosecution as though the floor tipped, and it didn't help that Kya sat rigid and detached—carved from ice. He flicked his white hair from his forehead and approached the coroner for the cross-examination.

"Good morning, Dr. Cone."

"Good morning."

"Dr. Cone, you testified that the wound on the back of Chase Andrews's head was consistent with him going backward through the open hole. Isn't it true that if he stepped backward on his own and fell through the hole by accident, the results of hitting the back of his head would have been exactly the same?"

"Yes."

"Were there any bruises on his chest or arms that would coincide with him being pushed or shoved?"

"No. There was, of course, heavy bruising over his entire body from the fall. Mostly on the back of his body and legs. There were none that could be identified specifically as developing from a push or shove."

"In fact, isn't it true that there is no evidence whatsoever that Chase Andrews was pushed into the hole?"

"That is true. There's no evidence that I'm aware of that Chase Andrews was pushed."

"So, Dr. Cone, there is no evidence from your professional examination of Chase Andrews's body that proves this was a murder and not an accident?"

"No."

Tom took his time, letting this answer sink into the jury, then continued. "Now, let's talk about those red wool fibers found on Chase's jacket. Is there any way to determine how long the fibers had been on the jacket?"

"No. We can say where they came from, but not when."

"In other words, those fibers could have been on that jacket for a year, even four years?"

"That's correct."

"Even if the jacket had been washed?"

"Yes."

"So there's no evidence that those fibers became attached to that jacket the night Chase died?"

"No."

"There has been testimony that the defendant knew Chase Andrews for four years prior to his death. So you're saying that anytime during those four years, when they met wearing those items of clothing, it's possible the fibers were transferred from the cap to the jacket."

"From what I have seen, yes."

"So the red fibers do not prove that Miss Clark was with Chase Andrews the night he died. Was there any evidence at all that Miss Clark was in close proximity to Chase Andrews that night? For example, her skin fragments on his body, under his fingernails, or her fingerprints on the buttons or snaps of his jacket? Strands of her hair on his clothes or body?"

"No."

"So, in fact, since the red fibers could have been on his jacket for as long as four years, there's no evidence whatsoever that Miss Catherine Clark was near Chase Andrews the night of his death?"

"From my examination that is correct."

"Thank you. No more questions."

Judge Sims declared an early lunch recess.

Tom touched Kya's elbow gently and whispered that it had been a good cross-examination. She nodded slightly as people stood and stretched. Almost all stayed long enough to watch Kya being hand-cuffed and led from the room.

As Jacob's steps echoed down the hall after leaving her in her cell, Kya sat hard on her bed. When she was first incarcerated, they hadn't allowed her to bring her knapsack into the cell but let her take some of its contents with her in a brown paper bag. She reached into the bag then and pulled out the scrap of paper with Jodie's phone number and address. Since being there, she'd looked at it almost every day and thought of phoning her brother, asking him to come be with her. She knew he would, and Jacob had said she could use the phone to call him. But she had not. How would she say the words: *Please come; I'm in jail, charged with murder.*

Carefully, she put the paper back into the bag and lifted out the World War I compass Tate had given her. She let the needle swing north and watched it settle true. She held it against her heart. Where else would one need a compass more than in this place?

Then she whispered Emily Dickinson's words:

> The sweeping up the heart,
> And putting Love away
> We shall not want to use again
> Until Eternity.

46.

King of the World

1969

The September sea and sky glistened pale blue from a soft sun as Kya churned in her little boat toward Jumpin's to get the bus schedule. The thought of busing with strange people to a strange town unnerved her, but she wanted to meet her editor, Robert Foster. For more than two years, they had exchanged short notes—and even some long letters— mostly discussing editorial adjustments for the prose and art in her books, but the correspondence, written so often in biological phrases blended with poetic descriptions, had become a bond welded in its own language. She wanted to meet this person on the other end of the mail line, who knew how ordinary light is shattered by microscopic prisms in the feathers of hummingbirds, creating the iridescence of its golden-red throat. And how to say it in words as startling as the colors.

As she stepped onto the wharf, Jumpin' greeted her and asked if she needed gas.

"No thanks, not this time. I need to write down the bus schedule. You have a copy, right?"

"Sho' do. Tacked up right on the wall, left a' the doah. Hep yurself."

After she stepped from the shop with the schedule, he asked, "Ya goin' on a trip somewheres, Miss Kya?"

"I might. My editor invited me to Greenville to meet him. Not sure yet."

"Well then, thata' be mighty fine. It's a fur piece over there, but a trip a' do ya good."

As Kya turned to get back into her boat, Jumpin' leaned in and looked at her more closely. "Miss Kya, what's done happened to yo' eye, yo' face? Look like you been beat up, Miss Kya." Quickly she turned her face away. The bruise from Chase's slug, almost a month old, was faded to a faint yellowish stain, which Kya thought no one would notice.

"No, I just walked into a door in—"

"Don't ya go tellin' me a story now, Miss Kya. I didn't jus' fall off the turnip truck. Who done hit ya like that?"

She stood silent.

"Was it Mr. Chase done this to ya? Ya know ya can tell me. In fact, we gwine stand right here tills ya tell me."

"Yes, it was Chase." Kya could barely believe the words came from her mouth. She never thought she had anyone to tell such things. She turned away again, fighting tears.

Jumpin's entire face frowned. He didn't speak for several seconds. And then, "What else he done?"

"Nothing, I swear. He tried, Jumpin', but I fought him off."

"That man gotta be horsewhupped, then run outta this town."

"Jumpin', please. You can't tell anybody. You know you can't tell the sheriff or anybody. They'd drag me into the sheriff's office and make me describe what happened to a bunch of men. I can't live through that." Kya dropped her face in her hands.

"Well, sump'm gotta be done. He cain't go an' do a thing like that, and then just go on boatin' 'round in that fancy boat a' his. King of the World."

"Jumpin', you know how it is. They'll take his side. They'll say I'm just stirring up trouble. Trying to get money out of his parents or something. Think what would happen if one of the girls from Colored Town accused Chase Andrews of assault and attempted rape. They'd do nothing. Zero." Kya's voice became more and more shrill. "It would end in big trouble for that girl. Write-ups in the newspaper. People accusing her of whoring. Well, it'd be the same for me, and you know it. Please promise me you won't tell anybody." She ended in a sob.

"Ya right, Miss Kya. I know ya right. Ya don't gotta worry 'bout me doin' anythang to make this thang worse. But how d'ya know he ain't comin' after ya again? And ya a'ways on yo' lonesome out there?"

"I've always protected myself before; I just slipped up this time because I didn't hear him coming. I'll stay safe, Jumpin'. If I decide to go to Greenville, when I come back, maybe I could live out at my reading cabin awhile. I don't think Chase knows about it."

"A'right, then. But I wantcha to come in here more of'en, I wantcha to come by and let me know how things're goin'. Ya know ya can always come out and stay with Mabel and me, ya know that."

"Thank you, Jumpin'. I know."

"When ya goin' over to Greenville?"

"I'm not sure. The editor's letter mentioned late October. I haven't made arrangements, haven't even accepted the invitation." She knew now she couldn't go unless the bruise had disappeared completely.

"Well, ya let me know when ya gwine over thar and when ya get back. Ya hear? I gotta know if ya outer town. 'Cause, if'n I don't see ya fer more'n a day or so, I'm goin' out to yo' place maself. Bring along a posse if need be."

"I will. Thank you, Jumpin'."

47.

The Expert

1970

Prosecutor Eric Chastain had been questioning the sheriff about the two boys who discovered Chase Andrews's body at the base of the fire tower on October 30, the doctor's examination, and the initial investigation.

Eric continued. "Sheriff, please tell us what led you to believe that Chase Andrews had not fallen from the tower by accident. What made you think a crime had been committed?"

"Well, one of the first things I noticed was there weren't any footprints around Chase's body, not even his own. Except those made by the boys who found him, so I figured somebody had destroyed them to cover up a crime."

"Isn't it also true, Sheriff, that there were no fingerprints and no vehicle tracks at the scene?"

"Yeah, that's correct. The lab reports stated there were no fresh fingerprints on the tower. Not even on the grate, which somebody had to open. My deputy and I searched for vehicle tracks, and there weren't any of those either. All this indicated that someone had purposely destroyed evidence."

"So when the lab reports proved that red wool fibers from Miss Clark's hat were found on Chase's clothing that night, you . . ."

"Objection, Your Honor," Tom said. "Leading the witness. And besides, testimony has already established that the red fibers could have been transferred from Miss Clark's clothing to those of Mr. Andrews prior to the night of October 29 to 30."

"Sustained," the judge boomed.

"No more questions. Your witness." Eric had known the sheriff's testimony would be somewhat weak for the prosecution—what can you do with no murder weapon and no finger-, foot-, or truck prints—but there was still enough meat and gravy to convince the jury someone had murdered Chase, and considering the red fibers, that someone could've been Miss Clark.

Tom Milton walked to the witness box. "Sheriff, did you or anybody else ask an expert to look for footprints or for evidence that footprints were wiped out?"

"That wasn't necessary. I am the expert. Footprint examination is part of my official training. I didn't need another expert."

"I see. So was there evidence that footprints had been wiped off the ground? I mean, for example, were there marks from a brush or branch to cover tracks? Or was there mud moved on top of other mud? Any evidence, any photographs of such an act?"

"No. I'm here to testify as an expert that there were no footprints under the tower except ours and the boys'. So somebody had to have wiped them out."

"Okay. But, Sheriff, it's a physical characteristic of the marsh that as the tides come in and out, the groundwater—even far beyond the tide—goes up and down, making areas dry for a while, then a few hours later the water rises again. In many places, as the water rises it soaks the area, wiping out any marks in the mud, such as footprints. Clean slate. Isn't that true?"

"Well, yeah, it can be like that. But there's no evidence that something like that occurred."

"I have here the tide table for the night of October 29 and the morning of October 30, and see, Sheriff Jackson, it shows that low tide was around midnight. So, at the time Chase arrived at the tower and walked to the steps, he would have made tracks in the wet mud. Then when the tide came in and the groundwater rose, his tracks were wiped out. That's the reason you and the boys made deep tracks, and the same reason that Chase's prints were gone. Do you agree that this is possible?"

Kya nodded slightly—her first reaction to testimony since the trial began. Many times she'd seen marsh waters swallow yesterday's story: deer prints by a creek or bobcat tracks near a dead fawn, vanished.

The sheriff answered, "Well, I've never seen it wipe out anything so complete as that, so I don't know."

"But, Sheriff, as you said, you're the expert, trained in footprint examination. And now you say you don't know if this common occurrence happened that night or not."

"Well, it wouldn't be that hard to prove one way or the other, would it? Just go out there at low tide, make some tracks, and see if they are wiped out when the tide comes in."

"Yes, it wouldn't be that hard to determine one way or the other, so why wasn't it done? Here we are in court, and you have no proof whatsoever that a person wiped away footprints to cover a crime. It's more likely that Chase Andrews did leave prints under the tower and that they were washed away by the rising groundwater. And if some friends had been with him to climb the tower for fun, their footprints would have been washed away as well. Under these very likely circumstances, there is no suggestion whatsoever of a crime. Isn't that correct, Sheriff?"

Ed's eyes darted left, right, left, right, as if the answer were on the walls. People shifted on the benches.

"Sheriff?" Tom repeated.

"In my professional opinion, it seems unlikely that a normal cycle of rising groundwater would completely wash away footprints to the extent that they disappeared in this case. However, since there was no sign of a cover-up, the absence of footprints does not, by itself, prove there was a crime. But—"

"Thank you." Tom turned toward the jury and repeated the sheriff's words. "The absence of footprints does not prove there was a crime. Now, moving on, Sheriff, what about the grate that was left open on the floor of the fire tower? Did you examine it for Miss Clark's fingerprints?"

"Yes, of course we did."

"And did you find Miss Clark's fingerprints on the grate or anywhere on the tower?"

"No. No, but we didn't find any other fingerprints either, so . . ."

The judge leaned over. "Only answer the questions, Ed."

"What about hair? Miss Clark has long black hair—if she had climbed all the way to the top and was busy on the platform, opening a grate and such, I would expect there to be strands of her hair. Did you find any?"

"No." The sheriff's brow glistened.

"The coroner testified that, after examining Chase's body, there was no evidence that Miss Clark was in close proximity to him that night. Oh, there were those fibers, but they could have been four years old.

And now, you're telling us that there is no evidence whatsoever that Miss Clark was even on the fire tower that night. Is that a correct statement?"

"Yes."

"So we have no evidence that proves Miss Clark was on the fire tower the night Chase Andrews fell to his death. Correct?"

"That's what I said."

"So that's a yes."

"Yeah, that's a yes."

"Sheriff, isn't it true that those grates on top of the tower were left open quite frequently by kids playing up there?"

"Yeah, they were left open sometimes. But like I said earlier, it was usually the one you had to open to climb on top, not the other ones."

"But isn't it true that the grate by the stairs and occasionally the others were left open so often and considered so dangerous that your office submitted a written request to the U.S. Forest Service to remedy the situation?" Tom held a document out to the sheriff. "Is this the official request to the Forest Service on July 18 of last year?" The sheriff looked at the page.

"Yeah. That's it."

"Who exactly wrote this request?"

"I did it myself."

"So only three months before Chase Andrews fell to his death through an open grate on the fire tower, you submitted a written request to the Forest Service asking them to close the tower or secure the grates so that no one would be hurt. Is that correct?"

"Yeah."

"Sheriff, would you please read to the court the last sentence of this document that you wrote to the Forest Service? Just the last sentence, here." He handed the document to the sheriff, pointing at the last line.

The sheriff read out loud to the court, "'I must repeat, these grates are very dangerous and if action is not taken, a serious injury or even death will occur.'"

"I have no further questions."

48.

A Trip

1969

On October 28, 1969, Kya eased up to Jumpin's dock to tell him good-bye, as promised, then motored to the town wharf, where fishermen and shrimpers as always stopped their work to watch her. Ignoring them, she tied up and carried a faded cardboard suitcase—pulled from the back of Ma's old closet—onto Main Street. She had no purse, but toted her knapsack packed with books, some ham and biscuits, and a small amount of cash, after burying most of her royalty money in a tin can near the lagoon. For once, she looked quite normal, dressed in a brown Sears, Roebuck skirt, white blouse, and flats. Shopkeepers bus-ied about, tending customers, sweeping the sidewalk, every one of them staring at her.

She stood on the corner under the *Bus Stop* sign and waited until the Trailways bus, its air brakes hissing, pulled up, blocking the ocean. Nobody got off or on as Kya stepped forward and bought a ticket to Greenville from the driver. When she asked about the return dates and times, he handed her a printed schedule and then stowed her suitcase. She held tightly to her knapsack and boarded. And before she had time to think much about it, the bus, which seemed as long as the town, drove out of Barkley Cove.

Two days later, at 1:16 in the afternoon, Kya stepped off the Trail-ways from Greenville. Now even more villagers were about, staring and whispering as she tossed her long hair over her shoulder and took her suitcase from the driver. She crossed the street to the wharf, stepped into her boat, and motored straight home. She wanted to stop by and tell Jumpin' that she was back, as she had promised to do, but other boats were lined up waiting for gas at his wharf, so she figured she'd come back the next day. Besides, this way she'd get back to the gulls faster.

So, the next morning, October 31, as she pulled up to Jumpin's wharf, she called to him, and he stepped out from the small store.

"Hey, Jumpin', I'm just letting you know I'm home. Got back yes-terday." He said nothing as he walked toward her.

As soon as she stepped onto his wharf, he said, "Miss Kya. I . . ."

She cocked her head. "What is it? What's wrong?"

He stood looking at her. "Kya, have ya heard the news 'bout Mr. Chase?"

"No. What news?"

He shook his head. "Chase Andrews is dead. Died in tha middle of the night while ya were over'n Greenval."

"What?" Both Kya and Jumpin' looked deep into the other's eyes.

"They found 'im yestadee mornin' at the bottom of the ol' far towa with a . . . well, they say his neck broke an' his skull smashed right in. They reckon he fell right off from the top."

Kya's lips remained parted.

Jumpin' went on. "Whole town's buzzed up. Some folks're puttin' it down as a accident, but the word is, the sheriff itn't so sure. Chase's mama's all riled up, says there was foul play. It's a sho'-nuff mess."

Kya asked, "Why do they think foul play was . . . ?"

"One a' them grates on the towa flo' was left wide open, and he fell plumb through, and they reckoned that was suspicious. Some people're sayin' them grates are left open all the time with kids always messin' 'round up there, and Mr. Chase coulda fell through by accident. But some folks cryin' murder."

Kya was silent, so Jumpin' continued. "One reason was, when Mr. Chase was found, he wan't wearin' that shell necklace he wore ever' day fer years, and his wife says he was wearin' it that very night when he lef' the house, 'fore he went to his folks for dinah. A'ways wore it, she said."

Her mouth went dry at the mention of the necklace.

"Then, those two young'uns that found Chase, well, they heard the sheriff say thar weren't no footprints at the scene. Nary a one. Like somebody done rubbed out evidence. Them boys been yappin' all over town 'bout it."

Jumpin' told her when the funeral would be but knew Kya wouldn't go. What a spectacle that would be for the sewing bees and Bible study groups. For sure, the speculation and gossip would include Kya. *Thank tha Lawd she'd been in Greenval at the time 'a his death, or they'd'a put this on 'er,* Jumpin' thought.

Kya nodded at Jumpin' and churned home. She stood on the mud bank of the lagoon, whispering one of Amanda Hamilton's verses:

"Never underrate
the heart,
Capable of deeds
The mind cannot conceive.
The heart dictates as well as feels.
How else can you explain
The path I have taken,
That you have taken
The long way through this pass?"

49

Disguises

1970

Stating his name as Mr. Larry Price—a man with curly white hair, cut short, and dressed in a blue suit that shone cheaply—and that he drove the Trailways bus on varying routes in this area of North Carolina, the next witness was sworn in. As Eric questioned him, Mr. Price confirmed that it was possible to bus from Greenville to Barkley Cove and back again on the same night. He also stated that he was driving the bus from Greenville bound for Barkley Cove the night Chase died, and none of the passengers looked like Miss Clark.

Eric said, "Now, Mr. Price, you told the sheriff during his investigation that there was a skinny passenger on that bus who could've been a tall woman disguised as a man. Is that correct? Please describe this passenger."

"Yeah, that's right. A young white man. Reckon he was 'bout five ten, and his pants just hung on him like sheets on a fence post. He wore a big bulky cap, blue. Kept his head down, didn't look at anybody."

"And now that you've seen Miss Clark, do you believe it's possible that the skinny man on the bus was Miss Clark in disguise? Could her long hair have been hidden in that bulky cap?"

"Yeah, I do."

Eric asked the judge to request that Kya stand up, and she did so with Tom Milton by her side.

"You can sit back down, Miss Clark," Eric said, and then to the witness, "Would you say that the young man on the bus was the same height and stature as Miss Clark?"

"I'd say 'bout exactly the same," Mr. Price said.

"So all things considered, would you say that it's likely that the skinny man on the 11:50 P.M. bus traveling from Greenville to Barkley Cove on the night of October 29 of last year was in fact the defendant Miss Clark?"

"Yeah, I'd say that's very possible."

"Thank you, Mr. Price. No further questions. Your witness."

Tom stood in front of the witness stand and, after five minutes of questioning Mr. Price, he summed up. "What you've told us is this: one, there was no woman who looked like the defendant on the bus from Greenville to Barkley Cove on the night of October 29, 1969; two, there was a tall, thin man on the bus, but at the time, even though you saw his face very close, you didn't think of him as a woman in disguise; three, this idea of disguise only came to you when the sheriff suggested it."

Tom continued before the witness could respond. "Mr. Price, tell us how you're sure the thin man was on the 11:50 P.M. bus of October 29? Did you take notes, write it down? Maybe it was the night before or the night after. Are you one hundred percent sure it was October 29?"

"Well, I see what you gettin' at. And, when the sheriff was jogging my memory, it seemed like that man was on that bus, but now, I reckon I can't be one hundred percent sure."

"Also, Mr. Price, wasn't the bus very late that night? In fact, it was twenty-five minutes late and didn't arrive in Barkley Cove until 1:40 in the morning. Is that correct?"

"Yeah." Mr. Price looked at Eric. "I'm just trying to help out here, do the right thing."

Tom reassured him. "You've been a great help, Mr. Price. Thank you very much. No further questions."

Eric called his next witness, the driver for the 2:30 A.M. bus from Barkley Cove to Greenville on the morning of October 30, a Mr. John King. He testified that the defendant, Miss Clark, was not on the bus, but there was an older lady, ". . . tall like Miss Clark, who had gray hair, short with curls, like a permanent wave."

"Looking at the defendant, Mr. King, is it possible that if Miss Clark had disguised herself as an older lady, she would have looked similar to the woman on the bus?"

"Well, it's hard to picture it. Maybe."

"So it's possible?"

"Yes, I guess."

On cross, Tom said, "We cannot accept the word *guess* in a murder trial. Did you see the defendant, Miss Clark, on the 2:30 A.M. bus from Barkley Cove to Greenville in the early morning of October 30, 1969?"

"No, I did not."

"And was there another bus from Barkley Cove to Greenville that night?"

"No."

50.

The Journal

1970

When Kya was led into the courtroom the next day, she glanced toward Tate, Jumpin', and Mabel and held her breath at seeing a full uniform, a slight smile across a scarred face. Jodie. She nodded slightly, wondering how he'd learned of her trial. Probably the Atlanta paper. She tucked her head in shame.

Eric stood. "Your Honor, if it please the court, the People call Mrs. Sam Andrews." The room breathed out as Patti Love, the grieving mother, made her way to the witness stand. Watching the woman she'd once hoped would be her mother-in-law, Kya now realized the absurdity of that notion. Even in this sullen setting, Patti Love, dressed in the finest black silks, seemed preoccupied with her own appearance and importance. She sat straight with her glossy purse perched on her lap, dark hair swept into the perfect bun under a hat, tipped just so, with dramatic black netting obscuring her eyes. Never would she have taken a barefoot marsh dweller as a daughter-in-law.

"Mrs. Andrews, I know this is difficult for you, so I'll be as brief as possible. Is it true that your son, Chase Andrews, wore a rawhide necklace hung with a shell?"

"Yes, that's true."

"And when, how often, did he wear that necklace?"

"All the time. He never took it off. For four years I never saw him without that necklace."

Eric handed a leather journal to Mrs. Andrews. "Can you identify this book for the court?"

Kya stared at the floor, working her lips, enraged at this invasion of her privacy as the prosecutor held her journal for all the court to see. She'd made it for Chase very soon after they met. Most of her life, she'd been denied the joy of giving gifts, a deprivation few understand. After working for days and nights on the journal, she'd wrapped it in brown paper and decorated it with striking green ferns and white feathers from snow geese. She'd held it out as Chase stepped from his boat onto the lagoon shore.

"What's this?"

"Just something from me," she had said, and smiled.

A painted story of their times together. The first, an ink sketch of them sitting against the driftwood, Chase playing the harmonica. The Latin names of the sea oats and scattered shells were printed in Kya's hand. A swirl of watercolors revealed his boat drifting in moonlight. The next was an abstract image of curious porpoises circling the boat, with the words of "Michael Row the Boat Ashore" drifting in the clouds. Another of her swirling among silver gulls on a silver beach.

Chase had turned the pages in wonder. Ran his fingers lightly over some of the drawings, laughed at some, but mostly was silent, nodding.

"I've never had anything like this." Leaning over to embrace her, he

317

had said, "Thank you, Kya." They sat on the sand awhile, wrapped in blankets, talking, holding hands.

Kya remembered how her heart had pounded at the joy of giving, never imagining anyone else would see the journal. Certainly not as evidence at her murder trial.

She didn't look at Patti Love when she answered Eric's question. "It's a collection of paintings that Miss Clark made for Chase. She gave it to him as a present." Patti Love remembered finding the journal under a stack of albums while cleaning his room. Apparently hidden from her. She'd sat on Chase's bed and opened the thick cover. There, in detailed ink, her son lying against driftwood with that girl. The Marsh Girl. Her Chase with trash. She could barely breathe. *What if people find out?* First cold, then sweaty, her body reeled.

"Mrs. Andrews, would you please explain what you see in this picture painted by the defendant, Miss Clark."

"That's a painting of Chase and Miss Clark on the top of the fire tower." A murmur moved through the room.

"What else is going on?"

"There—between their hands, she is giving him the shell necklace."

And he never took it off again, Patti Love thought. *I believed that he told me everything. I thought I'd bonded with my son more than other mothers; that's what I told myself. But I knew nothing.*

"So, because he told you and because of this journal, you knew your son was seeing Miss Clark, and you knew she gave him the necklace?"

"Yes."

"When Chase came to your house for dinner on the night of October 29, was he wearing the necklace?"

"Yes, he didn't leave our house until after eleven, and he was wearing the necklace."

"Then when you went into the clinic the next day to identify Chase, did he have the necklace on?"

"No, he did not."

"Do you know of any reason why any of his friends or anyone else, besides Miss Clark, would want to take the necklace off Chase?"

"No."

"Objection, Your Honor," Tom called quickly from his seat. "Hearsay. Calls for speculation. She can't speak to the reasoning of other people."

"Sustained. Jurors, you must disregard the last question and answer." Then, lowering his head ganderlike at the prosecutor, the judge said, "Watch your step, Eric. For crying out loud! You know better than that."

Eric, unfazed, continued. "All right, we know from her own drawings that the defendant, Miss Clark, climbed the fire tower with Chase at least once; we know she gave the shell necklace to him. After that, he wore it continuously until the night he died. At which time it disappeared. Is all that correct?"

"Yes."

"Thank you. No further questions. Your witness."

"No questions," Tom said.

51.

Waning Moon

1970

The language of the court was, of course, not as poetic as the language of the marsh. Yet Kya saw similarities in their natures. The judge, obviously the alpha male, was secure in his position, so his posture was imposing, but relaxed and unthreatened as the territorial boar. Tom Milton, too, exuded confidence and rank with easy movements and stance. A powerful buck, acknowledged as such. The prosecutor, on the other hand, relied on wide, bright ties and broad-shouldered suit jackets to enhance his status. He threw his weight by flinging his arms or raising his voice. A lesser male needs to shout to be noticed. The bailiff represented the lowest-ranking male and depended on his belt hung with glistening pistol, clanging wad of keys, and clunky radio to bolster his position. *Dominance hierarchies enhance stability in natural populations, and some less natural,* Kya thought.

The prosecutor, wearing a scarlet tie, stepped boldly to the front and called his next witness, Hal Miller, a rake-thin twenty-eight-year-old with moppy brown hair.

"Mr. Miller, please tell us where you were and what you saw the night of October 29 to 30, 1969, at about 1:45 A.M."

"Me and Allen Hunt were crewing for Tim O'Neal on his shrimp boat, and we were headed back to Barkley Cove Harbor late, and we seen her, Miz Clark, in her boat, about a mile out, east of the bay, headed north-northwest."

"And where would that course take her?"

"Right smack to that cove near the fire tower."

Judge Sims banged his gavel at the outburst, which rumbled for a full minute.

"Could she not have been going somewhere else?"

"Well, I reckon, but there's nothing up that way but miles of swamped-out woods. No other destination I know of 'cept the fire tower."

Ladies' funeral fans pumped against the warming, unsettled room. Sunday Justice, sleeping on the windowsill, flowed to the floor and walked to Kya. For the first time in the courtroom, he rubbed against her leg, then jumped onto her lap and settled. Eric stopped talking and looked at the judge, perhaps considering an objection for such an open display of partiality, but there seemed no legal precedent.

"How can you be sure it was Miss Clark?"

"Oh, we all know her boat. She's been boatin' around on her own fer years."

"Were there lights on her boat?"

"No, no lights. Might've run her over if we hadn't seen her."

"But isn't it illegal to operate a boat after dark without lights?"

"Yeah, she was s'posed to have lights. But she didn't."

"So on the night that Chase Andrews died at the fire tower, Miss Clark was boating in exactly that direction, just minutes before the time of his death. Is that correct?"

"Yeah, that's what we seen."

Eric sat down.

Tom walked toward the witness. "Good morning, Mr. Miller."

"Good mornin'."

"Mr. Miller, how long have you been serving as a crew member on Tim O'Neal's shrimp boat?"

"Going on three years now."

"And tell me, please, what time did the moon rise the night of October 29 to the 30?"

"It was waning, and didn't rise till after we docked in Barkley. Sometime after two A.M. I reckon."

"I see. So when you saw the small boat motoring near Barkley Cove that night, there was no moon. It must have been very dark."

"Yeah. It was dark. There was some starlight but, yeah, pretty dark."

"Would you please tell the court what Miss Clark was wearing as she motored past you in her boat that night."

"Well, we weren't near close enough to see what she was wearing."

"Oh? You weren't near enough to see her clothes." Tom looked at the jury as he said this. "Well, how far away were you?"

"I reckon we was a good sixty yards away at least."

"Sixty yards." Tom looked at the jury again. "That's quite a distance to identify a small boat in the dark. Tell me, Mr. Miller, what characteristics, what features of this person in this boat made you so sure it was Miss Clark?"

"Well, like I said, 'bout everybody in this town knows her boat, how it looks from close and far. We know the shape of the boat and the figure she cuts sittin' in the stern, tall, thin like that. A very particular shape."

"A particular shape. So anybody with this same shape, any person who was tall and thin in this type of boat would have looked like Miss Clark. Correct?"

"I guess somebody else coulda looked like her, but we get to know boats and their owners real good, you know, being out there all the time."

"But, Mr. Miller, may I remind you, this is a murder trial. It cannot get more serious than this, and in these cases we have to be certain. We can't go by shapes or forms that are seen from sixty yards away in the dark. So, please can you tell the court you are certain the person you saw on the night of October 29 to October 30, 1969, was Miss Clark?"

"Well, no, I can't be completely sure. Never said I could be completely sure it was her. But I'm pretty—"

"That will be all, Mr. Miller. Thank you."

Judge Sims asked, "Redirect, Eric?"

From his seat, Eric asked, "Hal, you testified that you've been seeing and recognizing Miss Clark in her boat for at least three years. Tell me, have you ever thought you saw Miss Clark in her boat from a distance and then once you got closer, you discovered that it wasn't Miss Clark after all? Has that ever happened?"

"No, not once."

"Not once in three years?"

"Not once in three years."

"Your Honor, the State rests."

52.

Three Mountains Motel

1970

Judge Sims entered the courtroom and nodded at the defense table. "Mr. Milton, are you ready to call your first witness for the defense?"

"I am, Your Honor."

"Proceed."

After the witness was sworn and seated, Tom said, "Please state your name and what you do in Barkley Cove." Kya raised her head enough to see the short, elderly woman with the purplish-white hair and tight perm who years ago asked her why she always came alone to the grocery. Perhaps she was shorter and her curls tighter, but she looked remarkably the same. Mrs. Singletary had seemed nosey and bossy, but she had given Kya the net Christmas stocking with the blue whistle inside the winter after Ma left. It was all the Christmas Kya had.

"I'm Sarah Singletary, and I clerk at the Piggly Wiggly market in Barkley Cove."

"Sarah, is it correct that from your cash register within the Piggly Wiggly, you can see the Trailways bus stop?"

"Yes, I can see it clearly."

"On October 28 of last year, did you see the defendant, Miss Catherine Clark, waiting at the bus stop at 2:30 P.M.?"

"Yes, I saw Miss Clark standing there." At this, Sarah glanced at Kya and remembered the little girl coming barefoot into the market for so many years. No one would ever know, but before Kya could count, Sarah had given the child extra change—money she had to take from her own purse to balance the register. Of course, Kya was dealing with small sums to start with, so Sarah contributed only nickels and dimes, but it must have helped.

"How long did she wait? And did you actually see her step onto the 2:30 P.M. bus?"

"She waited about ten minutes, I think. We all saw her buy her ticket from the driver, give him her suitcase, and step onto the bus. It drove away, and she was most definitely inside."

"And I believe you also saw her return two days later on October 30 on the 1:16 P.M. bus. Is that correct?"

"Yes, two days later, a little after 1:15 in the afternoon, I looked up as the bus stopped, and there was Miss Clark stepping off it. I pointed her out to the other checkout ladies."

"Then what did she do?"

"She walked to the wharf, got in her boat, and headed south."

"Thank you, Sarah. That will be all."

Judge Sims asked, "Any questions, Eric?"

"No, Your Honor, I have no questions. In fact, I see from the witness list that the defense intends to call several townspeople to testify that Miss Clark got on and off the Trailways bus on the dates and times

Mrs. Singletary has stated. The prosecution does not refute this testimony. Indeed, it is consistent with our case that Miss Clark traveled on those buses at those times and, if it please the court, it is not necessary to hear from other witnesses on this matter."

"All right. Mrs. Singletary, you can step down. What about you, Mr. Milton? If the prosecution accepts the fact that Miss Clark got on the 2:30 bus on October 28, 1969, and returned at about 1:16 on October 30, 1969, do you need to call other witnesses to this effect?"

"No, Your Honor." His face appeared calm, but Tom swore inside. Kya's alibi of being out of town at the time of Chase's death was one of the strongest points for the defense. But Eric had successfully diluted the alibi simply by accepting it, even stating that he didn't need to hear testimony that Kya traveled to and from Greenville during the day. It didn't matter to the prosecution's case because they claimed Kya had returned to Barkley at night and committed the murder. Tom had foreseen the risk but thought it crucial that the jury hear testimony, to visualize Kya leaving town in daylight and not returning until after the incident. Now, they'd think her alibi wasn't important enough even to be confirmed.

"Noted. Please proceed with your next witness."

Bald and fubsy, his coat buttoned tight against a round belly, Mr. Lang Furlough testified that he owned and operated the Three Mountains Motel in Greenville and that Miss Clark had stayed at the motel from October 28 until October 30, 1969.

Kya detested listening to this oily-haired man, who she never thought she'd see again, and here he was talking about her as though she weren't present. He explained how he had shown her to her motel room but failed to mention he had lingered too long. Kept thinking of reasons to stay in her room until she opened the door, hinting for him to leave. When Tom asked how he could be sure of Miss Clark's comings and goings from the motel, he chuckled and said she was the kind of woman men notice. He added how strange she was, not knowing how to use the telephone, walking from the bus station with a cardboard suitcase, and bringing her own bagged dinner.

"Mr. Furlough, on the next night, that being October 29, 1969, the night Chase Andrews died, you worked at the reception desk all night. Is that correct?"

"Yes."

"After Miss Clark returned to her room at ten P.M. after dinner with her editor, did you see her leave again? At any time during the night of October 29 or the early-morning hours of October 30, did you see her leave or return to her room?"

"No. I was there all night and I never saw her leave her room. Like I said, her room was directly across from the reception counter, so I would have seen her leave."

"Thank you, Mr. Furlough, that's all. Your witness."

After several minutes of cross-examination, Eric continued. "Okay, Mr. Furlough, so far we have you leaving the reception area altogether to walk to your apartment twice, use the restroom, and return; the pizza boy bringing pizza; you paying him, et cetera; four guests checking in, two checking out; and in between all that, you completed your receipts account. Now I'd submit, Mr. Furlough, that during all that commotion, there were plenty of times that Miss Clark could have quietly walked out of her room, quickly crossed the street, and you would never have seen her. Isn't that entirely possible?"

"Well, I guess it's possible. But I never saw a thing. I didn't see her leave her room that night—is what I'm saying."

"I understand that, Mr. Furlough. And what I'm saying is that it's very possible that Miss Clark left her room, walked to the bus station, bused to Barkley Cove, murdered Chase Andrews, and returned to her room, and you never saw her because you were very busy doing your job. No more questions."

After the lunch recess, just as everyone was settled and the judge had taken his seat, Scupper stepped inside the courtroom. Tate turned to see his father, still in his overalls and yellow marine boots, walking down the aisle. Scupper had not attended the trial because of his work, he'd said, but mostly because his son's long attachment to Miss Clark confounded him. It seemed Tate had never had feelings for any other girl, and even as a grown, professional man, he still loved this strange, mysterious woman. A woman now accused of murder.

Then, that noon, standing on his boat, nets pooled around his boots, Scupper breathed out heavily. His face blazed with shame as he realized that he—like some of the ignorant villagers—had been preju-diced against Kya because she had grown up in the marsh. He remem-bered Tate proudly showing him Kya's first book on shells and how Scupper himself was taken aback by her scientific and artistic prowess. He had bought himself a copy of each of her books but hadn't men-tioned that to Tate. What bullshit.

He was so proud of his son, how he had always known what he wanted and how to achieve it. Well, Kya had done the same against much bigger odds.

How could he not be there for Tate? Nothing mattered except sup-porting his son. He dropped the net at his feet, left the boat wallowing against the pier, and walked directly to the courthouse.

When he reached the first row, Jodie, Jumpin', and Mabel stood to allow him to squeeze by and sit next to Tate. Father and son nodded at each other, and tears swelled in Tate's eyes.

Tom Milton waited for Scupper to sit, the silence in the room complete, then said, "Your Honor, the defense calls Robert Foster." Dressed in a tweed jacket, tie, and khaki pants, Mr. Foster was trim, of medium height, and had a neat beard and kind eyes. Tom asked his name and occupation.

"My name is Robert Foster, and I'm a senior editor for Harrison Morris Publishing Company in Boston, Massachusetts." Kya, hand to her forehead, stared at the floor. Her editor was the only person she knew who didn't think of her as the Marsh Girl, who had respected her, even seemed awed at her knowledge and talent. Now he was in court seeing her at the defendant's table, charged with murder.

"Are you the editor for Miss Catherine Clark's books?"

"Yes, I am. She is a very talented naturalist, artist, and writer. One of our favorite authors."

"Can you confirm that you traveled to Greenville, North Carolina, on October 28, 1969, and that you had meetings with Miss Clark on both the twenty-ninth and the thirtieth?"

"That is correct. I was attending a small conference there, and knew I would have some extra time while in town but wouldn't have enough time to travel to her place, so I invited Miss Clark to Greenville so we could meet."

"Can you tell us the exact time that you drove her back to her motel on the night of October 29, last year?"

"After our meetings, we dined at the hotel and then I drove Kya back to her motel at 9:55 P.M."

Kya recalled standing on the threshold of the dining room, filled with candlelit tables under soft chandeliers. Tall wineglasses on white tablecloths. Stylishly dressed diners conversed in quiet voices, while she wore the plain skirt and blouse. She and Robert dined on almond-crusted North Carolina trout, wild rice, creamed spinach, and yeast rolls. Kya felt comfortable as he kept the conversation going with easy grace, sticking to subjects about nature familiar to her.

Remembering it now, she was astonished how she had carried it off. But in fact, the restaurant, with all its glitter, wasn't nearly as grand as her favorite picnic. When she was fifteen, Tate had boated to her shack one dawn and, after he'd wrapped a blanket around her shoulders, they cruised inland through a maze of waterways to a forest she'd never seen. They hiked a mile to the edge of a waterlogged meadow where fresh grass sprouted through mud, and there he laid the blanket under ferns as large as umbrellas.

"Now we wait," he'd said, as he poured hot tea from a thermos and offered her "coon balls," a baked mixture of biscuit dough, hot sausage, and sharp cheddar cheese he had cooked for the occasion. Even now in this cold courtroom setting, she remembered the warmth of his shoulders touching hers under the blanket, as they nibbled and sipped the breakfast picnic.

They didn't have to wait long. Moments later, a ruckus as loud as cannons sounded from the north. "Here they come," Tate had said.

A thin, black cloud appeared on the horizon and, as it moved toward them, it soared skyward. The shrieking rose in intensity and volume as the cloud rapidly filled the sky until not one spot of blue remained. Hundreds of thousands of snow geese, flapping, honking, and gliding, covered the world. Swirling masses wheeled and banked for landing. Perhaps a half million white wings flared in unison, as pink-orange feet dangled down, and a blizzard of birds came in to land. A true whiteout as everything on Earth, near and far, disappeared. One at a time, then ten at a time, then hundreds of geese landed only yards from where Kya and Tate had sat under the ferns. The sky emptied as the wet meadow filled until it was covered in downy snow.

No fancy dining room could compare to that, and the coon balls offered more spice and flare than almond-crusted trout.

"You saw Miss Clark go into her room?"

"Of course. I opened her door and saw her safely inside before I drove away."

"Did you see Miss Clark the next day?"

"We had arranged to meet for breakfast, so I picked her up at 7:30 A.M. We ate at the Stack 'Em High pancake place. I took her back to her motel at 9:00. And that was the last I saw of her until today." He glanced at Kya, but she looked down at the table.

"Thank you, Mr. Foster. I have no further questions."

Eric stood and asked, "Mr. Foster, I was wondering why you stayed at the Piedmont Hotel, which is the best hotel in the area, while your publishing company only paid for Miss Clark—such a talented author, one of the favorites, as you put it—to stay in a very basic motel, the Three Mountains?"

"Well, of course, we offered, even recommended that Miss Clark stay at the Piedmont, but she insisted on staying at the motel."

"Is that so? Did she know the motel's name? Did she specifically request to stay at the Three Mountains?"

"Yes, she wrote a note saying she preferred to stay at the Three Mountains."

"Did she say why?"

"No, I don't know why."

"Well, I have an idea. Here's a tourist map of Greenville." Eric waved the map around as he approached the witness stand. "You can see here, Mr. Foster, that the Piedmont Hotel—the four-star hotel that you offered to Miss Clark—is located in the downtown area. The Three Mountains Motel, on the other hand, is on Highway 258, near the Trailways bus station. In fact, if you study the map as I have, you will see that the Three Mountains is the closest motel to the bus station . . ."

"Objection, Your Honor," Tom called out. "Mr. Foster is not an authority on the layout of Greenville."

"No, but the map is. I see where you're going, Eric, and I'll allow it. Proceed."

"Mr. Foster, if someone were planning a quick trip to the bus station in the middle of the night, it is logical that they would choose the Three Mountains over the Piedmont. Especially if they planned to walk. All I need from you is the confirmation that Miss Clark asked specifically to stay at the Three Mountains and not the Piedmont."

"As I said, she requested the Three Mountains."

"I have nothing more."

"Redirect?" Judge Sims asked.

"Yes, Your Honor. Mr. Foster, how many years have you worked with Miss Clark?"

"Three years."

"And even though you didn't meet her until the visit in Greenville last October, would you say that you've gotten to know Miss Clark quite well through correspondence over those years? If so, how would you describe her?"

"Yes, I have. She is a shy, gentle person, I believe. She prefers to be alone in the wilderness; it took some time for me to convince her to come to Greenville. Certainly she would avoid a crowd of people."

"A crowd of people like one would encounter at a large hotel such as the Piedmont?"

"Yes."

"In fact, wouldn't you say, Mr. Foster, that it is not surprising that Miss Clark—who likes to keep to herself—would choose a small, rather remote motel over a large bustling hotel right in town? That this choice would fit her character?"

"Yes, I would say that."

"Also, doesn't it make sense if Miss Clark, who is not familiar with public transport and knew she had to walk from the bus station to her hotel and back again, carrying a suitcase, that she would select a hotel or motel closest to the station?"

"Yes."

"Thank you. That will be all."

When Robert Foster left the witness stand, he sat with Tate, Scupper, Jodie, Jumpin', and Mabel, behind Kya.

That afternoon, Tom called the sheriff back as his next witness.

Kya knew from Tom's list of witnesses that there weren't many more to be called, and the thought sickened her. The closing arguments came next, then the verdict. As long as a stream of witnesses supported her, she could hope for acquittal or at least a delay of conviction. If the court proceedings trailed on forever, a judgment would never be handed down. She tried to lead her mind into fields-of-snow-geese distractions as she had since the trial began, but instead she saw only images of jail, bars, clammy cement walls. Mental inserts now and then of an electric chair. Lots of straps.

Suddenly, she felt she couldn't breathe, couldn't sit here any longer, her head too heavy to hold up. She sagged slightly, and Tom turned from the sheriff to Kya as her head dropped onto her hands. He rushed to her.

"Your Honor, I request a short recess. Miss Clark needs a break."

"Granted. Court dismissed for a fifteen-minute recess."

Tom helped her stand and whisked her out the side door and into the small conference room, where she sank into a chair. Sitting next to her, he said, "What is it? Kya, what's wrong?"

She buried her head in her hands. "How can you ask that? Isn't it obvious? How does anyone live through this? I feel too sick, too tired to sit there. Do I have to? Can't the trial continue without me?" All she was capable of, all she wanted, was to return to her cell and curl up with Sunday Justice.

"No, I'm afraid not. In a capital case, such as this, the law requires your presence."

"What if I can't? What if I refuse? All they can do is throw me in jail."

"Kya, it's the law. You have to attend, and anyway, it's better for you to be present. It's easier for a jury to convict an absent defendant. But, Kya, it won't be for much longer."

"That doesn't make me feel any better, don't you see? What comes next is worse than this."

"We don't know that. Don't forget, we can appeal if this doesn't go our way."

Kya didn't answer. Thoughts of an appeal sickened her more, the same forced march through different courtrooms, farther from the marsh. Probably large towns. Some gull-less sky. Tom stepped out of the room and returned with a glass of sweet iced tea and a package of salted peanuts. She sipped at the tea; refused the nuts. A few minutes later, the bailiff knocked on the door and led them back into court. Kya's mind faded in and out of reality, catching only snippets of the testimony.

"Sheriff Jackson," Tom said, "the prosecution is claiming that Miss Clark snuck out of her motel late at night and walked from the Three

Mountains Motel to the bus station—a trip of at least twenty minutes. That she then took the 11:50 P.M. night bus from Greenville to Barkley Cove, but the bus was late, so she couldn't have arrived in Barkley until 1:40 A.M. They claim that from the Barkley bus stop, she walked to the town wharf—three or four minutes—then she boated to the cove near the water tower—at least twenty minutes—walked to the tower, another eight minutes; climbed it in pitch dark, say, four to five minutes at least; opened the grate, a few seconds; waited for Chase—no time estimate—and then all of this in reverse.

"Those actions would have taken one hour seven minutes minimum, and that does not count time supposedly waiting for Chase. But the bus back to Greenville, which she had to catch, departed only fifty minutes after she arrived. Therefore, it is a simple fact: there was not enough time for her to commit this alleged crime. Isn't that correct, Sheriff?"

"It would've been tight, that's true. But she could've jogged from her boat to the tower and back, she could've cut a minute here and there."

"A minute here and there won't do it. She would have needed twenty extra minutes. At least. How could she have saved twenty minutes?"

"Well, maybe she didn't go in her boat at all; maybe she walked or ran from the bus stop on Main, down the sandy track to the tower. That would be much quicker than going by sea." From his seat at the prosecution table, Eric Chastain glared at the sheriff. He had convinced the jury there was enough time for Kya to commit the crime and return to the bus. They didn't need much convincing. In addition, they had a superior witness, the shrimper, who testified that he had seen Miss Clark headed to the tower by boat.

"Do you have any evidence whatsoever that Miss Clark went by land to the tower, Sheriff?"

"No. But going by land is a good theory."

"*Theory!*" Tom turned to the jury. "The time for *theories* was before you arrested Miss Clark, before you held her in jail for two months. The fact is you cannot prove that she went by land, and there was not enough time for her to go by sea. No more questions."

Eric faced the sheriff for the cross. "Sheriff, isn't it true that the waters near Barkley Cove are subjected to strong currents, riptides, and undertows that can influence the speed of a boat?"

"Yeah, that's true. Everybody lives here knows that."

"Someone who knew how to take advantage of such a current could boat very quickly to the tower from the harbor. In such a case, it would be very feasible to cut twenty minutes off the round trip. Isn't that correct?" Eric was annoyed that he had to suggest yet another theory, but all he needed was some plausible concept the jurors could latch on to and pull them in.

"Yeah, that's correct."

"Thank you." As soon as Eric turned from the witness stand, Tom stood for the redirect.

"Sheriff, yes or no, do you have any evidence that a current, riptide, or strong wind occurred on the night of October 29 to the 30 that could have decreased the time for someone to boat from the Barkley Cove Harbor to the fire tower, or any evidence that Miss Clark went to the tower by land?"

"No, but I'm sure there—"

"Sheriff, it doesn't make any difference what you're sure of or not. Do you have any evidence that a strong riptide was flowing the night of October 29, 1969?"

"No, I don't."

53.

Missing Link

1970

The next morning, Tom had only one more witness. His last card.

He called Tim O'Neal, who had operated his own shrimping boat in the waters off Barkley Cove for thirty-eight years. Tim, nearing sixty-five, tall yet stout, had thick brown hair with only whispers of gray, yet a full beard, nearly white. Folks knew him to be quiet and serious, honest and gracious, always opening doors for ladies. The perfect last witness.

"Tim, is it correct that on the night of October 29 to the 30 of last year, you were skippering your boat into Barkley Cove Harbor at approximately 1:45 to 2:00 A.M.?"

"Yes."

"Two of your crew members, Mr. Hal Miller, who testified here, and Mr. Allen Hunt, who signed an affidavit, both claim they saw Miss Clark motoring north past the harbor in her boat at approximately the times mentioned. Are you aware of their declarations?"

"Yes."

"Did you see the same boat, at that time and place, that both Mr. Miller and Mr. Hunt saw?"

"Yes, I did."

"And do you agree with their statements that it was Miss Clark in her boat that you saw motoring north?"

"No. I do not."

"Why not?"

"It was dark. There was no moon until later. And that boat was too far away to recognize with any certainty. I know everybody 'round here with that kinda boat, and I've seen Miss Clark in hers plenty a' times, and known right away it was her. But that night, it was too dark to recognize that boat or who was in it."

"Thank you, Tim. No more questions."

Eric walked up close to the witness stand. "Tim, even if you could not identify that boat, or who exactly was in it, do you agree that a rig about the same size and shape as Miss Clark's boat was headed toward the Barkley Cove Fire Tower at approximately 1:45 A.M. the night Chase Andrews died at the fire tower around that time?"

"Yes, I can say the boat was a similar shape and size as Miss Clark's."

"Thank you very much."

On redirect, Tom rose and spoke from where he stood. "Tim, to confirm, you testified that you have recognized Miss Clark in her boat many times, but on that evening, you saw nothing at all to identify that boat or boater to be Miss Clark in her rig. Correct?"

"Correct."

"And can you tell us, are there very many boats the same size and shape as Miss Clark's boat operating in this area?"

"Oh yes, hers is one of the most common types of boat around. There's lots of boats just like hers operating here."

"So the boater you saw that night could have been any number of other persons in a similar boat?"

"Absolutely."

"Thank you. Your Honor, the defense rests."

Judge Sims said, "We'll recess for twenty minutes. Court dismissed."

For his closing, Eric wore a tie with wide gold and burgundy stripes. The gallery was quietly expectant as he approached the jury and stood at the railing, passing his eyes deliberately from one to the next.

"Ladies and gentlemen of the jury, you are members of a community, of a proud and unique town. Last year you lost one of your own sons. A young man, a shining star of your neighborhood, looking forward to a long life with his beautiful . . ."

Kya barely heard him as he repeated his account of how she murdered Chase Andrews. She sat, elbows on the table, her head in her hands, catching only fragments of his discourse.

". . . Two well-known men in this community saw Miss Clark and Chase in the woods . . . heard her saying the words *I will kill you!* . . . a red wool cap that left fibers on his denim jacket . . . Who else would want to remove that necklace . . . you know these currents and winds can drastically increase the speed . . .

"We know from her lifestyle that she is very capable of boating at night, of climbing the tower in the dark. It all fits together like clockwork. Every single move she made that night is clear. You can and must find that the defendant is guilty of first-degree murder. Thank you for doing your duty."

Judge Sims nodded at Tom, who approached the jury box.

"Ladies and gentlemen of the jury, I grew up in Barkley Cove, and when I was a younger man I heard the tall tales about the Marsh Girl. Yes, let's just get this out in the open. We called her the Marsh Girl. Many still call her that. Some people whispered that she was part wolf or the missing link between ape and man. That her eyes glowed in the dark. Yet in reality, she was only an abandoned child, a little girl surviving on her own in a swamp, hungry and cold, but we didn't help her. Except for one of her only friends, Jumpin', not one of our churches or community groups offered her food or clothes. Instead we labeled and rejected her because we thought she was different. But, ladies and gentlemen, did we exclude Miss Clark because she was different, or was she different because we excluded her? If we had taken her in as one of our own—I think that is what she would be today. If we had fed, clothed, and loved her, invited her into our churches and homes, we wouldn't be prejudiced against her. And I believe she would not be sitting here today accused of a crime.

"The job of judging this shy, rejected young woman has fallen on your shoulders, but you must base that judgment on the facts presented in this case, in this courtroom, not on rumors or feelings from the past twenty-four years.

"What are the true and solid facts?" Just as with the prosecution, Kya's mind caught only snippets. ". . . the prosecution has not even proved that this incident was indeed a murder and not simply a tragic accident. No murder weapon, no wounds from being pushed, no witnesses, no fingerprints . . .

"One of the most important and proven facts is that Miss Clark has a sound alibi. We know she was in Greenville the night Chase died . . .

no evidence that she dressed as a man, bused to Barkley . . . In fact, the prosecution has failed to prove that she was in Barkley Cove that night at all, failed to prove that she went to the tower. I say again: there is not one single piece of evidence that proves Miss Clark was on the fire tower, in Barkley Cove, or killed Chase Andrews.

". . . and the skipper, Mr. O'Neal, who has operated his own shrimp boat for thirty-eight years, testified that it was too dark to identify that boat.

". . . fibers on his jacket, which could have been there for four years . . . These are uncontested facts . . .

"Not one of the witnesses for the prosecution was sure of what they saw, not one. Yet in her defense, every witness is one hundred percent certain . . ."

Tom stood for a moment in front of the jury. "I know most of you very well, and I know you can set aside any former prejudices against Miss Clark. Even though she only went to school one day in her life—because the other children harassed her—she educated herself and became a well-known naturalist and author. We called her the Marsh Girl; now scientific institutions recognize her as the Marsh Expert.

"I believe you can put all of the rumors and tall tales aside. I believe you will come to a judgment based on the facts you heard in this courtroom, not the false rumors you have heard for years.

"It is time, at last, for us to be fair to the Marsh Girl."

54.

Vice Versa

1970

Motioning toward mismatched chairs in a small conference room, Tom offered seats to Tate, Jodie, Scupper, and Robert Foster. They sat around the rectangular table, stained with coffee-mug circles. The walls were two tones of flaking plaster: lime green around the top, dark green around the bottom. An odor of dankness—as much from the walls as from the marsh—permeated.

"You can wait in here," Tom said, closing the door behind him. "There's a coffee machine down the hall across from the assessor's, but it's not fit for a three-eyed mule. The diner has okay coffee. Let's see, it's a little after eleven. We'll make a plan for lunch later."

Tate walked to the window, which was crisscrossed with a mesh of white bars, as if other verdict-waiters had tried escape. He asked Tom, "Where'd they take Kya? To her cell? Does she have to wait in there alone?"

"Yes, she's in her cell. I'm going to see her now."

"How long do you think the jury will take?" Robert asked.

"It's impossible to say. When you think it'll be quick, they take days, and vice versa. Most of them have probably already decided—and not in Kya's favor. If a few jurors have doubts and try to convince the others that guilt has not been proven definitively, we have a chance."

They nodded silently, weighed down by the word *definitively*, as though guilt had been proven, just not absolutely.

"Okay," Tom continued. "I'm going to see Kya and then get to work. I have to prepare the appeals request and even a motion for a mistrial due to prejudice. Please keep in mind, if she's convicted, this is not the end of the road. Not by any means. I'll be in and out, and I'll certainly let you know if there's any news."

"Thanks," Tate said, then added, "Please tell Kya we're here, and will sit with her if she wants." This, though she had refused to see anyone but Tom for the last few days and almost no one for two months.

"Sure. I'll tell her." Tom left.

Jumpin' and Mabel had to wait for the verdict outside among the palmettos and saw grass of the square, along with the few other blacks. Just as they spread colorful quilts on the ground and unpacked biscuits and sausage from paper bags, a rain shower sent them grabbing things and running for cover under the overhang of the Sing Oil. Mr. Lane shouted that they had to wait outside—a fact they'd known for a hundred years—and not to get in the way of any customers. Some whites crowded in the diner or the Dog-Gone for coffee, and others clustered in the street beneath bright umbrellas. Kids splashed in sudden puddles and ate Cracker Jacks, expecting a parade.

Tutored by millions of minutes alone, Kya thought she knew lonely. A life of staring at the old kitchen table, into empty bedrooms, across endless stretches of sea and grass. No one to share the joy of a found feather or a finished watercolor. Reciting poetry to gulls.

But after Jacob closed her cell with the clank of bars, disappeared down the hall, and locked the heavy door with a final thud, a cold silence settled. Waiting for the verdict of her own murder trial brought a loneliness of a different order. The question of whether she lived or died did not surface on her mind, but sank beneath the greater fear of years alone without her marsh. No gulls, no sea in a starless place.

The annoying cellmates down the hall had been released. She almost missed their constant nattering—a human presence no matter how lowly. Now she alone inhabited this long cement tunnel of locks and bars.

She knew the scale of the prejudices against her and that an early verdict would mean there had been little deliberation, which would mean conviction. Lockjaw came to mind—the twisting, tortured life of being doomed.

Kya thought of moving the crate under the window and searching for raptors over the marsh. Instead she just sat there. In the silence.

Two hours later, at one in the afternoon, Tom opened the door into the room where Tate, Jodie, Scupper, and Robert Foster waited. "Well, there's some news."

"What?" Tate jerked his head up. "Not a verdict already?"

"No, no. Not a verdict. But I think it's good news. The jurors have asked to see the court record of the bus drivers' testimonies. This means, at least, they're thinking things through—not simply jumping to a verdict. The bus drivers are key, of course, and both said they were certain Kya was not on their respective buses and weren't certain about the disguises either. Sometimes seeing testimony in black and white makes it more definitive to the jurors. We'll see, but it's a glimmer of hope."

"We'll take a glimmer," Jodie said.

"Look, it's past lunchtime. Why don't y'all go over to the diner? I promise, I'll get you if anything happens."

"I don't think so," Tate said. "They'll all be talking about how guilty she is over there."

"I understand. I'll send my clerk for some burgers. How's that?"

"Fine, thanks," Scupper said, and pulled some dollars from his wallet.

At 2:15, Tom returned to tell them the jurors had asked to see the coroner's testimony. "I'm not sure if this is favorable or not."

"Shit!" Tate swore. "How does anybody live through this?"

"Try to relax; this may take days. I'll keep you posted."

Unsmiling and drawn, Tom opened the door again at four o'clock. "Well, gentlemen, the jurors have a verdict. The judge has ordered everyone back to the courtroom."

Tate stood. "What does it mean? Happening so fast like this."

"Come on, Tate." Jodie touched his arm. "Let's go."

In the hallway, they joined the stream of townspeople jostling shoulder to shoulder from outside. Dank air, smelling of cigarette smoke, rain-wet hair, and damp clothes, flowed with them.

The courtroom filled in less than ten minutes. Many couldn't get a seat and bunched in the hall or on the front steps. At 4:30 the bailiff led Kya toward her seat. For the first time, he supported her by her elbow, and indeed, it appeared she might drop if he did not. Her eyes never moved from the floor. Tate watched every twitch in her face. His breath labored against nausea.

Miss Jones, the recorder, entered and took her seat. Then, like a funeral choir, solemn and cheerless, the jurors filed into their box. Mrs. Culpepper glanced at Kya. The others kept their eyes ahead. Tom tried to read their faces. There was not one cough or shuffle from the gallery.

"All rise."

Judge Sims's door opened, and he sat at his bench. "Please be seated. Mr. Foreman, is it correct that the jury has reached a verdict?"

Mr. Tomlinson, a quiet man who owned the Buster Brown Shoe Shop, stood in the first row. "We have, Your Honor."

Judge Sims looked at Kya. "Would the defendant please rise for the reading of the verdict." Tom touched Kya's arm, then guided her up. Tate placed his hand on the railing as close to Kya as he could get. Jumpin' lifted Mabel's hand and held it.

No one in the room had ever experienced this collective heart pounding, this shared lack of breath. Eyes shifted, hands sweated. The shrimper crew, Hal Miller, knotted his mind, fighting to confirm that it truly was Miss Clark's boat he had seen that night. Suppose he'd been wrong. Most stared, not at the back of Kya's head, but at the floor, the walls. It seemed that the village—not Kya—awaited judgment, and few felt the salacious joy they had expected at this juncture.

The foreman, Mr. Tomlinson, handed a small piece of paper to the bailiff, who passed it to the judge. He unfolded it and read it with a vacant face. The bailiff then took it from Judge Sims and handed it to Miss Jones, the recorder.

"Would somebody read it to us," Tate spat.

Miss Jones stood and faced Kya, unfolded the paper, and read: "We the jury find Miss Catherine Danielle Clark not guilty as charged in the first-degree murder of Mr. Chase Andrews." Kya buckled and sat. Tom followed.

Tate blinked. Jodie sucked in air. Mabel sobbed. The gallery sat motionless. Surely they had misunderstood. "Did she say not guilty?" A stream of whispers quickly rose in pitch and volume to angry questions. Mr. Lane called out, "This ain't right."

The judge hammered his gavel. "Silence! Miss Clark, the jury has found you not guilty as charged. You are free to go, and I apologize on behalf of this State that you served two months in jail. Jury, we thank you for your time and for serving this community. Court dismissed."

A small covey gathered around Chase's parents. Patti Love wept. Sarah Singletary scowled like everybody else but discovered that she was greatly relieved. Miss Pansy hoped no one saw her jaw relax. A lone tear trailed down Mrs. Culpepper's cheek, and then a shadow smile for the little swamp truant escaping again.

A group of men in overalls stood near the back. "Them jurors have some explainin' to do."

"Cain't Eric declare a mistrial? Do the whole thing over?"

"No. Remember? Cain't be tried for murder twice. She's free. Got away with the whole thing."

"It's the sheriff who messed it up for Eric. Couldn't keep his story straight, kep' makin' it up as he went. Theory this, theory that."

"Been struttin' 'round like he's on *Gunsmoke.*"

But this small band of disgruntlement fell apart quickly, some wandering out the door, talking about work to catch up on; how the rain had cooled things down.

Jodie and Tate had rushed through the wooden gate to the defense table. Scupper, Jumpin', Mabel, and Robert followed and encircled Kya. They did not touch her, but stood close as she sat there unmoving.

Jodie said, "Kya, you can go home. Do you want me to drive you?"

"Yes, please."

Kya stood and thanked Robert for coming all the way from Boston. He smiled. "You just forget about this nonsense and continue your amazing work." She touched Jumpin's hand, and Mabel hugged her into her cushy bosom. Then Kya turned to Tate. "Thank you for the things you brought me." She turned to Tom and lost words. He simply enfolded her in his arms. Then she looked at Scupper. She'd never been introduced to him, but knew from his eyes who he was. She nodded a soft thank-you, and to her surprise, he put his hand on her shoulder and squeezed gently.

Then, following the bailiff, she walked with Jodie toward the back door of the courtroom and, as she passed the windowsill, reached out and touched Sunday Justice's tail. He ignored her, and she admired his perfected pretense of not needing good-bye.

When the door opened she felt the breath of the sea on her face.

55.

Grass Flowers

1970

As Jodie's truck bumped off the pavement onto the sandy marsh road, he talked gently to Kya, saying she'd be fine; it would just take some time. She scanned cattails and egrets, pines and ponds flashing past. Craned her neck to watch two beavers paddling. Like a migrating tern who has flown ten thousand miles to her natal shore, her mind pounded with the longing and expectation of home; she barely heard Jodie's prattle. Wished he would be quiet and listen to the wilderness within him. Then he might see.

Her breath caught as Jodie turned the last bend of the winding lane, and the old shack came into view, waiting there beneath the oaks. The Spanish moss tossed gently in the breeze above the rusted roof, and the heron balanced on one leg in the shadows of the lagoon. As soon as Jodie stopped the truck, Kya jumped out and ran into the shack, touching the bed, the table, the stove. Knowing what she would want, he'd left a bag of crumbs on the counter, and, finding new energy, she ran to the beach with it, tears streaming her cheeks as the gulls flew toward her from up and down the shore. Big Red landed and tramped around her, his head bobbing.

Kneeling on the beach, surrounded by a bird frenzy, she trembled. "I never asked people for anything. Maybe now they'll leave me alone."

Jodie took her few belongings into the house and made tea in the old pot. He sat at the table and waited. Finally, he heard the porch door open, and as she stepped into the kitchen, she said, "Oh, you're still here." Of course, he was still there—his truck was in plain view outside.

"Please sit down a minute, would you?" he said. "I'd like to talk."

She didn't sit. "I'm fine, Jodie. Really."

"So, does that mean you want me to go? Kya, you've been alone in that cell for two months, thinking a whole town was against you. You've hardly let anyone visit you. I understand all that, I do, but I don't think I should drive away and leave you alone. I want to stay with you a few days. Would that be okay?"

"I've lived alone almost all my life, not two months! And I didn't *think*, I *knew* a whole town was against me."

"Kya, don't let this horrible thing drive you further from people. It's been a soul-crushing ordeal, but this seems to be a chance to start over. The verdict is maybe their way of saying they will accept you."

"Most people don't have to be acquitted of murder to be accepted."

"I know, and you have every reason in the world to hate people. I don't blame you, but . . ."

"That's what nobody understands about me." She raised her voice, "I never hated people. *They* hated *me*. *They* laughed at *me*. *They* left *me*. *They* harassed *me*. *They* attacked *me*. Well, it's true; I learned to live without them. Without you. Without Ma! Or anybody!"

He tried to hold her, but she jerked away.

"Jodie, maybe I'm just tired right now. In fact, I'm exhausted.

Please, I need to get over all this—the trial, jail, *the thought of being executed*—by myself, because *by myself* is all I've ever known. I don't know how to be consoled. I'm too tired to even have this conversation. I . . ." Her voice trailed off.

She didn't wait for an answer but walked from the shack and into the oak forest. Knowing it was futile, he didn't go after her. He would wait. The day before, he'd supplied the shack with groceries—just in case of acquittal—and now set about chopping vegetables for her favorite: homemade chicken pie. But as the sun set he couldn't stand keeping her from her shack another minute, so he left the hot, bubbling pie on the stovetop and walked out the door. She had circled to the beach, and when she heard his truck driving slowly down the lane, she ran home.

Whiffs of golden pastry filled the shack to the ceiling, but Kya still wasn't hungry. In the kitchen she took out her paints and planned her next book on marsh grasses. People rarely noticed grasses except to mow, trample, or poison them. She swept her brush madly across the canvas in a color more black than green. Dark images emerged, maybe dying meadows under storm cells. It was hard to tell.

She dropped her head and sobbed. "Why am I angry now? Why now? Why was I so mean to Jodie?" Limp, she slid to the floor like a rag doll. Curling into a ball, still crying, she wished she could snuggle with the only one who'd ever accepted her as she was. But the cat was back at the jail.

Just before dark, Kya walked back to the beach where the gulls were preening and settling in for the night. As she waded into the surf, shards of shells and chips of crabs brushed her toes as they tumbled back to the sea. She reached down and picked up two pelican feathers just like the one Tate had put in the *P* section of the dictionary he had given her for Christmas years ago.

She whispered a verse by Amanda Hamilton:

"You came again,
Blinding my eyes
Like the shimmer of sun upon the sea.
Just as I feel free
The moon casts your face upon the sill.
Each time I forget you
Your eyes haunt my heart and it falls still.
And so farewell
Until the next time you come,
Until at last I do not see you."

The next morning before dawn, Kya sat up in her porch bed and breathed the rich scents of the marsh into her heart. As faint light filtered into the kitchen, she cooked herself some grits, scrambled eggs, and biscuits, as light and fluffy as Ma's. She ate every bite. Then, as the sun rose, she rushed to her boat and chugged across the lagoon, dipping her fingers into the clear, deep water.

Churning through the channel, she spoke to the turtles and egrets and lifted her arms high above her head. Home. "I'll collect all day, anything I want," she said. Deeper in her mind was the thought that she might see Tate. Maybe he'd be working nearby and she'd come across him. She could invite him back to the shack to share the chicken pie Jodie had baked.

Less than a mile away, Tate waded through shallow water, dipping samples in tiny vials. A wake of gentle ripples fanned out from each step, from each dip. He planned to stay near Kya's place. Maybe she'd boat out into the marsh, and they'd meet. If not, he'd go to her shack that evening. He hadn't decided exactly what he'd say to her, but kissing some sense into her came to mind.

In the distance an angry engine roared, higher-pitched and much louder than a motorboat—defeating the soft sounds of the marsh. He tracked the noise as it moved in his direction, and suddenly one of those new airboats, which he hadn't seen, raced into view. It glided and gloated above the water, above even the grasses, sending behind a fantail of spray. Emitting the noise of ten sirens.

Crushing shrubs and grasses, the boat broke its own trail across the marsh and then sped across the estuary. Herons and egrets squawking. Three men stood at its helm, and seeing Tate, they turned in his direction. As they neared, he recognized Sheriff Jackson, his deputy, and another man.

The flashy boat sat back on its haunches as it slowed and eased near. The sheriff shouted something to Tate, but even cupping his ears with his hands and leaning toward them, he couldn't hear above the din. They maneuvered even closer until the boat wallowed next to Tate, sloshing water up his thighs. The sheriff leaned down, hollering.

Nearby, Kya had also heard the strange boat and, as she boated toward it, she saw it approaching Tate. She backed into a thicket and watched him take in the sheriff's words, then stand very still, head lowered, shoulders sagging in surrender. Even from this distance she read despair in his posture. The sheriff shouted again, and Tate finally reached up and let the deputy pull him into the boat. The other man hopped into the water and climbed into Tate's cruiser. Chin lowered, eyes downcast, Tate stood between the two uniformed men as they turned around and sped back through the marsh toward Barkley Cove, followed by the other man driving Tate's boat.

Kya stared until both boats disappeared behind a point of eelgrass.

Why had they apprehended Tate? Was it something to do with Chase's death? Had they arrested him?

Agony ripped her. Finally, after a lifetime, she admitted it was the chance of seeing Tate, the hope of rounding a creek bend and watching him through reeds, that had pulled her into the marsh every day of her life since she was seven. She knew his favorite lagoons and paths through difficult quagmires; always following him at a safe distance. Sneaking about, stealing love. Never sharing it. You can't get hurt when you love someone from the other side of an estuary. All the years she rejected him, she survived because he was somewhere in the marsh, waiting. But now perhaps he would no longer be there.

She stared at the fading noise of the strange boat. Jumpin' knew everything—he'd know why the sheriff had taken Tate in and what she could do about it.

She pull-cranked her engine and sped through the marsh.

56.

The Night Heron

1970

The Barkley Cove graveyard trailed off under tunnels of dark oaks. Spanish moss hung in long curtains, creating cavelike sanctuaries for old tombstones—the remains of a family here, a loner there, in no order at all. Fingers of gnarled roots had torn and twisted gravestones into hunched and nameless forms. Markers of death all weathered into nubbins by elements of life. In the distance, the sea and sky sang too bright for this serious ground.

Yesterday the cemetery moved with villagers, like constant ants, including all the fishermen and shopkeepers, who had come to bury Scupper. People clustered in awkward silence as Tate moved among familiar townspeople and unfamiliar relatives. Ever since the sheriff found him in the marsh to tell him his father had died, Tate simply stepped and acted as guided—a hand behind his back, a nudge to his side. He remembered none of it and walked back to the cemetery today to say good-bye.

During all those months, pining for Kya, then trying to visit her in jail, he'd spent almost no time with Scupper. Guilt and regret needed clawing away. Had he not been so obsessed with his own heart, perhaps he would have noticed his father's was failing. Before her arrest, Kya had shown signs of coming back—gifting him a copy of her first book, coming onto his boat to look through the microscope, laughing at the hat toss—but once the trial began she had pulled away more than ever. Jail could do that to a person, he thought.

Even now, walking toward the new grave, carrying a brown plastic case, he found himself thinking more of Kya than of his dad and swore at that. He approached the fresh-scarred mound under the oaks, the wide sea beyond. The grave lay next to his mother's; his sister's on the far side, all enclosed in a small wall of rough stones and mortar embedded with shells. Enough space left for him. It didn't feel as if his dad were here at all. "I should've had you cremated like Sam McGee," Tate said, almost smiling. Then, looking over the ocean, he hoped Scupper had a boat wherever he was. A red boat.

He set the plastic case—a battery-operated record player—on the ground next to the grave and put a 78 on the turntable. The needle arm wobbled, then dropped, and Miliza Korjus's silvery voice lifted over the trees. He sat between his mother's grave and the flower-covered mound. Oddly, the sweet, freshly turned earth smelled more like a beginning than an end.

Talking out loud, head low, he asked his dad to forgive him for spending so much time away, and he knew Scupper did. Tate remembered his dad's definition of a man: one who can cry freely, feel poetry and opera in his heart, and do whatever it takes to defend a woman. Scupper would have understood tracking love through mud. Tate sat there quite awhile, one hand on his mother, the other on his father.

Finally, he touched the grave one last time, walked back to his truck, and drove to his boat at the town wharf. He would go back to work, immerse himself in squirming life-forms. Several fishermen walked to him on the dock, and he stood awkwardly, accepting condolences just as awkward.

Head low, determined to leave before anyone else approached, he stepped onto the aft deck of his cabin cruiser. But before he sat behind the wheel, he saw a pale brown feather resting on the seat cushion. He knew right away it was the soft breast feather of a female night heron, a long-legged secretive creature who lives deep in the marsh, alone. Yet here it was too near the sea.

He looked around. No, she wouldn't be here, not this close to town. He turned the key, churned south through the sea, and finally the marsh.

Going too fast in the channels, he brushed past low branches that slapped at the boat. The agitated wake sloshed against the bank as he pulled into her lagoon and tied his boat next to hers. Smoke rose from the shack's chimney, billowing and free.

"Kya," he yelled. "Kya!"

She opened the porch door and stepped under the oak. She was dressed in a long, white skirt and pale blue sweater—the colors of wings—hair falling about her shoulders.

He waited for her to walk to him, then took her shoulders and held her against his chest. Then pushed back.

"I love you, Kya, you know that. You've known it for a long time."

"You left me like all the others," she said.

"I will never leave you again."

"I know," she said.

"Kya, do you love me? You've never spoken those words to me."

"I've always loved you. Even as a child—in a time I don't remember—I already loved you." She dipped her head.

"Look at me," he said gently. She hesitated, face downcast. "Kya, I need to know that the running and hiding are over. That you can love without being afraid."

She lifted her face and looked into his eyes, then led him through the woods to the oak grove, the place of the feathers.

57.

The Firefly

They slept the first night on the beach, and he moved into the shack with her the next day. Packing and unpacking within a single tide. As sand creatures do.

As they walked along the tide line in late afternoon, he took her hand and looked at her. "Will you marry me, Kya?"

"We are married. Like the geese," she said.

"Okay. I can live with that."

Each morning they rose at dawn and, while Tate percolated coffee, Kya fried corn fritters in Ma's old iron skillet—blackened and dented—or stirred grits and eggs as sunrise eased over the lagoon. The heron posing one-legged in the mist. They cruised estuaries, waded waterways, and slipped through narrow streams, collecting feathers and amoebas. In the evenings, they drifted in her old boat until sunset, then swam naked in moonlight or loved in beds of cool ferns.

Archbald Lab offered Kya a job, but she turned it down and continued writing her books. She and Tate hired the fix-it man again, and he built a lab and studio—of raw wood, hand-hewn posts, and tin roof—for her behind the shack. Tate gave her a microscope and in-stalled worktables, shelves, and closets for her specimens. Trays of in-struments and supplies. Then they refurbished the shack, adding a new bedroom and bath, a larger sitting room. She insisted on keeping the kitchen as it was and the exterior unpainted, so that the dwelling, more of a cabin now, remained weathered and real.

From a phone in Sea Oaks she called Jodie and invited him and his wife, Libby, for a visit. The four of them explored the marsh and fished some. When Jodie pulled in a large bream, Kya squealed, "Lookee there. You got one big as Alabamee!" They fried up fish and hush pup-pies big as "goose aigs."

Kya never went to Barkley Cove again in her life, and for the most part, she and Tate spent their time in the marsh alone. The villagers saw her only as a distant shape gliding through fog, and over the years the mysteries of her story became legend, told over and over with but-termilk pancakes and hot pork sausages at the diner. The theories and gossip over how Chase Andrews died never stopped.

As time passed, most everyone agreed the sheriff never should've ar-rested her. After all, there was no hard evidence against her, no real proof of a crime. It had been truly cruel to treat a shy, natural creature that way. Now and then a new sheriff—Jackson was never elected again—would open the folder, make some inquiries about other sus-pects, but not much came of it. Over the years the case, too, eased into legend. And though Kya was never completely healed from the scorn and suspicion surrounding her, a soft contentment, a near-happiness settled into her.

Kya lay on the soft duff near the lagoon one afternoon, waiting for Tate to return from a collecting trip. She breathed deep, knowing he would always come back, that for the first time in her life she would not be abandoned. She heard the deep purr of his cruiser, chugging up the channel; could feel the quiet rumble through the ground. She sat up as his boat pushed through the thickets and waved to him at the helm. He waved back but didn't smile. She stood.

He tied to the small wharf he had built and walked up to her on the shore.

"Kya, I'm so sorry. I have bad news. Jumpin' died last night in his sleep."

An ache pushed against her heart. All those who left her had chosen to do so. This was different. This was not rejection; this was like the Cooper's hawk returning to the sky. Tears rolled down her cheeks, and Tate held her.

Tate and almost everyone in town went to Jumpin's funeral. Kya did not. But after the services, she walked to Jumpin' and Mabel's house, with some blackberry jam long overdue.

Kya paused at the fence. Friends and family stood in the dirt yard, swept clean as a whistle. Some talked, some laughed at old Jumpin' stories, and some cried. As she opened the gate everyone looked at her, then stepped aside to make a path. Standing on the porch, Mabel rushed to Kya. They hugged, rocking back and forth, crying.

"Lawd, he loved ya like his own dawder," Mabel said.

"I know," Kya said, "and he was my pa."

Later, Kya walked to her beach and said farewell to Jumpin' in her own words, in her own way, alone.

And as she wandered the beach remembering Jumpin', thoughts of her mother pushed into her mind. As though Kya were once again the little girl of six, she saw Ma walking down the sandy lane in her old gator shoes, maneuvering the deep ruts. But in this version, Ma stopped at the end of the trail and looked back, waving her hand high in farewell. She smiled at Kya, turned onto the road, and disappeared into the forest. And this time, finally, it was okay.

With no tears or censure, Kya whispered, "Good-bye, Ma." She thought of the others briefly—Pa, her brother and sisters. But she didn't have enough of that bygone family to bid farewell.

That regret faded too when Jodie and Libby began bringing their two children—Murph and Mindy—to visit Kya and Tate several times a year. Once again the shack swelled with family around the old cookstove, serving up Ma's corn fritters, scrambled eggs, and sliced tomatoes. But this time there was laughter and love.

Barkley Cove changed over the years. A man from Raleigh built a fancy marina where Jumpin's shack had leaned for more than a hundred years. With bright blue awnings over each slip, yachts could pull in. Boaters from up and down the coastline moseyed up to Barkley Cove and paid $3.50 for an espresso.

Little sidewalk cafés with smart-colored umbrellas and art galleries with seascapes sprouted on Main. A lady from New York opened a gift shop that sold everything the villagers didn't need but every tourist had to have. Almost every shop had a special table displaying the books by *Catherine Danielle Clark ~ Local Author ~ Award-Winning Biologist*. Grits were listed on the menus as polenta in mushroom sauce and cost $6.00. And one day, some women from Ohio walked into the Dog-Gone Beer Hall, never imagining they were the first females to pass through the door, and ordered spicy shrimp in paper boats, and beer, now on draft. Adults of either sex or any color can walk through the door now, but the window, which was cut out of the wall so that women could order from the sidewalk, is still there.

Tate continued his job at the lab, and Kya published seven more award-winning books. And though she was granted many accolades—including an honorary doctorate from the University of North Carolina at Chapel Hill—she never once accepted the invitations to speak at universities and museums.

Tate and Kya hoped for a family, but a child never came. The disappointment wove them closer together, and they were seldom separated for more than a few hours of any day.

Sometimes Kya walked alone to the beach, and as the sunset streaked the sky, she felt the waves pounding her heart. She'd reach down and touch the sand, then stretch her arms toward the clouds. Feeling the *connections*. Not the connections Ma and Mabel had spoken of—Kya never had her troop of close friends, nor the connections Jodie described, for she never had her own family. She knew the years of isolation had altered her behavior until she was different from others, but it wasn't her fault she'd been alone. Most of what she knew, she'd learned from the wild. Nature had nurtured, tutored, and protected her when no one else would. If consequences resulted from her behaving differently, then they too were functions of life's fundamental core.

Tate's devotion eventually convinced her that human love is more than the bizarre mating competitions of the marsh creatures, but life also taught her that ancient genes for survival still persist in some undesirable forms among the twists and turns of man's genetic code.

For Kya, it was enough to be part of this natural sequence as sure as the tides. She was bonded to her planet and its life in a way few people are. Rooted solid in this earth. Born of this mother.

At sixty-four Kya's long black hair had turned as white as the sand. One evening she did not return from a collecting trip, so Tate puttered around in the marsh, searching. As dusk eased in, he came around a bend and saw her drifting in her boat in a lagoon surrounded by syca-mores touching the sky. She had slumped backward, her head lying against the old knapsack. He called her name softly, and, when she didn't move, he shouted, then screamed. Pulling his boat next to hers, he stumbled awkwardly into the stern of her boat. Reaching out his long arms, he took her shoulders and gently shook her. Her head slumped farther to the side. Her eyes not seeing.

"Kya, Kya, no. No!" he screamed.

Still young, so beautiful, her heart had quietly stopped. She had lived long enough to see the bald eagles make a comeback; for Kya that was long enough. Folding her in his arms, he rocked back and forth, weeping. He wrapped her in a blanket and towed her back to her la-goon in the old boat through the maze of creeks and estuaries, passing the herons and deer for the last time.

> And I'll hide the maid in a cypress tree,
> When the footstep of death is near.

He got special permission for her to be buried on her land under an oak overlooking the sea, and the whole town came out for the funeral. Kya would not have believed the long lines of slow-moving mourners. Of course, Jodie and his family came and all of Tate's cousins. Some curiosity-seekers attended, but most people came out of respect for how she had survived years alone in the wild. Some remembered the little girl, dressed in an oversized, shabby coat, boating to the wharf,

364

walking barefoot to the grocery to buy grits. Others came to her grave-side because her books had taught them how the marsh links the land to the sea, both needing the other.

By now, Tate understood that her nickname was not cruel. Only few become legend, so he chose as the epitaph for her tombstone:

CATHERINE DANIELLE CLARK

"KYA"

THE MARSH GIRL

1945–2009

The evening of her funeral, when everyone was finally gone, Tate stepped into her homemade lab. Her carefully labeled samples, more than fifty years' worth, was the longest-running, most complete collection of its kind. She had requested that it be donated to Archbald Lab, and someday he would do so, but parting with it now was unthinkable.

Walking into the shack—as she always called it—Tate felt the walls exhaling her breath, the floors whispering her steps so clear he called out her name. Then he stood against the wall, weeping. He lifted the old knapsack and held it to his chest.

The officials at the courthouse had asked Tate to look for her will and birth certificate. In the old back bedroom, which had once been her parents', he rummaged through the closet and found boxes of her life stuffed in the bottom, almost hidden, under some blankets. He pulled them onto the floor and sat beside them.

Ever so carefully he opened the old cigar box, the one where all the collecting began. The box still smelled of sweet tobacco and little girl. Among a few birds' feathers, insects' wings, and seeds was the small jar with the ashes from her ma's letter, and a bottle of Revlon fingernail polish, Barely Pink. The bits and bones of a life. The stones of her stream.

Tucked in the bottom was the deed for the property, which Kya had put in a conservation easement, protecting it from development. At least this fragment of the marsh would always be wild. But there was no will or personal papers, which did not surprise him; she would not have thought of such things. Tate planned to live out his days at her place, knowing she had wanted that and that Jodie would not object.

Late in the day, the sun dipping behind the lagoon, he stirred corn mush for the gulls and mindlessly glanced at the kitchen floor. He cocked his head as he noticed for the first time that the linoleum had not been installed under the woodpile or the old stove. Kya had kept firewood stacked high, even in summer, but now it was low, and he saw the edge of a cutout in the floorboard. He moved the remaining logs aside and saw a trapdoor in the plywood. Kneeling down, he slowly opened it to find an enclosed compartment between the joists, which held, among other things, an old cardboard box covered in dust. He pulled it out and found inside scores of manila envelopes and a smaller box. All the envelopes were marked with the initials *A.H.*, and from them he pulled out pages and pages of poetry by Amanda Hamilton, the local poet who had published simple verses in regional magazines. Tate had thought Hamilton's poems rather weak, but Kya had always saved the published clippings, and here were envelopes full of them. Some of the written pages were completed poems, but most of them were unfinished, with lines crossed out and some words rewritten in the margin in the poet's handwriting—*Kya's handwriting*.

Amanda Hamilton *was Kya*. Kya was the poet.

Tate's face grimaced in disbelief. Through the years she must have put the poems in the rusty mailbox, submitting them to local publications. Safe behind a nom de plume. Perhaps a reaching-out, a way to express her feelings to someone other than gulls. Somewhere for her words to go.

He glanced through some of the poems, most about nature or love. One was folded neatly in its own envelope. He pulled it out and read:

The Firefly

Luring him was as easy
As flashing valentines.
But like a lady firefly
They hid a secret call to die.

A final touch,
Unfinished;
The last step, a trap.
Down, down he falls,
His eyes still holding mine
Until they see another world.

I saw them change.
First a question,
Then an answer,
Finally an end.

And love itself passing
To whatever it was before it began. A.H.

Still kneeling on the floor, he read it again. He held the paper next to his heart, throbbing inside his chest. He looked out the window, making certain no one was coming down the lane—not that they would, why would they? But to be sure. Then he opened the small box, knowing what he would find. There, laid out carefully on cotton, was the shell necklace Chase had worn until the night he died.

Tate sat at the kitchen table for a long while, taking it in, imagining her riding on night buses, catching a riptide, planning around the moon. Softly calling to Chase in the darkness. Pushing him backward. Then, squatting in mud at the bottom, lifting his head, heavy with death, to retrieve the necklace. Covering her footprints; leaving no trace.

Breaking kindling into bits, Tate built a fire in the old woodstove and, envelope by envelope, burned the poems. Maybe he didn't need to burn them all, maybe he should have destroyed just the one, but he wasn't thinking clearly. The old, yellowed papers made a great *whoosh* a foot high, then smoldered. He took the shell off the rawhide, dropped the rawhide in the fire, and put the boards back in the floor.

Then, in near dusk, he walked to the beach and stood on a sharp bed of white and cracked mollusks and crab pieces. For a second he stared at Chase's shell in his open palm and then dropped it on the sand. Looking the same as all the others, it vanished. The tide was coming in, and a wave flowed over his feet, taking with it hundreds of seashells back into the sea. Kya had been of this land and of this water; now they would take her back. Keep her secrets deep.

And then the gulls came. Seeing him there, they spiraled above his head. Calling. Calling.

As night fell, Tate walked back toward the shack. But when he reached the lagoon, he stopped under the deep canopy and watched hundreds of fireflies beckoning far into the dark reaches of the marsh. Way out yonder, where the crawdads sing.

Acknowledgments

To my twin brother, Bobby Dykes, my deepest thanks for a lifetime of unimaginable encouragement and support. Thank you to my sister, Helen Cooper, for always being there for me, and to my brother Lee Dykes, for believing in me. I am so grateful to my forever friends and family for their unwavering support, encouragement, and laughter: Amanda Walker Hall, Margaret Walker Weatherly, Barbara Clark Copeland, Joanne and Tim Cady, Mona Kim Brown, Bob Ivey and Jill Bowman, Mary Dykes, Doug Kim Brown, Ken Eastwell, Jesse Chastain, Steve O'Neil, Andy Vann, Napier Murphy, Linda Denton (and for the horse and ski trails), Sabine Dahlmann, and Greg and Alicia Johnson.

For reading and commenting on the manuscript, I thank: Joanne and Tim Cady (multiple readings!), Jill Bowman, Bob Ivey, Carolyn Testa, Dick Burgheim, Helen Cooper, Peter Matson, Mary Dykes, Alexandra Fuller, Mark Owens, Dick Houston, Janet Gause, Jennifer Durbin, John O'Connor, and Leslie Anne Keller.

To my agent, Russell Galen, thank you for loving and understanding Kya and fireflies, and for your enthusiastic determination to get this story told.

Thank you, G. P. Putnam's Sons, for publishing my words. I am so

Acknowledgments

grateful to my editor, Tara Singh Carlson, for all your encouragement, beautiful editing, and vision for my novel. Also at Putnam, my thanks to Helen Richard for helping at every turn.

Special thanks to Hannah Cady for your cheerful assistance with some of the more mundane and gritty jobs—like the bonfires—of writing a novel.

CRY OF THE KALAHARI

Paperback coming in 2022

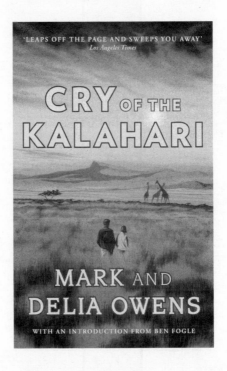

The incredible memoir by the author of *Where the Crawdads Sing*, Delia Owens and fellow nature conservationist Mark Owens is out now. Charting their time researching wildlife in the Kalahari Desert, *Cry of the Kalahari* is a gripping account of how they survived the dangers of living in one of the last and largest pristine areas on Earth and will be reissued with full colour photographs for the first time since its original publication in 1984.